Selected Works of
Sir Arthur Conan Doyle

maple press

SELECTED WORKS OF SIR ARTHUR CONAN DOYLE

Published by

MAPLE PRESS PRIVATE LIMITED
office: A-63, Sector 58, Noida 201301, U.P., India
phone: +91 120 455 3581, 455 3583
email: info@maplepress.co.in
website: www.maplepress.co.in

Reprinted in 2019

ISBN: 978-93-88304-13-9

CONTENTS

ESSAYS/ ARTICLES

PLAY

The Case Book of
Sherlock Holmes

PREFACE

I fear that Mr. Sherlock Holmes may become like one of those popular tenors who, having outlived their time, are still tempted to make repeated farewell bows to their indulgent audiences. This must cease and he must go the way of all flesh, material or imaginary. One likes to think that there is some fantastic limbo for the children of imagination, some strange, impossible place where the beaux of Fielding may still make love to the belles of Richardson, where Scott's heroes still may strut, Dickens's delightful Cockneys still raise a laugh, and Thackeray's worldlings continue to carry on their reprehensible careers. Perhaps in some humble corner of such a Valhalla, Sherlock and his Watson may for a time find a place, while some more astute sleuth with some even less astute comrade may fill the stage which they have vacated.

His career has been a long one - though it is possible to exaggerate it; decrepit gentlemen who approach me and declare that his adventures formed the reading of their boyhood do not meet the response from me which they seem to expect. One is not anxious to have one's personal dates handled so unkindly. As a matter of cold fact, Holmes made his debut in A Study in Scarlet and in The Sign of Four, two small booklets which appeared between 1887 and 1889. It was in 1891 that "A Scandal in Bohemia," the first of the long series of short stories, appeared in The Strand Magazine. The public seemed appreciative and desirous of more, so that from that date, thirty-nine years ago, they have been produced in a broken series which now contains no fewer than fifty-six stories, republished in The Adventures, The Memoirs, The Return, and His Last Bow. and there remain these twelve published during the last few years which are here produced under the title of The Case Book of Sherlock Holmes. He began his adventures in the very heart of the later Victorian era, carried it through the all-too-short reign of Edward, and has managed to hold his own little niche even in these feverish days. Thus it would be true to say that those who first read of him, as young men, have lived to see their own grown-up children following the same adventures in the same magazine. It is a striking example of the patience and loyalty of the British public.

I had fully determined at the conclusion of The Memoirs to bring Holmes to an end, as I felt that my literary energies should not be directed too much into one channel. That pale, clear-cut face and loose-limbed figure were taking up an undue share of my imagination. I did the deed, but fortunately no coroner had pronounced upon the remains, and so, after a long interval, it was not difficult for me to respond to the flattering demand and to explain my rash act away. I have never regretted it, for I have not in actual practice found that these lighter sketches have prevented me from exploring and finding my limitations in such varied branches of literature as history, poetry, historical novels, psychic research, and the drama. Had Holmes never existed I could not have done more, though he may perhaps have stood a little in the way of the recognition of my more serious literary work.

And so, reader, farewell to Sherlock Holmes! I thank you for your past constancy, and can but hope that some return has been made in the shape of that distraction from the worries of life and stimulating change of thought which can only be found in the fairy kingdom of romance.

Arthur Conan Doyle

THE ADVENTURE OF THE ILLUSTRIOUS CLIENT

"It can't hurt now," was Mr. Sherlock Holmes's comment when, for the tenth time in as many years, I asked his leave to reveal the following narrative. So it was that at last I obtained permission to put on record what was, in some ways, the supreme moment of my friend's career.

Both Holmes and I had a weakness for the Turkish bath. It was over a smoke in the pleasant lassitude of the drying-room that I have found him less reticent and more human than anywhere else. On the upper floor of the Northumberland Avenue establishment there is an isolated corner where two couches lie side by side, and it was on these that we lay upon September 3, 1902, the day when my narrative begins. I had asked him whether anything was stirring, and for answer he had shot his long, thin, nervous arm out of the sheets which enveloped him and had drawn an envelope from the inside pocket of the coat which hung beside him.

"It may be some fussy, self-important fool; it may be a matter of life or death," said he as he handed me the note. "I know no more than this message tells me."

It was from the Carlton Club and dated the evening before. This is what I read:

Sir James Damery presents his compliments to Mr. Sherlock Holmes and will call upon him at 4:30 to-morrow. Sir James begs to say that the matter upon which he desires to consult Mr. Holmes is very delicate and also very important. He trusts, therefore, that Mr. Holmes will make every effort to grant this interview, and that he will confirm it over the telephone to the Carlton Club.

"I need not say that I have confirmed it, Watson," said Holmes as I returned the paper. "Do you know anything of this man Damery?"

"Only that this name is a household word in society."

"Well, I can tell you a little more than that. He has rather a reputation for arranging delicate matters which are to be kept out of the papers. You may remember his negotiations with Sir George Lewis over the Hammerford Will case. He is a man of the world with a natural turn for diplomacy. I am bound, therefore, to hope that it is not a false scent and that he has some real need for our assistance."

"Our?"

"Well, if you will be so good, Watson."

"I shall be honoured."

"Then you have the hour - 4:30. Until then we can put the matter out of our heads."

I was living in my own rooms in Queen Anne Street at the time, but I was round at Baker Street before the time named. Sharp to the half-hour, Colonel Sir James Damery was announced. It is hardly necessary to describe him, for many will remember that large, bluff, honest personality, that broad, cleanshaven face, and, above all, that pleasant, mellow voice. Frankness shone from his gray Irish eyes, and good humour played round his mobile, smiling lips. His lucent top-hat, his dark frock-coat, indeed, every detail, from the pearl pin in the black satin cravat to the lavender spats over the varnished shoes, spoke of the meticulous care in dress for which he was famous. The big, masterful aristocrat dominated the little room.

"Of course, I was prepared to find Dr. Watson," he remarked with a courteous bow. "His collaboration may be very necessary, for we are dealing on this occasion, Mr. Holmes, with a man to whom violence is familiar and who will, literally, stick at nothing. I should say that there is no more dangerous man in Europe."

"I have had several opponents to whom that flattering term has been applied," said Holmes with a smile. "Don't you smoke? Then you will excuse me if I light my pipe. If your man is more dangerous than the late Professor Moriarty, or than the living Colonel Sebastian Moran, then he is indeed worth meeting. May I ask his name?"

"Have you ever heard of Baron Gruner?"

"You mean the Austrian murderer?"

Colonel Damery threw up his kid-gloved hands with a laugh. "There is no getting past you, Mr. Holmes! Wonderful! So you have already sized him up as a murderer?"

"It is my business to follow the details of Continental crime. Who could possibly have read what happened at Prague and have any doubts as to the man's guilt! It was a purely technical legal point and the suspicious death of a witness that saved him! I am as sure that he killed his wife when the socalled 'accident' happened in the Splugen Pass as if I had seen him do it. I knew, also, that he had come to England and had a presentiment that sooner or later he would find me some work to do. Well, what has Baron Gruner been up to? I presume it is not this old tragedy which has come up again?"

"No, it is more serious than that. To revenge crime is important, but to prevent it is more so. It is a terrible thing, Mr. Holmes, to see a dreadful event, an atrocious situation, preparing itself before your eyes, to clearly understand whither it will lead and yet to be utterly unable to avert it. Can a human being be placed in a more trying position?"

"Perhaps not."

"Then you will sympathize with the client in whose interests I am acting."

"I did not understand that you were merely an intermediary. Who is the principal?"

"Mr. Holmes, I must beg you not to press that question. It is important that I should be able to assure him that his honoured name has been in no way dragged into the matter. His motives are, to the last degree, honourable and chivalrous, but he prefers to remain unknown. I need not say that your fees will be assured and that you will be given a perfectly free hand. Surely the actual name of your client is immaterial?"

"I am sorry," said Holmes. "I am accustomed to have mystery at one end of my cases, but to have it at both ends is too confusing. I fear, Sir James, that I must decline to act."

Our visitor was greatly disturbed. His large, sensitive face was darkened with emotion and disappointment.

"You hardly realize the effect of your own action, Mr. Holmes," said he. "You place me in a most serious dilemma for I am perfectly certain that you would be proud to take over the case if I could give you the facts, and yet a promise forbids me from revealing them all. May I, at least, lay all that I can before you?"

"By all means, so long as it is understood that I commit myself to nothing."

"That is understood. In the first place, you have no doubt heard of General de Merville?"

"De Merville of Khyber fame? Yes, I have heard of him."

"He has a daughter, Violet de Merville, young, rich, beautiful, accomplished, a wonder-woman in every way. It is this daughter, this lovely, innocent girl, whom we are endeavouring to save from the clutches of a fiend."

"Baron Gruner has some hold over her, then?"

"The strongest of all holds where a woman is concerned - the hold of love. The fellow is, as you may have heard, extraordinarily handsome, with a most fascinating manner. a gentle voice and that air of romance and mystery which means so much to a woman. He is said to have the whole sex at his mercy and to have made ample use of the fact."

"But how came such a man to meet a lady of the standing of Miss Violet de Merville?"

"It was on a Mediterranean yachting voyage. The company, though select, paid their own passages. No doubt the promoters hardly realized the Baron's true character until it was too late. The villain attached himself to the lady, and with such effect that he has completely and absolutely won her heart. To say that she loves him hardly expresses it. She dotes upon him, she is obsessed by him. Outside of him there is nothing on earth. She will not hear one word against him. Everything has been done to cure her of her madness, but in vain. To sum up, she proposes to marry him next month. As she is of age and has a will of iron, it is hard to know how to prevent her."

"Does she know about the Austrian episode?"

"The cunning devil has told her every unsavoury public scandal of his past life, but always in such a way as to make himself out to be an innocent martyr. She absolutely accepts his version and will listen to no other."

"Dear me! But surely you have inadvertently let out the name of your client? It is no doubt General de Merville."

Our visitor fidgeted in his chair.

"I could deceive you by saying so, Mr. Holmes, but it would not be true. De Merville is a broken man. The strong soldier has been utterly demoralized by this incident. He has lost the nerve which never failed him on the battlefield and has become a weak, doddering old man, utterly incapable of contending with a brilliant, forceful rascal like this Austrian. My client however is an old friend, one who has known the General intimately for many years and taken a paternal interest in this young girl since she wore short frocks. He cannot see this tragedy consummated without some attempt to stop it. There is nothing in which Scotland Yard can act. It was his own suggestion that you should be called in, but it was, as I have said, on the express stipulation that he should not be personally involved in the matter. I have no doubt, Mr. Holmes, with your great powers you could easily trace my client back through me, but I must ask you, as a point of honour, to refrain from doing so, and not to break in upon his incognito."

Holmes gave a whimsical smile.

"I think I may safely promise that," said he. "I may add that your problem interests me, and that I shall be prepared to look into it. How shall I keep in touch with you?"

"The Carlton Club will find me. But in case of emergency, there is a private telephone call, 'XX.31.'"

Holmes noted it down and sat, still smiling, with the open memorandum-book upon his knee.

"The Baron's present address, please?"

"Vernon Lodge, near Kingston. It is a large house. He has been fortunate in some rather shady speculations and is a rich man, which naturally makes him a more dangerous antagonist."

"Is he at home at present?"

"Yes."

"Apart from what you have told me, can you give me any further information about the man?"

"He has expensive tastes. He is a horse fancier. For a short time he played polo at Hurlingham, but then this Prague affair got noised about and he had to leave. He collects books and pictures. He is a man with a considerable artistic side to his nature. He is, I believe, a recognized authority upon Chinese pottery and has written a book upon the subject."

"A complex mind," said Holmes. "All great criminals have that. My old friend Charlie Peace was a violin virtuoso. Wainwright was no mean artist. I could quote many more. Well, Sir James, you will inform your client that I am turning my mind upon Baron Gruner. I can say no more. I have some sources of information of my own, and I dare say we may find some means of opening the matter up."

When our visitor had left us Holmes sat so long in deep thought that it seemed to me that he had forgotten my presence. At last, however, he came briskly back to earth.

"Well, Watson, any views?" he asked.

"I should think you had better see the young lady herself."

"My dear Watson, if her poor old broken father cannot move her, how shall I, a stranger, prevail? And yet there is something in the suggestion if all else fails. But I think we must begin from a different angle. I rather fancy that Shinwell Johnson might be a help."

I have not had occasion to mention Shinwell Johnson in these memoirs because I have seldom drawn my cases from the latter phases of my friend's career . During the first years of the century he became a valuable assistant. Johnson, I grieve to say, made his name first as a very dangerous villain and served two terms at Parkhurst. Finally he repented and allied himself to Holmes, acting as his agent in the huge criminal underworld of London and obtaining information which often proved to be of vital importance. Had Johnson been a "nark" of the police he would soon have been exposed, but as he dealt with cases which never came directly into the courts, his activities were never realized by his companions. With the glamour of his two convictions upon him, he had the entree of every night-club, doss house, and gambling den in the town, and his quick observation and active brain made him an ideal agent for gaining information. It was to him that Sherlock Holmes now proposed to turn.

It was not possible for me to follow the immediate steps taken by my friend, for I had some pressing professional business of my own, but I met him by appointment that evening at Simpson's, where, sitting at a small table in the front window and looking down at the rushing stream of life in the Strand, he told me something of what had passed.

"Johnson is on the prowl," said he. "He may pick up some garbage in the darker recesses of the underworld, for it is down there, amid the black roots of crime, that we must hunt for this man's secrets."

"But if the lady will not accept what is already known, why should any fresh discovery of yours turn her from her purpose?"

"Who knows, Watson? Woman's heart and mind are insoluble puzzles to the male. Murder might be condoned or explained, and yet some smaller offence might rankle. Baron Gruner remarked to me -"

"He remarked to you!"

"Oh, to be sure, I had not told you of my plans. Well, Watson, I love to come to close grips with my man. I like to meet him eye to eye and read for myself the stuff that he is made of. When I had given Johnson his instructions I took a cab out to Kingston and found the Baron in a most affable mood."

"Did he recognize you?"

"There was no difficulty about that, for I simply sent in my card. He is an excellent antagonist, cool as ice, silky voiced and soothing as one of your fashionable consultants, and poisonous as a cobra. He has breeding in him - a real aristocrat of crime with a superficial suggestion of afternoon tea and all the cruelty of the grave behind it. Yes, I am glad to have had my attention called to Baron Adelbert Gruner."

"You say he was affable?"

"A purring cat who thinks he sees prospective mice. Some people's affability is more deadly than the violence of coarser souls. His greeting was characteristic. 'I rather thought I should see you sooner or later,

Mr. Holmes,' said he. 'You have been engaged, no doubt by General de Merville, to endeavour to stop my marriage with his daughter, Violet. That is so, is it not?'"

I acquiesced.

"My dear man," said he. "You will only ruin your own well-deserved reputation. It is not a case in which you can possibly succeed. You will have barren work, to say nothing of incurring some danger. Let me very strongly advise you to draw off at once."

"It is curious," I answered, "but that was the very advice which I had intended to give you. I have a respect for your brains, Baron, and the little which I have seen of your personality has not lessened it. Let me put it to you as man to man. No one wants to rake up your past and make you unduly uncomfortable. It is over, and you are now in smooth waters, but if you persist in this marriage you will raise up a swarm of powerful enemies who will never leave you alone until they have made England too hot to hold you. Is the game worth it? Surely you would be wiser if you left the lady alone. It would not be pleasant for you if these facts of your past were brought to her notice."

"The Baron has little waxed tips of hair under his nose, like the short antennae of an insect. These quivered with amusement as he listened, and he finally broke into a gentle chuckle."

"Excuse my amusement, Mr. Holmes," said he, "but it is really funny to see you trying to play a hand with no cards in it. I don't think anyone could do it better, but it is rather pathetic all the same. Not a colour card there, Mr. Holmes, nothing but the smallest of the small."

"So you think."

"So I know. Let me make the thing clear to you, for my own hand is so strong that I can afford to show it. I have been fortunate enough to win the entire affection of this lady. This was given to me in spite of the fact that I told her very clearly of all the unhappy incidents in my past life. I also told her that certain wicked and designing persons - I hope you recognize yourself - would come to her and tell her these things and I warned her how to treat them. You have heard of post-hypnotic suggestion Mr. Holmes. Well you will see how it works for a man of personality can use hypnotism without any vulgar passes or tomfoolery. So she is ready for you and, I have no doubt, would give you an appointment, for she is quite amenable to her father's will - save only in the one little matter."

"Well, Watson, there seemed to be no more to say, so I took my leave with as much cold dignity as I could summon, but, as I had my hand on the door-handle, he stopped me."

"By the way, Mr. Holmes," said he, "did you know Le Brun, the French agent?"

"Yes," said I.

"Do you know what befell him?"

"I heard that he was beaten by some Apaches in the Montmartre district and crippled for life."

"Quite true, Mr. Holmes. By a curious coincidence he had been inquiring into my affairs only a week before. Don't do it, Mr. Holmes; it's not a lucky thing to do. Several have found that out. My last word to you is, go your own way and let me go mine. Good-bye!"

"So there you are, Watson. You are up to date now."

"The fellow seems dangerous."

"Mighty dangerous. I disregard the blusterer, but this is the sort of man who says rather less than he means."

"Must you interfere? Does it really matter if he marries the girl?"

"Considering that he undoubtedly murdered his last wife, I should say it mattered very much. Besides, the client! Well, well, we need not discuss that. When you have finished your coffee you had best come home with me, for the blithe Shinwell will be there with his report."

We found him sure enough, a huge, coarse, red-faced, scorbutic man, with a pair of vivid black eyes which were the only external sign of the very cunning mind within. It seems that he had dived down into what was peculiarly his kingdom, and beside him on the settee was a brand which he had brought up in the shape of a slim, flame-like young woman with a pale, intense face, youthful, and yet so worn with sin and sorrow that one read the terrible years which had left their leprous mark upon her.

"This is Miss Kitty Winter," said Shinwell Johnson, waving his fat hand as an introduction. "What she don't know - well, there, she'll speak for herself. Put my hand right on her, Mr. Holmes, within an hour of your message."

"I'm easy to find," said the young woman. "Hell, London, gets me every time. Same address for Porky Shinwell. We're old mates, Porky, you and I. But, by cripes! there is another who ought to be down in a lower hell than we if there was any justice in the world! That is the man you are after, Mr. Holmes."

Holmes smiled. "I gather we have your good wishes, Miss Winter."

"If I can help to put him where he belongs, I'm yours to the rattle," said our visitor with fierce energy. There was an intensity of hatred in her white, set face and her blazing eyes such as woman seldom and man never can attain.

"You needn't go into my past, Mr. Holmes. That's neither here nor there. But what I am Adelbert Gruner made me. If I could pull him down!" She clutched frantically with her hands into the air. "Oh, if I could only pull him into the pit where he has pushed so many!"

"You know how the matter stands?"

"Porky Shinwell has been telling me. He's after some other poor fool and wants to marry her this time. You want to stop it. Well, you surely know enough about this devil to prevent any decent girl in her senses wanting to be in the same parish with him."

"She is not in her senses. She is madly in love. She has been told all about him. She cares nothing."

"Told about the murder?"

"Yes."

"My Lord, she must have a nerve!"

"She puts them all down as slanders."

"Couldn't you lay proofs before her silly eyes?"

"Well, can you help us do so?"

"Ain't I a proof myself? If I stood before her and told her how he used me -"

"Would you do this?"

"Would I? Would I not!"

"Well, it might be worth trying. But he has told her most of his sins and had pardon from her, and I understand she will not reopen the question."

"I'll lay he didn't tell her all," said Miss Winter. "I caught a glimpse of one or two murders besides the one that made such a fuss. He would speak of someone in his velvet way and then look at me with a steady eye and say: 'He died within a month.' It wasn't hot air, either. But I took little notice - you see, I loved him myself at that time. Whatever he did went with me, same as with this poor fool! There was just one thing that shook me. Yes, by cripes! if it had not been for his poisonous, lying tongue that explains and soothes. I'd have left him that very night. It's a book he has - a brown leather book with a lock and his arms in gold on the outside. I think he was a bit drunk that night, or he would not have shown it to me."

"What was it, then?"

"I tell you. Mr. Holmes. This man collects women, and takes a pride in his collection. as some men collect moths or butterflies. He had it all in that book. Snapshot photographs. names, details, everything about them. It was a beastly book - a book no man, even if he had come from the gutter, could have put together. But it was Adelbert Gruner's book all the same. 'Souls I have ruined.' He could have put that on the outside if he had been so minded. However, that's neither here nor there, for the book would not serve you, and, if it would, you can't get it."

"Where is it?"

"How can I tell you where it is now? It's more than a year since I left him. I know where he kept it then. He's a precise, tidy cat of a man in many of his ways, so maybe it is still in the pigeon-hole of the old bureau in the inner study. Do you know his house?"

"I've been in the study," said Holmes.

"Have you. thought? You haven't been slow on the job if you only started this morning. Maybe dear Adelbert has met his match this time. The outer study is the one with the Chinese crockery in it - big glass cupboard between the windows. Then behind his desk is the door that leads to the inner study - a small room where he keeps papers and things."

"Is he not afraid of burglars?"

"Adelbert is no coward. His worst enemy couldn't say that of him. He can look after himself. There's a burglar alarm at night. Besides, what is there for a burglar - unless they got away with all this fancy crockery?"

"No good," said Shinwell Johnson with the decided voice of the expert. "No fence wants stuff of that sort that you can neither melt nor sell."

"Quite so," said Holmes. "Well, now, Miss Winter. If you would call here tomorrow evening at five. I would consider in the meanwhile whether your suggestion of seeing this lady personally may not be arranged. I am exceedingly obliged to your cooperation. I need not say that my clients will consider liberally -"

"None of that, Mr. Holmes," cried the young woman. "I am not out for money. Let me see this man in the mud, and I've got all I've worked for - in the mud with my foot on his cursed face. That's my price. I'm with you tomorrow or any other day so long as you are on his track. Porky here can tell you always where to find me."

I did not see Holmes again until the following evening when we dined once more at our Strand restaurant. He shrugged his shoulders when I asked him what luck he had had in his interview. Then he told the story, which I would repeat in this way. His hard, dry statement needs some little editing to soften it into the terms of real life.

"There was no difficulty at all about the appointment," said Holmes, "for the girl glories in showing abject filial obedience in all secondary things in an attempt to atone for her flagrant breach of it in her engagement. The General phoned that all was ready, and the fiery Miss W. turned up according to schedule, so that at half-past five a cab deposited us outside 104 Berkeley Square, where the old soldier resides - one of those awful gray London castles which would make a church seem frivolous. A footman showed us into a great yellow-curtained drawing-room, and there was the lady awaiting us, demure, pale, self-contained, as inflexible and remote as a snow image on a mountain."

"I don't quite know how to make her clear to you, Watson. Perhaps you may meet her before we are through, and you can use your own gift of words. She is beautiful, but with the ethereal other-world beauty of some fanatic whose thoughts are set on high. I have seen such faces in the pictures of the old masters of the Middle Ages. How a beastman could have laid his vile paws upon such a being of the beyond I cannot imagine. You may have noticed how extremes call to each other, the spiritual to the animal, the cave-man to the angel. You never saw a worse case than this."

"She knew what we had come for, of course - that villain had lost no time in poisoning her mind against us. Miss Winter's advent rather amazed her, I think, but she waved us into our respective chairs like a reverend abbess receiving two rather leprous mendicants. If your head is inclined to swell. my dear Watson, take a course of Miss Violet de Merville.

"Well, sir," said she in a voice like the wind from an iceberg, "your name is familiar to me, you have called, as I understand, to malign my fiance, Baron Gruner. It is only by my father's request that I see you at all, and I warn you in advance that anything you can say could not possibly have the slightest effect upon my mind."

"I was sorry for her, Watson. I thought of her for the moment as I would have thought of a daughter of my own. I am not often eloquent. I use my head, not my heart. But I really did plead with her with all the warmth of words that I could find in my nature. I pictured to her the awful position of the woman who only wakes to a man's character after she is his wife - a woman who has to submit to be caressed by bloody hands and lecherous lips. I spared her nothing - the shame, the fear, the agony, the hopelessness of it all. All my hot words could not bring one tinge of colour to those ivory cheeks or one gleam of emotion to those abstracted eyes. I thought of what the rascal had said about a post-hypnotic influence. One could really believe that she was living above the earth in some ecstatic dream. Yet there was nothing indefinite in her replies."

"I have listened to you with patience, Mr. Holmes," said she. "The effect upon my mind is exactly as predicted. I am aware that Adelbert, that my fiance, has had a stormy life in which he has incurred bitter hatreds and most unjust aspersions. You are only the last of a series who have brought their slanders before me. Possibly you mean well, though I learn that you are a paid agent who would have been equally willing to act for the Baron as against him. But in any case I wish you to understand once for all that I love him and that he loves me, and that the opinion of all the world is no more to me than the twitter of those birds outside the window. If his noble nature has ever for an instant fallen, it may be that I have been specially sent to raise it to its true and lofty level. I am not clear" - here she turned eyes upon my companion - "who this young lady may be."

"I was about to answer when the girl broke in like a whirlwind. If ever you saw flame and ice face to face, it was those two women."

"I'll tell you who I am," she cried, springing out of her chair, her mouth all twisted with passion - "I am his last mistress. I am one of a hundred that he has tempted and used and ruined and thrown into the refuse heap, as he will you also. Your refuse heap is more likely to be a grave, and maybe that's the best. I tell you, you foolish woman, if you marry this man he'll be the death of you. It may be a broken heart or it may be a broken neck, but he'll have you one way or the other. It's not out of love for you I'm speaking. I don't care a tinker's curse whether you live or die. It's out of hate for him and to spite him and to get back on him for what he did to me. But it's all the same, and you needn't look at me like that, my fine lady, for you may be lower than I am before you are through with it."

"I should prefer not to discuss such matters," said Miss de Merville coldly. "Let me say once for all that I am aware of three passages in my fiance's life in which he became entangled with designing women, and that I am assured of his hearty repentance for any evil that he may have done."

"Three passages!" screamed my companion. "You fool! You unutterable fool!"

"Mr. Holmes, I beg that you will bring this interview to an end," said the icy voice. "I have obeyed my father's wish in seeing you, but I am not compelled to listen to the ravings of this person."

"With an oath Miss Winter darted forward, and if I had not caught her wrist she would have clutched this maddening woman by the hair. I dragged her towards the door and was lucky to get her back into the cab without a public scene, for she was beside herself with rage. In a cold way I felt pretty furious myself, Watson, for there was something indescribably annoying in the calm aloofness and supreme self-complaisance of the woman whom we were trying to save. So now once again you know exactly how we stand, and it is clear that I must plan some fresh opening move, for this gambit won't work. I'll keep in touch with you, Watson, for it is more than likely that you will have your part to play, though it is just possible that the next move may lie with them rather than with us."

And it did. Their blow fell - or his blow rather, for never could I believe that the lady was privy to it. I think I could show you the very paving-stone upon which I stood when my eyes fell upon the placard, and a pang of horror passed through my very soul. It was between the Grand Hotel and Charing Cross Station, where a one-legged news-vender displayed his evening papers. The date was just two days after the last conversation. There, black upon yellow, was the terrible news-sheet:

MURDEROUS ATTACK UPON SHERLOCK HOLMES

I think I stood stunned for some moments. Then I have a confused recollection of snatching at a paper. Of the remonstrance of the man, whom I had not paid, and, finally, of standing in the doorway of a chemist's shop while I turned up the fateful paragraph. This was how it ran:

We learn with regret that Mr. Sherlock Holmes, the well-known private detective, was the victim this morning of a murderous assault which has left him in a precarious position. There are no exact details to hand, but the event seems to have occurred about twelve o'clock in Regent Street, outside the Cafe Royal. The attack was made by two men armed with sticks, and Mr. Holmes was beaten about the head and body, receiving injuries which the doctors describe as most serious. He was carried to Charing Cross Hospital and afterwards insisted upon being taken to his rooms in Baker Street. The miscreants who attacked him appear to have been respectably dressed men, who escaped from the bystanders by passing through the Cafe Royal and out into Glasshouse Street behind it.

No doubt they belonged to that criminal fraternity which has so often had occasion to bewail the activity and ingenuity of the injured man.

I need not say that my eyes had hardly glanced over the paragraph before I had sprung into a hansom and was on my way to Baker Street. I found Sir Leslie Oakshott, the famous surgeon, in the hall and his brougham waiting at the curb.

"No immediate danger," was his report. "Two lacerated scalp wounds and some considerable bruises. Several stitches have been necessary. Morphine has been injected and quiet is essential, but an interview of a few minutes would not be absolutely forbidden."

With this permission I stole into the darkened room. The sufferer was wide awake, and I heard my name in a hoarse whisper. The blind was three-quarters down, but one ray of sunlight slanted through and struck the bandaged head of the injured man. A crimson patch had soaked through the white linen compress. I sat beside him and bent my head.

"All right, Watson. Don't look so scared," he muttered in a very weak voice. "It's not as bad as it seems."

"Thank God for that!"

"I'm a bit of a single-stick expert, as you know. I took most of them on my guard. It was the second man that was too much for me."

"What can I do, Holmes? Of course, it was that damned fellow who set them on. I'll go and thrash the hide off him if you give the word."

"Good old Watson! No, we can do nothing there unless the police lay their hands on the men. But their get-away had been well prepared. We may be sure of that. Wait a little. I have my plans. The first thing is to exaggerate my injuries. They'll come to you for news. Put it on thick, Watson. Lucky if I live the week out concussion delirium - what you like! You can't overdo it."

"But Sir Leslie Oakshott?"

"Oh, he's all right. He shall see the worst side of me. I'll look after that."

"Anything else?"

"Yes. Tell Shinwell Johnson to get that girl out of the way. Those beauties will be after her now. They know, of course, that she was with me in the case. If they dared to do me in it is not likely they will neglect her. That is urgent. Do it to-night."

"I'll go now. Anything more?"

"Put my pipe on the table - and the tobacco-slipper. Right! Come in each morning and we will plan our campaign."

I arranged with Johnson that evening to take Miss Winter to a quiet suburb and see that she lay low until the danger was past.

For six days the public were under the impression that Holmes was at the door of death. The bulletins were very grave and there were sinister paragraphs in the papers. My continual visits assured me that it was not so bad as that. His wiry constitution and his determined will were working wonders. He was recovering fast, and I had suspicions at times that he was really finding himself faster than he pretended even to me. There was a curious secretive streak in the man which led to many dramatic effects, but left even his closest friend guessing as to what his exact plans might be. He pushed to an extreme the axiom that the only safe plotter was he who plotted alone. I was nearer him than anyone else, and yet I was always conscious of the gap between.

On the seventh day the stitches were taken out, in spite of which there was a report of erysipelas in the evening papers. The same evening papers had an announcement which I was bound, sick or well, to carry to my friend. It was simply that among the passengers on the Cunard boat Ruritania, starting from Liverpool on Friday, was the Baron Adelbert Gruner, who had some important financial business to settle in the States before his impending wedding to Miss Violet de Merville, only daughter of, etc., etc. Holmes listened to the news with a cold, concentrated look upon his pale face, which told me that it hit him hard.

"Friday!" he cried. "Only three clear days. I believe the rascal wants to put himself out of danger's way. But he won't, Watson! By the Lord Harry, he won't! Now, Watson, I want you to do something for me."

"I am here to be used, Holmes."

"Well, then, spend the next twenty-four hours in an intensive study of Chinese pottery."

He gave no explanations and I asked for none. By long experience I had learned the wisdom of obedience. But when I had left his room I walked down Baker Street, revolving in my head how on earth I was to carry out so strange an order. Finally I drove to the London Library in St. James's Square, put the matter to my friend Lomax, the sub-librarian, and departed to my rooms with a goodly volume under my arm.

It is said that the barrister who crams up a case with such care that he can examine an expert witness upon the Monday has forgotten all his forced knowledge before the Saturday. Certainly I should not like now to pose as an authority upon ceramics. And yet all that evening, and all that night with a short interval for rest, and all next morning, I was sucking in knowledge and committing names to memory. There I learned of the hall-marks of the great artist-decorators, of the mystery of cyclical dates, the marks of the Hung-wu and the beauties of the Yung-lo, the writings of Tang-ying, and the glories of the primitive period of the Sung and the Yuan. I was charged with all this information when I called upon Holmes next evening. He was out of bed now, though you would not have guessed it from the published reports, and he sat with his much-bandaged head resting upon his hand in the depth of his favourite armchair.

"Why, Holmes," I said, "if one believed the papers, you are dying."

"That," said he, "is the very impression which I intended to convey. And now, Watson, have you learned your lessons?"

"At least I have tried to."

"Good. You could keep up an intelligent conversation on the subject?"

"I believe I could."

"Then hand me that little box from the mantelpiece."

He opened the lid and took out a small object most carefully wrapped in some fine Eastern silk. This he unfolded, and disclosed a delicate little saucer of the most beautiful deep-blue colour.

"It needs careful handling, Watson. This is the real egg-shell pottery of the Ming dynasty. No finer piece ever passed through Christie's. A complete set of this would be worth a king's ransom - in fact, it is doubtful if there is a complete set outside the imperial palace of Peking. The sight of this would drive a real connoisseur wild."

"What am I to do with it?"

Holmes handed me a card upon which was printed: "Dr. Hill Barton, 369 Half Moon Street."

"That is your name for the evening, Watson. You will call upon Baron Gruner. I know something of his habits, and at half-past eight he would probably be disengaged. A note will tell him in advance that you are about to call, and you will say that you are bringing him a specimen of an absolutely unique set of Ming china. You may as well be a medical man, since that is a part which you can play without duplicity. You are a collector this set has come your way, you have heard of the Baron's interest in the subject, and you are not averse to selling at a price."

"What price?"

"Well asked, Watson. You would certainly fall down badly if you did not know the value of your own wares. This saucer was got for me by Sir James, and comes, I understand, from the collection of his client. You will not exaggerate if you say that it could hardly be matched in the world."

"I could perhaps suggest that the set should be valued by an expert."

"Excellent, Watson! You scintillate to-day. Suggest Christie or Sotheby. Your delicacy prevents your putting a price for yourself."

"But if he won't see me?"

"Oh, yes, he will see you. He has the collection mania in its most acute form - and especially on this subject, on which he is an acknowledged authority. Sit down, Watson, and I will dictate the letter. No answer needed. You will merely say that you are coming, and why."

It was an admirable document, short, courteous, and stimulating to the curiosity of the connoisseur. A district messenger was duly dispatched with it. On the same evening, with the precious saucer in my hand and the card of Dr. Hill Barton in my pocket, I set off on my own adventure.

The beautiful house and grounds indicated that Baron Gruner was, as Sir James had said, a man of considerable wealth. A long winding drive, with banks of rare shrubs on either side, opened out into a great gravelled square adorned with statues. The place had been built by a South African gold king in the days of the great boom, and the long, low house with the turrets at the corners, though an architectural nightmare, was imposing in its size and solidity. A butler, who would have adorned a bench of bishops, showed me in and handed me over to a plush-clad footman, who ushered me into the Baron's presence.

He was standing at the open front of a great case which stood between the windows and which contained part of his Chinese collection. He turned as I entered with a small brown vase in his hand.

"Pray sit down, Doctor," said he. "I was looking over my own treasures and wondering whether I could really afford to add to them. This little Tang specimen, which dates from the seventh century, would probably interest you. I am sure you never saw finer workmanship or a richer glaze. Have you the Ming saucer with you of which you spoke?"

I carefully unpacked it and handed it to him. He seated himself at his desk, pulled over the lamp, for it was growing dark, and set himself to examine it. As he did so the yellow light beat upon his own features, and I was able to study them at my ease.

He was certainly a remarkably handsome man. His European reputation for beauty was fully deserved. In figure he was not more than of middle size, but was built upon graceful and active lines. His face was swarthy, almost Oriental, with large, dark, languorous eyes which might easily hold an irresistible fascination for women. His hair and moustache were raven black, the latter short, pointed, and carefully waxed. His features were regular and pleasing, save only his straight, thin-lipped mouth. If ever I saw a murderer's mouth it was there - a cruel, hard gash in the face, compressed, inexorable, and terrible. He was ill-advised to train his moustache away from it, for it was Nature's danger-signal, set as a warning to his victims. His voice was engaging and his manners perfect. In age I should have put him at little over thirty, though his record afterwards showed that he was forty-two.

"Very fine - very fine indeed!" he said at last. "And you say you have a set of six to correspond. What puzzles me is that I should not have heard of such magnificent specimens. I only know of one in England to match this, and it is certainly not likely to be in the market. Would it be indiscreet if I were to ask you, Dr. Hill Barton, how you obtained this?"

"Does it really matter?" I asked with as careless an air as I could muster.

"You can see that the piece is genuine, and, as to the value, I am content to take an expert's valuation."

"Very mysterious," said he with a quick, suspicious flash of his dark eyes. "In dealing with objects of such value, one naturally wishes to know all about the transaction. That the piece is genuine is certain. I have no doubts at all about that. But suppose - I am bound to take every possibility into account - that it should prove afterwards that you had no right to sell?"

"I would guarantee you against any claim of the son."

"That, of course, would open up the question as to what your guarantee was worth."

"My bankers would answer that."

"Quite so. And yet the whole transaction strikes me as rather unusual."

"You can do business or not," said I with indifference. "I have given you the first offer as I understood that you were a connoisseur, but I shall have no difficulty in other quaerers."

"Who told you I was a connoisseur?"

"I was aware that you had written a book upon the subject."

"Have you read the book?"

"No."

"Dear me, this becomes more and more difficult for me to understand! You are a connoisseur and collector with a very valuable piece in your collection, and yet you have never troubled to consult the one book which would have told you of the real meaning and value of what you held. How do you explain that?"

"I am a very busy man. I am a doctor in practice."

"That is no answer. If a man has a hobby he follows it up, whatever his other pursuits may be. You said in your note that you were a connoisseur."

"So I am."

"Might I ask you a few questions to test you? I am obliged to tell you, Doctor - if you are indeed a doctor - that the incident becomes more and more suspicious. I would ask you what do you know of the Emperor Shomu and how do you associate him with the Shoso-in near Nara? Dear me, does that puzzle you? Tell me a little about the Nonhern Wei dynasty and its place in the history of ceramics."

I sprang from my chair in simulated anger.

"This is intolerable, sir," said I. "I came here to do you a favour, and not to be examined as if I were a schoolboy. My knowledge on these subjects may be second only to your own, but I certainly shall not answer questions which have been put in so offensive a way."

He looked at me steadily. The languor had gone from his eyes. They suddenly glared. There was a gleam of teeth from between those cruel lips.

"What is the game? You are here as a spy. You are an emissary of Holmes. This is a trick that you are playing upon me. The fellow is dying I hear, so he sends his tools to keep watch upon me. You've made your way in here without leave, and, by God! you may find it harder to get out than to get in."

He had sprung to his feet, and I stepped back, bracing myself for an attack, for the man was beside himself with rage. He may have suspected me from the first; certainly this cross-examination had shown him the truth; but it was clear that I could not hope to deceive him. He dived his hand into a side-drawer and rummaged furiously. Then something struck upon his ear, for he stood listening intently.

"Ah!" he cried. "Ah!" and dashed into the room behind him.

Two steps took me to the open door, and my mind will ever carry a clear picture of the scene within. The window leading out to the garden was wide open. Beside it, looking like some terrible ghost, his head gin with bloody bandages, his face drawn and white, stood Sherlock Holmes. The next instant he was through the gap, and I heard the crash of his body among the laurel bushes outside. With a howl of rage the master of the house rushed after him to the open window.

And then! It was done in an instant, and yet I clearly saw it. An arm - a woman's arm - shot out from among the leaves. At the same instant the Baron uttered a horrible cry - a yell which will always ring in my memory. He clapped his two hands to his face and rushed round the room, beating his head horribly against the walls. Then he fell upon the carpet, rolling and writhing, while scream after scream resounded through the house.

"Water! For God's sake, water!" was his cry.

I seized a carafe from a side-table and rushed to his aid. At the same moment the butler and several footmen ran in from the hall. I remember that one of them fainted as I knelt by the injured man and turned that awful face to the light of the lamp. The vitriol was eating into it everywhere and dripping from the ears and the chin. One eye was already white and glazed. The other was red and inflamed. The features which I had admired a few minutes before were now like some beautiful painting over which the artist has passed a wet and foul sponge. They were blurred, discoloured, inhuman, and terrible.

In a few words I explained exactly what had occurred, so far as the vitriol attack was concerned. Some had climbed through the window and others had rushed out on to the lawn, but it was dark and it had begun to rain. Between his screams the victim raged and raved against the avenger. "It was that hell-cat, Kitty Winter!" he cried. "Oh, the she-devil! She shall pay for it! She shall pay! Oh, God in heaven, this pain is more than I can bear!"

I bathed his face in oil, put cotton wadding on the raw surfaces, and administered a hypodermic of morphia. All suspicion of me had passed from his mind in the presence of this shock, and he clung to my hands as if I might have the power even yet to clear those dead-fish eyes which glazed up at me. I could have wept over the ruin had I not remembered very clearly the vile life which had led up to so hideous a change. It was loathsome to feel the pawing of his burning hands, and I was relieved when his family surgeon, closely followed by a specialist, came to relieve me of my charge. An inspector of police had also arrived, and to him I handed my real card. It would have been useless as well as foolish to do otherwise, for I was nearly as well known by sight at the Yard as Holmes himself. Then I left that house of gloom and terror. Within an hour I was at Baker Street.

Holmes was seated in his familiar chair, looking very pale and exhausted. Apart from his injuries, even his iron nerves had been shocked by the events of the evening, and he listened with horror to my account of the Baron's transformation.

"The wages of sin, Watson - the wages of sin!" said he. "Sooner or later it will always come. God knows, there was sin enough," he added, taking up a brown volume from the table. "Here is the book the woman talked of. If this will not break off the marriage, nothing ever could. But it will, Watson. It must. No self-respecting woman could stand it."

"It is his love diary?"

"Or his lust diary. Call it what you will. The moment the woman told us of it I realized what a tremendous weapon was there if we could but lay our hands on it. I said nothing at the time to indicate my thoughts, for this woman might have given it away. But I brooded over it. Then this assault upon me gave me the chance of letting the Baron think that no precautions need be taken against me. That was all to the good. I would have waited a little longer, but his visit to America forced my hand. He would never have left so compromising a document behind him. Therefore we had to act at once. Burglary at night is impossible. He takes precautions. But there was a chance in the evening if I could only be sure that his attention was engaged. That was where you and your blue saucer came in. But I had to be sure of the position of the book, and I knew I had only a few minutes in which to act, for my time was limited by your knowledge of Chinese pottery. Therefore I gathered the girl up at the last moment. How could I guess what the little packet was that she carried so carefully under her cloak? I thought she had come altogether on my business, but it seems she had some of her own."

"He guessed I came from you."

"I feared he would. But you held him in play just long enough for me to get the book, though not long enough for an unobserved escape. Ah, Sir James, I am very glad you have come!"

Our courtly friend had appeared in answer to a previous summons. He listened with the deepest attention to Holmes's account of what had occurred.

"You have done wonders - wonders!" he cried when he had heard the narrative. "But if these injuries are as terrible as Dr. Watson describes, then surely our purpose of thwarting the marriage is sufficiently gained without the use of this horrible book."

Holmes shook his head.

"Women of the De Merville type do not act like that. She would love him the more as a disfigured martyr. No, no. It is his moral side, not his physical, which we have to destroy. That book will bring her back to earth -nd I know nothing else that could. It is in his own writing. She cannot get past it."

Sir James carried away both it and the precious saucer. As I was myself overdue, I went down with him into the street. A brougham was waiting for him. He sprang in, gave a hurried order to the cockaded coachman, and drove swiftly away. He flung his overcoat half out of the window to cover the armorial bearings upon the panel, but I had seen them in the glare of our fanlight none the less. I gasped with surprise. Then I turned back and ascended the stair to Holmes's room.

"I have found out who our client is," I cried, bursting with my great news. "Why, Holmes, it is -"

"It is a loyal friend and a chivalrous gentleman," said Holmes, holding up a restraining hand. "Let that now and forever be enough for us."

I do not know how the incriminating book was used. Sir James may have managed it. Or it is more probable that so delicate a task was entrusted to the young lady's father. The effect, at any rate, was all that could be desired.

Three days later appeared a paragraph in the Morning Post to say that the marriage between Baron Adelbert Gruner and Miss Violet de Merville would not take place. The same paper had the first police-court hearing of the proceedings against Miss Kitty Winter on the grave charge of vitriol-throwing. Such extenuating circumstances came out in the trial that the sentence, as will be remembered was the lowest that was possible for such an offence. Sherlock Holmes was threatened with a prosecution for burglary, but when an object is good and a client is sufficiently illustrious, even the rigid British law becomes human and elastic. My friend has not yet stood in the dock.

THE ADVENTURE OF THE BLANCHED SOLDIER

The ideas of my friend Watson, though limited, are exceedingly pertinacious. For a long time he has worried me to write an experience of my own. Perhaps I have rather invited this persecution, since I have often had occasion to point out to him how superficial are his own accounts and to accuse him of pandering to popular taste instead of confining himself rigidly to facts and figures. "Try it yourself, Holmes!" he has retorted, and I am compelled to admit that, having taken my pen in my hand, I do begin to realize that the matter must be presented in such a way as may interest the reader. The following case can hardly fail to do so, as it is among the strangest happenings in my collection though it chanced that Watson had no note of it in his collection. Speaking of my old friend and biographer, I would take this opportunity to remark that if I burden myself with a companion in my various little inquiries it is not done out of sentiment or caprice, but it is that Watson has some remarkable characteristics of his own to which in his modesty he has given small attention amid his exaggerated estimates of my own performances. A confederate who foresees your conclusions and course of action is always dangerous, but one to whom each development comes as a perpetual surprise, and to whom the future is always a closed book, is indeed an ideal helpmate.

I find from my notebook that it was in January, 1903, just after the conclusion of the Boer War, that I had my visit from Mr. James M. Dodd, a big, fresh, sunburned, upstanding Briton. The good Watson had at that time deserted me for a wife, the only selfish action which I can recall in our association. I was alone.

It is my habit to sit with my back to the window and to place my visitors in the opposite chair, where the light falls full upon them.

Mr. James M. Dodd seemed somewhat at a loss how to begin the interview. I did not attempt to help him, for his silence gave me more time for observation. I have found it wise to impress clients with a sense of power, and so I gave him some of my conclusions.

"From South Africa, sir, I perceive."

"Yes, sir," he answered, with some surprise.

"Imperial Yeomanry, I fancy."

"Exactly."

"Middlesex Corps, no doubt."

"That is so. Mr. Holmes, you are a wizard."

I smiled at his bewildered expression.

"When a gentleman of virile appearance enters my room with such tan upon his face as an English sun could never give, and with his handkerchief in his sleeve instead of in his pocket, it is not difficult to place him. You wear a short beard, which shows that you were not a regular. You have the cut of a riding-man. As to Middlesex, your card has already shown me that you are a stockbroker from Throgmorton Street. What other regiment would you join?"

"You see everything."

"I see no more than you, but I have trained myself to notice what I see. However, Mr. Dodd, it was not to discuss the science of observation that you called upon me this morning. What has been happening at Tuxbury Old Park?"

"Mr. Holmes -!"

"My dear sir, there is no mystery. Your letter came with that heading, and as you fixed this appointment in very pressing terms it was clear that something sudden and important had occurred."

"Yes, indeed. But the letter was written in the afternoon, and a good deal has happened since then. If Colonel Emsworth had not kicked me out -"

"Kicked you out!"

"Well, that was what it amounted to. He is a hard nail, is Colonel Emsworth. The greatest martinet in the Army in his day, and it was a day of rough language, too. I couldn't have stuck the colonel if it had not been for Godfrey's sake."

I lit my pipe and leaned back in my chair.

"Perhaps you will explain what you are talking about."

My client grinned mischievously.

"I had got into the way of supposing that you knew everything without being told," said he. "But I will give you the facts, and I hope to God that you will be able to tell me what they mean. I've been awake all night puzzling my brain, and the more I think the more incredible does it become."

"When I joined up in January, 1901 - just two years ago - young Godfrey Emsworth had joined the same squadron. He was Colonel Emsworth's only son - Emsworth the Crimean V.C. - and he had the fighting blood in him, so it is no wonder he volunteered. There was not a finer lad in the regiment. We formed a friendship - the sort of friendship which can only be made when one lives the same life and shares the same joys and sorrows. He was my mate - and that means a good deal in the Army. We took the rough and the smooth together for a year of hard fighting. Then he was hit with a bullet from an elephant gun in the action near Diamond Hill outside - Pretoria. I got one letter from the hospital at Cape Town and one from Southampton. Since then not a word - not one word, Mr. Holmes, for six months and more, and he my closest pal."

"Well, when the war was over, and we all got back, I wrote to his father and asked where Godfrey was. No answer. I waited a bit and then I wrote again. This time I had a reply, short and gruff. Godfrey had gone on a voyage round the world, and it was not likely that he would be back for a year. That was all."

"I wasn't satisfied, Mr. Holmes. The whole thing seemed to me so damned unnatural. He was a good lad, and he would not drop a pal like that. It was not like him. Then, again, I happened to know that he was heir to a lot of money, and also that his father and he did not always hit it off too well. The old man was sometimes a bully, and young Godfrey had too much spirit to stand it. No, I wasn't satisfied, and I determined that I would get to the root of the matter. It happened, however, that my own affairs needed a lot of straightening out, after two years' absence, and so it is only this week that I have been able to take up Godfrey's case again. But since I have taken it up I mean to drop everything in order to see it through."

Mr. James M. Dodd appeared to be the sort of person whom it would be better to have as a friend than as an enemy. His blue eyes were stern and his square jaw had set hard as he spoke.

"Well, what have you done?" I asked.

"My first move was to get down to his home, Tuxbury Old Park, near Bedford, and to see for myself how the ground lay. I wrote to the mother, therefore - I had had quite enough of the curmudgeon of a father - and I made a clean frontal attack: Godfrey was my chum, I had a great deal of interest which I might tell her of our common experiences, I should be in the neighbourhood, would there be any objection, et cetera? In reply I had quite an amiable answer from her and an offer to put me up for the night. That was what took me down on Monday."

"Tuxbury Old Hall is inaccessible - five miles from anywhere. There was no trap at the station, so I had to walk, carrying my suitcase, and it was nearly dark before I arrived. It is a great wandering house, standing in a considerable park. I should judge it was of all sorts of ages and styles, starting on a half-timbered Elizabethan foundation and ending in a Victorian portico. Inside it was all panelling and tapestry and half-effaced old pictures, a house of shadows and mystery. There was a butler, old Ralph, who seemed about the same age as the house, and there was his wife, who might have been older. She had been Godfrey's nurse, and I had heard him speak of her as second only to his mother in his affections, so I was drawn to her in spite of her queer appearance. The mother I liked also - a gentle little white mouse of a woman. It was only the colonel himself whom I barred."

"We had a bit of barney right away, and I should have walked back to the station if I had not felt that it might be playing his game for me to do so. I was shown straight into his study, and there I found him, a huge, bow-backed man with a smoky skin and a straggling gray beard, seated behind his littered desk. A red-veined nose jutted out like a vulture's beak, and two fierce gray eyes glared at me from under tufted brows. I could understand now why Godfrey seldom spoke of his father."

"Well, sir", said he in a rasping voice, "I should be interested to know the real reasons for this visit."

"I answered that I had explained them in my letter to his wife."

"Yes, yes, you said that you had known Godfrey in Africa. We have, of course, only your word for that."

"I have his letters to me in my pocket."

"Kindly let me see them."

He glanced at the two which I handed him, and then he tossed them back.

"Well, what then?" he asked.

"I was fond of your son Godfrey, sir. Many ties and memories united us. Is it not natural that I should wonder at his sudden silence and should wish to know what has become of him?"

"I have some recollections, sir, that I had already corresponded with you and had told you what had become of him. He has gone upon a voyage round the world. His health was in a poor way after his African experiences, and both his mother and I were of opinion that complete rest and change were needed. Kindly pass that explanation on to any other friends who may be interested in the matter."

"Certainly," I answered. "But perhaps you would have the goodness to let me have the name of the steamer and of the line by which he sailed, together with the date. I have no doubt that I should be able to get a letter through to him."

My request seemed both to puzzle and to irritate my host. His great eyebrows came down over his eyes, and he tapped his fingers impatiently on the table. He looked up at last with the expression of one who has seen his adversary make a dangerous move at chess, and has decided how to meet it.

"Many people, Mr. Dodd," said he, "would take offence at your infernal pertinacity and would think that this insistence had reached the point of damned impertinence."

"You must put it down, sir, to my real love for your son."

"Exactly. I have already made every allowance upon that score. I must ask you, however, to drop these inquiries. Every family has its own inner knowledge and its own motives, which cannot always be made clear to outsiders, however well-intentioned. My wife is anxious to hear something of Godfrey's past which you are in a position to tell her, but I would ask you to let the present and the future alone. Such inquiries serve no useful purpose, sir, and place us in a delicate and difficult position."

"So I came to a dead end, Mr. Holmes. There was no getting past it. I could only pretend to accept the situation and register a vow inwardly that I would never rest until my friend's fate had been cleared up. It was a dull evening. We dined quietly, the three of us, in a gloomy, faded old room. The lady questioned me eagerly about her son, but the old man seemed morose and depressed. I was so bored by the whole proceeding that I made an excuse as soon as I decently could and retired to my bedroom. It was a large, bare room on the ground floor, as gloomy as the rest of the house, but after a year of sleeping upon the veldt, Mr. Holmes, one is not too particular about one's quarters. I opened the curtains and looked out into the garden, remarking that it was a fine night with a bright half-moon. Then I sat down by the roaring fire with the lamp on a table beside me, and endeavoured to distract my mind with a novel. I was interrupted, however, by Ralph, the old butler, who came in with a fresh supply of coals."

"I thought you might run short in the night-time, sir. It is bitter weather and these rooms are cold."

"He hesitated before leaving the room, and when I looked round he was standing facing me with a wistful look upon his wrinkled face."

"Beg your pardon, sir, but I could not help hearing what you said of young Master Godfrey at dinner. You know, sir, that my wife nursed him, and so I may say I am his foster-father. It's natural we should take an interest. And you say he carried himself well, sir?"

"There was no braver man in the regiment. He pulled me out once from under the rifles of the Boers, or maybe I should not be here."

The old butler rubbed his skinny hands.

"Yes, sir, yes, that is Master Godfrey all over. He was always courageous. There's not a tree in the park, sir, that he has not climbed. Nothing would stop him. He was a fine boy and oh, sir, he was a fine man."

I sprang to my feet.

"Look here!" I cried. "You say he was. You speak as if he were dead. What is all this mystery? What has become of Godfrey Emsworth?"

"I gripped the old man by the shoulder, but he shrank away.

"I don't know what you mean, sir. Ask the master about Master Godfrey. He knows. It is not for me to interfere."

He was leaving the room, but I held his arm

"Listen," I said. "You are going to answer one question before you leave if I have to hold you all night. Is Godfrey dead?"

"He could not face my eyes. He was like a man hypnotized. The answer was dragged from his lips. It was a terrible and unexpected one."

"I wish to God he was!" he cried, and, tearing himself free he dashed from the room.

"You will think, Mr. Holmes, that I returned to my chair in no very happy state of mind. The old man's words seemed to me to bear only one interpretation. Clearly my poor friend had become involved in some criminal or, at the least, disreputable transaction which touched the family honour. That stern old man had sent his son away and hidden him from the world lest some scandal should come to light. Godfrey was a reckless fellow. He was easily influenced by those around him. No doubt he had fallen into bad hands and been misled to his ruin. It was a piteous business, if it was indeed so, but even now it was my duty to hunt him out and see if I could aid him. I was anxiously pondering the matter when I looked up, and there was Godfrey Emsworth standing before me."

My client had paused as one in deep emotion.

"Pray continue," I said. "Your problem presents some very unusual features."

"He was outside the window, Mr. Holmes, with his face pressed against the glass. I have told you that I looked out at the night. When I did so I left the curtains partly open. His figure was framed in this gap. The window came down to the ground and I could see the whole length of it, but it was his face which held my gaze. He was deadly pale - never have I seen a man so white. I reckon ghosts may look like that; but his eyes met mine, and they were the eyes of a living man. He sprang back when he saw that I was looking at him, and he vanished into the darkness."

"There was something shocking about the man, Mr. Holmes. It wasn't merely that ghastly face glimmering as white as cheese in the darkness. It was more subtle than that - something slinking, something furtive, something guilty - something very unlike the frank, manly lad that I had known. It left a feeling of horror in my mind."

"But when a man has been soldiering for a year or two with brother Boer as a playmate, he keeps his nerve and acts quickly. Godfrey had hardly vanished before I was at the window. There was an awkward catch, and I was some little time before I could throw it up. Then I nipped through and ran down the garden path in the direction that I thought he might have taken."

"It was a long path and the light was not very good, but it seemed to me something was moving ahead of me. I ran on and called his name, but it was no use. When I got to the end of the path there were several others branching in different directions to various outhouses. I stood hesitating, and as I did so I heard distinctly the sound of a closing door. It was not behind me in the house, but ahead of me, somewhere in the darkness. That was enough, Mr. Holmes, to assure me that what I had seen was not a vision. Godfrey had run away from me, and he had shut a door behind him. Of that I was certain."

"There was nothing more I could do, and I spent an uneasy night turning the matter over in my mind and trying to find some theory which would cover the facts. Next day I found the colonel rather more conciliatory, and as his wife remarked that there were some places of interest in the neighbourhood, it gave me an opening to ask whether my presence for one more night would incommode them. A somewhat grudging acquiescence from the old man gave me a clear day in which to make my observations. I was already perfectly convinced that Godfrey was in hiding somewhere near, but where and why remained to be solved."

"The house was so large and so rambling that a regiment might be hid away in it and no one the wiser. If the secret lay there it was difficult for me to penetrate it. But the door which I had heard close was certainly not in the house. I must explore the garden and see what I could find. There was no difficulty in the way, for the old people were busy in their own fashion and left me to my own devices."

"There were several small outhouses, but at the end of the garden there was a detached building of some size - large enough for a gardener's or a gamekeeper's residence. Could this be the place whence the sound of that shutting door had come? I approached it in a careless fashion as though I were strolling aimlessly round the grounds. As I did so, a small, brisk, bearded man in a black coat and bowler hat - not at all the gardener type - came out of the door. To my surprise, he locked it after him and put the key in his pocket. Then he looked at me with some surprise on his face."

"Are you a visitor here?" he asked.

"I explained that I was and that I was a friend of Godfrey's."

"What a pity that he should be away on his travels, for he would have so liked to see me," I continued.

"Quite so. Exactly," said he with a rather guilty air. "No doubt you will renew your visit at some more propitious time." He passed on, but when I turned I observed that he was standing watching me, half-concealed by the laurels at the far end of the garden.

I had a good look at the little house as I passed it, but the windows were heavily curtained, and, so far as one could see, it was empty. I might spoil my own game and even be ordered off the premises if I were too audacious, for I was still conscious that I was being watched. Therefore, I strolled back to the house and waited for night before I went on with my inquiry. When all was dark and quiet I slipped out of my window and made my way as silently as possible to the mysterious lodge.

"I have said that it was heavily curtained, but now I found that the windows were shuttered as well. Some light, however, was breaking through one of them, so I concentrated my attention upon this. I was in luck, for the curtain had not been quite closed, and there was a crack in the shutter, so that I could see the inside of the room. It was a cheery place enough, a bright lamp and a blazing fire. Opposite to me was seated the little man whom I had seen in the morning. He was smoking a pipe and reading a paper."

"What paper?" I asked.

My client seemed annoyed at the interruption of his narrative.

"Can it matter?" he asked.

"It is most essential."

"I really took no notice."

"Possibly you observed whether it was a broad-leafed paper or of that smaller type which one associates with weeklies."

"Now that you mention it, it was not large. It might have been the Spectator. However, I had little thought to spare upon such details, for a second man was seated with his back to the window, and I could swear that this second man was Godfrey. I could not see his face, but I knew the familiar slope of his shoulders. He was leaning upon his elbow in an attitude of great melancholy, his body turned towards the fire. I was hesitating as to what I should do when there was a sharp tap on my shoulder, and there was Colonel Emsworth beside me."

"This way, sir!" said he in a low voice. He walked in silence to the house, and I followed him into my own bedroom. He had picked up a time-table in the hall.

"There is a train to London at 8:30," said he. "The trap will be at the door at eight."

He was white with rage, and, indeed, I felt myself in so difficult a position that I could only stammer out a few incoherent apologies in which I tried to excuse myself by urging my anxiety for my friend.

"The matter will not bear discussion," said he abruptly. "You have made a most damnable intrusion into the privacy of our family. You were here as a guest and you have become a spy. I have nothing more to say, sir, save that I have no wish ever to see you again."

"At this I lost my temper, Mr. Holmes," and I spoke with some warmth.

"I have seen your son, and I am convinced that for some reason of your own you are concealing him from the world. I have no idea what your motives are in cutting him off in this fashion, but I am sure that he is no longer a free agent. I warn you, Colonel Emsworth, that until I am assured as to the safety and well-being of my friend I shall never desist in my efforts to get to the bottom of the mystery, and I shall certainly not allow myself to be intimidated by anything which you may say or do."

"The old fellow looked diabolical, and I really thought he was about to attack me. I have said that he was a gaunt, fierce old giant, and though

I am no weakling I might have been hard put to it to hold my own against him. However, after a long glare of rage he turned upon his heel and walked out of the room. For my part, I took the appointed train in the morning, with the full intention of coming straight to you and asking for your advice and assistance at the appointment for which I had already written."

Such was the problem which my visitor laid before me. It presented, as the astute reader will have already perceived, few difficulties in its solution, for a very limited choice of alternatives must get to the root of the matter. Still, elementary as it was, there were points of interest and novelty about it which may excuse my placing it upon record. I now proceeded, using my familiar method of logical analysis, to narrow down the possible solutions.

"The servants," I asked; "how many were in the house?"

"To the best of my belief there were only the old butler and his wife. They seemed to live in the simplest fashion."

"There was no servant, then, in the detached house?"

"None, unless the little man with the beard acted as such. He seemed, however, to be quite a superior person."

"That seems very suggestive. Had you any indication that food was conveyed from the one house to the other?"

"Now that you mention it, I did see old Ralph carrying a basket down the garden walk and going in the direction of this house. The idea of food did not occur to me at the moment."

"Did you make any local inquiries?"

"Yes, I did. I spoke to the station-master and also to the innkeeper in the village. I simply asked if they knew anything of my old comrade, Godfrey Emsworth. Both of them assured me that he had gone for a voyage round the world. He had come home and then had almost at once started off again. The story was evidently universally accepted."

"You said nothing of your suspicions?"

"Nothing."

"That was very wise. The matter should certainly be inquired into. I will go back with you to Tuxbury Old Park."

"To-day?"

It happened that at the moment I was clearing up the case which my friend Watson has described as that of the Abbey School, in which the Duke of Greyminster was so deeply involved. I had also a commission from the Sultan of Turkey which called for immediate action, as political consequences of the gravest kind might arise from its neglect. Therefore it was not until the beginning of the next week, as my diary records, that I was able to start forth on my mission to Bedfordshire in company with Mr. James M. Dodd. As we drove to Eustonn we picked up a grave and taciturn gentleman of iron-gray aspect, with whom I had made the necessary arrangements.

"This is an old friend," said I to Dodd. "It is possible that his presence may be entirely unnecessary, and, on the other hand, it may be essential. It is not necessary at the present stage to go further into the matter."

The narratives of Watson have accustomed the reader, no doubt, to the fact that I do not waste words or disclose my thoughts while a case is actually under consideration. Dodd seemed surprised, but nothing more was said, and the three of us continued our journey together. In the train I asked Dodd one more question which I wished our companion to hear.

"You say that you saw your friend's face quite clearly at the window, so clearly that you are sure of his identity?"

"I have no doubt about it whatever. His nose was pressed against the glass. The lamplight shone full upon him."

"It could not have been someone resembling him?"

"No, no, it was he."

"But you say he was changed?"

"Only in colour. His face was - how shall I describe it? - it was of a fish-belly whiteness. It was bleached."

"Was it equally pale all over?"

"I think not. It was his brow which I saw so clearly as it was pressed against the window."

"Did you call to him?"

"I was too startled and horrified for the moment. Then I pursued him, as I have told you, but without result."

My case was practically complete, and there was only one small incident needed to round it off. When, after a considerable drive, we arrived at the strange old rambling house which my client had described, it was Ralph, the elderly butler, who opened the door. I had requisitioned the carriage for the day and had asked my elderly friend to remain within it unless we should summon him. Ralph, a little wrinkled old fellow, was in the conventional costume of black coat and pepper-and-salt trousers, with only one curious variant. He wore brown leather gloves, which at sight of us he instantly shuffled off, laying them down on the hall-table as we passed in. I have, as my friend Watson may have remarked, an abnormally acute set of senses, and a faint but incisive scent was apparent. It seemed to centre on the hall table. I turned, placed my hat there, knocked it off, stooped to pick it up, and contrived to bring my nose within a foot of the gloves. Yes, it was undoubtedly from them that the curious tarry odour was oozing. I passed on into the study with my case complete. Alas, that I should have to show my hand so when I tell my own story! It was by concealing such links in the chain that Watson was enabled to produce his meretricious finales.

Colonel Emsworth was not in his room, but he came quickly enough on receipt of Ralph's message. We heard his quick, heavy step in the passage. The door was flung open and he rushed in with bristling beard and twisted features, as terrible an old man as ever I have seen. He held our cards in his hand, and he tore them up and stamped on the fragments.

"Have I not told you, you infernal busybody, that you are warned off the premises? Never dare to show your damned face here again. If you enter again without my leave I shall be within my rights if I use violence. I'll shoot you, sir! By God, I will! As to you, sir," turning upon me, "I extend the same warning to you. I am familiar with your ignoble profession, but you must take your reputed talents to some other field. There is no opening for them here."

"I cannot leave here," said my client firmly, "until I hear from Godfrey's own lips that he is under no restraint."

Our involuntary host rang the bell.

"Ralph," he said, "telephone down to the county police and ask the inspector to send up two constables. Tell him there are burglars in the house."

"One moment," said I. "You must be aware, Mr. Dodd, that Colonel Emsworth is within his rights and that we have no legal status within his house. On the other hand, he should recognize that your action is prompted entirely by solicitude for his son. I venture to hope that if I were allowed to have five minutes conversation with Colonel Emsworth I could certainly alter his view of the matter."

"I am not so easily altered," said the old soldier. "Ralph, do what I have told you. What the devil are you waiting for? Ring up the police!"

"Nothing of the sort," I said, putting my back to the door. "Any police interference would bring about the very catastrophe which you dread." I took out my notebook and scribbled one word upon a loose sheet. "That," said I as I handed it to Colonel Emsworth, "is what has brought us here."

He stared at the writing with a face from which every expression save amazement had vanished.

"How do you know?" he gasped, sitting down heavily in his chair.

"It is my business to know things. That is my trade."

He sat in deep thought, his gaunt hand tugging at his straggling beard. Then he made a gesture of resignation.

"Well, if you wish to see Godfrey, you shall. It is no doing of mine, but you have forced my hand. Ralph, tell Mr. Godfrey and Mr. Kent that in five minutes we shall be with them."

At the end of that time we passed down the garden path and found ourselves in front of the mystery house at the end. A small bearded man stood at the door with a look of considerable astonishment upon his face.

"This is very sudden, Colonel Emsworth," said he. "This will disarrange all our plans."

"I can't help it, Mr. Kent. Our hands have been forced. Can Mr. Godfrey see us?"

"Yes, he is waiting inside." He turned and led us into a large plainly furnished front room. A man was standing with his back to the fire, and at the sight of him my client sprang forward with outstretched hand.

"Why, Godfrey, old man, this is fine!"

But the other waved him back.

"Don't touch me, Jimmie. Keep your distance. Yes, you may well stare! I don't quite look the smart Lance-Corporal Emsworth, of B Squadron, do I?"

His appearance was certainly extraordinary. One could see that he had indeed been a handsome man with clear-cut features sunburned by an African sun, but mottled in patches over this darker surface were curious whitish patches which had bleached his skin.

"That's why I don't court visitors," said he. "I don't mind you, Jimmie, but I could have done without your friend. I suppose there is some good reason for it, but you have me at a disadvantage."

"I wanted to be sure that all was well with you, Godfrey. I saw you that night when you looked into my window, and I could not let the matter rest till I had cleared things up."

"Old Ralph told me you were there, and I couldn't help taking a peep at you. I hoped you would not have seen me, and I had to run to my burrow when I heard the window go up."

"But what in heaven's name is the matter?"

"Well, it's not a long story to tell," said he, lighting a cigarette. "You remember that morning fight at Buffelspruit, outside Pretoria, on the Eastern railway line? You heard I was hit?"

"Yes, I heard that but I never got particulars."

Three of us got separated from the others. It was very broken country, you may remember. There was Simpson - the fellow we called Baldy Simpson - and Anderson, and I. We were clearing brother Boer, but he lay low and got the three of us. The other two were killed. I got an elephant bullet through my shoulder. I stuck on to my horse, however, and he galloped several miles before I fainted and rolled off the saddle.

When I came to myself it was nightfall, and I raised myself up, feeling very weak and ill. To my surprise there was a house close beside me, a fairly large house with a broad stoep and many windows. It was deadly cold. You remember the kind of numb cold which used to come at evening, a deadly, sickening sort of cold, very different from a crisp healthy frost. Well, I was chilled to the bone, and my only hope seemed to lie in reaching that house. I staggered to my feet and dragged myself along, hardly conscious of what I did. I have a dim memory of slowly ascending the steps, entering a wide-opened door, passing into a large room which contained several beds, and throwing myself down with a gasp of satisfaction upon one of them. It was unmade, but that troubled me not at all. I drew the clothes over my shivering body and in a moment I was in a deep sleep.

It was morning when I wakened, and it seemed to me that instead of coming out into a world of sanity I had emerged into some extraordinary nightmare. The African sun flooded through the big, curtainless windows, and every detail of the great, bare, whitewashed dormitory stood out hard and clear. In front of me was standing a small, dwarf-like man with a huge, bulbous head, who was jabbering excitedly in Dutch, waving two horrible hands which looked to me like brown sponges. Behind him stood a group of people who seemed to be intensely amused by the situation, but a chill came over me as I looked at them. Not one of them was a normal human being. Everyone was twisted or swollen or disfigured in some strange way. The laughter of these strange monstrosities was a dreadful thing to hear.

It seemed that none of them could speak English, but the situation wanted clearing up, for the creature with the big head was growing furiously angry, and, uttering wild-beast cries, he had laid his deformed hands upon me and was dragging me out of bed, regardless of the fresh flow of blood from my wound. The little monster was as strong as a bull, and I don't know what he might have done to me had not an elderly man who was clearly in authority been attracted to the room by the hubbub; He said a few stern words in Dutch, and my persecutor shrank away. Then he turned upon me, gazing at me in the utmost amazement.

"How in the world did you come here?" he asked in amazement. "Wait a bit! I see that you are tired out and that wounded shoulder of yours wants looking after. I am a doctor, and I'll soon have you tied up. But, man alive! you are in far greater danger here than ever you were on the battlefield. You are in the Leper Hospital, and you have slept in a leper's bed."

"Need I tell you more, Jimmie? It seems that in view of the approaching battle all these poor creatures had been evacuated the day before. Then, as the British advanced, they had been brought back by this, their medical superintendent, who assured me that, though he believed he was immune to the disease, he would none the less never have dared to do what I had done. He put me in a private room, treated me kindly, and within a week or so I was removed to the general hospital at Pretoria."

"So there you have my tragedy. I hoped against hope, but it was not until I had reached home that the terrible signs which you see upon my face told me that I had not escaped. What was I to do? I was in this lonely house. We had two servants whom we could utterly trust. There was a house where I could live. Under pledge of secrecy, Mr. Kent, who is a surgeon, was prepared to stay with me. It seemed simple enough on those lines. The alternative was a dreadful one - segregation for life among strangers with never a hope of release. But absolute secrecy was necessary, or even in this quiet countryside there would have been an outcry, and I should have been dragged to my horrible doom. Even you, Jimmie - even you had to be kept in the dark. Why my father has relented I cannot imagine."

Colonel Emsworth pointed to me.

"This is the gentleman who forced my hand." He unfolded the scrap of paper on which I had written the word "Leprosy." "It seemed to me that if he knew so much as that it was safer that he should know all."

"And so it was," said I. "Who knows but good may come of it? I understand that only Mr. Kent has seen the patient. May I ask, sir, if you are an authority on such complaints, which are, I understand, tropical or semi-tropical in their nature?"

"I have the ordinary knowledge of the educated medical man," he observed with some stiffness.

"I have no doubt, sir, that you are fully competent, but I am sure that you will agree that in such a case a second opinion is valuable. You have avoided this, I understand, for fear that pressure should be put upon you to segregate the patient."

"That is so," said Colonel Emsworth.

"I foresaw this situation," I explained, "and I have brought with me a friend whose discretion may absolutely be trusted. I was able once to do him a professional service, and he is ready to advise as a friend rather than as a specialist. His name is Sir James Saunders."

The prospect of an interview with Lord Roberts would not have excited greater wonder and pleasure in a raw subaltern than was now reflected upon the face of Mr. Kent.

"I shall indeed be proud," he murmured.

"Then I will ask Sir James to step this way. He is at present in the carriage outside the door. Meanwhile, Colonel Emsworth, we may perhaps assemble in your study, where I could give the necessary explanations."

And here it is that I miss my Watson. By cunning questions and ejaculations of wonder he could elevate my simple art, which is but systematized common sense, into a prodigy. When I tell my own story I have no such aid. And yet I will give my process of thought even as I gave it to my small audience, which included Godfrey's mother in the study of Colonel Emsworth.

"That process," said I, "starts upon the supposition that when you have eliminated all which is impossible, then whatever remains, however improbable, must be the truth. It may well be that several explanations remain, in which case one tries test after test until one or other of them has a convincing amount of support. We will now apply this principle to the case in point. As it was first presented to me, there were three possible explanations of the seclusion or incarceration of this gentleman in an outhouse of his father's mansion. There was the explanation that he was in hiding for a crime, or that he was mad and that they wished to avoid an asylum, or that he had some disease which caused his segregation. I could think of no other adequate solutions. These, then, had to be sifted and balanced against each other."

"The criminal solution would not bear inspection. No unsolved crime had been reported from that district. I was sure of that. If it were some crime not yet discovered, then clearly it would be to the interest of the family to get rid of the delinquent and send him abroad rather than keep him concealed at home. I could see no explanation for such a line of conduct."

"Insanity was more plausible. The presence of the second person in the outhouse suggested a keeper. The fact that he locked the door when he came out strengthened the supposition and gave the idea of constraint. On the other hand, this constraint could not be severe or the young man could not have got loose and come down to have a look at his friend. You will remember, Mr. Dodd, that I felt round for points, asking you, for example, about the paper which Mr. Kent was reading. Had it been the Lancet or the British Medical Journal it would have helped me. It is not illegal, however, to keep a lunatic upon private premises so long as there is a qualified person in attendance and that the authorities have been duly notified. Why, then, all this desperate desire for secrecy? Once again I could not get the theory to fit the facts."

"There remained the third possibility, into which, rare and unlikely as it was, everything seemed to fit. Leprosy is not uncommon in South Africa. By some extraordinary chance this youth might have contracted it. His people would be placed in a very dreadful position, since they would desire to save him from segregation. Great secrecy would be needed to prevent rumours from getting about and subsequent interference by the authorities. A devoted medical man, if sufficiently paid, would easily be found to take charge of the sufferer. There would be no reason why the latter should not be allowed freedom after dark. Bleaching of the skin is a common result of the disease. The case was a strong one - so strong that I determined to act as if it were actually proved. When on arriving here I noticed that Ralph, who carries out the meals, had gloves which are impregnated with disinfectants, my last doubts were removed. A single word showed you, sir, that your secret was discovered, and if I wrote rather than said it, it was to prove to you that my discretion was to be trusted."

I was finishing this little analysis of the case when the door was opened and the austere figure of the great dermatologist was ushered in. But for once his sphinx-like features had relaxed and there was a warm humanity in his eyes. He strode up to Colonel Emsworth and shook him by the hand.

"It is often my lot to bring ill-tidings and seldom good," said he. "This occasion is the more welcome. It is not leprosy."

"What?"

"A well-marked case of pseudo-leprosy or ichthyosis, a scale-like affection of the skin, unsightly, obstinate, but possibly curable, and certainly non-infective. Yes, Mr. Holmes, the coincidence is a remarkable one. But is it coincidence? Are there not subtle forces at work of which we know little? Are we assured that the apprehension from which this young man has no doubt suffered terribly since his exposure to its contagion may not produce a physical effect which simulates that which it fears? At any rate, I pledge my professional reputation - But the lady has fainted! I think that Mr. Kent had better be with her until she recovers from this joyous shock."

THE ADVENTURE OF THE MAZARIN STONE

It was pleasant to Dr. Watson to find himself once more in the untidy room of the first floor in Baker Street which had been the starting-point of so many remarkable adventures. He looked round him at the scientific charts upon the wall, the acid-charred bench of chemicals, the violin-case leaning in the corner, the coal-scuttle, which contained of old the pipes and tobacco. Finally, his eyes came round to the fresh and smiling face of Billy, the young but very wise and tactful page, who had helped a little to fill up the gap of loneliness and isolation which surrounded the saturnine figure of the great detective.

"It all seems very unchanged, Billy. You don't change, either. I hope the same can be said of him?"

Billy glanced with some solicitude at the closed door of the bedroom.

"I think he's in bed and asleep," he said.

It was seven in the evening of a lovely summer's day, but Dr. Watson was sufficiently familiar with the irregularity of his old friend's hours to feel no surprise at the idea.

"That means a case, I suppose?"

"Yes, sir, he is very hard at it just now. I'm frightened for his health. He gets paler and thinner, and he eats nothing. 'When will you be pleased to dine, Mr. Holmes?' Mrs. Hudson asked. 'Seven-thirty, the day after to-morrow,' said he. You know his way when he is keen on a case."

"Yes, Billy, I know."

"He's following someone. Yesterday he was out as a workman looking for a job. To-day he was an old woman. Fairly took me in, he did, and I ought to know his ways by now." Billy pointed with a grin to a very baggy parasol which leaned against the sofa. "That's part of the old woman's outfit," he said.

"But what is it all about, Billy?"

Billy sank his voice, as one who discusses great secrets of State. "I don't mind telling you, sir, but it should go no farther. It's this case of the Crown diamond."

"What - the hundred-thousand-pound burglary?"

"Yes, sir. They must get it back, sir. Why, we had the Prime Minister and the Home Secretary both sitting on that very sofa. Mr. Holmes was very nice to them. He soon put them at their ease and promised he would do all he could. Then there is Lord Cantlemere -"

"Ah!"

"Yes, sir, you know what that means. He's a stiff 'un, sir, if I may say so. I can get along with the Prime Minister, and I've nothing against the Home Secretary, who seemed a civil, obliging sort of man, but I can't stand his Lordship. Neither can Mr. Holmes, sir. You see, he don't believe in Mr. Holmes and he was against employing him. He'd rather he failed."

"And Mr. Holmes knows it?"

"Mr. Holmes always knows whatever there is to know."

"Well, we'll hope he won't fail and that Lord Cantlemere will be confounded. But I say, Billy, what is that curtain for across the window?"

"Mr. Holmes had it put up there three days ago. We've got something funny behind it."

Billy advanced and drew away the drapery which screened the alcove of the bow window.

Dr. Watson could not restrain a cry of amazement. There was a facsimile of his old friend, dressing-gown and all, the face turned three-quarters towards the window and downward, as though reading an invisible book, while the body was sunk deep in an armchair. Billy detached the head and held it in the air.

"We put it at different angles, so that it may seem more lifelike. I wouldn't dare touch it if the blind were not down. But when it's up you can see this from across the way."

"We used something of the sort once before."

"Before my time," said Billy. He drew the window curtains apart and looked out into the street. "There are folk who watch us from over yonder. I can see a fellow now at the window. Have a look for yourself."

Watson had taken a step forward when the bedroom door opened, and the long, thin form of Holmes emerged, his face pale and drawn, but his step and bearing as active as ever. With a single spring he was at the window, and had drawn the blind once more.

"That will do, Billy," said he. "You were in danger of your life then, my boy, and I can't do without you just yet. Well, Watson, it is good to see you in your old quarters once again. You come at a critical moment."

"So I gather."

"You can go, Billy. That boy is a problem, Watson. How far am I justified in allowing him to be in danger?"

"Danger of what, Holmes?"

"Of sudden death. I'm expecting something this evening."

"Expecting what?"

"To be murdered, Watson."

"No, no, you are joking, Holmes!"

"Even my limited sense of humour could evolve a better joke than that. But we may be comfortable in the meantime, may we not? Is alcohol permitted? The gasogene and cigars are in the old place. Let me see you once more in the customary armchair. You have not, I hope, learned to despise my pipe and my lamentable tobacco? It has to take the place of food these days."

"But why not eat?"

"Because the faculties become refined when you starve them. Why, surely, as a doctor, my dear Watson, you must admit that what your digestion gains in the way of blood supply is so much lost to the brain. I am a brain, Watson. The rest of me is a mere appendix. Therefore, it is the brain I must consider."

"But this danger, Holmes?"

"Ah. yes, in case it should come off, it would perhaps be as well that you should burden your memory with the name and address of the murderer. You can give it to Scotland Yard, with my love and a parting blessing. Sylvius is the name - Count Negretto Sylvius. Write it down, man, write it down! 136 Moorside Gardens, N.W. Got it?"

Watson's honest face was twitching with anxiety. He knew only too well the immense risks taken by Holmes and was well aware that what he said was more likely to be under-statement than exaggeration. Watson was always the man of action, and he rose to the occasion.

"Count me in, Holmes. I have nothing to do for a day or two."

"Your morals don't improve, Watson. You have added fibbing to your other vices. You bear every sign of the busy medical man, with calls on him every hour."

"Not such important ones. But can't you have this fellow arrested?"

"Yes, Watson, I could. That's what worries him so."

"But why don't you?"

"Because I don't know where the diamond is."

"Ah! Billy told me - the missing Crown jewel!"

"Yes, the great yellow Mazarin stone. I've cast my net and I have my fish. But I have not got the stone. What is the use of taking them? We can make the world a better place by laying them by the heels. But that is not what I am out for. It's the stone I want."

"And is this Count Sylvius one of your fish?"

"Yes, and he's a shark. He bites. The other is Sam Merton the boxer. Not a bad fellow, Sam, but the Count has used him. Sam's not a shark. He is a great big silly bull-headed gudgeon. But he is flopping about in my net all the same."

"Where is this Count Sylvius?"

"I've been at his very elbow all the morning. You've seen me as an old lady, Watson. I was never more convincing. He actually picked up my parasol for me once. 'By your leave, madame,' said he - half-Italian, you know, and with the Southern graces of manner when in the mood, but a devil incarnate in the other mood. Life is full of whimsical happenings, Watson."

"It might have been tragedy."

"Well, perhaps it might. I followed him to old Straubenzee's workshop in the Minories. Straubenzee made the air-gun - a very pretty bit of work, as I understand, and I rather fancy it is in the opposite window at the present moment. Have you seen the dummy? Of course, Billy showed it to you. Well, it may get a bullet through its beautiful head at any moment.

Ah, Billy, what is it?"

The boy had reappeared in the room with a card upon a tray. Holmes glanced at it with raised eyebrows and an amused smile.

"The man himself. I had hardly expected this. Grasp the nettle, Watson! A man of nerve. Possibly you have heard of his reputation as a shooter of big game. It would indeed be a triumphant ending to his excellent sporting record if he added me to his bag. This is a proof that he feels my toe very close behind his heel."

"Send for the police."

"I probably shall. But not just yet. Would you glance carefully out of the window, Watson, and see if anyone is hanging about in the street?"

Watson looked warily round the edge of the curtain.

"Yes, there is one rough fellow near the door."

"That will be Sam Merton -the faithful but rather fatuous Sam. Where is this gentleman, Billy?"

"In the waiting-room, sir."

"Show him up when I ring."

"Yes, sir."

"If I am not in the room, show him in all the same."

"Yes, sir."

Watson waited until the door was closed, and then he turned earnestly to his companion.

"Look here, Holmes, this is simply impossible. This is a desperate man, who sticks at nothing. He may have come to murder you."

"I should not be surprised."

"I insist upon staying with you."

"You would be horribly in the way."

"In his way?"

"No, my dear fellow - in my way."

"Well, I can't possibly leave you."

"Yes, you can, Watson. And you will, for you have never failed to play the game. I am sure you will play it to the end. This man has come for his own purpose, but he may stay for mine."

Holmes took out his notebook and scribbled a few lines. "Take a cab to Scotland Yard and give this to Youghal of the C.I.D. Come back with the police. The fellow's arrest will follow."

"I'll do that with joy."

"Before you return I may have just time enough to find out where the stone is." He touched the bell. "I think we will go out through the bedroom. This second exit is exceedingly useful. I rather want to see my shark without his seeing me, and I have, as you will remember, my own way of doing it."

It was, therefore, an empty room into which Billy, a minute later, ushered Count Sylvius. The famous game-shot, sportsman, and man-about-town was a big, swarthy fellow, with a formidable dark moustache shading a cruel, thin-lipped mouth, and surmounted by a long, curved nose like the beak of an eagle. He was well dressed, but his brilliant necktie, shining pin, and glittering rings were flamboyant in their effect. As the door closed behind him he looked round him with fierce, startled eyes, like one who suspects a trap at every turn. Then he gave a violent start as he saw the impassive head and the collar of the dressing-gown which projected above the armchair in the window. At first his expression was one of pure amazement. Then the light of a horrible hope gleamed in his dark, murderous eyes. He took one more glance round to see that there were no witnesses, and then, on tiptoe, his thick stick half raised, he approached the silent figure. He was crouching for his final spring and blow when a cool, sardonic voice greeted him from the open bedroom door:

"Don't break it, Count! Don't break it!"

The assassin staggered back, amazement in his convulsed face. For an instant he half raised his loaded cane once more, as if he would turn his violence from the effigy to the original; but there was something in that steady gray eye and mocking smile which caused his hand to sink to his side.

"It's a pretty little thing," said Holmes, advancing towards the image. "Tavernier, the French modeller, made it. He is as good at waxworks as your friend Straubenzee is at air-guns."

"Air-guns, sir! What do you mean?"

"Put your hat and stick on the side-table. Thank you! Pray take a seat. Would you care to put your revolver out also? Oh, very good, if you prefer to sit upon it. Your visit is really most opportune, for I wanted badly to have a few minutes' chat with you."

The Count scowled, with heavy, threatening eyebrows.

"I, too, wished to have some words with you, Holmes. That is why I am here. I won't deny that I intended to assault you just now."

Holmes swung his leg on the edge of the table.

"I rather gathered that you had some idea of the sort in your head," said he. "But why these personal attentions?"

"Because you have gone out of your way to annoy me. Because you have put your creatures upon my track."

"My creatures! I assure you no!"

"Nonsense! I have had them followed. Two can play at that game, Holmes."

"It is a small point, Count Sylvius, but perhaps you would kindly give me my prefix when you address me. You can understand that, with my routine of work, I should find myself on familiar terms with half the rogues' gallery, and you will agree that exceptions are invidious."

"Well, Mr. Holmes, then."

"Excellent! But I assure you you are mistaken about my alleged agents."

Count Sylvius laughed contemptuously.

"Other people can observe as well as you. Yesterday there was an old sporting man. To-day it was an elderly woman. They held me in view all day."

"Really, sir, you compliment me. Old Baron Dowson said the night before he was hanged that in my case what the law had gained the stage had lost. And now you give my little impersonations your kindly praise?"

"It was you - you yourself?"

Holmes shrugged his shoulders. "You can see in the corner the parasol which you so politely handed to me in the Minories before you began to suspect."

"If I had known, you might never -"

"Have seen this humble home again. I was well aware of it. We all have neglected opportunities to deplore. As it happens, you did not know, so here we are!"

The Count's knotted brows gathered more heavily over his menacing eyes. "What you say only makes the matter worse. It was not your agents but your play-acting, busybody self! You admit that you have dogged me. Why?"

"Come now, Count. You used to shoot lions in Algeria."

"Well?"

"But why?"

"Why? The sport - the excitement - the danger!"

"And, no doubt, to free the country from a pest?"

"Exactly!"

"My reasons in a nutshell!"

The Count sprang to his feet, and his hand involuntarily moved back to his hip-pocket.

"Sit down, sir, sit down! There was another, more practical, reason. I want that yellow diamond!"

Count Sylvius lay back in his chair with an evil smile.

"Upon my word!" said he.

"You knew that I was after you for that. The real reason why you are here to-night is to find out how much I know about the matter and how far my removal is absolutely essential. Well, I should say that, from your point of view, it is absolutely essential, for I know all about it, save only one thing, which you are about to tell me."

"Oh, indeed! And pray, what is this missing fact?"

"Where the Crown diamond now is."

The Count looked sharply at his companion. "Oh, you want to know that, do you? How the devil should I be able to tell you where it is?"

"You can, and you will."

"Indeed!"

"You can't bluff me, Count Sylvius." Holmes's eyes, as he gazed at him, contracted and lightened until they were like two menacing points of steel. "You are absolute plate-glass. I see to the very back of your mind."

"Then, of course, you see where the diamond is!"

Holmes clapped his hands with amusement, and then pointed a derisive finger. "Then you do know. You have admitted it!"

"I admit nothing."

"Now, Count, if you will be reasonable we can do business. If not, you will get hurt."

Count Sylvius threw up his eyes to the ceiling. "And you talk about bluff!" said he.

Holmes looked at him thoughtfully like a master chess-player who meditates his crowning move. Then he threw open the table drawer and drew out a squat notebook.

"Do you know what I keep in this book?"

"No, sir, I do not!"

"You!"

"Me!"

"Yes, sir, you! You are all here - every action of your vile and dangerous life."

"Damn you, Holmes!" cried the Count with blazing eyes. "There are limits to my patience!"

"It's all here, Count. The real facts as to the death of old Mrs. Harold, who left you the Blymer estate, which you so rapidly gambled away."

"You are dreaming!"

"And the complete life history of Miss Minnie Warrender."

"Tut! You will make nothing of that!"

"Plenty more here, Count. Here is the robbery in the train de-luxe to the Riviera on February 13, 1892. Here is the forged check in the same year on the Credit Lyonnais."

"No, you're wrong there."

"Then I am right on the others! Now, Count, you are a card-player. When the other fellow has all the trumps, it saves time to throw down your hand."

"What has all this talk to do with the jewel of which you spoke?"

"Gently, Count. Restrain that eager mind! Let me get to the points in my own humdrum fashion. I have all this against you; but, above all, I have a clear case against both you and your fighting bully in the case of the Crown diamond."

"Indeed!"

"I have the cabman who took you to Whitehall and the cabman who brought you away. I have the commissionaire who saw you near the case. I have Ikey Sanders, who refused to cut it up for you. Ikey has peached, and the game is up."

The veins stood out on the Count's forehead. His dark, hairy hands were clenched in a convulsion of restrained emotion. He tried to speak, but the words would not shape themselves.

"That's the hand I play from," said Holmes. "I put it all upon the table. But one card is missing. It's the king of diamonds. I don't know where the stone is."

"You never shall know."

"No? Now, be reasonable, Count. Consider the situation. You are going to be locked up for twenty years. So is Sam Merton. What good are you going to get out of your diamond? None in the world. But if you hand it over - well, I'll compound a felony. We don't want you or Sam. We want the stone. Give that up, and so far as I am concerned you can go free so long as you behave yourself in the future. If you make another slip well, it will be the last. But this time my commission is to get the stone, not you."

"But if I refuse?"

"Why, then - alas! - it must be you and not the stone."

Billy had appeared in answer to a ring.

"I think, Count, that it would be as well to have your friend Sam at this conference. After all, his interests should be represented. Billy, you will see a large and ugly gentleman outside the front door. Ask him to come up."

"If he won't come, sir?"

"No violence, Billy. Don't be rough with him. If you tell him that Count Sylvius wants him he will certainly come."

"What are you going to do now?" asked the Count as Billy disappeared.

"My friend Watson was with me just now. I told him that I had a shark and a gudgeon in my net; now I am drawing the net and up they come together."

The Count had risen from his chair, and his hand was behind his back. Holmes held something half protruding from the pocket of his dressing-gown.

"You won't die in your bed, Holmes."

"I have often had the same idea. Does it matter very much? After all, Count, your own exit is more likely to be perpendicular than horizontal. But these anticipations of the future are morbid. Why not give ourselves up to the unrestrained enjoyment of the present?"

A sudden wild-beast light sprang up in the dark, menacing eyes of the master criminal. Holmes's figure seemed to grow taller as he grew tense and ready.

"It is no use your fingering your revolver, my friend," he said in a quiet voice. "You know perfectly well that you dare not use it, even if I gave you time to draw it. Nasty, noisy things, revolvers, Count. Better stick to air-guns. Ah! I think I hear the fairy footstep of your estimable partner. Good day, Mr. Merton. Rather dull in the street, is it not?"

The prize-fighter, a heavily built young man with a stupid, obstinate, slab-sided face, stood awkwardly at the door, looking about him with a puzzled expression. Holmes's debonair manner was a new experience, and though he vaguely felt that it was hostile, he did not know how to counter it. He turned to his more astute comrade for help.

"What's the game now, Count? What's this fellow want? What's up?" His voice was deep and raucous.

The Count shrugged his shoulders, and it was Holmes who answered.

"If I may put it in a nutshell, Mr. Merton, I should say it was all up."

The boxer still addressed his remarks to his associate.

"Is this cove trying to be funny, or what? I'm not in the funny mood myself."

"No, I expect not," said Holmes."I think I can promise you that you will feel even less humorous as the evening advances. Now, look here,

64

Count Sylvius. I'm a busy man and I can't waste time. I'm going into that bedroom. Pray make yourselves quite at home in my absence. You can explain to your friend how the matter lies without the restraint of my presence. I shall try over the Hoffman 'Barcarole' upon my violin. In five minutes I shall return for your final answer. You quite grasp the alternative, do you not? Shall we take you, or shall we have the stone?"

Holmes withdrew, picking up his violin from the corner as he passed. A few moments later the long-drawn, wailing notes of that most haunting of tunes came faintly through the closed door of the bedroom.

"What is it, then?" asked Merton anxiously as his companion turned to him. "Does he know about the stone?"

"He knows a damned sight too much about it. I'm not sure that he doesn't know all about it."

"Good Lord!" The boxer's sallow face turned a shade whiter.

"Ikey Sanders has split on us."

"He has, has he? I'll do him down a thick 'un for that if I swing for it."

"That won't help us much. We've got to make up our minds what to do."

"Half a mo," said the boxer, looking suspiciously at the bedroom door. "He's a leary cove that wants watching. I suppose he's not listening?"

"How can he be listening with that music going?"

"That's right. Maybe somebody's behind a curtain. Too many curtains in this room." As he looked round he suddenly saw for the first time the effigy in the window, and stood staring and pointing, too amazed for words.

"Tut! it's only a dummy," said the Count.

"A fake, is it? Well, strike me! Madame Tussaud ain't in it. It's the living spit of him, gown and all. But them curtains Count!"

"Oh, confound the curtains! We are wasting our time, and there is none too much. He can lag us over this stone."

"The deuce he can!"

"But he'll let us slip if we only tell him where the swag is."

"What! Give it up? Give up a hundred thousand quid?"

"It's one or the other."

Merton scratched his short-cropped pate.

"He's alone in there. Let's do him in. If his light were out we should have nothing to fear."

The Count shook his head.

"He is armed and ready. If we shot him we could hardly get away in a place like this. Besides, it's likely enough that the police know whatever evidence he has got. Hallo! What was that?"

There was a vague sound which seemed to come from the window. Both men sprang round, but all was quiet. Save for the one strange figure seated in the chair, the room was certainly empty.

"Something in the street," said Merton. "Now look here, guv'nor, you've got the brains. Surely you can think a way out of it. If slugging is no use then it's up to you."

"I've fooled better men than he," the Count answered. "The stone is here in my secret pocket. I take no chances leaving it about. It can be out of England to-night and cut into four pieces in Amsterdam before Sunday. He knows nothing of Van Seddar."

"I thought Van Seddar was going next week."

"He was. But now he must get off by the next boat. One or other of us must slip round with the stone to Lime Street and tell him."

"But the false bottom ain't ready."

"Well, he must take it as it is and chance it. There's not a moment to lose." Again, with the sense of danger which becomes an instinct with the sportsman, he paused and looked hard at the window. Yes, it was surely from the street that the faint sound had come.

"As to Holmes," he continued, "we can fool him easily enough. You see, the damned fool won't arrest us if he can get the stone. Well, we'll promise him the stone. We'll put him on the wrong track about it, and before he finds that it is the wrong track it will be in Holland and we out of the country."

"That sounds good to me!" cried Sam Merton with a grin.

"You go on and tell the Dutchman to get a move on him. I'll see this sucker and fill him up with a bogus confession. I'll tell him that the stone is in Liverpool. Confound that whining music; it gets on my nerves! By the time he finds it isn't in Liverpool it will be in quarters and we on the blue water. Come back here, out of a line with that keyhole. Here is the stone."

"I wonder you dare carry it."

"Where could I have it safer? If we could take it out of Whitehall someone else could surely take it out of my lodgings."

"Let's have a look at it."

Count Sylvius cast a somewhat unflattering glance at his associate and disregarded the unwashed hand which was extended towards him.

"What - d'ye think I'm going to snatch it off you? See here, mister, I'm getting a bit tired of your ways."

"Well, well, no offence, Sam. We can't afford to quarrel. Come over to the window if you want to see the beauty properly. Now hold it to the light! Here!"

"Thank you!"

With a single spring Holmes had leaped from the dummy's chair and had grasped the precious jewel. He held it now in one hand, while his other pointed a revolver at the Count's head. The two villains staggered back in utter amazement. Before they had recovered Holmes had pressed the electric bell.

"No violence, gentlemen - no violence, I beg of you! Consider the furniture! It must be very clear to you that your position is an impossible one. The police are waiting below."

The Count's bewilderment overmastered his rage and fear.

"But how the deuce -?" he gasped.

"Your surprise is very natural. You are not aware that a second door from my bedroom leads behind that curtain. I fancied that you must have heard me when I displaced the figure, but luck was on my side. It gave me a chance of listening to your racy conversation which would have been painfully constrained had you been aware of my presence."

The Count gave a gesture of resignation.

"We give you best, Holmes. I believe you are the devil himself."

"Not far from him, at any rate," Holmes answered with a polite smile.

Sam Merton's slow intellect had only gradually appreciated the situation. Now, as the sound of heavy steps came from the stairs outside, he broke silence at last.

"A fair cop!" said he. "But, I say, what about that bloomin' fiddle! I hear it yet."

"Tut, tut!" Holmes answered. "You are perfectly right. Let it play! These modern gramophones are a remarkable invention."

There was an inrush of police, the handcuffs clicked and the criminals were led to the waiting cab. Watson lingered with Holmes, congratulating him upon this fresh leaf added to his laurels. Once more their conversation was interrupted by the imperturbable Billy with his card-tray.

"Lord Cantlemere sir."

"Show him up, Billy. This is the eminent peer who represents the very highest interests," said Holmes. "He is an excellent and loyal person, but rather of the old regime. Shall we make him unbend? Dare we venture upon a slight liberty? He knows, we may conjecture, nothing of what has occurred."

The door opened to admit a thin, austere figure with a hatchet face and drooping mid-Victorian whiskers of a glossy blackness which hardly corresponded with the rounded shoulders and feeble gait. Holmes advanced affably, and shook an unresponsive hand.

"How do you do, Lord Cantlemere? It is chilly for the time of year, but rather warm indoors. May I take your overcoat?"

"No, I thank you; I will not take it off."

Holmes laid his hand insistently upon the sleeve.

"Pray allow me! My friend Dr. Watson would assure you that these changes of temperature are most insidious."

His Lordship shook himself free with some impatience.

"I am quite comfortable, sir. I have no need to stay. I have simply looked in to know how your self-appointed task was progressing."

"It is difficult - very difficult."

"I feared that you would find it so."

There was a distinct sneer in the old courtier's words and manner.

"Every man finds his limitations, Mr. Holmes, but at least it cures us of the weakness of self-satisfaction."

"Yes, sir, I have been much perplexed."

"No doubt."

"Especially upon one point. Possibly you could help me upon

"You apply for my advice rather late in the day. I thought that you had your own all-sufficient methods. Still, I am ready to help you."

"You see, Lord Cantlemere, we can no doubt frame a case against the actual thieves."

"When you have caught them."

"Exactly. But the question is - how shall we proceed against the receiver?"

"Is this not rather premature?"

"It is as well to have our plans ready. Now, what would you regard as final evidence against the receiver?"

"The actual possession of the stone."

"You would arrest him upon that?"

"Most undoubtedly."

Holmes seldom laughed, but he got as near it as his old friend Watson could remember.

"In that case, my dear sir, I shall be under the painful necessity of advising your arrest."

Lord Cantlemere was very angry. Some of the ancient fires flickered up into his sallow cheeks.

"You take a great liberty, Mr. Holmes. In fifty years of official life I cannot recall such a case. I am a busy man, sir engaged upon important affairs, and I have no time or taste for foolish jokes. I may tell you frankly, sir, that I have never been a believer in your powers, and that I have always been of the opinion that the matter was far safer in the hands of the regular police force. Your conduct confirms all my conclusions. I have the honour, sir, to wish you good-evening."

Holmes had swiftly changed his position and was between the peer and the door.

"One moment, sir," said he. "To actually go off with the Mazarin stone would be a more serious offence than to be found in temporary possession of it."

"Sir, this is intolerable! Let me pass."

"Put your hand in the right-hand pocket of your overcoat."

"What do you mean, sir?"

"Come - come, do what I ask."

An instant later the amazed peer was standing, blinking and stammering, with the great yellow stone on his shaking palm.

"What! What! How is this, Mr. Holmes?"

"Too bad, Lord Cantlemere, too bad!" cried Holmes. "My old friend here will tell you that I have an impish habit of practical joking. Also that I can never resist a dramatic situation. I took the liberty - the very great liberty, I admit - of putting the stone into your pocket at the beginning of our interview."

The old peer stared from the stone to the smiling face before him.

"Sir, I am bewildered. But - yes - it is indeed the Mazarin stone. We are greatly your debtors, Mr. Holmes. Your sense of humour may, as you admit, be somewhat perverted, and its exhibition remarkably untimely, but at least I withdraw any reflection I have made upon your amazing professional powers. But how -"

"The case is but half finished; the details can wait. No doubt, Lord Cantlemere, your pleasure in telling of this successful result in the exalted circle to which you return will be some small atonement for my practical joke. Billy, you will show his Lordship out, and tell Mrs. Hudson that I should be glad if she would send up dinner for two as soon as possible."

THE ADVENTURE OF THE THREE GABLES

I don't think that any of my adventures with Mr. Sherlock Holmes opened quite so abruptly, or so dramatically, as that which I associate with The Three Gables. I had not seen Holmes for some days and had no idea of the new channel into which his activities had been directed. He was in a chatty mood that morning, however, and had just settled me into the well-worn low armchair on one side of the fire, while he had curled down with his pipe in his mouth upon the opposite chair, when our visitor arrived. If I had said that a mad bull had arrived it would give a clearer impression of what occurred.

The door had flown open and a huge negro had burst into the room. He would have been a comic figure if he had not been terrific, for he was dressed in a very loud gray check suit with a flowing salmon-coloured tie. His broad face and flattened nose were thrust forward, as his sullen dark eyes, with a smouldering gleam of malice in them, turned from one of us to the other.

"Which of you gen'l'men is Masser Holmes?" he asked.

Holmes raised his pipe with a languid smile.

"Oh! it's you, is it?" said our visitor, coming with an unpleasant, stealthy step round the angle of the table. "See here, Masser Holmes, you keep your hands out of other folks' business. Leave folks to manage their own affairs. Got that, Masser Holmes?"

"Keep on talking," said Holmes. "It's fine."

"Oh! it's fine, is it?" growled the savage. "It won't be so damn fine if I have to trim you up a bit. I've handled your kind before now, and they didn't look fine when I was through with them. Look at that, Masser Holmes!"

He swung a huge knotted lump of a fist under my friend's nose. Holmes examined it closely with an air of great interest.

"Were you born so?" he asked. "Or did it come by degrees?"

It may have been the icy coolness of my friend, or it may have been the slight clatter which I made as I picked up the poker. In any case, our visitor's manner became less flamboyant.

"Well, I've given you fair warnin'," said he. "I've a friend that's interested out Harrow way - you know what I'm meaning - and he don't intend to have no buttin' in by you. Got that? You ain't the law, and I ain't the law either, and if you come in I'll be on hand also. Don't you forget it."

"I've wanted to meet you for some time," said Holmes. "I won't ask you to sit down, for I don't like the smell of you, but aren't you Steve Dixie, the bruiser?"

"That's my name, Masser Holmes, and you'll get put through it for sure if you give me any lip."

"It is certainly the last thing you need," said Holmes, staring at our visitor's hideous mouth. "But it was the killing of young Perkins outside the Holborn - Bar What! you're not going?"

The negro had sprung back, and his face was leaden. "I won't listen to no such talk," said he. "What have I to do with this 'ere Perkins, Masser Holmes? I was trainin' at the Bull Ring in Birmingham when this boy done gone get into trouble."

"Yes, you'll tell the magistrate about it, Steve," said Holmes. "I've been watching you and Barney Stockdale -"

"So help me the Lord! Masser Holmes -"

"That's enough. Get out of it. I'll pick you up when I want you."

"Good-mornin', Masser Holmes. I hope there ain't no hard feelin's about this 'ere visit?"

"There will be unless you tell me who sent you."

"Why, there ain't no secret about that, Masser Holmes. It was that same gen'l'man that you have just done gone mention."

"And who set him on to it?"

"S'elp me. I don't know, Masser Holmes. He just say, 'Steve, you go see Mr. Holmes, and tell him his life ain't safe if he go down Harrow way.' That's the whole truth." Without waiting for any further questioning, our visitor bolted out of the room almost as precipitately as he had entered. Holmes knocked out the ashes of his pipe with a quiet chuckle.

"I am glad you were not forced to break his woolly head, Watson. I observed your manoeuvres with the poker. But he is really rather a harmless fellow, a great muscular, foolish, blustering baby, and easily cowed, as you have seen. He is one of the Spencer John gang and has taken part in some dirty work of late which I may clear up when I have time. His immediate principal, Barney, is a more astute person. They specialize in assaults, intimidation, and the like. What I want to know is, who is at the back of them on this panicular occasion?"

"But why do they want to intimidate you?"

"It is this Harrow Weald case. It decides me to look into the matter, for if it is worth anyone's while to take so much trouble, there must be something in it."

"But what is it?"

"I was going to tell you when we had this comic interlude. Here is Mrs. Maberley's note. If you care to come with me we will wire her and go out at once."

DEAR MR. SHERLOCK HOLMES [I read]:

I have had a succession of strange incidents occur to me in connection with this house, and I should much value your advice. You would find me at home any time to-morrow. The house is within a short walk of the Weald Station. I believe that my late husband, Mortimer Maberley, was one of your early clients.

Yours faithfully,

MARY MABERLEY

The address was "The Three Gables, Harrow Weald."

"So that's that!" said Holmes. "And now, if you can spare the time, Watson, we will get upon our way."

A short railway journey, and a shorter drive, brought us to the house, a brick and timber villa, standing in its own acre of undeveloped grassland. Three small projections above. the upper windows made a feeble attempt to justify its name. Behind was a grove of melancholy, half-grown pines, and the whole aspect of the place was poor and depressing. None the less, we found the house to be well furnished, and the lady who received us was a most engaging elderly person, who bore every mark of refinement and culture.

"I remember your husband well, madam," said Holmes, "though it is some years since he used my services in some trifling matter."

"Probably you would be more familiar with the name of my son Douglas."

Holmes looked at her with great interest.

"Dear me! Are you the mother of Douglas Maberley? I knew him slightly. But of course all London knew him. What a magnificent creature he was! Where is he now?"

"Dead, Mr. Holmes, dead! He was attache at Rome, and he died there of pneumonia last month."

"I am sorry. One could not connect death with such a man. I have never known anyone so vitally alive. He lived intensely - every fibre of him!"

"Too intensely, Mr. Holmes. That was the ruin of him. You remember him as he was - debonair and splendid. You did not see the moody, morose, brooding creature into which he developed. His heart was broken. In a single month I seemed to see my gallant boy turn into a worn-out cynical man."

"A love affair - a woman?"

"Or a fiend. Well, it was not to talk of my poor lad that I asked you to come, Mr. Holmes."

"Dr. Watson and I are at your service."

"There have been some very strange happenings. I have been in this house more than a year now, and as I wished to lead a retired life I have seen little of my neighbours. Three days ago I had a call from a man who said that he was a house agent. He said that this house would exactly suit a client of his, and that if I would part with it money would be no object. It seemed to me very strange as there are several empty houses on the market which appear to be equally eligible, but naturally I was interested in what he said. I therefore named a price which was five hundred pounds more than I gave. He at once closed with the offer, but added that his client desired to buy the furniture as well and would I put a price upon it. Some of this furniture is from my old home, and it is, as you see, very good, so that I named a good round sum. To this also he at once agreed. I had always wanted to travel, and the bargain was so good a one that it really seemed that I should be my own mistress for the rest of my life.

"Yesterday the man arrived with the agreement all drawn out. Luckily I showed it to Mr. Sutro, my lawyer, who lives in Harrow. He said to me, 'This is a very strange document. Are you aware that if you sign it you could not legally take anything out of the house - not even your own private possessions?' When the man came again in the evening I pointed this out, and I said that I meant only to sell the furniture.

"No, no, everything," said he.

"But my clothes? My jewels?"

"Well, well, some concession might be made for your personal effects. But nothing shall go out of the house unchecked. My client is a very liberal man, but he has his fads and his own way of doing things. It is everything or nothing with him."

"Then it must be nothing," said I. And there the matter was left, but the whole thing seemed to me to be so unusual that I thought -

Here we had a very extraordinary interruption.

Holmes raised his hand for silence. Then he strode across the room, flung open the door, and dragged in a great gaunt woman whom he had seized by the shoulder. She entered with ungainly struggle like some huge awkward chicken, torn, squawking, out of its coop.

"Leave me alone! What are you a-doin' of?" she screeched.

"Why, Susan, what is this?"

"Well, ma'am, I was comin' in to ask if the visitors was stayin' for lunch when this man jumped out at me."

"I have been listening to her for the last five minutes, but did not wish to interrupt your most interesting narrative. Just a little wheezy, Susan, are you not? You breathe too heavily for that kind of work."

Susan turned a sulky but amazed face upon her captor. "Who be you, anyhow, and what right have you a-pullin' me about like this?"

"It was merely that I wished to ask a question in your presence. Did you, Mrs. Maberley, mention to anyone that you were going to write to me and consult me?"

"No, Mr. Holmes, I did not."

"Who posted your letter?"

"Susan did."

"Exactly. Now, Susan, to whom was it that you wrote or sent a message to say that your mistress was asking advice from me?"

"It's a lie. I sent no message."

"Now, Susan, wheezy people may not live long, you know. It's a wicked thing to tell fibs. Whom did you tell?"

"Susan!" cried her mistress, "I believe you are a bad, treacherous woman. I remember now that I saw you speaking to someone over the hedge."

"That was my own business," said the woman sullenly.

"Suppose I tell you that it was Barney Stockdale to whom you spoke?" said Holmes.

"Well, if you know, what do you want to ask for?"

"I was not sure, but I know now. Well now, Susan, it will be worth ten pounds to you if you will tell me who is at the back of Barney."

"Someone that could lay down a thousand pounds for every ten you have in the world."

"So, a rich man? No; you smiled - a rich woman. Now we have got so far, you may as well give the name and earn the tenner."

"I'll see you in hell first."

"Oh, Susan! Language!"

"I am clearing out of here. I've had enough of you all. I'll send for my box to-morrow." She flounced for the door.

"Good-bye, Susan. Paregoric is the stuff... Now," he continued, turning suddenly from lively to severe when the door had closed behind the flushed and angry woman, "this gang means business. Look how close they play the game. Your letter to me had the 10 P.M. postmark. And yet Susan passes the word to Barney. Barney has time to go to his employer and get instructions; he or she - I incline to the latter from Susan's grin when she thought I had blundered - forms a plan. Black Steve is called in, and I am warned off by eleven o'clock next morning. That's quick work, you know."

"But what do they want?"

"Yes, that's the question. Who had the house before you?"

"A retired sea captain called Ferguson."

"Anything remarkable about him?"

"Not that ever I heard of."

"I was wondering whether he could have buried something. Of course, when people bury treasure nowadays they do it in the Post-Office bank. But there are always some lunatics about. It would be a dull world without them. At first I thought of some buried valuable. But why, in that case, should they want your furniture? You don't happen to have a Raphael or a first folio Shakespeare without knowing it?"

"No, I don't think I have anything rarer than a Crown Derby tea-set."

"That would hardly justify all this mystery. Besides, why should they not openly state what they want? If they covet your tea-set, they can surely offer a price for it without buying you out, lock, stock, and barrel. No, as I read it, there is something which you do not know that you have, and which you would not give up if you did know."

"That is how I read it," said I.

"Dr. Watson agrees, so that settles it."

"Well, Mr. Holmes, what can it be?"

"Let us see whether by this purely mental analysis we can get it to a finer point. You have been in this house a year."

"Nearly two."

"All the better. During this long period no one wants anything from you. Now suddenly within three or four days you have urgent demands. What would you gather from that?"

"It can only mean," said I, "that the object, whatever it may be, has only just come into the house."

"Settled once again," said Holmes. "Now, Mrs. Maberley has any object just arrived?"

"No, I have bought nothing new this year."

"Indeed! That is very remarkable. Well, I think we had best let matters develop a little further until we have clearer data. Is that lawyer of yours a capable man?"

"Mr. Sutro is most capable."

"Have you another maid, or was the fair Susan, who has just banged your front door alone?"

"I have a young girl."

"Try and get Sutro to spend a night or two in the house. You might possibly want protection."

"Against whom?"

"Who knows? The matter is certainly obscure. If I can't find what they are after, I must approach the matter from the other end and try to get at the principal. Did this house-agent man give any address?"

"Simply his card and occupation. Haines-Johnson, Auctioneer and Valuer."

"I don't think we shall find him in the directory. Honest business men don't conceal their place of business. Well, you will let me know any fresh development. I have taken up your case, and you may rely upon it that I shall see it through."

As we passed through the hall Holmes's eyes, which missed nothing, lighted upon several trunks and cases which were piled in a corner. The labels shone out upon them.

"'Milano.' 'Lucerne.' These are from Italy."

"They are poor Douglas's things."

"You have not unpacked them? How long have you had them?"

"They arrived last week."

"But you said - why, surely this might be the missing link. How do we know that there is not something of value there?"

"There could not possibly be, Mr. Holmes. Poor Douglas had only his pay and a small annuity. What could he have of value?"

Holmes was lost in thought.

"Delay no longer, Mrs. Maberley," he said at last. "Have these things taken upstairs to your bedroom. Examine them as soon as possible and see what they cohtain. I will come tomorrow and hear your report."

It was quite evident that The Three Gables was under very close surveillance, for as we came round the high hedge at the end of the lane there was the negro prize-fighter standing in the shadow. We came on him quite suddenly, and a grim and menacing figure he looked in that lonely place. Holmes clapped his hand to his pocket.

"Lookin' for your gun, Masser Holmes?"

"No, for my scent-bottle, Steve."

"You are funny, Masser Holmes, ain't you?"

"It won't be funny for you, Steve, if I get after you. I gave you fair warning this morning."

"Well, Masser Holmes, I done gone think over what you said, and I don't want no more talk about that affair of Masser Perkins. S'pose I can help you, Masser Holmes, I will."

"Well, then, tell me who is behind you on this job."

"So help me the Lord! Masser Holmes, I told you the truth before. I don't know. My boss Barney gives me orders and that's all."

"Well, just bear in mind, Steve, that the lady in that house, and everything under that roof, is under my protection. Don't forget it."

"All right, Masser Holmes. I'll remember."

"I've got him thoroughly frightened for his own skin, Watson," Holmes remarked as we walked on. "I think he would double-cross his employer if he knew who he was. It was lucky I had some knowledge of the Spencer John crowd, and that Steve was one of them. Now, Watson, this is a case for Langdale Pike, and I am going to see him now. When I get back I may be clearer in the matter."

I saw no more of Holmes during the day, but I could well imagine how he spent it, for Langdale Pike was his human book of reference upon all matters of social scandal. This strange, languid creature spent his waking hours in the bow window of a St. James's Street club and was the receiving station as well as the transmitter for all the gossip of the metropolis. He made, it was said, a four-figure income by the paragraphs which he contributed every week to the garbage papers which cater to an inquisitive public. If ever, far down in the turbid depths of London life, there was some strange swirl or eddy, it was marked with automatic exactness by this human dial upon the surface. Holmes discreetly helped Langdale to knowledge, and on occasion was helped in turn.

When I met my friend in his room early next morning, I was conscious from his bearing that all was well, but none the less a most unpleasant surprise was awaiting us. It took the shape of the following telegram.

Please come out at once. Client's house burgled in the night. Police in possession.

SUTRO

Holmes whistled. "The drama has come to a crisis, and quicker than I had expected. There is a great driving-power at the back of this business, Watson, which does not surprise me after what I have heard. This Sutro, of course, is her lawyer. I made a mistake, I fear, in not asking you to spend the night on guard. This fellow has clearly proved a broken reed. Well, there is nothing for it but another journey to Harrow Weald."

We found The Three Gables a very different establishment to the orderly household of the previous day. A small group of idlers had assembled at the garden gate, while a couple of constables were examining the windows and the geranium beds. Within we met a gray old gentleman, who introduced himself as the lawyer together with a bustling, rubicund inspector, who greeted Holmes as an old friend.

"Well, Mr. Holmes, no chance for you in this case, I'm afraid. Just a common, ordinary burglary, and well within the capacity of the poor old police. No experts need apply."

"I am sure the case is in very good hands," said Holmes. "Merely a common burglary, you say?"

"Quite so. We know pretty well who the men are and where to find them. It is that gang of Barney Stockdale, with the big nigger in it - they've been seen about here."

"Excellent! What did they get?"

"Well, they don't seem to have got much. Mrs. Maberley was chloroformed and the house was - Ah! here is the lady herself."

Our friend of yesterday, looking very pale and ill, had entered the room, leaning upon a little maidservant.

"You gave me good advice, Mr. Holmes," said she, smiling ruefully. "Alas, I did not take it! I did not wish to trouble Mr. Sutro, and so I was unprotected."

"I only heard of it this morning," the lawyer explained.

"Mr. Holmes advised me to have some friend in the house. I neglected his advice, and I have paid for it."

"You look wretchedly ill," said Holmes. "Perhaps you are hardly equal to telling me what occurred."

"It is all here," said the inspector, tapping a bulky notebook.

"Still, if the lady is not too exhausted -"

"There is really so little to tell. I have no doubt that wicked Susan had planned an entrance for them. They must have known the house to an inch. I was conscious for a moment of the chloroform rag which was thrust over my mouth, but I have no notion how long I may have been senseless. When I woke, one man was at the bedside and another was rising with a bundle in his hand from among my son's baggage, which was partially opened and littered over the floor. Before he could get away I sprang up and seized him."

"You took a big risk," said the inspector.

"I clung to him, but he shook me off, and the other may have struck me, for I can remember no more. Mary the maid heard the noise and began screaming out of the window. That brought the police, but the rascals had got away."

"What did they take?"

"Well, I don't think there is anything of value missing. I am sure there was nothing in my son's trunks."

"Did the men leave no clue?"

"There was one sheet of paper which I may have torn from the man that I grasped. It was lying all crumpled on the floor. It is in my son's handwriting."

"Which means that it is not of much use," said the inspector. "Now if it had been in the burglar's -"

"Exactly," said Holmes. "What rugged common sense! None the less, I should be curious to see it."

The inspector drew a folded sheet of foolscap from his pocketbook.

"I never pass anything, however trifling," said he with some pomposity. "That is my advice to you, Mr. Holmes. In twenty five years' experience I have learned my lesson. There is always the chance of finger-marks or something."

Holmes inspected the sheet of paper.

"What do you make of it, Inspector?"

"Seems to be the end of some queer novel, so far as I can see."

"It may certainly prove to be the end of a queer tale," said Holmes. "You have noticed the number on the top of the page. It is two hundred and forty-five. Where are the odd two hundred and forty-four pages?"

"Well, I suppose the burglars got those. Much good may it do them!"

"It seems a queer thing to break into a house in order to steal such papers as that. Does it suggest anything to you, Inspector?"

"Yes, sir, it suggests that in their hurry the rascals just grabbed at what came first to hand. I wish them joy of what they got."

"Why should they go to my son's things?" asked Mrs. Maberley.

"Well, they found nothing valuable downstairs, so they tried their luck upstairs. That is how I read it. What do you make of it, Mr. Holmes?"

"I must think it over, Inspector. Come to the window, Watson." Then, as we stood together, he read over the fragment of paper. It began in the middle of a sentence and ran like this:

"... face bled considerably from the cuts and blows, but it was nothing to the bleeding of his heart as he saw that lovely face, the face for which he had been prepared to sacrifice his very life, looking out at his agony and humiliation. She smiled - yes, by Heaven! she smiled, like the heartless fiend she was, as he looked up at her. It was at that moment that love died and hate was born. Man must live for something. If it is not for your embrace, my lady, then it shall surely be for your undoing and my complete revenge."

"Queer grammar!" said Holmes with a smile as he handed the paper back to the inspector. "Did you notice how the 'he' suddenly changed to 'my'? The writer was so carried away by his own story that he imagined himself at the supreme moment to be the hero."

"It seemed mighty poor stuff," said the inspector as he replaced it in his book. "What! are you off, Mr. Holmes?"

"I don't think there is anything more for me to do now that the case is in such capable hands. By the way, Mrs. Maberley, did you say you wished to travel?"

"It has always been my dream, Mr. Holmes."

"Where would you like to go - Cairo, Madeira, the Riviera?"

"Oh if I had the money I would go round the world."

"Quite so. Round the world. Well, good-morning. I may drop you a line in the evening." As we passed the window I caught a glimpse of the inspector's smile and shake of the head. "These clever fellows have always a touch of madness." That was what I read in the inspector's smile.

"Now, Watson, we are at the last lap of our little journey," said Holmes when we were back in the roar of central London once more. "I think we had best clear the matter up at once, and it would be well that you should come with me, for it is safer to have a witness when you are dealing with such a lady as Isadora Klein."

We had taken a cab and were speeding to some address in Grosvenor Square. Holmes had been sunk in thought, but he roused himself suddenly.

"By the way, Watson, I suppose you see it all clearly?"

"No, I can't say that I do. I only gather that we are going to see the lady who is behind all this mischief."

"Exactly! But does the name Isadora Klein convey nothing to you? She was, of course, the celebrated beauty. There was never a woman to touch her. She is pure Spanish, the real blood of the masterfui Conquistadors, and her people have been leaders in Pernambuco for generations. She married the aged German sugar king, Klein, and presently found herself the richest as well as the most lovely widow upon earth. Then there was an interval of adventure when she pleased her own tastes. She had several lovers, and Douglas Maberley, one of the most striking men in London, was one of them. It was by all accounts more than an adventure with him.

He was not a society butterfly but a strong, proud man who gave and expected all. But she is the 'belle dame sans merci' of fiction. When her caprice is satisfied the matter is ended, and if the other party in the matter can't take her word for it she knows how to bring it home to him."

"Then that was his own story -"

"Ah! you are piecing it together now. I hear that she is about to marry the young Duke of Lomond, who might almost be her son. His Grace's ma might overlook the age, but a big scandal would be a different matter, so it is imperative - Ah! here we are."

It was one of the finest corner-houses of the West End. A machine-like footman took up our cards and returned with word that the lady was not at home. "Then we shall wait until she is," said Holmes cheerfully.

The machine broke down.

"Not at home means not at home to you," said the footman.

"Good," Holmes answered. "That means that we shall not have to wait. Kindly give this note to your mistress."

He scribbled three or four words upon a sheet of his notebook, folded it, and handed it to the man.

"What did you say, Holmes?" I asked.

"I simply wrote: 'Shall it be the police, then?' I think that should pass us in."

It did - with amazing celerity. A minute later we were in an Arabian Nights drawing-room, vast and wonderful, in a half gloom, picked out with an occasional pink electric light. The lady had come, I felt, to that time of life when even the proudest beauty finds the half light more welcome. She rose from a settee as we entered: tall, queenly, a perfect figure, a lovely mask-like face, with two wonderful Spanish eyes which looked murder at us both.

"What is this intrusion and this insulting message?" she asked, holding up the slip of paper.

"I need not explain, madame. I have too much respect for your intelligence to do so - though I confess that intelligence has been surprisingly at fault of late."

"How so, sir?"

"By supposing that your hired bullies could frighten me from my work. Surely no man would take up my profession if it were not that danger attracts him. It was you, then, who forced me to examine the case of young Maberley."

"I have no idea what you are talking about. What have I to do with hired bullies?"

Holmes turned away wearily.

"Yes, I have underrated your intelligence. Well, good-afternoon!"

"Stop! Where are you going?"

"To Scotland Yard."

We had not got halfway to the door before she had overtaken us and was holding his arm. She had turned in a moment from steel to velvet.

"Come and sit down, gentlemen. Let us talk this matter over. I feel that I may be frank with you, Mr. Holmes. You have the feelings of a gentleman. How quick a woman's instinct is to find it out. I will treat you as a friend."

"I cannot promise to reciprocate, madame. I am not the law, but I represent justice so far as my feeble powers go. I am ready to listen, and then I will tell you how I will act."

"No doubt it was foolish of me to threaten a brave man like yourself."

"What was really foolish, madame, is that you have placed yourself in the power of a band of rascals who may blackmail or give you away."

"No, no! I am not so simple. Since I have promised to be frank, I may say that no one, save Barney Stockdale and Susan, his wife, have the least idea who their employer is. As to them, well, it is not the first -" She smiled and nodded with a charming coquettish intimacy.

"I see. You've tested them before."

"They are good hounds who run silent."

"Such hounds have a way sooner or later of biting the hand that feeds them. They will be arrested for this burglary. The police are already after them."

"They will take what comes to them. That is what they are paid for. I shall not appear in the matter."

"Unless I bring you into it."

"No, no, you would not. You are a gentleman. It is a woman's secret."

"In the first place, you must give back this manuscript."

She broke into a ripple of laughter and walked to the fireplace. There was a calcined mass which she broke up with the poker. "Shall I give this back?" she asked. So roguish and exquisite did she look as she stood before us with a challenging smile that I felt of all Holmes's criminals this was the one whom he would find it hardest to face. However, he was immune from sentiment.

"That seals your fate," he said coldly. "You are very prompt in your actions, madame, but you have overdone it on this occasion."

She threw the poker down with a clatter.

"How hard you are!" she cried. "May I tell you the whole story?"

"I fancy I could tell it to you."

"But you must look at it with my eyes, Mr. Holmes. You must realize it from the point of view of a woman who sees all her life's ambition about to be ruined at the last moment. Is such a woman to be blamed if she protects herself?"

"The original sin was yours."

"Yes, yes! I admit it. He was a dear boy, Douglas, but it so chanced that he could not fit into my plans. He wanted marriage-marriage, Mr. Holmes - with a penniless commoner. Nothing less would serve him. Then he became pertinacious. Because I had given he seemed to think that I still must give, and to him only. It was intolerable. At last I had to make him realize it."

"By hiring ruffians to beat him under your own window."

"You do indeed seem to know everything. Well, it is true. Barney and the boys drove him away, and were, I admit, a little rough in doing so. But what did he do then? Could I have believed that a gentleman would do such an act? He wrote a book in which he described his own story. I, of course, was the wolf; he the lamb. It was all there, under different names, of course; but who in all London would have failed to recognize it? What do you say to that, Mr. Holmes?"

"Well, he was within his rights."

"It was as if the air of Italy had got into his blood and brought with it the old cruel Italian spirit. He wrote to me and sent me a copy of his book that I might have the torture of anticipation. There were two copies, he said - one for me, one for his publisher."

"How did you know the publisher's had not reached him?"

"I knew who his publisher was. It is not his only novel, you know. I found out that he had not heard from Italy. Then came Douglas's sudden death. So long as that other manuscript was in the world there was no safety for me. Of course, it must be among his effects, and these would be returned to his mother. I set the gang at work. One of them got into the house as servant. I wanted to do the thing honestly. I really and truly did. I was ready to buy the house and everything in it. I offered any price she cared to ask. I only tried the other way when everything else had failed. Now, Mr. Holmes, granting that I was too hard on Douglas - and, God knows, I am sorry for it! - what else could I do with my whole future at stake?"

Sherlock Holmes shrugged his shoulders.

"Well, well," said he, "I suppose I shall have to compound a felony as usual. How much does it cost to go round the world in first-class style?"

The lady stared in amazement.

"Could it be done on five thousand pounds?"

"Well, I should think so, indeed!"

"Very good. I think you will sign me a check for that, and I will see that it comes to Mrs. Maberley. You owe her a little change of air. Meantime, lady" - he wagged a cautionary forefinger - "have a care! Have a care! You can't play with edged tools forever without cutting those dainty hands."

THE ADVENTURE OF THE SUSSEX VAMPIRE

Holmes had read carefully a note which the last post had brought him. Then, with the dry chuckle which was his nearest approach to a laugh, he tossed it over to me.

"For a mixture of the modern and the mediaeval, of the practical and of the wildly fanciful, I think this is surely the limit," said he. "What do you make of it, Watson?"

I read as follows:

46, OLD JEWRY,

Nov. 19th

Re Vampires

SIR:

Our client, Mr. Robert Ferguson, of Ferguson and Muirhead, tea brokers, of Mincing Lane, has made some inquiry from us in a communication of even date concerning vampires. As our firm specializes entirely upon the assessment of machinery the matter hardly comes within our purview, and we have therefore recommended Mr. Ferguson to call upon you and lay the matter before you. We have not forgotten your successful action in the case of Matilda Briggs.

We are, sir,

Faithfully yours,

MORRISON, MORRISON, AND DODD

per E.J.C.

"Matilda Briggs was not the name of a young woman, Watson," said Holmes in a reminiscent voice. "It was a ship which is associated with the giant rat of Sumatra, a story for which the world is not yet prepared. But what do we know about vampires? Does it come within our purview either? Anything is better than stagnation, but really we seem to have been switched on to a Grimms' fairy tale. Make a long arm, Watson, and see what V has to say."

I leaned back and took down the great index volume to which he referred. Holmes balanced it on his knee, and his eyes moved slowly and lovingly over the record of old cases, mixed with the accumulated information of a lifetime.

"Voyage of the Gloria Scott," he read. "That was a bad business. I have some recollection that you made a record of it, Watson, though I was unable to congratulate you upon the result. Victor Lynch, the forger. Venomous lizard or gila. Remarkable case, that! Vittoria, the circus belle. Vanderbilt and the Yeggman. Vipers. Vigor, the Hammersmith wonder. Hullo! Hullo! Good old index. You can't beat it. Listen to this, Watson. Vampirism in Hungary. And again, Vampires in Transylvania." He turned over the pages with eagerness, but after a short intent perusal he threw down the great book with a snarl of disappointment.

"Rubbish, Watson, rubbish! What have we to do with walking corpses who can only be held in their grave by stakes driven through their hearts? It's pure lunacy."

"But surely," said I, "the vampire was not necessarily a dead man? A living person might have the habit. I have read, for example, of the old sucking the blood of the young in order to retain their youth."

"You are right, Watson. It mentions the legend in one of these references. But are we to give serious attention to such things? This agency stands flat-footed upon the ground, and there it must remain. The world is big enough for us. No ghosts need apply. I fear that we cannot take Mr. Robert Ferguson very seriously. Possibly this note may be from him and may throw some light upon what is worrying him."

He took up a second letter which had lain unnoticed upon the table while he had been absorbed with the first. This he began to read with a smile of amusement upon his face which gradually faded away into an expression of intense interest and concentration. When he had finished he sat for some little time lost in thought with the letter dangling from his fingers. Finally, with a start, he aroused himself from his reverie.

"Cheeseman's, Lamberley. Where is Lamberley, Watson?"

"It is in Sussex, South of Horsham."

"Not very far, eh? And Cheeseman's?"

"I know that country, Holmes. It is full of old houses which are named after the men who built them centuries ago. You get Odley's and Harvey's and Carriton's - the folk are forgotten but their names live in their houses."

"Precisely," said Holmes coldly. It was one of the peculiarities of his proud, self-contained nature that though he docketed any fresh information very quietly and accurately in his brain, he seldom made any acknowledgment to the giver. "I rather fancy we shall know a good deal more about Cheeseman's, Lamberley, before we are through. The letter is, as I had hoped, from Robert Ferguson. By the way, he claims acquaintance with you."

"With me!"

"You had better read it."

He handed the letter across. It was headed with the address quoted.

DEAR MR HOLMES [it said]:

I have been recommended to you by my lawyers, but indeed the matter is so extraordinarily delicate that it is most difficult to discuss. It concerns a friend for whom I am acting. This gentleman married some five years ago a Peruvian lady the daughter of a Peruvian merchant, whom he had met in connection with the importation of nitrates. The lady was very beautiful, but the fact of her foreign birth and of her alien religion always caused a separation of interests and of feelings between husband and wife, so that after a time his love may have cooled towards her and he may have come to regard their union as a mistake. He felt there were sides of her character which he could never explore or understand. This was the more painful as she was as loving a wife as a man could have - to all appearance absolutely devoted.

Now for the point which I will make more plain when we meet. Indeed, this note is merely to give you a general idea of the situation and to ascertain whether you would care to interest yourself in the matter. The lady began to show some curious traits quite alien to her ordinarily sweet and gentle disposition. The gentleman had been married twice and he had one son by the first wife. This boy was now fifteen, a very charming and affectionate youth, though unhappily injured through an accident in childhood. Twice the wife was caught in the act of assaulting this poor lad in the most unprovoked way. Once she struck him with a stick and left a great weal on his arm.

This was a small matter, however, compared with her conduct to her own child, a dear boy just under one year of age. On one occasion about a month ago this child had been left by its nurse for a few minutes. A loud cry from the baby, as of pain, called the nurse back. As she ran into the room she saw her employer, the lady, leaning over the baby and apparently biting his neck. There was a small wound in the neck from which a stream of blood had escaped. The nurse was so horrified that she wished to call the husband, but the lady implored her not to do so and actually gave her five pounds as a price for her silence. No explanation was ever given, and for the moment the matter was passed over.

It left, however, a terrible impression upon the nurse's mind, and from that time she began to watch her mistress closely and to keep a closer guard upon the baby, whom she tenderly loved. It seemed to her that even as she watched the mother, so the mother watched her, and that every time she was compelled to leave the baby alone the mother was waiting to get at it. Day and night the nurse covered the child, and day and night the silent, watchful mother seemed to be lying in wait as a wolf waits for a lamb. It must read most incredible to you, and yet I beg you to take it seriously, for a child's life and a man's sanity may depend upon it.

At last there came one dreadful day when the facts could no longer be concealed from the husband. The nurse's nerve had given way; she could stand the strain no longer, and she made a clean breast of it all to the man. To him it seemed as wild a tale as it may now seem to you. He knew his wife to be a loving wife, and, save for the assaults upon her stepson, a loving mother. Why, then, should she wound her own dear little baby? He told the nurse that she was dreaming, that her suspicions were those of a lunatic, and that such libels upon her mistress were not to be tolerated. While they were talking a sudden cry of pain was heard. Nurse and master rushed together to the nursery.

Imagine his feelings, Mr. Holmes, as he saw his wife rise from a kneeling position beside the cot and saw blood upon the child's exposed neck and upon the sheet. With a cry of horror, he turned his wife's face to the light and saw blood all round her lips. It was she - she beyond all question - who had drunk the poor baby's blood.

So the matter stands. She is now confined to her room. There has been no explanation. The husband is half demented. He knows, and I know, little of vampirism beyond the name. We had thought it was some wild tale of foreign parts. And yet here in the very heart of the English Sussex -well, all this can be discussed with you in the morning. Will you see me? Will you use your great powers in aiding a distracted man? If so, kindly wire to Ferguson, Cheeseman's, Lamberley, and I will be at your rooms by ten o'clock.

Yours faithfully,
ROBERT FERGUSON

P.S. I believe your friend Watson played Rugby for Blackheath when I was three-quarter for Richmond. It is the only personal introduction which I can give.

"Of course I remembered him," said I as I laid down the letter. "Big Bob Ferguson, the finest three-quarter Richmond ever had. He was always a good-natured chap. It's like him to be so concerned over a friend's case."

Holmes looked at me thoughtfully and shook his head.

"I never get your limits, Watson," said he. "There are unexplored possibilities about you. Take a wire down, like a good fellow. 'Will examine your case with pleasure.'"

"Your case!"

"We must not let him think that this agency is a home for the weak-minded. Of course it is his case. Send him that wire and let the matter rest till morning."

Promptly at ten o'clock next morning Ferguson strode into our room. I had remembered him as a long, slab-sided man with loose limbs and a fine turn of speed which had carried him round many an opposing back. There is surely nothing in life more painful than to meet the wreck of a fine athlete whom one has known in his prime. His great frame had fallen in, his flaxen hair was scanty, and his shoulders were bowed. I fear that I roused corresponding emotions in him.

"Hullo, Watson," said he, and his voice was still deep and hearty. "You don't look quite the man you did when I threw you over the ropes into the crowd at the Old Deer Park. I expect I have changed a bit also. But it's this last day or two that has aged me. I see by your telegram, Mr. Holmes, that it is no use my pretending to be anyone's deputy."

"It is simpler to deal direct," said Holmes.

"Of course it is. But you can imagine how difficult it is when you are speaking of the one woman whom you are bound to protect and help. What can I do? How am I to go to the police with such a story? And yet the kiddies have got to be protected. Is it madness, Mr. Holmes? Is it something in the blood? Have you any similar case in your experience? For God's sake, give me some advice, for I am at my wit's end."

"Very naturally, Mr. Ferguson. Now sit here and pull yourself together and give me a few clear answers. I can assure you that I am very far from being at my wit's end, and that I am confident we shall find some solution. First of all, tell me what steps you have taken. Is your wife still near the children?"

"We had a dreadful scene. She is a most loving woman, Mr. Holmes. If ever a woman loved a man with all her heart and soul, she loves me. She was cut to the heart that I should have discovered this horrible, this incredible, secret. She would not even speak. She gave no answer to my reproaches, save to gaze at me with a sort of wild, despairing look in her eyes. Then she rushed to her room and locked herself in. Since then she has refused to see me. She has a maid who was with her before her marriage, Dolores by name - a friend rather than a servant. She takes her food to her."

"Then the child is in no immediate danger?"

"Mrs. Mason, the nurse, has sworn that she will not leave it night or day. I can absolutely trust her. I am more uneasy about poor little Jack, for, as I told you in my note, he has twice been assaulted by her."

"But never wounded?"

"No, she struck him savagely. It is the more terrible as he is a poor little inoffensive cripple." Ferguson's gaunt features softened as he spoke of his boy. "You would think that the dear lad's condition would soften anyone's heart. A fall in childhood and a twisted spine, Mr. Holmes. But the dearest, most loving heart within."

Holmes had picked up the letter of yesterday and was reading it over. "What other inmates are there in your house, Mr. Ferguson?"

"Two servants who have not been long with us. One stablehand, Michael, who sleeps in the house. My wife, myself, my boy Jack, baby, Dolores, and Mrs. Mason. That is all."

"I gather that you did not know your wife well at the time of your marriage?"

"I had only known her a few weeks."

"How long had this maid Dolores been with her?"

"Some years."

"Then your wife's character would really be better known by Dolores than by you?"

"Yes, you may say so."

Holmes made a note.

"I fancy," said he, "that I may be of more use at Lamberley than here. It is eminently a case for personal investigation. If the lady remains in her room, our presence could not annoy or inconvenience her. Of course, we would stay at the inn."

Ferguson gave a gesture of relief.

"It is what I hoped, Mr. Holmes. There is an excellent train at two from Victoria if you could come."

"Of course we could come. There is a lull at present. I can give you my undivided energies. Watson, of course, comes with us. But there are one or two points upon which I wish to be very sure before I start. This unhappy lady, as I understand it, has appeared to assault both the children, her own baby and your little son?"

"That is so."

"But the assaults take different forms, do they not? She has beaten your son."

"Once with a stick and once very savagely with her hands."

"Did she give no explanation why she struck him?"

"None save that she hated him. Again and again she said so."

"Well, that is not unknown among stepmothers. A posthumous jealousy, we will say. Is the lady jealous by nature?"

"Yes, she is very jealous - jealous with all the strength of her fiery tropical love."

"But the boy - he is fifteen, I understand, and probably very developed in mind, since his body has been circumscribed in action. Did he give you no explanation of these assaults?"

"No, he declared there was no reason."

"Were they good friends at other times?"

"No, there was never any love between them."

"Yet you say he is affectionate?"

"Never in the world could there be so devoted a son. My life is his life. He is absorbed in what I say or do."

Once again Holmes made a note. For some time he sat lost in thought.

"No doubt you and the boy were great comrades before this second marriage. You were thrown very close together, were you not?"

"Very much so."

"And the boy, having so affectionate a nature, was devoted, no doubt, to the memory of his mother?"

"Most devoted."

"He would certainly seem to be a most interesting lad. There is one other point about these assaults. Were the strange attacks upon the baby and the assaults upon yow son at the same period?"

"In the first case it was so. It was as if some frenzy had seized her, and she had vented her rage upon both. In the second case it was only Jack who suffered. Mrs. Mason had no complaint to make about the baby."

"That certainly complicates matters."

"I don't quite follow you, Mr. Holmes."

"Possibly not. One forms provisional theories and waits for time or fuller knowledge to explode them. A bad habit, Mr. Ferguson, but human nature is weak. I fear that your old friend here has given an exaggerated view of my scientific methods. However, I will only say at the present stage that your problem does not appear to me to be insoluble, and that you may expect to find us at Victoria at two o'clock."

It was evening of a dull, foggy November day when, having left our bags at the Chequers, Lamberley, we drove through the Sussex clay of a long winding lane and finally reached the isolated and ancient farmhouse in which Ferguson dwelt. It was a large, straggling building, very old in the centre, very new at the wings with towering Tudor chimneys and a lichen-spotted, high-pitched roof of Horsham slabs. The doorsteps were worn into curves, and the ancient tiles which lined the porch were marked with the rebus of a cheese and a man after the original builder. Within, the ceilings were corrugated with heavy oaken beams, and the uneven floors sagged into sharp curves. An odour of age and decay pervaded the whole crumbling building.

There was one very large central room into which Ferguson led us. Here, in a huge old-fashioned fireplace with an iron screen behind it dated 1670, there blazed and spluttered a splendid log fire.

The room, as I gazed round, was a most singular mixture of dates and of places. The half-panelled walls may well have belonged to the original yeoman farmer of the seventeenth century. They were ornamented, however, on the lower part by a line of well-chosen modern water-colours; while above, where yellow plaster took the place of oak, there was hung a fine collection of South American utensils and weapons, which had been brought, no doubt, by the Peruvian lady upstairs. Holmes rose, with that quick curiosity which sprang from his eager mind, and examined them with some care. He returned with his eyes full of thought.

"Hullo!" he cried. "Hullo!"

A spaniel had lain in a basket in the corner. It came slowly forward towards its master, walking with difficulty. Its hind legs moved irregularly and its tail was on the ground. It licked Ferguson's hand.

"What is it, Mr. Holmes?"

"The dog. What's the matter with it?"

"That's what puzzled the vet. A sort of paralysis. Spinal meningitis, he thought. But it is passing. He'll be all right soon - won't you, Carlo?"

A shiver of assent passed through the drooping tail. The dog's mournful eyes passed from one of us to the other. He knew that we were discussing his case.

"Did it come on suddenly?"

"In a single night."

"How long ago?"

"It may have been four months ago."

"Very remarkable. Very suggestive."

"What do you see in it, Mr. Holmes?"

"A confirmation of what I had already thought."

"For God's sake, what do you think, Mr. Holmes? It may be a mere intellectual puzzle to you, but it is life and death to me! My wife a would-be murderer - my child in constant danger! Don't play with me, Mr. Holmes. It is too terribly serious."

The big Rugby three-quarter was trembling all over. Holmes put his hand soothingly upon his arm.

"I fear that there is pain for you, Mr. Ferguson, whatever the solution may be," said he. "I would spare you all I can. I cannot say more for the instant, but before I leave this house I hope I may have something definite."

"Please God you may! If you will excuse me, gentlemen, I will go up to my wife's room and see if there has been any change."

He was away some minutes, during which Holmes resumed his examination of the curiosities upon the wall. When our host returned it was clear from his downcast face that he had made no progress. He brought with him a tall, slim, brown-faced girl.

"The tea is ready, Dolores," said Ferguson. "See that your mistress has everything she can wish."

"She very ill," cried the girl, looking with indignant eyes at her master. "She no ask for food. She very ill. She need doctor. I frightened stay alone with her without doctor."

Ferguson looked at me with a question in his eyes.

"I should be so glad if I could be of use."

"Would your mistress see Dr. Watson?"

"I take him. I no ask leave. She needs doctor."

"Then I'll come with you at once."

I followed the girl, who was quivering with strong emotion, up the staircase and down an ancient corridor. At the end was an iron-clamped and massive door. It struck me as I looked at it that if Ferguson tried to force his way to his wife he would find it no easy matter. The girl drew a key from her pocket, and the heavy oaken planks creaked upon their old hinges. I passed in and she swiftly followed, fastening the door behind her.

On the bed a woman was lying who was clearly in a high fever. She was only half conscious, but as I entered she raised a pair of frightened but beautiful eyes and glared at me in apprehension. Seeing a stranger, she appeared to be relieved and sank back with a sigh upon the pillow. I stepped up to her with a few reassuring words, and she lay still while I took her pulse and temperature. Both were high, and yet my impression was that the condition was rather that of mental and nervous excitement than of any actual seizure.

"She lie like that one day, two day. I 'fraid she die," said the girl.

The woman turned her flushed and handsome face towards me.

"Where is my husband?"

"He is below and would wish to see you."

"I will not see him. I will not see him." Then she seemed to wander off into delirium. "A fiend! A fiend! Oh, what shall I do with this devil?"

"Can I help you in any way?"

"No. No one can help. It is finished. All is destroyed. Do what I will, all is destroyed."

The woman must have some strange delusion. I could not see honest Bob Ferguson in the character of fiend or devil.

"Madame," I said, "your husband loves you dearly. He is deeply grieved at this happening."

Again she turned on me those glorious eyes.

"He loves me. Yes. But do I not love him? Do I not love him even to sacrifice myself rather than break his dear heart? That is how I love him. And yet he could think of me - he could speak of me so."

"He is full of grief, but he cannot understand."

"No, he cannot understand. But he should trust."

"Will you not see him?" I suggested.

"No, no, I cannot forget those terrible words nor the look upon his face. I will not see him. Go now. You can do nothing for me. Tell him only one thing. I want my child. I have a right to my child. That is the only message I can send him." She turned her face to the wall and would say no more.

I returned to the room downstairs, where Ferguson and Holmes still sat by the fire. Ferguson listened moodily to my account of the interview.

"How can I send her the child?" he said. "How do I know what strange impulse might come upon her? How can I ever forget how she rose from beside it with its blood upon her lips?" He shuddered at the recollection. "The child is safe with Mrs. Mason, and there he must remain."

A smart maid, the only modern thing which we had seen in the house, had brought in some tea. As she was serving it the door opened and a youth entered the room. He was a remarkable lad, pale-faced and fair-haired, with excitable light blue eyes which blazed into a sudden flame of emotion and joy as they rested upon his father. He rushed forward and threw his arms round his neck with the abandon of a loving girl.

"Oh, daddy," he cried, "I did not know that you were due yet. I should have been here to meet you. Oh, I am so glad to see you!"

Ferguson gently disengaged himself from the embrace with some little show of embarrassment.

"Dear old chap," said he, patting the flaxen head with a very tender hand. "I came early because my friends, Mr. Holmes and Dr. Watson, have been persuaded to come down and spend an evening with us."

"Is that Mr. Holmes, the detective?"

"Yes."

The youth looked at us with a very penetrating and, as it seemed to me, unfriendly gaze.

"What about your other child, Mr. Ferguson?" asked Holmes. "Might we make the acquaintance of the baby?"

"Ask Mrs. Mason to bring baby down," said Ferguson. The boy went off with a curious, shambling gait which told my surgical eyes that he was suffering from a weak spine. Presently he returned, and behind him came a tall, gaunt woman bearing in her arms a very beautiful child, dark-eyed, golden-haired, a wonderful mixture of the Saxon and the Latin. Ferguson was evidently devoted to it, for he took it into his arms and fondled it most tenderly.

"Fancy anyone having the heart to hurt him," he muttered as he glanced down at the small, angry red pucker upon the cherub throat.

It was at this moment that I chanced to glance at Holmes and saw a most singular intentness in his expression. His face was as set as if it had been carved out of old ivory, and his eyes, which had glanced for a moment at father and child, were now fixed with eager curiosity upon something at the other side of the room. Following his gaze I could only guess that he was looking out through the window at the melancholy, dripping garden. It is true that a shutter had half closed outside and obstructed the view, but none the less it was certainly at the window that Holmes was fixing his concentrated attention. Then he smiled, and his eyes came back to the baby. On its chubby neck there was this small puckered mark. Without speaking, Holmes examined it with care. Finally he shook one of the dimpled fists which waved in front of him.

"Good-bye, little man. You have made a strange start in life. Nurse, I should wish to have a word with you in private."

He took her aside and spoke earnestly for a few minutes. I only heard the last words, which were: "Your anxiety will soon, I hope, be set at rest." The woman, who seemed to be a sour, silent kind of creature, withdrew with the child.

"What is Mrs. Mason like?" asked Holmes.

"Not very prepossessing externally, as you can see, but a heart of gold, and devoted to the child."

"Do you like her, Jack?" Holmes turned suddenly upon the boy. His expressive mobile face shadowed over, and he shook his head.

"Jacky has very strong likes and dislikes," said Ferguson, putting his arm round the boy. "Luckily I am one of his likes."

The boy cooed and nestled his head upon his father's breast. Ferguson gently disengaged him.

"Run away, little Jacky," said he, and he watched his son with loving eyes until he disappeared. "Now, Mr. Holmes," he continued when the boy was gone, "I really feel that I have brought you on a fool's errand, for what can you possibly do save give me your sympathy? It must be an exceedingly delicate and complex affair from your point of view."

"It is certainly delicate," said my friend with an amused smile, "but I have not been struck up to now with its complexity. It has been a case for intellectual deduction, but when this original intellectual deduction is confirmed point by point by quite a number of independent incidents, then the subjective becomes objective and we can say confidently that we have reached our goal. I had, in fact, reached it before we left Baker Street, and the rest has merely been observation and confirmation."

Ferguson put his big hand to his furrowed forehead.

"For heaven's sake, Holmes," he said hoarsely; "if you can see the truth in this matter, do not keep me in suspense. How do I stand? What shall I do? I care nothing as to how you have found your facts so long as you have really got them."

"Certainly I owe you an explanation, and you shall have it. But you will permit me to handle the matter in my own way? Is the lady capable of seeing us, Watson?"

"She is ill, but she is quite rational."

"Very good. It is only in her presence that we can clear the matter up. Let us go up to her."

"She will not see me," cried Ferguson.

"Oh, yes, she will," said Holmes. He scribbled a few lines upon a sheet of paper. "You at least have the entree, Watson. Will you have the goodness to give the lady this note?"

I ascended again and handed the note to Dolores, who cautiously opened the door. A minute later I heard a cry from within, a cry in which joy and surprise seemed to be blended. Dolores looked out.

"She will see them. She will listen," said she.

At my summons Ferguson and Holmes came up. As we entered

the room Ferguson took a step or two towards his wife, who had raised herself in the bed, but she held out her hand to repulse him. He sank into an armchair, while Holmes seated himself beside him, after bowing to the lady, who looked at him with wide-eyed amazement.

"I think we can dispense with Dolores," said Holmes. "Oh, very well, madame, if you would rather she stayed I can see no objection. Now, Mr. Ferguson, I am a busy man wlth many calls, and my methods have to be short and direct. The swiftest surgery is the least painful. Let me first say what will ease your mind. Your wife is a very good, a very loving, and a very ill-used woman."

Ferguson sat up with a cry of joy.

"Prove that, Mr. Holmes, and I am your debtor forever."

"I will do so, but in doing so I must wound you deeply in another direction."

"I care nothing so long as you clear my wife. Everything on earth is insignificant compared to that."

"Let me tell you, then, the train of reasoning which passed through my mind in Baker Street. The idea of a vampire was to me absurd. Such things do not happen in criminal practice in England. And yet your observation was precise. You had seen the lady rise from beside the child's cot with the blood upon her lips."

"I did."

"Did it not occur to you that a bleeding wound may be sucked for some other purpose than to draw the blood from it? Was there not a queen in English history who sucked such a wound to draw poison from it?"

"Poison!"

"A South American household. My instinct felt the presence of those weapons upon the wall before my eyes ever saw them. It might have been other poison, but that was what occurred to me. When I saw that little empty quiver beside the small birdbow, it was just what I expected to see. If the child were pricked with one of those arrows dipped in curare or some other devilish drug, it would mean death if the venom were not sucked out.

"And the dog! If one were to use such a poison, would one not try it first in order to see that it had not lost its power? I did not foresee the dog, but at least I understand him and he fitted into my reconstruction.

"Now do you understand? Your wife feared such an attack. She saw it made and saved the child's life, and yet she shrank from telling you all the truth, for she knew how you loved the boy and feared lest it break your heart."

"Jacky!"

"I watched him as you fondled the child just now. His face was clearly reflected in the glass of the window where the shutter formed a background. I saw such jealousy, such cruel hatred, as I have seldom seen in a human face."

"My Jacky!"

"You have to face it, Mr. Ferguson. It is the more painful because it is a distorted love, a maniacal exaggerated love for you, and possibly for his dead mother, which has prompted his action. His very soul is consumed with hatred for this splendid child, whose health and beauty are a contrast to his own weakness."

"Good God! It is incredible!"

"Have I spoken the truth, madame?"

The lady was sobbing, with her face buried in the pillows. Now she turned to her husband.

"How could I tell you, Bob? I felt the blow it would be to you. It was better that I should wait and that it should come from some other lips than mine. When this gentleman, who seems to have powers of magic, wrote that he knew all, I was glad."

"I think a year at sea would be my prescription for Master Jacky," said Holmes, rising from his chair. "Only one thing is still clouded, madame. We can quite understand your attacks upon Master Jacky. There is a limit to a mother's patience. But how did you dare to leave the child these last two days?"

"I had told Mrs. Mason. She knew."

"Exactly. So I imagined."

Ferguson was standing by the bed, choking, his hands outstretched and quivering.

"This, I fancy, is the time for our exit, Watson," said Holmes in a whisper. "If you will take one elbow of the too faithful Dolores, I will take the other. There, now," he added as he closed the door behind him, "I think we may leave them to settle the rest among themselves."

I have only one further note of this case. It is the letter which Holmes wrote in final answer to that with which the narrative begins. It ran thus:

BAKER STREET,

Nov. 21st

Re Vampires

SIR:

Referring to your letter of the 19th, I beg to state that I have looked into the inquiry of your client, Mr. Robert Ferguson, of Ferguson and Muirhead, tea brokers, of Mincing Lane, and that the matter has been brought to a satisfactory conclusion. With thanks for your recommendation, I am, sir,

Faithfully yours,

SHERLOCK HOLMES

THE ADVENTURE OF THE THREE GARRIDEBS

It may have been a comedy, or it may have been a tragedy. It cost one man his reason, it cost me a blood-letting, and it cost yet another man the penalties of the law. Yet there was certainly an element of comedy. Well, you shall judge for yourselves.

I remember the date very well, for it was in the same month that Holmes refused a knighthood for services which may perhaps someday be described. I only refer to the matter in passing, for in my position of partner and confidant I am obliged to be particularly careful to avoid any indiscretion. I repeat, however, that this enables me to fix the date, which was the latter end of June, 1902, shortly after the conclusion of the South African War. Holmes had spent several days in bed, as was his habit from time to time, but he emerged that morning with a long foolscap document in his hand and a twinkle of amusement in his austere gray eyes.

"There is a chance for you to make some money. friend Watson," said he. "Have you ever heard the name of Garrideb?"

I admitted that I had not.

"Well, if you can lay your hand upon a Garrideb, there's money in it."

"Why?"

"Ah, that's a long story - rather a whimsical one, too. I don't think in all our explorations of human complexities we have ever come upon anything more singular. The fellow will be here presently for cross-examination, so I won't open the matter up till he comes. But, meanwhile, that's the name we want."

The telephone directory lay on the table beside me, and I turned over the pages in a rather hopeless quest. But to my amazement there was this strange name in its due place. I gave a cry of triumph.

"Here you are, Holmes! Here it is!"

Holmes took the book from my hand.

"'Garrideb, N.,'" he read, "'136 Little Ryder Street, W.' Sorry to disappoint you, my dear Watson, but this is the man himself. That is the address upon his letter. We want another to match him."

Mrs. Hudson had come in with a card upon a tray. I took it up and glanced at it.

"Why, here it is!" I cried in amazement. "This is a different initial. John Garrideb, Counsellor at Law, Moorville, Kansas, U.S.A."

Holmes smiled as he looked at the card. "I am afraid you must make yet another effort, Watson," said he. "This gentleman is also in the plot already, though I certainly did not expect to see him this morning. However, he is in a position to tell us a good deal which I want to know."

A moment later he was in the room. Mr. John Garrideb, Counsellor at Law, was a short, powerful man with the round, fresh, clean-shaven face characteristic of so many American men of affairs. The general effect was chubby and rather childlike, so that one received the impression of quite a young man with a broad set smile upon his face. His eyes, however, were arresting. Seldom in any human head have I seen a pair which bespoke a more intense inward life, so bright were they, so alert, so responsive to every change of thought. His accent was American, but was not accompanied by any eccentricity of speech.

"Mr. Holmes?" he asked, glancing from one to the other. "Ah, yes! Your pictures are not unlike you, sir, if I may say so. I believe you have had a letter from my namesake, Mr. Nathan Garrideb, have you not?"

"Pray sit down," said Sherlock Holmes. "We shall, I fancy, have a good deal to discuss." He took up his sheets of foolscap. "You are, of course, the Mr. John Garrideb mentioned in this document. But surely you have been in England some time?"

"Why do you say that, Mr. Holmes?" I seemed to read sudden suspicion in those expressive eyes.

"Your whole outfit is English."

Mr. Garrideb forced a laugh. "I've read of your tricks, Mr. Holmes, but I never thought I would be the subject of them. Where do you read that?"

"The shoulder cut of your coat, the toes of your boots - could anyone doubt it?"

"Well, well, I had no idea I was so obvious a Britisher. But business brought me over here some time ago, and so, as you say, my outfit is nearly all London. However, I guess your time is of value, and we did not meet to talk about the cut of my socks. What about getting down to that paper you hold in your hand?"

Holmes had in some way ruffled our visitor, whose chubby face had assumed a far less amiable expression.

"Patience! Patience, Mr. Garrideb!" said my friend in a soothing voice. "Dr. Watson would tell you that these little digressions of mine sometimes prove in the end to have some bearing on the matter. But why did Mr. Nathan Garrideb not come with you?"

"Why did he ever drag you into it at all?" asked our visitor with a sudden outflame of anger. "What in thunder had you to do with it? Here was a bit of professional business between two gentlemen, and one of them must needs call in a detective! I saw him this morning, and he told me this fool-trick he had played me, and that's why I am here. But I feel bad about it, all the same."

"There was no reflection upon you, Mr. Garrideb. It was simply zeal upon his part to gain your end - an end which is, I understand, equally vital for both of you. He knew that I had means of getting information, and, therefore, it was very natural that he should apply to me."

Our visitor's angry face gradually cleared.

"Well, that puts it different," said he. "When I went to see him this morning and he told me he had sent to a detective, I just asked for your address and came right away. I don't want police butting into a private matter. But if you are content just to help us find the man, there can be no harm in that."

"Well, that is just how it stands," said Holmes. "And now, sir, since you are here, we had best have a clear account from your own lips. My friend here knows nothing of the details."

Mr. Garrideb surveyed me with not too friendly a gaze.

"Need he know?" he asked.

"We usually work together."

"Well, there's no reason it should be kept a secret. I'll give you the facts as short as I can make them. If you came from Kansas I would not need to explain to you who Alexander Hamilton Garrideb was. He made his money in real estate, and afterwards in the wheat pit at Chicago, but he spent it in buying up as much land as would make one of your counties, lying along the Arkansas River, west of Fort Dodge. It's grazing-land and lumber-land and arable-land and mineralized-land, and just every sort of land that brings dollars to the man that owns it.

"He had no kith nor kin - or, if he had, I never heard of it. But he took a kind of pride in the queerness of his name. That was what brought us together. I was in the law at Topeka, and one day I had a visit from the old man, and he was tickled to death to meet another man with his own name. It was his pet fad, and he was dead set to find out if there were any more Garridebs in the world. 'Find me another!' said he. I told him I was a busy man and could not spend my life hiking round the world in search of Garridebs. 'None the less,' said he, 'that is just what you will do if things pan out as I planned them.' I thought he was joking, but there was a powerful lot of meaning in the words, as I was soon to discover.

"For he died within a year of saying them, and he left a will behind him. It was the queerest will that has ever been filed in the State of Kansas. His property was divided into three parts and I was to have one on condition that I found two Garridebs who would share the remainder. It's five million dollars for each if it is a cent, but we can't lay a finger on it until we all three stand in a row.

"It was so big a chance that I just let my legal practice slide and I set forth looking for Garridebs. There is not one in the United States. I went through it, sir, with a fine-toothed comb and never a Garrideb could I catch. Then I tried the old country. Sure enough there was the name in the London telephone directory. I went after him two days ago and explained the whole matter to him. But he is a lone man, like myself, with some women relations, but no men. It says three adult men in the will. So you see we still have a vacancy, and if you can help to fill it we will be very ready to pay your charges."

"Well, Watson," said Holmes with a smile, "I said it was rather whimsical, did I not? I should have thought, sir, that your obvious way was to advertise in the agony columns of the papers."

"I have done that, Mr. Holmes. No replies."

"Dear me! Well, it is certainly a most curious little problem. I may take a glance at it in my leisure. By the way, it is curious that you should have come from Topeka. I used to have a correspondent - he is dead now - old Dr. Lysander Starr, who was mayor in 1890."

"Good old Dr. Starr!" said our visitor. "His name is still honoured. Well, Mr. Holmes, I suppose all we can do is to report to you and let you know how we progress. I reckon you will hear within a day or two." With this assurance our American bowed and departed.

Holmes had lit his pipe, and he sat for some time with a curious smile upon his face.

"Well?" I asked at last.

"I am wondering, Watson - just wondering!"

"At what?"

Holmes took his pipe from his lips.

"I was wondering, Watson, what on earth could be the object of this man in telling us such a rigmarole of lies. I nearly asked him so - for there are times when a brutal frontal attack is the best policy - but I judged it better to let him think he had fooled us. Here is a man with an English coat frayed at the elbow and trousers bagged at the knee with a year's wear, and yet by this document and by his own account he is a provincial American lately landed in London. There have been no advertisements in the agony columns. You know that I miss nothing there. They are my favourite covert for putting up a bird, and I would never have overlooked such a cock pheasant as that. I never knew a Dr. Lysander Starr, of Topeka. Touch him where you would he was false. I think the fellow is really an American, but he has worn his accent smooth with years of London. What is his game, then, and what motive lies behind this preposterous search for Garridebs? It's worth our attention, for, granting that the man is a rascal, he is certainly a complex and ingenious one. We must now find out if our other correspondent is a fraud also. Just ring him up, Watson."

I did so, and heard a thin, quavering voice at the other end of the line.

"Yes, yes, I am Mr. Nathan Garrideb. Is Mr. Holmes there? I should very much like to have a word with Mr. Holmes."

My friend took the instrument and I heard the usual syncopated dialogue.

"Yes, he has been here. I understand that you don't know him... How long? ... Only two days! ... Yes, yes, of course, it is a most captivating prospect. Will you be at home this evening? I suppose your namesake will not be there? ... Very good, we will come then, for I would rather have a chat without him... Dr. Watson will come with me... I understand from your note that you did not go out often... Well, we shall be round about six. You need not mention it to the American lawyer... Very good. Good-bye!"

It was twilight of a lovely spring evening, and even Little Ryder Street, one of the smaller offshoots from the Edgware Road, within a stone-cast of old Tyburn Tree of evil memory, looked golden and wonderful in the slanting rays of the setting sun. The particular house to which we were directed was a large, old-fashioned, Early Georgian edifice, with a flat brick face broken only by two deep bay windows on the ground floor. It was on this ground floor that our client lived, and, indeed, the low windows proved to be the front of the huge room in which he spent his waking hours. Holmes pointed as we passed to the small brass plate which bore the curious name.

"Up some years, Watson," he remarked, indicating its discoloured surface. "It's his real name, anyhow, and that is something to note."

The house had a common stair, and there were a number of names painted in the hall, some indicating offices and some private chambers. It was not a collection of residential flats, but rather the abode of Bohemian bachelors. Our client opened the door for us himself and apologized by saying that the woman in charge left at four o'clock. Mr. Nathan Garrideb proved to be a very tall, loose jointed, round-backed person, gaunt and bald, some sixty-odd years of age. He had a cadaverous face, with the dull dead skin of a man to whom exercise was unknown. Large round spectacles and a small projecting goat's beard combined with his stooping attitude to give him an expression of peering curiosity. The general effect, however, was amiable, though eccentric.

The room was as curious as its occupant. It looked like a small museum. It was both broad and deep, with cupboards and cabinets all round, crowded with specimens, geological and anatomical. Cases of butterflies and moths flanked each side of the entrance. A large table in the centre was littered with all sorts of debris, while the tall brass tube of a powerful microscope bristled up among them. As I glanced round I was surprised at the universality of the man's interests. Here was a case of ancient coins. There was a cabinet of flint instruments. Behind his central table was a large cupboard of fossil bones. Above was a line of plaster skulls with such names as "Neanderthal," "Heidelberg," "Cro-Magnon" printed beneath them. It was clear that he was a student of many subjects. As he stood in front of us now, he held a piece of chamois leather in his right hand with which he was polishing a coin.

"Syracusan - of the best period," he explained, holding it up. "They degenerated greatly towards the end. At their best I hold them supreme, though some prefer the Alexandrian school. You will find a chair here, Mr. Holmes. Pray allow me to clear these bones. And you, sir - ah, yes, Dr. Watson - if you would have the goodness to put the Japanese vase to one side. You see round me my little interests in life. My doctor lectures me about never going out, but why should I go out when I have so much to hold me here? I can assure you that the adequate cataloguing of one of those cabinets would take me three good months."

Holmes looked round him with curiosity.

"But do you tell me that you never go out?" he said.

"Now and again I drive down to Sotheby's or Christie's. Otherwise I very seldom leave my room. I am not too strong, and my researches are very absorbing. But you can imagine, Mr. Holmes, what a terrific shock - pleasant but terrific - it was for me when I heard of this unparalleled good fortune. It only needs one more Garrideb to complete the matter, and surely we can find one. I had a brother, but he is dead, and female relatives are disqualified. But there must surely be others in the world. I had heard that you handled strange cases, and that was why I sent to you. Of course, this American gentleman is quite right, and I should have taken his advice first, but I acted for the best."

"I think you acted very wisely indeed," said Holmes. "But are you really anxious to acquire an estate in America?"

"Certainly not, sir. Nothing would induce me to leave my collection. But this gentleman has assured me that he will buy me out as soon as we have established our claim. Five million dollars was the sum named. There are a dozen specimens in the market at the present moment which fill gaps in my collection, and which I am unable to purchase for want of a few hundred pounds. Just think what I could do with five million dollars. Why, I have the nucleus of a national collection. I shall be the Hans Sloane of my age."

His eyes gleamed behind his great spectacles. It was very clear that no pains would be spared by Mr. Nathan Garrideb in finding a namesake.

"I merely called to make your acquaintance, and there is no reason why I should interrupt your studies," said Holmes. "I prefer to establish personal touch with those with whom I do business. There are few questions I need ask, for I have your very clear narrative in my pocket, and I filled up the blanks when this American gentleman called. I understand that up to this week you were unaware of his existence."

"That is so. He called last Tuesday."

"Did he tell you of our interview to-day?"

"Yes, he came straight back to me. He had been very angry."

"Why should he be angry?"

"He seemed to think it was some reflection on his honour. But he was quite cheerful again when he returned."

"Did he suggest any course of action?"

"No, sir, he did not."

"Has he had, or asked for, any money from you?"

"No, sir, never!"

"You see no possible object he has in view?"

"None, except what he states."

"Did you tell him of our telephone appointment?"

"Yes, sir, I did."

Holmes was lost in thought. I could see that he was puzzled.

"Have you any articles of great value in your collection?"

"No, sir. I am not a rich man. It is a good collection, but not a very valuable one."

"You have no fear of burglars?"

"Not the least."

"How long have you been in these rooms?"

"Nearly five years."

Holmes's cross-examination was interrupted by an imperative knocking at the door. No sooner had our client unlatched it than the American lawyer burst excitedly into the room.

"Here you are!" he cried, waving a paper over his head. "I thought I should be in time to get you. Mr. Nathan Garrideb, my congratulations! You are a rich man, sir. Our business is happily finished and all is well. As to you, Mr. Holmes, we can only say we are sorry if we have given you any useless trouble."

He handed over the paper to our client, who stood staring at a marked advertisement. Holmes and I leaned forward and read it over his shoulder. This is how it ran:

HOWARD GARRIDEB
CONSTRUCTOR OF ACRICULTURAL MACHINERY

Binders, reapers, steam and hand plows, drills, harrows, farmer's carts, buckboards, and all other appliances.

Estimates for Artesian Wells.

Apply Grosvenor Buildings, Aston

"Glorious!" gasped our host. "That makes our third man."

"I had opened up inquiries in Birmingham," said the American, "and my agent there has sent me this advertisement from a local paper. We must hustle and put the thing through. I have written to this man and told him that you will see him in his office to-morrow afternoon at four o'clock."

"You want me to see him?"

"What do you say, Mr. Holmes? Don't you think it would be wiser? Here am I, a wandering American with a wonderful tale. Why should he believe what I tell him? But you are a Britisher with solid references, and he is bound to take notice of what you say. I would go with you if you wished, but I have a very busy day to-morrow, and I could always follow you if you are in any trouble."

"Well, I have not made such a journey for years."

"It is nothing, Mr. Garrideb. I have figured out our connections. You leave at twelve and should be there soon after two. Then you can be back the same night. All you have to do is to see this man, explain the matter, and get an affidavit of his existence. By the Lord!" he added hotly, "considering I've come all the way from the centre of America, it is surely little enough if you go a hundred miles in order to put this matter through."

"Quite so," said Holmes. "I think what this gentleman says is very true."

Mr. Nathan Garrideb shrugged his shoulders with a disconsolate air. "Well, if you insist I shall go," said he. "It is certainly hard for me to refuse you anything, considering the glory of hope that you have brought into my life."

"Then that is agreed," said Holmes, "and no doubt you will let me have a report as soon as you can."

"I'll see to that," said the American. "Well," he added looking at his watch, "I'll have to get on. I'll call to-morrow, Mr. Nathan, and see you off to Birmingham. Coming my way, Mr. Holmes? Well, then, good-bye, and we may have good news for you to-morrow night."

I noticed that my friend's face cleared when the American left the room, and the look of thoughtful perplexity had vanished.

"I wish I could look over your collection, Mr. Garrideb," said he. "In my profession all sorts of odd knowledge comes useful, and this room of yours is a storehouse of it."

Our client shone with pleasure and his eyes gleamed from behind his big glasses.

"I had always heard, sir, that you were a very intelligent man," said he. "I could take you round now if you have the time."

"Unfortunately, I have not. But these specimens are so well labelled and classified that they hardly need your personal explanation. If I should be able to look in to-morrow, I presume that there would be no objection to my glancing over them?"

"None at all. You are most welcome. The place will, of course, be shut up, but Mrs. Saunders is in the basement up to four o'clock and would let you in with her key."

"Well, I happen to be clear to-morrow afternoon. If you would say a word to Mrs. Saunders it would be quite in order. By the way, who is your house-agent?"

Our client was amazed at the sudden question.

"Holloway and Steele, in the Edgware Road. But why?"

"I am a bit of an archaeologist myself when it comes to houses," said Holmes, laughing. "I was wondering if this was Queen Anne or Georgian."

"Georgian, beyond doubt."

"Really. I should have thought a little earlier. However, it is easily ascertained. Well, good-bye, Mr. Garrideb, and may you have every success in your Birmingham journey."

The house-agent's was close by, but we found that it was closed for the day, so we made our way back to Baker Street. It was not till after dinner that Holmes reverted to the subject.

"Our little problem draws to a close," said he. "No doubt you have outlined the solution in your own mind."

"I can make neither head nor tail of it."

"The head is surely clear enough and the tail we should see to-morrow. Did you notice nothing curious about that advertisement?"

"I saw that the word 'plough' was misspelt."

"Oh, you did notice that, did you? Come, Watson, you improve all the time. Yes, it was bad English but good American. The printer had set it up as received. Then the buckboards. That is American also. And artesian wells are commoner with them than with us. It was a typical American advertisement, but purporting to be from an English firm. What do you make of that?"

"I can only suppose that this American lawyer put it in himself. What his object was I fail to understand."

"Well, there are alternative explanations. Anyhow, he wanted to get this good old fossil up to Birmingham. That is very clear. I might have told him that he was clearly going on a wild-goose chase, but, on second thoughts, it seemed better to clear the stage by letting him go. To-morrow, Watson - well, to-morrow will speak for itself."

Holmes was up and out early. When he returned at lunchtime I noticed that his face was very grave.

"This is a more serious matter than I had expected, Watson," said he. "It is fair to tell you so, though I know it will only be an additional reason to you for running your head into danger. I should know my Watson by now. But there is danger, and you should know it."

"Well, it is not the first we have shared, Holmes. I hope it may not be the last. What is the particular danger this time?"

"We are up against a very hard case. I have identified Mr. John Garrideb, Counsellor at Law. He is none other than 'Killer' Evans, of sinister and murderous reputation."

"I fear I am none the wiser."

"Ah, it is not part of your profession to carry about a portable Newgate Calendar in your memory. I have been down to see friend Lestrade at the Yard. There may be an occasional want of imaginative intuition down there, but they lead the world for thoroughness and method. I had an idea that we might get on the track of our American friend in their records. Sure enough, I found his chubby face smiling up at me from the rogues' portrait gallery. 'James Winter, alias Morecroft, alias Killer Evans,' was the inscription below." Holmes drew an envelope from his pocket. "I scribbled down a few points from his dossier: Aged forty-four. Native of Chicago. Known to have shot three men in the States. Escaped from penitentiary through political influence. Came to London in 1893. Shot a man over cards in a night-club in the Waterloo Road in January, 1895. Man died, but he was shown to have been the aggressor in the row. Dead man was identified as Rodger Prescott, famous as forger and coiner in Chicago. Killer Evans released in 1901. Has been under police supervision since, but so far as known has led an honest life. Very dangerous man, usually carries arms and is prepared to use them. That is our bird, Watson - a sporting bird, as you must admit."

"But what is his game?"

"Well, it begins to define itself. I have been to the houseagent's. Our client, as he told us, has been there five years. It was unlet for a year before then. The previous tenant was a gentleman at large named Waldron. Waldron's appearance was well remembered at the office. He had suddenly vanished and nothing more been heard of him. He was a tall, bearded man with very dark features. Now, Prescott, the man whom Killer Evans had shot, was, according to Scotland Yard, a tall, dark man with a beard. As a working hypothesis, I think we may take it that Prescott, the American criminal, used to live in the very room which our innocent friend now devotes to his museum. So at last we get a link, you see."

"And the next link?"

"Well, we must go now and look for that."

He took a revolver from the drawer and handed it to me.

"I have my old favourite with me. If our Wild West friend tries to live up to his nickname, we must be ready for him. I'll give you an hour for a siesta, Watson, and then I think it will be time for our Ryder Street adventure."

It was just four o'clock when we reached the curious apartment of Nathan Garrideb. Mrs. Saunders, the caretaker, was about to leave, but she had no hesitation in admitting us, for the door shut with a spring lock, and Holmes promised to see that all was safe before we left. Shortly afterwards the outer door closed, her bonnet passed the bow window, and we knew that we were alone in the lower floor of the house. Holmes made a rapid examination of the premises. There was one cupboard in a dark corner which stood out a little from the wall. It was behind this that we eventually crouched while Holmes in a whisper outlined his intentions.

"He wanted to get our amiable friend out of his room - that is very clear, and, as the collector never went out, it took some planning to do it. The whole of this Garrideb invention was apparently for no other end. I must say, Watson, that there is a certain devilish ingenuity about it, even if the queer name of the tenant did give him an opening which he could hardly have expected. He wove his plot with remarkable cunning.

"But what did he want?"

"Well, that is what we are here to find out. It has nothing whatever to do with our client, so far as I can read the situation. It is something connected with the man he murdered - the man who may have been his confederate in crime. There is some guilty secret in the room. That is how I read it. At first I thought our friend might have something in his collection more valuable than he knew - something worth the attention of a big criminal. But the fact that Rodger Prescott of evil memory inhabited these rooms points to some deeper reason. Well, Watson, we can but possess our souls in patience and see what the hour may bring."

That hour was not long in striking. We crouched closer in the shadow as we heard the outer door open and shut. Then came the sharp, metallic snap of a key, and the American was in the room. He closed the door softly behind him, took a sharp glance around him to see that all was safe, threw off his overcoat, and walked up to the central table with the brisk manner of one who knows exactly what he has to do and how to do it. He pushed the table to one side, tore up the square of carpet on which it rested, rolled it completely back, and then, drawing a jemmy from his inside pocket, he knelt down and worked vigorously upon the floor. Presently we heard the sound of sliding boards, and an instant later a square had opened in the planks. Killer Evans struck a match, lit a stump of candle, and vanished from our view.

Clearly our moment had come. Holmes touched my wrist as a signal, and together we stole across to the open trap-door. Gently as we moved, however, the old floor must have creaked under our feet, for the head of our American, peering anxiously round, emerged suddenly from the open space. His face turned upon us with a glare of baffled rage, which gradually softened into a rather shamefaced grin as he realized that two pistols were pointed at his head.

"Well, well!" said he coolly as he scrambled to the surface. "I guess you have been one too many for me, Mr. Holmes. Saw through my game, I suppose, and played me for a sucker from the first. Well, sir, I hand it to you; you have me beat and -"

In an instant he had whisked out a revolver from his breast and had fired two shots. I felt a sudden hot sear as if a red-hot iron had been pressed to my thigh. There was a crash as Holmes's pistol came down on the man's head. I had a vision of him sprawling upon the floor with blood running down his face while Holmes rummaged him for weapons. Then my friend's wiry arms were round me, and he was leading me to a chair.

"You're not hurt, Watson? For God's sake, say that you are not hurt!"

It was worth a wound - it was worth many wounds - to know the depth of loyalty and love which lay behind that cold mask. The clear, hard eyes were dimmed for a moment, and the firm lips were shaking. For the one and only time I caught a glimpse of a great heart as well as of a great brain. All my years of humble but single-minded service culminated in that moment of revelation.

"It's nothing, Holmes. It's a mere scratch."

He had ripped up my trousers with his pocket-knife.

"You are right," he cried with an immense sigh of relief. "It is quite superficial." His face set like flint as he glared at our prisoner, who was sitting up with a dazed face. "By the Lord, it is as well for you. If you had killed Watson, you would not have got out of this room alive. Now, sir, what have you to say for yourself?"

He had nothing to say for himself. He only sat and scowled. I leaned on Holmes's arm, and together we looked down into the small cellar which had been disclosed by the secret flap. It was still illuminated by the candle which Evans had taken down with him. Our eyes fell upon a mass of rusted machinery, great rolls of paper, a litter of bottles, and, neatly arranged upon a small table, a number of neat little bundles.

"A printing press - a counterfeiter's outfit," said Holmes.

"Yes, sir," said our prisoner, staggering slowly to his feet and then sinking into the chair. "The greatest counterfeiter London ever saw. That's Prescott's machine, and those bundles on the table are two thousand of Prescott's notes worth a hundred each and fit to pass anywhere. Help yourselves, gentlemen. Call it a deal and let me beat it."

Holmes laughed.

"We don't do things like that, Mr. Evans. There is no bolthole for you in this country. You shot this man Prescott, did you not?"

"Yes, sir, and got five years for it, though it was he who pulled on me.

Five years - when I should have had a medal the size of a soup plate. No living man could tell a Prescott from a Bank of England, and if I hadn't put him out he would have flooded London with them. I was the only one in the world who knew where he made them. Can you wonder that I wanted to get to the place? And can you wonder that when I found this crazy boob of a bug-hunter with the queer name squatting right on the top of it, and never quitting his room, I had to do the best I could to shift him? Maybe I would have been wiser if I had put him away. It would have been easy enough, but I'm a soft-hearted guy that can't begin shooting unless the other man has a gun also. But say, Mr. Holmes, what have I done wrong, anyhow? I've not used this plant. I've not hurt this old stiff. Where do you get me?"

"Only attempted murder, so far as I can see," said Holmes. "But that's not our job. They take that at the next stage. What we wanted at present was just your sweet self. Please give the Yard a call, Watson. It won't be entirely unexpected."

So those were the facts about Killer Evans and his remarkable invention of the three Garridebs. We heard later that our poor old friend never got over the shock of his dissipated dreams. When his castle in the air fell down, it buried him beneath the ruins. He was last heard of at a nursing-home in Brixton. It was a glad day at the Yard when the Prescott outfit was discovered, for, though they knew that it existed, they had never been able, after the death of the man, to find out where it was. Evans had indeed done great service and caused several worthy C.I.D. men to sleep the sounder, for the counterfeiter stands in a class by himself as a public danger. They would willingly have subscribed to that soup-plate medal of which the criminal had spoken, but an unappreciative bench took a less favourable view, and the Killer returned to those shades from which he had just emerged.

THE PROBLEM OF THOR BRIDGE

Somewhere in the vaults of the bank of Cox and Co., at Charing Cross, there is a travel-worn and battered tin dispatch box with my name, John H. Watson, M.D., Late Indian Army, painted upon the lid. It is crammed with papers, nearly all of which are records of cases to illustrate the curious problems which Mr. Sherlock Holmes had at various times to examine. Some, and not the least interesting, were complete failures, and as such will hardly bear narrating, since no final explanation is forthcoming. A problem without a solution may interest the student, but can hardly fail to annoy the casual reader. Among these unfinished tales is that of Mr. James Phillimore, who, stepping back into his own house to get his umbrella, was never more seen in this world. No less remarkable is that of the cutter Alicia, which sailed one spring morning into a small patch of mist from where she never again emerged, nor was anything further ever heard of herself and her crew. A third case worthy of note is that of Isadora Persano, the well-known journalist and duellist, who was found stark staring mad with a match box in front of him which contained a remarkable worm said to be unknown to science. Apart from these unfathomed cases, there are some which involve the secrets of private families to an extent which would mean consternation in many exalted quarters if it were thought possible that they might find their way into print. I need not say that such a breach of confidence is unthinkable, and that these records will be separated and destroyed now that my friend has time to turn his energies to the matter. There remain a considerable residue of cases of greater or less interest which I might have edited before had I not feared to give the public a surfeit which might react upon the reputation of the man whom above all others I revere. In some I was myself concerned and can speak as an eye-witness, while in others I was either not present or played so small a part that they could only be told as by a third person. The following narrative is drawn from my own experience.

It was a wild morning in October, and I observed as I was dressing how the last remaining leaves were being whirled from the solitary plane tree which graces the yard behind our house. I descended to breakfast prepared to find my companion in depressed spirits, for, like all great artists, he was easily impressed by his surroundings. On the contrary, I found that he had nearly finished his meal, and that his mood was particularly bright and joyous, with that somewhat sinister cheerfulness which was characteristic of his lighter moments.

"You have a case, Holmes?" I remarked.

"The faculty of deduction is certainly contagious, Watson," he answered. "It has enabled you to probe my secret. Yes, I have a case. After a month of trivialities and stagnation the wheels move once more."

"Might I share it?"

"There is little to share, but we may discuss it when you have consumed the two hard-boiled eggs with which our new cook has favoured us. Their condition may not be unconnected with the copy of the Family Herald which I observed yesterday upon the hall-table. Even so trivial a matter as cooking an egg demands an attention which is conscious of the passage of time and incompatible with the love romance in that excellent periodical."

A quarter of an hour later the table had been cleared and we were face to face. He had drawn a letter from his pocket.

"You have heard of Neil Gibson, the Gold King?" he said.

"You mean the American Senator?"

"Well, he was once Senator for some Western state, but is better known as the greatest gold-mining magnate in the world."

"Yes, I know of him. He has surely lived in England for some time. His name is very familiar."

"Yes, he bought a considerable estate in Hampshire some five years ago. Possibly you have already heard of the tragic end of his wife?"

"Of course. I remember it now. That is why the name is familiar. But I really know nothing of the details."

Holmes waved his hand towards some papers on a chair. "I had no idea that the case was coming my way or I should have had my extracts ready," said he. "The fact is that the problem, though exceedingly sensational, appeared to present no difficulty. The interesting personality of the accused does not obscure the clearness of the evidence. That was the view taken by the coroner's jury and also in the police-court proceedings. It is now referred to the Assizes at Winchester. I fear it is a thankless business. I can discover facts, Watson, but I cannot change them. Unless some entirely new and unexpected ones come to light I do not see what my client can hope for."

"Your client?"

"Ah, I forgot I had not told you. I am getting into your involved habit, Watson, of telling a story backward. You had best read this first."

The letter which he handed to me, written in a bold, masterful hand, ran as follows:

CLARIDGE'S HOTEL,

October 3rd

DEAR MR. SHERLOCK Holmes:

I can't see the best woman God ever made go to her death without doing all that is possible to save her. I can't explain things - I can't even try to explain them, but I know beyond all doubt that Miss Dunbar is innocent. You know the facts - who doesn't? It has been the gossip of the country. And never a voice raised for her! It's the damned injustice of it all that makes me crazy. That woman has a heart that wouldn't let her kill a fly. Well, I'll come at eleven to-morrow and see if you can get some ray of light in the dark. Maybe I have a clue and don't know it. Anyhow, all I know and all I have and all I am are for your use if only you can save her. If ever in your life you showed your powers, put them now into this case.

Yours faithfully,

J. NEIL GIBSON

"There you have it," said Sherlock Holmes, knocking out the ashes of his after-breakfast pipe and slowly refilling it. "That is the gentleman I await. As to the story, you have hardly time to master all these papers, so

I must give it to you in a nutshell if you are to take an intelligent interest in the proceedings. This man is the greatest financial power in the world, and a man, as I understand, of most violent and formidable character. He married a wife, the victim of this tragedy, of whom I know nothing save that she was past her prime, which was the more unfortunate as a very attractive governess superintended the education of two young children. These are the three people concerned, and the scene is a grand old manor house, the centre of a historical English state. Then as to the tragedy. The wife was found in the grounds nearly half a mile from the house, late at night, clad in her dinner dress, with a shawl over her shoulders and a revolver bullet through her brain. No weapon was found near her and there was no local clue as to the murder. No weapon near her, Watson - mark that! The crime seems to have been committed late in the evening, and the body was found by a gamekeeper about eleven o'clock, when it was examined by the police and by a doctor before being carried up to the house. Is this too condensed, or can you follow it clearly?"

"It is all very clear. But why suspect the governess?"

"Well, in the first place there is some very direct evidence. A revolver with one discharged chamber and a calibre which corresponded with the bullet was found on the floor of her wardrobe." His eyes fixed and he repeated in broken words, "On - the - floor - of - her - wardrobe." Then he sank into silence, and I saw that some train of thought had been set moving which I should be foolish to interrupt. Suddenly with a start he emerged into brisk life once more. "Yes, Watson, it was found. Pretty damning, eh? So the two juries thought. Then the dead woman had a note upon her making an appointment at that very place and signed by the governess. How's that? Finally there is the motive. Senator Gibson is an attractive person. If his wife dies, who more likely to succeed her than the young lady who had already by all accounts received pressing attentions from her employer? Love, fortune, power, all depending upon one middle aged life. Ugly, Watson - very ugly!"

"Yes, indeed, Holmes."

"Nor could she prove an alibi. On the contrary, she had to admit that she was down near Thor Bridge - that was the scene of the tragedy - about that hour. She couldn't deny it, for some passing villager had seen her there."

"That really seems final."

"And yet, Watson - and yet! This bridge - a single broad span of stone with balustraded sides - carries the drive over the narrowest part of a long, deep, reed-girt sheet of water. Thor Mere it is called. In the mouth of the bridge lay the dead woman. Such are the main facts. But here, if I mistake not, is our client, considerably before his time."

Billy had opened the door, but the name which he announced was an unexpected one. Mr. Marlow Bates was a stranger to both of us. He was a thin, nervous wisp of a man with frightened eyes and a twitching, hesitating manner - a man whom my own professional eye would judge to be on the brink of an absolute nervous breakdown.

"You seem agitated, Mr. Bates," said Holmes. "Pray sit down. I fear I can only give you a short time, for I have an appointment at eleven."

"I know you have," our visitor gasped, shooting out short sentences like a man who is out of breath. "Mr. Gibson is coming. Mr. Gibson is my employer. I am manager of his estate. Mr. Holmes, he is a villain - an infernal villain."

"Strong language, Mr. Bates."

"I have to be emphatic, Mr. Holmes, for the time is so limited. I would not have him find me here for the world. He is almost due now. But I was so situated that I could not come earlier. His secretary, Mr. Ferguson, only told me this morning of his appointment with you."

"And you are his manager?"

"I have given him notice. In a couple of weeks I shall have shaken off his accursed slavery. A hard man, Mr. Holmes, hard to all about him. Those public charities are a screen to cover his private iniquities. But his wife was his chief victim. He was brutal to her - yes, sir, brutal! How she came by her death I do not know, but I am sure that he had made her life a misery to her. She was a creature of the tropics, a Brazilian by birth, as no doubt you know."

"No, it had escaped me."

"Tropical by birth and tropical by nature. A child of the sun and of passion. She had loved him as such women can love, but when her own physical charms had faded - I am told that they once were great - there was nothing to hold him. We all liked her and felt for her and hated him for the way that he treated her. But he is plausible and cunning. That is all I have to say to you. Don't take him at his face value. There is more behind. Now I'll go. No, no, don't detain me! He is almost due."

With a frightened look at the clock our strange visitor literally ran to the door and disappeared.

"Well! Well!" said Holmes after an interval of silence. "Mr. Gibson seems to have a nice loyal household. But the warning is a useful one, and now we can only wait till the man himself appears."

Sharp at the hour we heard a heavy step upon the stairs, and the famous millionaire was shown into the room. As I looked upon him I understood not only the fears and dislike of his manager but also the execrations which so many business rivals have heaped upon his head. If I were a sculptor and desired to idealize the successful man of affairs, iron of nerve and leathery of conscience, I should choose Mr. Neil Gibson as my model. His tall, gaunt, craggy figure had a suggestion of hunger and rapacity. An Abraham Lincoln keyed to base uses instead of high ones would give some idea of the man. His face might have been chiselled in granite, hard-set, craggy, remorseless, with deep lines upon it, the scars of many a crisis. Cold gray eyes, looking shrewdly out from under bristling brows, surveyed us each in turn. He bowed in perfunctory fashion as Holmes mentioned my name, and then with a masterful air of possession he drew a chair up to my companion and seated himself with his bony knees almost touching him.

"Let me say right here, Mr. Holmes," he began, "that money is nothing to me in this case. You can burn it if it's any use in lighting you to the truth. This woman is innocent and this woman has to be cleared, and it's up to you to do it. Name your figure!"

"My professional charges are upon a fixed scale," said Holmes coldly. "I do not vary them, save when I remit them altogether."

"Well, if dollars make no difference to you, think of the reputation. If you pull this off every paper in England and America will be booming you. You'll be the talk of two continents."

"Thank you, Mr. Gibson, I do not think that I am in need of booming. It may surprise you to know that I prefer to work anonymously, and that it is the problem itself which attracts me. But we are wasting time. Let us get down to the facts."

"I think that you will find all the main ones in the press reports. I don't know that I can add anything which will help you. But if there is anything you would wish more light upon - well, I am here to give it."

"Well, there is just one point."

"What is it?"

"What were the exact relations between you and Miss Dunbar?"

The Gold King gave a violent start and half rose from his chair. Then his massive calm came back to him.

"I suppose you are within your rights - and maybe doing your duty - in asking such a question, Mr. Holmes."

"We will agree to suppose so," said Holmes.

"Then I can assure you that our relations were entirely and always those of an employer towards a young lady whom he never conversed with, or ever saw, save when she was in the company of his children."

Holmes rose from his chair.

"I am a rather busy man, Mr. Gibson," said he, "and I have no time or taste for aimless conversations. I wish you good morning."

Our visitor had risen also, and his great loose figure towered above Holmes. There was an angry gleam from under those bristling brows and a tinge of colour in the sallow cheeks.

"What the devil do you mean by this, Mr. Holmes? Do you dismiss my case?"

"Well, Mr. Gibson, at least I dismiss you. I should have thought my words were plain."

"Plain enough, but what's at the back of it? Raising the price on me, or afraid to tackle it, or what? I've a right to a plain answer."

"Well, perhaps you have," said Holmes. "I'll give you one. This case is quite sufficiently complicated to start with without the further difficulty of false information."

"Meaning that I lie."

"Well, I was trying to express it as delicately as I could, but if you insist upon the word I will not contradict you."

I sprang to my feet, for the expression upon the millionaire's face was fiendish in its intensity, and he had raised his great knotted fist. Holmes smiled languidly and reached his hand out for his pipe.

"Don't be noisy, Mr. Gibson. I find that after breakfast even the smallest argument is unsettling. I suggest that a stroll in the morning air and a little quiet thought will be greatly to your advantage."

With an effort the Gold King mastered his fury. I could not but admire him, for by a supreme self-command he had turned in a minute from a hot flame of anger to a frigid and contemptuous indifference.

"Well, it's your choice. I guess you know how to run your own business. I can't make you touch the case against your will. You've done yourself no good this morning, Mr. Holmes, for I have broken stronger men than you. No man ever crossed me and was the better for it."

"So many have said so, and yet here I am," said Holmes, smiling. "Well, good-morning, Mr. Gibson. You have a good deal yet to learn."

Our visitor made a noisy exit, but Holmes smoked in imperturbable silence with dreamy eyes fixed upon the ceiling.

"Any views, Watson?" he asked at last.

"Well, Holmes, I must confess that when I consider that this is a man who would certainly brush any obstacle from his path, and when I remember that his wife may have been an obstacle and an object of dislike, as that man Bates plainly told us, it seems to me -"

"Exactly. And to me also."

"But what were his relations with the governess, and how did you discover them?"

"Bluff, Watson, bluff! When I considered the passionate, unconventional, unbusinesslike tone of his letter and contrasted it with his self-contained manner and appearance, it was pretty clear that there was some deep emotion which centred upon the accused woman rather than upon the victim. We've got to understand the exact relations of those three people if we are to reach the truth. You saw the frontal attack which I made upon him, and how imperturbably he received it. Then I bluffed him by giving him the impression that I was absolutely certain, when in reality I was only extremely suspicious."

"Perhaps he will come back?"

"He is sure to come back. He must come back. He can't leave it where it is. Ha! isn't that a ring? Yes, there is his footstep. Well, Mr. Gibson, I was just saying to Dr. Watson that you were somewhat overdue."

The Gold King had reentered the room in a more chastened mood than he had left it. His wounded pride still showed in his resentful eyes, but his common sense had shown him that he must yield if he would attain his end.

"I've been thinking it over, Mr. Holmes, and I feel that I have been hasty in taking your remarks amiss. You are justified in getting down to the facts, whatever they may be, and I think the more of you for it. I can assure you, however, that the relations between Miss Dunbar and me don't really touch this case."

"That is for me to decide, is it not?"

"Yes, I guess that is so. You're like a surgeon who wants every symptom before he can give his diagnosis."

"Exactly. That expresses it. And it is only a patient who has an object in deceiving his surgeon who would conceal the facts of his case."

"That may be so, but you will admit, Mr. Holmes, that most men would shy off a bit when they are asked point-blank what their relations with a woman may be - if there is really some serious feeling in the case. I guess most men have a little private reserve of their own in some corner of their souls where they don't welcome intruders. And you burst suddenly into it. But the object excuses you, since it was to try and save her. Well, the stakes are down and the reserve open, and you can explore where you will. What is it you want?"

"The truth."

The Gold King paused for a moment as one who marshals his thoughts. His grim, deep-lined face had become even sadder and more grave.

"I can give it to you in a very few words, Mr. Holmes," said he at last. "There are some things that are painful as well as difficult to say, so I won't go deeper than is needful. I met my wife when I was gold-hunting in Brazil. Maria Pinto was the daughter of a government official at Manaos, and she was very beautiful. I was young and ardent in those days, but even now, as I look back with colder blood and a more critical eye, I can see that she was rare and wonderful in her beauty. It was a deep rich nature, too, passionate, whole-hearted, tropical, ill-balanced, very different from the American women whom I had known. Well, to make a long story short, I loved her and I married her. It was only when the romance had passed - and it lingered for years - that I realized that we had nothing - absolutely nothing - in common. My love faded. If hers had faded also it might have been easier. But you know the wonderful way of women! Do what I might, nothing could turn her from me. If I have been harsh to her, even brutal as some have said, it has been because I knew that if I could kill her love, or if it turned to hate, it would be easier for both of us. But nothing changed her. She adored me in those English woods as she had adored me twenty years ago on the banks of the Amazon. Do what I might, she was as devoted as ever.

"Then came Miss Grace Dunbar. She answered our advertisement and became governess to our two children. Perhaps you have seen her portrait in the papers. The whole world has proclaimed that she also is a very beautiful woman. Now, I make no pretence to be more moral than my neighbours, and I will admit to you that I could not live under the same roof with such a woman and in daily contact with her without feeling a passionate regard for her. Do you blame me, Mr. Holmes?"

"I do not blame you for feeling it. I should blame you if you expressed it, since this young lady was in a sense under your protection."

"Well, maybe so," said the millionaire, though for a moment the reproof had brought the old angry gleam into his eyes. "I'm not pretending to be any better than I am. I guess all my life I've been a man that reached out his hand for what he wanted, and I never wanted anything more than the love and possession of that woman. I told her so."

"Oh, you did, did you?"

Holmes could look very formidable when he was moved.

"I said to her that if I could marry her I would, but that it was out of my power. I said that money was no object and that all I could do to make her happy and comfortable would be done."

"Very generous, I am sure," said Holmes with a sneer.

"See here, Mr. Holmes. I came to you on a question of evidence, not on a question of morals. I'm not asking for your criticism."

"It is only for the young lady's sake that I touch your case at all," said Holmes sternly. "I don't know that anything she is accused of is really worse than what you have yourself admitted, that you have tried to ruin a defenseless girl who was under your roof. Some of you rich men have to be taught that all the world cannot be bribed into condoning your offences."

To my surprise the Gold King took the reproof with equanimity.

"That's how I feel myself about it now. I thank God that my plans did not work out as I intended. She would have none of it, and she wanted to leave the house instantly."

"Why did she not?"

"Well, in the first place, others were dependent upon her, and it was no light matter for her to let them all down by sacrificing her living. When I had sworn - as I did - that she should never be molested again, she consented to remain. But there was another reason. She knew the influence she had over me, and that it was stronger than any other influence in the world. She wanted to use it for good."

"How?"

"Well, she knew something of my affairs. They are large, Mr. Holmes - large beyond the belief of an ordinary man. I can make or break - and it is usually break. It wasn't individuals only. It was communities, cities, even nations. Business is a hard game, and the weak go to the wall. I played the game for all it was worth. I never squealed myself, and I never cared if the other fellow squealed. But she saw it different. I guess she was right. She believed and said that a fortune for one man that was more than he needed should not be built on ten thousand ruined men who were left without the means of life. That was how she saw it, and I guess she could see past the dollars to something that was more lasting. She found that I listened to what she said, and she believed she was serving the world by influencing my actions. So she stayed - and then this came along."

"Can you throw any light upon that?"

The Gold King paused for a minute or more, his head sunk in his hands, lost in deep thought.

"It's very black against her. I can't deny that. And women lead an inward life and may do things beyond the judgment of a man. At first I was so rattled and taken aback that I was ready to think she had been led away in some extraordinary fashion that was clean against her usual nature. One explanation came into my head. I give it to you, Mr. Holmes, for what it is worth. There is no doubt that my wife was bitterly jealous. There is a soul-jealousy that can be as frantic as anybody-jealousy, and though my wife had no cause - and I think she understood this - for the latter, she was aware that this English girl exerted an influence upon my mind and my acts that she herself never had. It was an influence for good, but that did not mend the matter. She was crazy with hatred and the heat of the Amazon was always in her blood. She might have planned to murder Miss Dunbar - or we will say to threaten her with a gun and so frighten her into leaving us. Then there might have been a scuffle and the gun gone off and shot the woman who held it."

"That possibility had already occurred to me," said Holmes. "Indeed, it is the only obvious alternative to deliberate murder."

"But she utterly denies it."

"Well, that is not final - is it? One can understand that a woman placed in so awful a position might hurry home still in her bewilderment holding the revolver. She might even throw it down among her clothes, hardly knowing what she was doing, and when it was found she might try to lie her way out by a total denial, since all explanation was impossible. What is against such a supposition?"

"Miss Dunbar herself."

"Well, perhaps."

Holmes looked at his watch. "I have no doubt we can get the necessary permits this morning and reach Winchester by the evening train. When I have seen this young lady it is very possible that I may be of more use to you in the matter, though I cannot promise that my conclusions will necessarily be such as you desire."

There was some delay in the official pass, and instead of reaching

Winchester that day we went down to Thor Place, the Hampshire estate of Mr. Neil Gibson. He did not accompany us himself, but we had the address of Sergeant Coventry, of the local police, who had first examined into the affair. He was a tall, thin, cadaverous man, with a secretive and mysterious manner which conveyed the idea that he knew or suspected a very great deal more than he dared say. He had a trick, too, of suddenly sinking his voice to a whisper as if he had come upon something of vital importance, though the information was usually commonplace enough. Behind these tricks of manner he soon showed himself to be a decent, honest fellow who was not too proud to admit that he was out of his depth and would welcome any help.

"Anyhow, I'd rather have you than Scotland Yard, Mr. Holmes," said he. "If the Yard gets called into a case, then the local loses all credit for success and may be blamed for failure. Now, you play straight, so I've heard."

"I need not appear in the matter at all," said Holmes to the evident relief of our melancholy acquaintance. "If I can clear it up I don't ask to have my name mentioned."

"Well, it's very handsome of you, I am sure. And your friend, Dr. Watson, can be trusted, I know. Now, Mr. Holmes, as we walk down to the place there is one question I should like to ask you. I'd breathe it to no soul but you." He looked round as though he hardly dare utter the words. "Don't you think there might be a case against Mr. Neil Gibson himself?"

"I have been considering that."

"You've not seen Miss Dunbar. She is a wonderful fine woman in every way. He may well have wished his wife out of the road. And these Americans are readier with pistols than our folk are. It was his pistol, you know."

"Was that clearly made out?"

"Yes, sir. It was one of a pair that he had."

"One of a pair? Where is the other?"

"Well, the gentleman has a lot of firearms of one sort and another. We never quite matched that particular pistol - but the box was made for two."

"If it was one of a pair you should surely be able to match it."

"Well, we have them all laid out at the house if you would care to look them over."

"Later, perhaps. I think we will walk down together and have a look at the scene of the tragedy."

This conversation had taken place in the little front room of Sergeant Coventry's humble cottage which served as the local police-station. A walk of half a mile or so across a wind-swept heath, all gold and bronze with the fading ferns, brought us to a side-gate opening into the grounds of the Thor Place estate. A path led us through the pheasant preserves, and then from a clearing we saw the widespread, half-timbered house, half Tudor and half Georgian, upon the crest of the hill. Beside us there was a long, reedy pool, constricted in the centre where the main carriage drive passed over a stone bridge, but swelling into small lakes on either side. Our guide paused at the mouth of this bridge, and he pointed to the ground.

"That was where Mrs. Gibson's body lay. I marked it by that stone."

"I understand that you were there before it was moved?"

"Yes, they sent for me at once."

"Who did?"

"Mr. Gibson himself. The moment the alarm was given and he had rushed down with others from the house, he insisted that nothing should be moved until the police should arrive."

"That was sensible. I gathered from the newspaper report that the shot was fired from close quarters."

"Yes, sir, very close."

"Near the right temple?"

"Just behind it, sir."

"How did the body lie?"

"On the back, sir. No trace of a struggle. No marks. No weapon. The short note from Miss Dunbar was clutched in her left hand."

"Clutched, you say?"

"Yes, sir, we could hardly open the fingers."

"That is of great importance. It excludes the idea that anyone could have placed the note there after death in order to furnish a false clue. Dear me! The note, as I remember, was quite short:

"I will be at Thor Bridge at nine o'clock."

"G. DUNBAR.

Was that not so?"

"Yes, sir."

"Did Miss Dunbar admit writing it?"

"Yes, sir."

"What was her explanation?"

"Her defense was reserved for the Assizes. She would say nothing."

"The problem is certainly a very interesting one. The point of the letter is very obscure, is it not?"

"Well, sir," said the guide, "it seemed, if I may be so bold as to say so, the only really clear point in the whole case."

Holmes shook his head.

"Granting that the letter is genuine and was really written, it was certainly received some time before - say one hour or two. Why, then, was this lady still clasping it in her left hand? Why should she carry it so carefully? She did not need to refer to it in the interview. Does it not seem remarkable?"

"Well, sir, as you put it, perhaps it does."

"I think I should like to sit quietly for a few minutes and think it out." He seated himself upon the stone ledge of the bridge, and I could see his quick gray eyes darting their questioning glances in every direction. Suddenly he sprang up again and ran across to the opposite parapet, whipped his lens from his pocket, and began to examine the stonework.

"This is curious," said he.

"Yes, sir, we saw the chip on the ledge. I expect it's been done by some passer-by."

The stonework was gray, but at this one point it showed white for a space not larger than a sixpence. When examined closely one could see that the surface was chipped as by a sharp blow.

"It took some violence to do that," said Holmes thoughtfully. With his cane he struck the ledge several times without leaving a mark. "Yes, it was a hard knock. In a curious place, too. It was not from above but from below, for you see that it is on the lower edge of the parapet."

"But it is at least fifteen feet from the body."

"Yes, it is fifteen feet from the body. It may have nothing to do with the matter, but it is a point worth noting. I do not think that we have anything more to learn here. There were no footsteps, you say?"

"The ground was iron hard, sir. There were no traces at all."

"Then we can go. We will go up to the house first and look over these weapons of which you speak. Then we shall get on to Winchester, for I should desire to see Miss Dunbar before we go farther."

Mr. Neil Gibson had not returned from town, but we saw in the house the neurotic Mr. Bates who had called upon us in the morning. He showed us with a sinister relish the formidable array of firearms of various shapes and sizes which his employer had accumulated in the course of an adventurous life.

"Mr. Gibson has his enemies, as anyone would expect who knew him and his methods," said he. "He sleeps with a loaded revolver in the drawer beside his bed. He is a man of violence, sir, and there are times when all of us are afraid of him. I am sure that the poor lady who has passed was often terrified."

"Did you ever witness physical violence towards her?"

"No, I cannot say that. But I have heard words which were nearly as bad - words of cold, cutting contempt, even before the servants."

"Our millionaire does not seem to shine in private life," remarked Holmes as we made our way to the station. "Well, Watson, we have come on a good many facts, some of them new ones, and yet I seem some way from my conclusion. In spite of the very evident dislike which Mr. Bates has to his employer, I gather from him that when the alarm came he was undoubtedly in his library. Dinner was over at 8:30 and all was normal up to then. It is true that the alarm was somewhat late in the evening, but the tragedy certainly occurred about the hour named in the note. There is no evidence at all that Mr. Gibson had been out of doors since his return from town at five o'clock. On the other hand, Miss Dunbar, as I understand it, admits that she had made an appointment to meet Mrs. Gibson at the bridge. Beyond this she would say nothing, as her lawyer had advised her to reserve her defence. We have several very vital questions to ask that young lady, and my mind will not be easy until we have seen her. I must confess that the case would seem to me to be very black against her if it were not for one thing."

"And what is that, Holmes?"

"The finding of the pistol in her wardrobe."

"Dear me, Holmes!" I cried, "that seemed to me to be the most damning incident of all."

"Not so, Watson. It had struck me even at my first perfunctory reading as very strange, and now that I am in closer touch with the case it is my only firm ground for hope. We must look for consistency. Where there is a want of it we must suspect deception."

"I hardly follow you."

"Well now, Watson, suppose for a moment that we visualize you in the character of a woman who, in a cold, premeditated fashion, is about to get rid of a rival. You have planned it. A note has been written. The victim has come. You have your weapon. The crime is done. It has been workmanlike and complete. Do you tell me that after carrying out so crafty a crime you would now ruin your reputation as a criminal by forgetting to fling your weapon into those adjacent reed-beds which would forever cover it, but you must needs carry it carefully home and put it in your own wardrobe, the very first place that would be searched? Your best friends would hardly call you a schemer, Watson, and yet I could not picture you doing anything so crude as that."

"In the excitement of the moment"

"No, no, Watson, I will not admit that it is possible. Where a crime is coolly premeditated, then the means of covering it are coolly premeditated also. I hope, therefore, that we are in the presence of a serious misconception."

"But there is so much to explain."

"Well, we shall set about explaining it. When once your point of view is changed, the very thing which was so damning becomes a clue to the truth. For example, there is this revolver. Miss Dunbar disclaims all knowledge of it. On our new theory she is speaking truth when she says so. Therefore, it was placed in her wardrobe. Who placed it there? Someone who wished to incriminate her. Was not that person the actual criminal? You see how we come at once upon a most fruitful line of inquiry."

We were compelled to spend the night at Winchester, as the formalities had not yet been completed, but next morning, in the company of Mr. Joyce Cummings, the rising barrister who was entrusted with the defense, we were allowed to see the young lady in her cell. I had expected from all that we had heard to see a beautiful woman, but I can never forget the effect which Miss Dunbar produced upon me. It was no wonder that even the masterful millionaire had found in her something more powerful than himself - something which could control and guide him. One felt, too, as one looked at the strong, clear-cut, and yet sensitive face, that even should she be capable of some impetuous deed, none the less there was an innate nobility of character which would make her influence always for the good. She was a brunette, tall, with a noble figure and commanding presence, but her dark eyes had in them the appealing, helpless expression of the hunted creature who feels the nets around it, but can see no way out from the toils. Now, as she realized the presence and the help of my famous friend, there came a touch of colour in her wan cheeks and a light of hope began to glimmer in the glance which she turned upon us.

"Perhaps Mr. Neil Gibson has told you something of what occurred between us?" she asked in a low, agitated voice.

"Yes," Holmes answered, "you need not pain yourself by entering into that part of the story. After seeing you, I am prepared to accept Mr. Gibson's statement both as to the influence which you had over him and as to the innocence of your relations with him. But why was the whole situation not brought out in court?"

"It seemed to me incredible that such a charge could be sustained. I thought that if we waited the whole thing must clear itself up without our being compelled to enter into painful details of the inner life of the family. But I understand that far from clearing it has become even more serious."

"My dear young lady," cried Holmes earnestly, "I beg you to have no illusions upon the point. Mr. Cummings here would assure you that all the cards are at present against us, and that we must do everything that is possible if we are to win clear. It would be a cruel deception to pretend that you are not in very great danger. Give me all the help you can, then, to get at the truth."

"I will conceal nothing."

"Tell us, then, of your true relations with Mr. Gibson's wife."

"She hated me, Mr. Holmes. She hated me with all the fervour of her tropical nature. She was a woman who would do nothing by halves, and the measure of her love for her husband was the measure also of her hatred for me. It is probable that she misunderstood our relations. I would not wish to wrong her, but she loved so vividly in a physical sense that she could hardly understand the mental, and even spiritual, tie which held her husband to me, or imagine that it was only my desire to influence his power to good ends which kept me under his roof. I can see now that I was wrong. Nothing could justify me in remaining where I was a cause of unhappiness, and yet it is certain that the unhappiness would have remained even if I had left the house."

"Now, Miss Dunbar," said Holmes, "I beg you to tell us exactly what occurred that evening."

"I can tell you the truth so far as I know it, Mr. Holmes, but I am in a position to prove nothing, and there are points - the most vital points - which I can neither explain nor can I imagine any explanation."

"If you will find the facts, perhaps others may find the explanation."

"With regard, then, to my presence at Thor Bridge that night, I received a note from Mrs. Gibson in the morning. It lay on the table of the schoolroom, and it may have been left there by her own hand. It implored me to see her there after dinner, said she had something important to say to me, and asked me to leave an answer on the sundial in the garden, as she desired no one to be in our confidence. I saw no reason for such secrecy, but I did as she asked, accepting the appointment. She asked me to destroy her note and I burned it in the schoolroom grate. She was very much afraid of her husband, who treated her with a harshness for which

I frequently reproached him, and I could only imagine that she acted in this way because she did not wish him to know of our interview."

"Yet she kept your reply very carefully?"

"Yes. I was surprised to hear that she had it in her hand when she died."

"Well, what happened then?"

"I went down as I had promised. When I reached the bridge she was waiting for me. Never did I realize till that moment how this poor creature hated me. She was like a mad woman - indeed, I think she was a mad woman, subtly mad with the deep power of deception which insane people may have. How else could she have met me with unconcern every day and yet had so raging a hatred of me in her heart? I will not say what she said. She poured her whole wild fury out in burning and horrible words. I did not even answer - I could not. It was dreadful to see her. I put my hands to my ears and rushed away. When I left her she was standing, still shrieking out her curses at me, in the mouth of the bridge."

"Where she was afterwards found?"

"Within a few yards from the spot."

"And yet, presuming that she met her death shortly after you left her, you heard no shot~"

"No, I heard nothing. But, indeed, Mr. Holmes, I was so agitated and horrified by this terrible outbreak that I rushed to get back to the peace of my own room, and I was incapable of noticing anything which happened."

"You say that you returned to your room. Did you leave it again before next morning?"

"Yes, when the alarm came that the poor creature had met her death I ran out with the others "

"Did you see Mr. Gibson?"

"Yes, he had just returned from the bridge when I saw him. He had sent for the doctor and the police."

"Did he seem to you much perturbed?"

"Mr. Gibson is a very strong, self-contained man. I do not think that he would ever show his emotions on the surface. But I, who knew him so well, could see that he was deeply concerned."

"Then we come to the all-important point. This pistol that was found in your room. Had you ever seen it before?"

"Never, I swear it."

"When was it found?"

"Next morning, when the police made their search."

"Among your clothes?"

"Yes, on the floor of my wardrobe under my dresses."

"You could not guess how long it had been there?"

"It had not been there the morning before."

"How do you know?"

"Because I tidied out the wardrobe."

"That is final. Then someone came into your room and placed the pistol there in order to inculpate you."

"It must have been so."

"And when?"

"It could only have been at meal-time, or else at the hours when I would be in the schoolroom with the children."

"As you were when you got the note?"

"Yes, from that time onward for the whole morning."

"Thank you, Miss Dunbar. Is there any other point which could help me in the investigation?"

"I can think of none."

"There was some sign of violence on the stonework of the bridge - a perfectly fresh chip just opposite the body. Could you suggest any possible explanation of that?"

"Surely it must be a mere coincidence."

"Curious, Miss Dunbar, very curious. Why should it appear at the very time of the tragedy, and why at the very place?"

"But what could have caused it? Only great violence could have such an effect."

Holmes did not answer. His pale, eager face had suddenly assumed that tense, far-away expression which I had learned to associate with the supreme manifestations of his genius. So evident was the crisis in his mind that none of us dared to speak, and we sat, barrister, prisoner, and myself, watching him in a concentrated and absorbed silence. Suddenly he sprang from his chair, vibrating with nervous energy and the pressing need for action.

"Come, Watson, come!" he cried.

"What is it, Mr. Holmes?"

"Never mind, my dear lady. You will hear from me, Mr. Cummings. With the help of the god of justice I will give you a case which will make England ring. You will get news by to-morrow, Miss Dunbar, and meanwhile take my assurance that the clouds are lifting and that I have every hope that the light of truth is breaking through."

It was not a long journey from Winchester to Thor Place, but it was long to me in my impatience, while for Holmes it was evident that it seemed endless; for, in his nervous restlessness he could not sit still, but paced the carriage or drummed with his long, sensitive fingers upon the cushions beside him. Suddenly, however, as we neared our destination he seated himself opposite to me - we had a first-class carriage to ourselves - and laying a hand upon each of my knees he looked into my eyes with the peculiarly mischievous gaze which was characteristic of his more imp-like moods.

"Watson," said he, "I have some recollection that you go armed upon these excursions of ours."

It was as well for him that I did so, for he took little care for his own safety when his mind was once absorbed by a problem so that more than once my revolver had been a good friend in need. I reminded him of the fact.

"Yes, yes, I am a little absent-minded in such matters. But have you your revolver on you?"

I produced it from my hip-pocket, a short, handy, but very serviceable little weapon. He undid the catch, shook out the cartridges, and examined it with care.

"It's heavy - remarkably heavy," said he.

"Yes, it is a solid bit of work."

He mused over it for a minute.

"Do you know, Watson," said he, "I believe your revolver is going to have a very intimate connection with the mystery which we are investigating."

"My dear Holmes, you are joking."

"No, Watson, I am very serious. There is a test before us. If the test comes off, all will be clear. And the test will depend upon the conduct of this little weapon. One cartridge out. Now we will replace the other five and put on the safety-catch. So! That increases the weight and makes it a better reproduction."

I had no glimmer of what was in his mind, nor did he enlighten me, but sat lost in thought until we pulled up in the little Hampshire station. We secured a ramshackle trap, and in a quarter of an hour were at the house of our confidential friend, the sergeant.

"A clue, Mr. Holmes? What is it?"

"It all depends upon the behaviour of Dr. Watson's revolver," said my friend. "Here it is. Now, officer, can you give me ten yards of string?"

The village shop provided a ball of stout twine.

"I think that this is all we will need," said Holmes. "Now, if you please, we will get off on what I hope is the last stage of our journey."

The sun was setting and turning the rolling Hampshire moor into a wonderful autumnal panorama. The sergeant, with many critical and incredulous glances, which showed his deep doubts of the sanity of my companion, lurched along beside us. As we approached the scene of the crime I could see that my friend under all his habitual coolness was in truth deeply agitated.

"Yes," he said in answer to my remark, "you have seen me miss my mark before, Watson. I have an instinct for such things, and yet it has sometimes played me false. It seemed a certainty when first it flashed across my mind in the cell at Winchester, but one drawback of an active mind is that one can always conceive alternative explanations which would make our scent a false one. And yet - and yet - Well, Watson, we can but try."

As he walked he had firmly tied one end of the string to the handle of the revolver. We had now reached the scene of the tragedy. With great care he marked out under the guidance of the policeman the exact spot where the body had been stretched. He then hunted among the heather and the ferns until he found a considerable stone. This he secured to the other end of his line of string, and he hung it over the parapet of the bridge so that it swung clear above the water. He then stood on the fatal spot, some distance from the edge of the bridge, with my revolver in his hand, the string being taut between the weapon and the heavy stone on the farther side.

"Now for it!" he cried.

At the words he raised the pistol to his head, and then let go his grip. In an instant it had been whisked away by the weight of the stone, had struck with a sharp crack against the parapet, and had vanished over the side into the water. It had hardly gone before Holmes was kneeling beside the stonework, and a joyous cry showed that he had found what he expected.

"Was there ever a more exact demonstration?" he cried. "See, Watson, your revolver has solved the problem!" As he spoke he pointed to a second chip of the exact size and shape of the first which had appeared on the under edge of the stone balustrade.

"We'll stay at the inn to-night," he continued as he rose and faced the astonished sergeant. "You will, of course, get a grappling-hook and you will easily restore my friend's revolver. You will also find beside it the revolver, string and weight with which this vindictive woman attempted to disguise her own crime and to fasten a charge of murder upon an innocent victim. You can let Mr. Gibson know that I will see him in the morning, when steps can be taken for Miss Dunbar's vindication."

Late that evening, as we sat together smoking our pipes in the village inn, Holmes gave me a brief review of what had passed.

"I fear, Watson," said he, "that you will not improve any reputation which I may have acquired by adding the case of the Thor Bridge mystery to your annals. I have been sluggish in mind and wanting in that mixture of imagination and reality which is the basis of my art. I confess that the chip in the stonework was a sufficient clue to suggest the true solution, and that I blame myself for not having attained it sooner.

"It must be admitted that the workings of this unhappy woman's mind were deep and subtle, so that it was no very simple matter to unravel her plot. I do not think that in our adventures we have ever come across a stranger example of what perverted love can bring about. Whether Miss Dunbar was her rival in a physical or in a merely mental sense seems to have been equally unforgivable in her eyes. No doubt she blamed this innocent lady for all those harsh dealings and unkind words with which her husband tried to repel her too demonstrative affection. Her first resolution was to end her own life. Her second was to do it in such a way as to involve her victim in a fate which was worse far than any sudden death could be.

"We can follow the various steps quite clearly, and they show a remarkable subtlety of mind. A note was extracted very cleverly from Miss Dunbar which would make it appear that she had chosen the scene of the crime. In her anxiety that it should be discovered she somewhat overdid it by holding it in her hand to the last. This alone should have excited my suspicions earlier than it did.

"Then she took one of her husband's revolvers - there was, as you saw, an arsenal in the house - and kept it for her own use. A similar one she concealed that morning in Miss Dunbar's wardrobe after discharging one barrel, which she could easily do in the woods without attracting attention. She then went down to the bridge where she had contrived this exceedingly ingenious method for getting rid of her weapon. When Miss Dunbar appeared she used her last breath in pouring out her hatred, and then, when she was out of hearing, carried out her terrible purpose. Every link is now in its place and the chain is complete. The papers may ask why the mere was not dragged in the first instance, but it is easy to be wise after the event, and in any case the expanse of a reed-filled lake is no easy matter to drag unless you have a clear perception of what you are looking for and where. Well, Watson, we have helped a remarkable woman, and also a formidable man. Should they in the future join their forces, as seems not unlikely, the financial world may find that Mr. Neil Gibson has learned something in that schoolroom of sorrow where our earthly lessons are taught."

THE ADVENTURE OF THE CREEPING MAN

Mr. Sherlock Holmes was always of opinion that I should publish the singular facts connected with Professor Presbury, if only to dispel once for all the ugly rumours which some twenty years ago agitated the university and were echoed in the learned societies of London. There were, however, certain obstacles in the way, and the true history of this curious case remained entombed in the tin box which contains so many records of my friend's adventures. Now we have at last obtained permission to ventilate the facts which formed one of the very last cases handled by Holmes before his retirement from practice. Even now a certain reticence and discretion have to be observed in laying the matter before the public.

It was one Sunday evening early in September of the year 1903 that I received one of Holmes's laconic messages:

Come at once if convenient - if inconvenient come all the same.

S.H.

The relations between us in those latter days were peculiar. He was a man of habits, narrow and concentrated habits, and I had become one of them. As an institution I was like the violin, the shag tobacco, the old black pipe, the index books, and others perhaps less excusable. When it was a case of active work and a comrade was needed upon whose nerve he could place some reliance, my role was obvious. But apart from this I had uses. I was a whetstone for his mind. I stimulated him. He liked to think aloud in my presence. His remarks could hardly be said to be made to me - many of them would have been as appropriately addressed to his bedstead - but none the less, having formed the habit, it had become in some way helpful that I should register and interject. If I irritated him by a certain methodical slowness in my mentality, that irritation served only to make his own flame-like intuitions and impressions flash up the more vividly and swiftly. Such was my humble role in our alliance.

When I arrived at Baker Street I found him huddled up in his armchair with updrawn knees, his pipe in his mouth and his brow furrowed with thought. It was clear that he was in the throes of some vexatious problem. With a wave of his hand he indicated my old armchair, but otherwise for half an hour he gave no sign that he was aware of my presence. Then with a start he seemed to come from his reverie, and with his usual whimsical smile he greeted me back to what had once been my home.

"You will excuse a certain abstraction of mind, my dear Watson," said he. "Some curious facts have been submitted to me within the last twenty-four hours, and they in turn have given rise to some speculations of a more general character. I have serious thoughts of writing a small monograph upon the uses of dogs in the work of the detective."

"But surely, Holmes, this has been explored," said I. "Bloodhounds - sleuth-hounds -"

"No, no, Watson, that side of the matter is, of course, obvious. But there is another which is far more subtle. You may recollect that in the case which you, in your sensational way, coupled with the Copper Beeches, I was able, by watching the mind of the child, to form a deduction as to the criminal habits of the very smug and respectable father."

"Yes, I remember it well."

"My line of thoughts about dogs is analogous. A dog reflects the family life. Whoever saw a frisky dog in a gloomy family, or a sad dog in a happy one? Snarling people have snarling dogs, dangerous people have dangerous ones. And their passing moods may reflect the passing moods of others."

I shook my head. "Surely, Holmes, this is a little far-fetched," said I.

He had refilled his pipe and resumed his seat, taking no notice of my comment.

"The practical application of what I have said is very close to the problem which I am investigating. It is a tangled skein, you understand. and I am looking for a loose end. One possible loose end lies in the question: Why does Professor Presbury's wolfhound, Roy, endeavour to bite him?"

I sank back in my chair in some disappointment. Was it for so trivial a question as this that I had been summoned from my work? Holmes glanced across at me.

"The same old Watson!" said he. "You never learn that the gravest issues may depend upon the smallest things. But is it not on the face of it strange that a staid, elderly philosopher - you've heard of Presbury, of course, the famous Camford physiologist? -that such a man, whose friend has been his devoted wolfhound, should now have been twice attacked by his own dog? What do you make of it?"

"The dog is ill."

"Well, that has to be considered. But he attacks no one else, nor does he apparently molest his master, save on very special occasions. Curious, Watson - very curious. But young Mr. Bennett is before his time if that is his ring. I had hoped to have a longer chat with you before he came."

There was a quick step on the stairs, a sharp tap at the door and a moment later the new client presented himself. He was a tall, handsome youth about thirty, well dressed and elegant, but with something in his bearing which suggested the shyness of the student rather than the self-possession of the man of the world. He shook hands with Holmes, and then looked with some surprise at me.

"This matter is very delicate, Mr. Holmes," he said. "Consider the relation in which I stand to Professor Presbury both privately and publicly. I really can hardly justify myself if I speak before any third person."

"Have no fear, Mr. Bennett. Dr. Watson is the very soul of discretion, and I can assure you that this is a matter in which I am very likely to need an assistant."

"As you like, Mr. Holmes. You will, I am sure, understand my having some reserves in the matter."

"You will appreciate it, Watson, when I tell you that this gentleman, Mr. Trevor Bennett, is professional assistant to the great scientist, lives under his roof, and is engaged to his only daughter. Certainly we must agree that the professor has every claim upon his loyalty and devotion. But it may best be shown by taking the necessary steps to clear up this strange mystery."

"I hope so, Mr. Holmes. That is my one object. Does Dr. Watson know the situation?"

"I have not had time to explain it."

"Then perhaps I had better go over the ground again before explaining some fresh developments."

"I will do so myself," said Holmes, "in order to show that I have the events in their due order. The professor, Watson, is a man of European reputation. His life has been academic. There has never been a breath of scandal. He is a widower with one daughter, Edith. He is, I gather, a man of very virile and positive, one might almost say combative, character. So the matter stood until a very few months ago.

"Then the current of his life was broken. He is sixty-one years of age, but he became engaged to the daughter of Professor Morphy, his colleague in the chair of comparative anatomy. It was not, as I understand, the reasoned courting of an elderly man but rather the passionate frenzy of youth, for no one could have shown himself a more devoted lover. The lady, Alice Morphy, was a very perfect girl both in mind and body, so that there was every excuse for the professor's infatuation. None the less, it did not meet with full approval in his own family."

"We thought it rather excessive," said our visitor.

"Exactly. Excessive and a little violent and unnatural. Professor Presbury was rich, however, and there was no objection upon the part of the father. The daughter, however, had other views, and there were already several candidates for her hand, who, if they were less eligible from a worldly point of view, were at least more of an age. The girl seemed to like the professor in spite of his eccentricities. It was only age which stood in the way.

"About this time a little mystery suddenly clouded the normal routine of the professor's life. He did what he had never done before. He left home and gave no indication where he was going. He was away a fortnight and returned looking rather travel-worn. He made no allusion to where he had been, although he was usually the frankest of men. It chanced, however, that our client here, Mr. Bennett, received a letter from a fellow student in Prague, who said that he was glad to have seen Professor Presbury there, although he had not been able to talk to him. Only in this way did his own household learn where he had been.

"Now comes the point. From that time onward a curious change came over the professor. He became furtive and sly. Those around him had always the feeling that he was not the man that they had known, but that he was under some shadow which had darkened his higher qualities. His intellect was not affected. His lectures were as brilliant as ever. But always there was something new, something sinister and unexpected. His daughter, who was devoted to him, tried again and again to resume the old relations and to penetrate this mask which her father seemed to have put on. You, sir, as I understand, did the same - but all was in vain. And now, Mr. Bennett, tell in your own words the incident of the letters."

"You must understand, Dr. Watson, that the professor had no secrets from me. If I were his son or his younger brother I could not have more completely enjoyed his confidence. As his secretary I handled every paper which came to him, and I opened and subdivided his letters. Shortly after his return all this was changed. He told me that certain letters might come to him from London which would be marked by a cross under the stamp. These were to be set aside for his own eyes only. I may say that several of these did pass through my hands, that they had the E.C. mark, and were in an illiterate handwriting. If he answered them at all the answers did not pass through my hands nor into the letterbasket in which our correspondence was collected."

"And the box," said Holmes.

"Ah, yes, the box. The professor brought back a little wooden box from his travels. It was the one thing which suggested a Continental tour, for it was one of those quaint carved things which one associates with Germany. This he placed in his instrument cupboard. One day, in looking for a canola, I took up the box. To my surprise he was very angry, and reproved me in words which were quite savage for my curiosity. It was the first time such a thing had happened, and I was deeply hurt. I endeavoured to explain that it was a mere accident that I had touched the box, but all the evening I was conscious that he looked at me harshly and that the incident was rankling in his mind." Mr. Bennett drew a little diary book from his pocket. "That was on July 2nd," said he.

"You are certainly an admirable witness," said Holmes. "I may need some of these dates which you have noted."

"I learned method among other things from my great teacher. From the time that I observed abnormality in his behaviour I felt that it was my duty to study his case. Thus I have it here that it was on that very day, July 2nd, that Roy attacked the professor as he came from his study into the hall. Again, on July 11th, there was a scene of the same sort, and then I have a note of yet another upon July 20th. After that we had to banish Roy to the stables. He was a dear, affectionate animal - but I fear I weary you."

Mr. Bennett spoke in a tone of reproach, for it was very clear that Holmes was not listening. His face was rigid and his eyes gazed abstractedly at the ceiling. With an effort he recovered himself.

"Singular! Most singular!" he murmured. "These details were new to me, Mr. Bennett. I think we have now fairly gone over the old ground, have we not? But you spoke of some fresh developments."

The pleasant, open face of our visitor clouded over, shadowed by some grim remembrance. "What I speak of occurred the night before last," said he. "I was lying awake about two in the morning, when I was aware of a dull muffled sound coming from the passage. I opened my door and peeped out. I should explain that the professor sleeps at the end of the passage -"

"The date being?" asked Holmes.

Our visitor was clearly annoyed at so irrelevant an interruption.

"I have said, sir, that it was the night before last - that is, September 4th."

Holmes nodded and smiled.

"Pray continue," said he.

"He sleeps at the end of the passage and would have to pass my door in order to reach the staircase. It was a really terrifying experience, Mr. Holmes. I think that I am as strong-nerved as my neighbours, but I was shaken by what I saw. The passage was dark save that one window halfway along it threw a patch of light. I could see that something was coming along the passage, something dark and crouching. Then suddenly it emerged into the light, and I saw that it was he. He was crawling, Mr. Holmes - crawling! He was not quite on his hands and knees. I should rather say on his hands and feet, with his face sunk between his hands. Yet he seemed to move with ease. I was so paralyzed by the sight that it was not until he had reached my door that I was able to step forward and ask if I could assist him. His answer was extraordinary. He sprang up, spat out some atrocious word at me, and hurried on past me, and down the staircase. I waited about for an hour, but he did not come back. It must have been daylight before he regained his room."

"Well, Watson, what make you of that?" asked Holmes with the air of the pathologist who presents a rare specimen.

"Lumbago, possibly. I have known a severe attack make a man walk in just such a way, and nothing would be more trying to the temper."

"Good, Watson! You always keep us flat-footed on the ground. But we can hardly accept lumbago, since he was able to stand erect in a moment."

"He was never better in health," said Bennett. "In fact, he is stronger than I have known him for years. But there are the facts, Mr. Holmes. It is not a case in which we can consult the police, and yet we are utterly at our wit's end as to what to do, and we feel in some strange way that we are drifting towards disaster. Edith - Miss Presbury - feels as I do, that we cannot wait passively any longer."

"It is certainly a very curious and suggestive case. What do you think, Watson?"

"Speaking as a medical man," said I, "it appears to be a case for an alienist. The old gentleman's cerebral processes were disturbed by the love affair. He made a journey abroad in the hope of breaking himself of the passion. His letters and the box may be connected with some other private transaction - a loan, perhaps, or share certificates, which are in the box."

"And the wolfhound no doubt disapproved of the financial bargain. No, no, Watson, there is more in it than this. Now, I can only suggest -"

What Sherlock Holmes was about to suggest will never be known, for at this moment the door opened and a young lady was shown into the room. As she appeared Mr. Bennett sprang up with a cry and ran forward with his hands out to meet those which she had herself outstretched.

"Edith, dear! Nothing the matter, I hope?"

"I felt I must follow you. Oh, Jack, I have been so dreadfully frightened! It is awful to be there alone."

"Mr. Holmes, this is the young lady I spoke of. This is my fiancee."

"We were gradually coming to that conclusion, were we not, Watson?" Holmes answered with a smile. "I take it, Miss Presbury, that there is some fresh development in the case, and that you thought we should know?"

Our new visitor, a bright, handsome girl of a conventional English type, smiled back at Holmes as she seated herself beside Mr. Bennett.

"When I found Mr. Bennett had left his hotel I thought I should probably find him here. Of course, he had told me that he would consult you. But, oh, Mr. Holmes, can you do nothing for my poor father?"

"I have hopes, Miss Presbury, but the case is still obscure. Perhaps what you have to say may throw some fresh light upon it."

"It was last night, Mr. Holmes. He had been very strange all day. I am sure that there are times when he has no recollection of what he does. He lives as in a strange dream. Yesterday was such a day. It was not my father with whom I lived. His outward shell was there, but it was not really he."

"'Tell me what happened."

"I was awakened in the night by the dog barking most furiously. Poor Roy, he is chained now near the stable. I may say that I always sleep with my door locked; for, as Jack - as Mr. Bennett - will tell you, we all have a feeling of impending danger. My room is on the second floor. It happened that the blind was up in my window, and there was bright moonlight outside. As I lay with my eyes fixed upon the square of light, listening to the frenzied barkings of the dog, I was amazed to see my father's face looking in at me. Mr. Holmes, I nearly died of surprise and horror. There it was pressed against the windowpane, and one hand seemed to be raised as if to push up the window. If that window had opened, I think I should have gone mad. It was no delusion, Mr. Holmes. Don't deceive yourself by thinking so. I dare say it was twenty seconds or so that I lay paralyzed and watched the face. Then it vanished, but I could not - I could not spring out of bed and look out after it. I lay cold and shivering till morning. At breakfast he was sharp and fierce in manner, and made no allusion to the adventure of the night. Neither did I, but I gave an excuse for coming to town -and here I am."

Holmes looked thoroughly surprised at Miss Presbury's narrative.

"My dear young lady, you say that your room is on the second floor. Is there a long ladder in the garden?"

"No, Mr. Holmes, that is the amazing part of it. There is no possible way of reaching the window - and yet he was there."

"The date being September 5th," said Holmes. "That certainly complicates matters."

It was the young lady's turn to look surprised. "This is the second time that you have alluded to the date, Mr. Holmes," said Bennett. "Is it possible that it has any bearing upon the case?"

"It is possible - very possible - and yet I have not my full material at present."

"Possibly you are thinking of the connection between insanity and phases of the moon?"

"No, I assure you. It was quite a different line of thought. Possibly you can leave your notebook with me, and I will check the dates. Now I think, Watson, that our line of action is perfectly clear. This young lady has informed us - and I have the greatest confidence in her intuition - that her father remembers little or nothing which occurs upon certain dates. We will therefore call upon him as if he had given us an appointment upon such a date. He will put it down to his own lack of memory. Thus we will open our campaign by having a good close view of him."

"That is excellent," said Mr. Bennett. "I warn you, however, that the professor is irascible and violent at times."

Holmes smiled. "There are reasons why we should come at once - very cogent reasons if my theories hold good. To-morrow, Mr. Bennett, will certainly see us in Camford. There is, if I remember right, an inn called the Chequers where the port used to be above mediocrity and the linen was above reproach. I think, Watson, that our lot for the next few days might lie in less pleasant places."

Monday morning found us on our way to the famous university town - an easy effort on the part of Holmes, who had no roots to pull up, but one which involved frantic planning and hurrying on my part, as my practice was by this time not inconsiderable. Holmes made no allusion to the case until after we had deposited our suitcases at the ancient hostel of which he had spoken.

"I think, Watson, that we can catch the professor just before lunch. He lectures at eleven and should have an interval at home."

"What possible excuse have we for calling?"

Holmes glanced at his notebook.

"There was a period of excitement upon August 26th. We will assume that he is a little hazy as to what he does at such times. If we insist that we are there by appointment I think he will hardly venture to contradict us. Have you the effrontery necessary to put it through?"

"We can but try."

"Excellent, Watson! Compound of the Busy Bee and Excelsior. We can but try - the motto of the firm. A friendly native will surely guide us."

Such a one on the back of a smart hansom swept us past a row of ancient colleges and, finally turning into a tree-lined drive, pulled up at the door of a charming house, girt round with lawns and covered with purple wisteria. Professor Presbury was certainly surrounded with every sign not only of comfort but of luxury. Even as we pulled up, a grizzled head appeared at the front window, and we were aware of a pair of keen eyes from under shaggy brows which surveyed us through large horn glasses. A moment later we were actually in his sanctum, and the mysterious scientist, whose vagaries had brought us from London, was standing before us. There was certainly no sign of eccentricity either in his manner or appearance, for he was a portly, large featured man, grave, tall, and frock-coated, with the dignity of bearing which a lecturer needs. His eyes were his most remarkable feature, keen, observant, and clever to the verge of cunning.

He looked at our cards. "Pray sit down, gentlemen. What can I do for you?"

Mr. Holmes smiled amiably.

"It was the question which I was about to put to you, Professor."

"To me, sir!"

"Possibly there is some mistake. I heard through a second person that Professor Presbury of Camford had need of my services."

"Oh, indeed!" It seemed to me that there was a malicious sparkle in the intense gray eyes. "You heard that, did you? May I ask the name of your informant?"

"I am sorry, Professor, but the matter was rather confidential. If I have made a mistake there is no harm done. I can only express my regret."

"Not at all. I should wish to go fun her into this matter. It interests me. Have you any scrap of writing, any letter or telegram, to bear out your assertion?"

"No, I have not."

"I presume that you do not go so far as to assert that I summoned you?"

"I would rather answer no questions," said Holmes.

"No, I dare say not," said the professor with asperity. "However, that particular one can be answered very easily without your aid."

He walked across the room to the bell. Our London friend Mr. Bennett, answered the call.

"Come in, Mr. Bennett. These two gentlemen have come from London under the impression that they have been summoned. You handle all my correspondence. Have you a note of anything going to a person named Holmes?"

"No, sir," Bennett answered with a flush.

"That is conclusive," said the professor, glaring angrily at my companion. "Now, sir" - he leaned forward with his two hands upon the table - "it seems to me that your position is a very questionable one."

Holmes shrugged his shoulders.

"I can only repeat that I am sorry that we have made a needless intrusion."

"Hardly enough, Mr. Holmes!" the old man cried in a high screaming voice, with extraordinary malignancy upon his face. He got between us and the door as he spoke, and he shook his two hands at us with furious passion. "You can hardly get out of it so easily as that." His face was convulsed, and he grinned and gibbered at us in his senseless rage. I am convinced that we should have had to fight our way out of the room if Mr. Bennett had not intervened.

"My dear Professor," he cried, "consider your position! Consider the scandal at the university! Mr. Holmes is a well known man. You cannot possibly treat him with such discourtesy."

Sulkily our host - if I may call him so - cleared the path to the door. We were glad to find ourselves outside the house and in the quiet of the tree-lined drive. Holmes seemed greatly amused by the episode.

"Our learned friend's nerves are somewhat out of order," said he. "Perhaps our intrusion was a little crude, and yet we have gained that personal contact which I desired. But, dear me, Watson, he is surely at our heels. The villain still pursues us."

There were the sounds of running feet behind, but it was, to my relief, not the formidable professor but his assistant who appeared round the curve of the drive. He came panting up to us.

"I am so sorry, Mr. Holmes. I wished to apologize."

"My dear sir, there is no need. It is all in the way of professional experience."

"I have never seen him in a more dangerous mood. But he grows more sinister. You can understand now why his daughter and I are alarmed. And yet his mind is perfectly clear."

"Too clear!" said Holmes. "That was my miscalculation. It is evident that his memory is much more reliable than I had thought. By the way, can we, before we go, see the window of Miss Presbury's room?"

Mr. Bennett pushed his way through some shrubs, and we had a view of the side of the house.

"It is there. The second on the left."

"Dear me, it seems hardly accessible. And yet you will observe that there is a creeper below and a water-pipe above which give some foothold."

"I could not climb it myself," said Mr. Bennett.

"Very likely. It would certainly be a dangerous exploit for any normal man."

"There was one other thing I wish to tell you, Mr. Holmes. I have the address of the man in London to whom the professor writes. He seems to have written this morning, and I got it from his blotting-paper. It is an ignoble position for a trusted secretary, but what else can I do?"

Holmes glanced at the paper and put it into his pocket.

"Dorak - a curious name. Slavonic, I imagine. Well, it is an important link in the chain. We return to London this afternoon, Mr. Bennett. I see no good purpose to be served by our remaining. We cannot arrest the professor because he has done no crime, nor can we place him under constraint, for he cannot be proved to be mad. No action is as yet possible."

"Then what on earth are we to do?"

"A little patience, Mr. Bennett. Things will soon develop. Unless I am mistaken, next Tuesday may mark a crisis. Certainly we shall be in Camford on that day. Meanwhile, the general position is undeniably unpleasant, and if Miss Presbury can prolong her visit."

"That is easy."

"Then let her stay till we can assure her that all danger is past. Meanwhile, let him have his way and do not cross him. So long as he is in a good humour all is well."

"There he is!" said Bennett in a startled whisper. Looking between the branches we saw the tall, erect figure emerge from the hall door and look around him. He stood leaning forward, his hands swinging straight before him, his head turning from side to side. The secretary with a last wave slipped off among the trees, and we saw him presently rejoin his employer, the two entering the house together in what seemed to be animated and even excited conversation.

"I expect the old gentleman has been putting two and two together," said Holmes as we walked hotel ward. "He struck me as having a particularly clear and logical brain from the little I saw of him. Explosive, no doubt, but then from his point of view he has something to explode about if detectives are put on his track and he suspects his own household of doing it. I rather fancy that friend Bennett is in for an uncomfortable time."

Holmes stopped at a post-office and sent off a telegram on our way. The answer reached us in the evening, and he tossed it across to me.

Have visited the Commercial Road and seen Dorak. Suave person, Bohemian, elderly. Keeps large general store.

MERCER

"Mercer is since your time," said Holmes. "He is my general utility man who looks up routine business. It was important to know something of the man with whom our professor was so secretly corresponding. His nationality connects up with the Prague visit."

"Thank goodness that something connects with something," said I. "At present we seem to be faced by a long series of inexplicable incidents with no bearing upon each other. "For example, what possible connection can there be between an angry wolfhound and a visit to Bohemia, or either of them with a man crawling down a passage at night? As to your dates, that is the biggest mystification of all."

Holmes smiled and rubbed his hands. We were, I may say, seated in the old sitting-room of the ancient hotel, with a bottle of the famous vintage of which Holmes had spoken on the table between us.

"Well, now, let us take the dates first," said he, his fingertips together and his manner as if he were addressing a class. "This excellent young man's diary shows that there was trouble upon July 2nd, and from then onward it seems to have been at nine-day intervals, with, so far as I remember, only one exception. Thus the last outbreak upon Friday was on September 3d, which also falls into the series, as did August 26th, which preceded it. The thing is beyond coincidence."

I was forced to agree.

"Let us, then, form the provisional theory that every nine days the professor takes some strong drug which has a passing but highly poisonous effect. His naturally violent nature is intensified by it. He learned to take this drug while he was in Prague, and is now supplied with it by a Bohemian intermediary in London. This all hangs together, Watson!"

"But the dog, the face at the window, the creeping man in the passage?"

"Well, well, we have made a beginning. I should not expect any fresh developments until next Tuesday. In the meantime we can only keep in touch with friend Bennett and enjoy the amenities of this charming town."

In the morning Mr. Bennett slipped round to bring us the latest report. As Holmes had imagined, times had not been easy with him. Without exactly accusing him of being responsible for our presence, the professor had been very rough and rude in his speech, and evidently felt some strong grievance. This morning he was quite himself again, however, and had delivered his usual brilliant lecture to a crowded class. "Apart from his queer fits," said Bennett, "he has actually more energy and vitality than I can ever remember, nor was his brain ever clearer. But it's not he - it's never the man whom we have known."

"I don't think you have anything to fear now for a week at least," Holmes answered. "I am a busy man, and Dr. Watson has his patients to attend to. Let us agree that we meet here at this hour next Tuesday, and I shall be surprised if before we leave you again we are not able to explain, even if we cannot perhaps put an end to, your troubles. Meanwhile, keep us posted in what occurs."

I saw nothing of my friend for the next few days, but on the following Monday evening I had a short note asking me to meet him next day at the train. From what he told me as we travelled up to Camford all was well, the peace of the professor's house had been unruffled, and his own conduct perfectly normal. This also was the report which was given us by Mr. Bennett himself when he called upon us that evening at our old quarters in the Chequers. "He heard from his London correspondent to-day. There was a letter and there was a small packet, each with the cross under the stamp which warned me not to touch them. There has been nothing else."

"That may prove quite enough," said Holmes grimly. "Now, Mr. Bennett, we shall, I think, come to some conclusion tonight. If my deductions are correct we should have an opportunity of bringing matters to a head. In order to do so it is necessary to hold the professor under observation. I would suggest, therefore, that you remain awake and on the lookout. Should you hear him pass your door, do not interrupt him, but follow him as discreetly as you can. Dr. Watson and I will not be far off. By the way, where is the key of that little box of which you spoke?"

"Upon his watch-chain."

"I fancy our researches must lie in that direction. At the worst the lock should not be very formidable. Have you any other able-bodied man on the premises?"

"There is the coachman, Macphail."

"Where does he sleep?"

"Over the stables."

"We might possibly want him. Well, we can do no more until we see how things develop, Good-bye - but I expect that we shall see you before morning."

It was nearly midnight before we took our station among some bushes immediately opposite the hall door of the professor. It was a fine night, but chilly, and we were glad of our warm overcoats. There was a breeze, and clouds were scudding across the sky, obscuring from time to time the half-moon. It would have been a dismal vigil were it not for the expectation and excitement which carried us along, and the assurance of my comrade that we had probably reached the end of the strange sequence of events which had engaged our attention.

"If the cycle of nine days holds good then we shall have the professor at his worst to-night," said Holmes. "The fact that these strange symptoms began after his visit to Prague, that he is in secret correspondence with a Bohemian dealer in London, who presumably represents someone in Prague, and that he received a packet from him this very day, all point in one direction. What he takes and why he takes it are still beyond our ken, but that it emanates in some way from Prague is clear enough. He takes it under definite directions which regulate this ninth-day system, which was the first point which attracted my attention. But his symptoms are most remarkable. Did you observe his knuckles?"

I had to confess that I did not.

"Thick and horny in a way which is quite new in my experience. Always look at the hands first, Watson. Then cuffs, trouser knees, and boots. Very curious knuckles which can only be explained by the mode of progression observed by -" Holmes paused and suddenly clapped his hand to his forehead. "Oh, Watson, Watson, what a fool I have been! It seems incredible, and yet it must be true. All points in one direction. How could I miss seeing the connection of ideas? Those knuckles how could I have passed those knuckles? And the dog! And the ivy! It's surely time that I disappeared into that little farm of my dreams. Look out, Watson! Here he is! We shall have the chance of seeing for ourselves."

The hall door had slowly opened, and against the lamp lit background we saw the tall figure of Professor Presbury. He was clad in his dressing gown. As he stood outlined in the doorway he was erect but leaning forward with dangling arms, as when we saw him last.

Now he stepped forward into the drive, and an extraordinary change came over him. He sank down into a crouching position and moved along upon his hands and feet, skipping every now and then as if he were overflowing with energy and vitality. He moved along the face of the house and then round the corner. As he disappeared Bennett slipped through the hall door and softly followed him.

"Come, Watson, come!" cried Holmes, and we stole as softly as we could through the bushes until we had gained a spot whence we could see the other side of the house, which was bathed in the light of the half-moon. The professor was clearly visible crouching at the foot of the ivy-covered wall. As we watched him he suddenly began with incredible agility to ascend it. From branch to branch he sprang, sure of foot and firm of grasp, climbing apparently in mere joy at his own powers, with no definite object in view. With his dressing-gown flapping on each side of him, he looked like some huge bat glued against the side of his own house, a great square dark patch upon the moonlit wall. Presently he tired of this amusement, and, dropping from branch to branch, he squatted down into the old attitude and moved towards the stables, creeping along in the same strange way as before. The wolfhound was out now, barking furiously, and more excited than ever when it actually caught sight of its master. It was straining on its chain and quivering with eagerness and rage. The professor squatted down very deliberately just out of reach of the hound and began to provoke it in every possible way. He took handfuls of pebbles from the drive and threw them in the dog's face, prodded him with a stick which he had picked up, flicked his hands about only a few inches from the gaping mouth, and endeavoured in every way to increase the animal's fury, which was already beyond all control. In all our adventures I do not know that I have ever seen a more strange sight than this impassive and still dignified figure crouching frog-like upon the ground and goading to a wilder exhibition of passion the maddened hound, which ramped and raged in front of him, by all manner of ingenious and calculated cruelty.

And then in a moment it happened! It was not the chain that broke, but it was the collar that slipped, for it had been made for a thick-necked Newfoundland. We heard the rattle of falling metal, and the next instant dog and man were rolling on the ground together, the one roaring in rage, the other screaming in a strange shrill falsetto of terror. It was a very narrow thing for the professor's life. The savage creature had him fairly by the throat, its fangs had bitten deep, and he was senseless before we could reach them and drag the two apart. It might have been a dangerous task for us, but Bennett's voice and presence brought the great wolfhound instantly to reason. The uproar had brought the sleepy and astonished coachman from his room above the stables. "I'm not surprised," said he, shaking his head. "I've seen him at it before. I knew the dog would get him sooner or later."

The hound was secured, and together we carried the professor up to his room, where Bennett, who had a medical degree, helped me to dress his torn throat. The sharp teeth had passed dangerously near the carotid artery, and the haemorrhage was serious. In half an hour the danger was past, I had given the patient an injection of morphia, and he had sunk into deep sleep. Then, and only then, were we able to look at each other and to take stock of the situation.

"I think a first-class surgeon should see him," said I.

"For God's sake, no!" cried Bennett. "At present the scandal is confined to our own household. It is safe with us. If it gets beyond these walls it will never stop. Consider his position at the university, his European reputation, the feelings of his daughter."

"Quite so," said Holmes. "I think it may be quite possible to keep the matter to ourselves, and also to prevent its recurrence now that we have a free hand. The key from the watch-chain, Mr. Bennett. Macphail will guard the patient and let us know if there is any change. Let us see what we can find in the professor's mysterious box."

There was not much, but there was enough - an empty phial, another nearly full, a hypodermic syringe, several letters in a crabbed, foreign hand. The marks on the envelopes showed that they were those which had disturbed the routine of the secretary, and each was dated from the Commercial Road and signed "A. Dorak." They were mere invoices to say that a fresh bottle was being sent to Professor Presbury, or receipt to acknowledge money. There was one other envelope, however, in a more educated hand and bearing the Austrian stamp with the postmark of Prague. "Here we have our material!" cried Holmes as he tore out the enclosure.

HONOURED COLLEAGUE [it ran]:

Since your esteemed visit I have thought much of your case, and though in your circumstances there are some special reasons for the treatment, I would none the less enjoin caution, as my results have shown that it is not without danger of a kind. It is possible that the serum of anthropoid would have been better. I have, as I explained to you, used black-faced langur because a specimen was accessible. Langur is, of course, a crawler and climber, while anthropoid walks erect and is in all ways nearer. I beg you to take every possible precaution that there be no premature revelation of the process. I have one other client in England, and Dorak is my agent for both. Weekly reports will oblige.

Yours with high esteem,

H. LOWENSTEIN

Lowenstein! The name brought back to me the memory of some snippet from a newspaper which spoke of an obscure scientist who was striving in some unknown way for the secret of rejuvenescence and the elixir of life. Lowenstein of Prague! Lowenstein with the wondrous strength-giving serum, tabooed by the profession because he refused to reveal its source. In a few words I said what I remembered. Bennett had taken a manual of zoology from the shelves." 'Langur.' "he read." "the great black-faced monkey of the Himalayan slopes, biggest and most human of climbing monkeys. Many details are added. Well, thanks to you, Mr. Holmes, it is very clear that we have traced the evil to its source."

"The real source," said Holmes, "lies, of course, in that untimely love affair which gave our impetuous professor the idea that he could only gain his wish by turning himself into a younger man. When one tries to rise above Nature one is liable to fall below it. The highest type of man may revert to the animal if he leaves the straight road of destiny." He sat musing for a little with the phial in his hand, looking at the clear liquid within. "When I have written to this man and told him that I hold him criminally responsible for the poisons which he circulates, we will have no more trouble. But it may recur. Others may find a better way. There is danger there - a very real danger to humanity. Consider, Watson, that the material, the sensual, the worldly would all prolong their worthless lives. The spiritual would not avoid the call to something higher. It would be the survival of the least fit. What sort of cesspool may not our poor world become?" Suddenly the dreamer disappeared, and Holmes, the man of action, sprang from his chair. "I think there is nothing more to be said, Mr. Bennett. The various incidents will now fit themselves easily into the general scheme. The dog, of course, was aware of the change far more quickly than you. His smell would insure that. It was the monkey, not the professor, whom Roy attacked, just as it was the monkey who teased Roy. Climbing was a joy to the creature, and it was a mere chance, I take it, that the pastime brought him to the young lady's window. There is an early train to town, Watson, but I think we shall just have time for a cup of tea at the Chequers before we catch it."

THE ADVENTURE OF THE LION'S MANE

It is a most singular thing that a problem which was certainly as abstruse and unusual as any which I have faced in my long professional career should have come to me after my retirement, and be brought, as it were, to my very door. It occurred after my withdrawal to my little Sussex home, when I had given myself up entirely to that soothing life of Nature for which I had so often yearned during the long years spent amid the gloom of London. At this period of my life the good Watson had passed almost beyond my ken. An occasional week-end visit was the most that I ever saw of him. Thus I must act as my own chronicler. Ah! had he but been with me, how much he might have made of so wonderful a happening and of my eventual triumph against every difficulty! As it is, however, I must needs tell my tale in my own plain way, showing by my words each step upon the difficult road which lay before me as I searched for the mystery of the Lion's Mane.

My villa is situated upon the southern slope of the downs, commanding a great view of the Channel. At this point the coast-line is entirely of chalk cliffs, which can only be descended by a single, long, tortuous path, which is steep and slippery. At the bottom of the path lie a hundred yards of pebbles and shingle, even when the tide is at full. Here and there, however, there are curves and hollows which make splendid swimming pools filled afresh with each flow. This admirable beach extends for some miles in each direction, save only at one point where the little cove and village of Fulworth break the line.

My house is lonely. I, my old housekeeper, and my bees have the estate all to ourselves. Half a mile off, however, is Harold Stackhurst's well-known coaching establishment, The Gables, quite a large place, which contains some score of young fellows preparing for various professions, with a staff of several masters. Stackhurst himself was a well-known rowing Blue in his day, and an excellent all-round scholar. He and I were always friendly from the day I came to the coast, and he was the one man who was on such terms with me that we could drop in on each other in the evenings without an invitation.

Towards the end of July, 1907, there was a severe gale, the wind blowing up-channel, heaping the seas to the base of the cliffs and leaving a lagoon at the turn of the tide. On the morning of which I speak the wind had abated, and all Nature was newly washed and fresh. It was impossible to work upon so delightful a day, and I strolled out before breakfast to enjoy the exquisite air. I walked along the cliff path which led to the steep descent to the beach. As I walked I heard a shout behind me, and there was Harold Stackhurst waving his hand in cheery greeting.

"What a morning, Mr. Holmes! I thought I should see you out."

"Going for a swim, I see."

"At your old tricks again," he laughed, patting his bulging pocket. "Yes. McPherson started early, and I expect I may find him there."

Fitzroy McPherson was the science master, a fine upstanding young fellow whose life had been crippled by heart trouble following rheumatic fever. He was a natural athlete, however, and excelled in every game which did not throw too great a strain upon him. Summer and winter he went for his swim, and, as I am a swimmer myself, I have often joined him.

At this moment we saw the man himself. His head showed above the edge of the cliff where the path ends. Then his whole figure appeared at the top, staggering like a drunken man. The next instant he threw up his hands and, with a terrible cry, fell upon his face. Stackhurst and I rushed forward - it may have been fifty yards - and turned him on his back. He was obviously dying. Those glazed sunken eyes and dreadful livid cheeks could mean nothing else. One glimmer of life came into his face for an instant, and he uttered two or three words with an eager air of warning. They were slurred and indistinct, but to my ear the last of them, which burst in a shriek from his lips, were "the Lion's Mane." It was utterly irrelevant and unintelligible, and yet I could twist the sound into no other sense. Then he half raised himself from the ground, threw his arms into the air, and fell forward on his side. He was dead.

My companion was paralyzed by the sudden horror of it, but I, as may well be imagined, had every sense on the alert. And I had need, for it was speedily evident that we were in the presence of an extraordinary case. The man was dressed only in his Burberry overcoat, his trousers, and an unlaced pair of canvas shoes. As he fell over, his Burberry, which had been simply thrown round his shoulders, slipped off, exposing his trunk. We stared at it in amazement. His back was covered with dark red lines as though he had been terribly flogged by a thin wire scourge. The instrument with which this punishment had been inflicted was clearly flexible, for the long, angry weals curved round his shoulders and ribs. There was blood dripping down his chin, for he had bitten through his lower lip in the paroxysm of his agony. His drawn and distorted face told how terrible that agony had been.

I was kneeling and Stackhurst standing by the body when a shadow fell across us, and we found that Ian Murdoch was by our side. Murdoch was the mathematical coach at the establishment, a tall, dark, thin man, so taciturn and aloof that none can be said to have been his friend. He seemed to live in some high abstract region of surds and conic sections, with little to connect him with ordinary life. He was looked upon as an oddity by the students, and would have been their butt, but there was some strange outlandish blood in the man, which showed itself not only in his coal-black eyes and swarthy face but also in occasional outbreaks of temper, which could only be described as ferocious. On one occasion, being plagued by a little dog belonging to McPherson, he had caught the creature up and hurled it through the plate-glass window, an action for which Stackhurst would certainly have given him his dismissal had he not been a very valuable teacher. Such was the strange complex man who now appeared beside us. He seemed to be honestly shocked at the sight before him, though the incident of the dog may show that there was no great sympathy between the dead man and himself.

"Poor fellow! Poor fellow! What can I do? How can I help?"

"Were you with him? Can you tell us what has happened?"

"No, no, I was late this morning. I was not on the beach at all. I have come straight from The Gables. What can I do?"

"You can hurry to the police-station at Fulworth. Report the matter at once."

Without a word he made off at top speed, and I proceeded to take the matter in hand, while Stackhurst, dazed at this tragedy, remained by the body. My first task naturally was to note who was on the beach. From the top of the path I could see the whole sweep of it, and it was absolutely deserted save that two or three dark figures could be seen far away moving towards the village of Fulworth. Having satisfied myself upon this point, I walked slowly down the path. There was clay or soft marl mixed with the chalk, and every here and there I saw the same footstep, both ascending and descending. No one else had gone down to the beach by this track that morning. At one place I observed the print of an open hand with the fingers towards the incline. This could only mean that poor McPherson had fallen as he ascended. There were rounded depressions, too, which suggested that he had come down upon his knees more than once. At the bottom of the path was the considerable lagoon left by the retreating tide. At the side of it McPherson had undressed, for there lay his towel on a rock. It was folded and dry, so that it would seem that, after all, he had never entered the water. Once or twice as I hunted round amid the hard shingle I came on little patches of sand where the print of his canvas shoe, and also of his naked foot, could be seen. The latter fact proved that he had made all ready to bathe, though the towel indicated that he had not actually done so.

And here was the problem clearly defined - as strange a one as had ever confronted me. The man had not been on the beach more than a quarter of an hour at the most. Stackhurst had followed him from The Gables, so there could be no doubt about that. He had gone to bathe and had stripped, as the naked footsteps showed. Then he had suddenly huddled on his clothes again - they were all dishevelled and unfastened - and he had returned without bathing, or at any rate without drying himself. And the reason for his change of purpose had been that he had been scourged in some savage, inhuman fashion, tortured until he bit his lip through in his agony, and was left with only strength enough to crawl away and to die. Who had done this barbarous deed? There were, it is true, small grottos and caves in the base of the cliffs, but the low sun shone directly into them, and there was no place for concealment. Then, again, there were those distant figures on the beach. They seemed too far away to have been connected with the crime, and the broad lagoon in which McPherson had intended to bathe lay between him and them, lapping up to the rocks. On the sea two or three fishing boats were at no great distance. Their occupants might be examined at our leisure. There were several roads for inquiry, but none which led to any very obvious goal.

When I at last returned to the body I found that a little group of wondering folk had gathered round it. Stackhurst was, of course, still there, and Ian Murdoch had just arrived with Anderson, the village constable, a big, ginger-moustached man of the slow, solid Sussex breed - a breed which covers much good sense under a heavy, silent exterior. He listened to everything, took note of all we said, and finally drew me aside.

"I'd be glad of your advice, Mr. Holmes. This is a big thing for me to handle, and I'll hear of it from Lewes if I go wrong."

I advised him to send for his immediate superior, and for a doctor; also to allow nothing to be moved, and as few fresh footmarks as possible to be made, until they came. In the meantime I searched the dead man's pockets. There were his handkerchief, a large knife, and a small folding card-case. From this projected a slip of paper, which I unfolded and handed to the constable. There was written on it in a scrawling, feminine hand:

I will be there, you may be sure.

MAUDIE

It read like a love affair, an assignation, though when and where were a blank. The constable replaced it in the card-case and returned it with the other things to the pockets of the Burberry. Then, as nothing more suggested itself, I walked back to my house for breakfast, having first arranged that the base of the cliffs should be thoroughly searched.

Stackhurst was round in an hour or two to tell me that the body had been removed to The Gables, where the inquest would be held. He brought with him some serious and definite news. As I expected, nothing had been found in the small caves below the cliff, but he had examined the papers in McPherson's desk and there were several which showed an intimate correspondence with a certain Miss Maud Bellamy, of Fulworth. We had then established the identity of the writer of the note.

"The police have the letters," he explained. "I could not bring them. But there is no doubt that it was a serious love affair. I see no reason, however, to connect it with that horrible happening save, indeed, that the lady had made an appointment with him."

"But hardly at a bathing-pool which all of you were in the habit of using," I remarked.

"It is mere chance," said he, "that several of the students were not with McPherson."

"Was it mere chance?"

Stackhurst knit his brows in thought.

"Ian Murdoch held them back," said he. "He would insist upon some algebraic demonstration before breakfast. Poor chap, he is dreadfully cut up about it all."

"And yet I gather that they were not friends."

"At one time they were not. But for a year or more Murdoch has been as near to McPherson as he ever could be to anyone. He is not of a very sympathetic disposition by nature."

"So I understand. I seem to remember your telling me once about a quarrel over the ill-usage of a dog."

"That blew over all right."

"But left some vindictive feeling, perhaps."

"No, no, I am sure they were real friends."

"Well, then, we must explore the matter of the girl. Do you know her?"

"Everyone knows her. She is the beauty of the neighbourhood -a real beauty, Holmes, who would draw attention everywhere. I knew that McPherson was attracted by her, but I had no notion that it had gone so far as these letters would seem to indicate."

"But who is she?"

"She is the daughter of old Tom Bellamy who owns all the boats and bathing-cots at Fulworth. He was a fisherman to start with, but is now a man of some substance. He and his son William run the business."

"Shall we walk into Fulworth and see them?"

"On what pretext?"

"Oh, we can easily find a pretext. After all, this poor man did not ill-use himself in this outrageous way. Some human hand was on the handle of that scourge, if indeed it was a scourge which inflicted the injuries. His circle of acquaintances in this lonely place was surely limited. Let us follow it up in every direction and we can hardly fail to come upon the motive, which in turn should lead us to the criminal."

It would have been a pleasant walk across the thyme-scented downs had our minds not been poisoned by the tragedy we had witnessed. The village of Fulworth lies in a hollow curving in a semicircle round the bay. Behind the old-fashioned hamlet several modern houses have been built upon the rising ground. It was to one of these that Stackhurst guided me.

"That's The Haven, as Bellamy called it. The one with the corner tower and slate roof. Not bad for a man who started with nothing but - By Jove, look at that!"

The garden gate of The Haven had opened and a man had emerged. There was no mistaking that tall, angular, straggling figure. It was Ian Murdoch, the mathematician. A moment later we confronted him upon the road.

"Hullo!" said Stackhurst. The man nodded, gave us a sideways glance from his curious dark eyes, and would have-passed us, but his principal pulled him up.

"What were you doing there?" he asked.

Murdoch's face flushed with anger. "I am your subordinate, sir, under your roof. I am not aware that I owe you any account of my private actions."

Stackhurst's nerves were near the surface after all he had endured. Otherwise, perhaps, he would have waited. Now he lost his temper completely.

"In the circumstances your answer is pure impertinence, Mr. Murdoch."

"Your own question might perhaps come under the same heading."

"This is not the first time that I have had to overlook your insubordinate ways. It will certainly be the last. You will kindly make fresh arrangements for your future as speedily as you can."

"I had intended to do so. I have lost to-day the only person who made The Gables habitable."

He strode off upon his way, while Stackhurst, with angry eyes, stood glaring after him. "Is he not an impossible, intolerable man?" he cried.

The one thing that impressed itself forcibly upon my mind was that Mr. Ian Murdoch was taking the first chance to open a path of escape from the scene of the crime. Suspicion, vague and nebulous, was now beginning to take outline in my mind. Perhaps the visit to the Bellamys might throw some further light upon the matter. Stackhurst pulled himself together, and we went forward to the house.

Mr. Bellamy proved to be a middle-aged man with a flaming red beard. He seemed to be in a very angry mood, and his face was soon as florid as his hair.

"No, sir, I do not desire any particulars. My son here" - indicating a powerful young man, with a heavy, sullen face, in the corner of the sitting-room - "is of one mind with me that Mr. McPherson's attentions to Maud were insulting. Yes, sir, the word 'marriage' was never mentioned, and yet there were letters and meetings, and a great deal more of which neither of us could approve. She has no mother, and we are her only guardians. We are determined -"

But the words were taken from his mouth by the appearance of the lady herself. There was no gainsaying that she would have graced any assembly in the world. Who could have imagined that so rare a flower would grow from such a root and in such an atmosphere? Women have seldom been an attraction to me, for my brain has always governed my heart, but I could not look upon her perfect clear-cut face, with all the soft freshness of the down lands in her delicate colouring, without realizing that no young man would cross her path unscathed. Such was the girl who had pushed open the door and stood now, wide-eyed and intense, in front of Harold Stackhurst.

"I know already that Fitzroy is dead," she said. "Do not be afraid to tell me the particulars."

"This other gentleman of yours let us know the news," explained the father.

"There is no reason why my sister should be brought into the matter," growled the younger man.

The sister turned a sharp, fierce look upon him. "This is my business, William. Kindly leave me to manage it in my own way. By all accounts there has been a crime committed. If I can help to show who did it, it is the least I can do for him who is gone."

She listened to a short account from my companion, with a composed concentration which showed me that she possessed strong character as well as great beauty. Maud Bellamy will always remain in my memory as a most complete and remarkable woman. It seems that she already knew me by sight, for she turned to me at the end.

"Bring them to justice, Mr. Holmes. You have my sympathy and my help, whoever they may be." It seemed to me that she glanced defiantly at her father and brother as she spoke.

"Thank you," said I. "I value a woman's instinct in such matters. You use the word 'they.' You think that more than one was concerned?"

"I knew Mr. McPherson well enough to be aware that he was a brave and a strong man. No single person could ever have inflicted such an outrage upon him."

"Might I have one word with you alone?"

"I tell you, Maud, not to mix yourself up in the matter," cried her father angrily.

She looked at me helplessly. "What can I do?"

"The whole world will know the facts presently, so there can be no harm if I discuss them here," said I. "I should have preferred privacy, but if your father will not allow it he must share the deliberations." Then I spoke of the note which had been found in the dead man's pocket. "It is sure to be produced at the inquest. May I ask you to throw any light upon it that you can?"

"I see no reason for mystery," she answered. "We were engaged to be married, and we only kept it secret because Fitzroy's uncle, who is very old and said to be dying, might have disinherited him if he had married against his wish. There was no other reason."

"You could have told us," growled Mr. Bellamy.

"So I would, father, if you had ever shown sympathy."

"I object to my girl picking up with men outside her own station."

"It was your prejudice against him which prevented us from telling you. As to this appointment" - she fumbled in her dress and produced a crumpled note - "it was in answer to this."

DEAREST [ran the message]:

The old place on the beach just after sunset on Tuesday.

It is the only time I can get away.

F.M.

"Tuesday was to-day, and I had meant to meet him to-night."

I turned over the paper. "This never came by post. How did you get it?"

"I would rather not answer that question. It has really nothing to do with the matter which you are investigating. But anything which bears upon that I will most freely answer."

She was as good as her word, but there was nothing which was helpful in our investigation. She had no reason to think that her fiance had any hidden enemy, but she admitted that she had had several warm admirers.

"May I ask if Mr. Ian Murdoch was one of them?"

She blushed and seemed confused.

"There was a time when I thought he was. But that was all changed when he understood the relations between Fitzroy and myself."

Again the shadow round this strange man seemed to me to be taking more definite shape. His record must be examined. His rooms must be privately searched. Stackhurst was a willing collaborator, for in his mind also suspicions were forming. We returned from our visit to The Haven with the hope that one free end of this tangled skein was already in our hands.

A week passed. The inquest had thrown no light upon the matter and had been adjourned for further evidence. Stackhurst had made discreet inquiry about his subordinate, and there had been a superficial search of his room, but without result. Personally, I had gone over the whole ground again, both physically and mentally, but with no new conclusions.

In all my chronicles the reader will find no case which brought me so completely to the limit of my powers. Even my imagination could conceive no solution to the mystery. And then there came the incident of the dog.

It was my old housekeeper who heard of it first by that strange wireless by which such people collect the news of the countryside.

"Sad story this, sir, about Mr. McPherson's dog," said she one evening.

I do not encourage such conversations, but the words arrested my attention.

"What of Mr. McPherson's dog?"

"Dead, sir. Died of grief for its master."

"Who told you this?"

"Why, sir, everyone is talking of it. It took on terrible, and has eaten nothing for a week. Then to-day two of the young gentlemen from The Gables found it dead - down on the beach, sir, at the very place where its master met his end."

"At the very place." The words stood out clear in my memory. Some dim perception that the matter was vital rose in my mind. That the dog should die was after the beautiful, faithful nature of dogs. But "in the very place"! Why should this lonely beach be fatal to it? Was it possible that it also had been sacrificed to some revengeful feud? Was it possible -? Yes, the perception was dim, but already something was building up in my mind. In a few minutes I was on my way to The Gables, where I found Stackhurst in his study. At my request he sent for Sudbury and Blount, the two students who had found the dog.

"Yes, it lay on the very edge of the pool," said one of them. "It must have followed the trail of its dead master."

I saw the faithful little creature, an Airedale terrier, laid out upon the mat in the hall. The body was stiff and rigid, the eyes projecting, and the limbs contorted. There was agony in every line of it.

From The Gables I walked down to the bathing-pool. The sun had sunk and the shadow of the great cliff lay black across the water, which glimmered dully like a sheet of lead. The place was deserted and there was no sign of life save for two sea-birds circling and screaming overhead. In the fading light I could dimly make out the little dog's spoor upon the sand round the very rock on which his master's towel had been laid. For a long time I stood in deep meditation while the shadows grew darker around me. My mind was filled with racing thoughts. You have known what it was to be in a nightmare in which you feel that there is some all-important thing for which you search and which you know is there, though it remains forever just beyond your reach. That was how I felt that evening as I stood alone by that place of death. Then at last I turned and walked slowly homeward.

I had just reached the top of the path when it came to me. Like a flash, I remembered the thing for which I had so eagerly and vainly grasped. You will know, or Watson has written in vain, that I hold a vast store of out-of-the-way knowledge without scientific system, but very available for the needs of my work. My mind is like a crowded box-room with packets of all sorts stowed away therein - so many that I may well have but a vague perception of what was there. I had known that there was something which might bear upon this matter. It was still vague, but at least I knew how I could make it clear. It was monstrous, incredible, and yet it was always a possibility. I would test it to the full.

There is a great garret in my little house which is stuffed with books. It was into this that I plunged and rummaged for an hour. At the end of that time I emerged with a little chocolate and silver volume. Eagerly I turned up the chapter of which I had a dim remembrance. Yes, it was indeed a far-fetched and unlikely proposition, and yet I could not be at rest until I had made sure if it might, indeed, be so. It was late when I retired, with my mind eagerly awaiting the work of the morrow.

But that work met with an annoying interruption. I had hardly swallowed my early cup of tea and was starting for the beach when I had a call from Inspector Bardle of the Sussex Constabulary - a steady, solid, bovine man with thoughtful eyes, which looked at me now with a very troubled expression.

"I know your immense experience, sir," said he. "This is quite unofficial, of course, and need go no farther. But I am fairly up against it in this McPherson case. The question is, shall I make an arrest, or shall I not?"

"Meaning Mr. Ian Murdoch?"

"Yes, sir. There is really no one else when you come to think of it. That's the advantage of this solitude. We narrow it down to a very small compass. If he did not do it, then who did?"

"What have you against him?"

He had gleaned along the same furrows as I had. There was Murdoch's character and the mystery which seemed to hang round the man. His furious bursts of temper, as shown in the incident of the dog. The fact that he had quarrelled with McPherson in the past, and that there was some reason to think that he might have resented his attentions to Miss Bellamy. He had all my points, but no fresh ones, save that Murdoch seemed to be making every preparation for departure.

"What would my position be if I let him slip away with all this evidence against him?" The burly, phlegmatic man was sorely troubled in his mind.

"Consider," I said, "all the essential gaps in your case. On the morning of the crime he can surely prove an alibi. He had been with his scholars till the last moment, and within a few minutes of McPherson's appearance he came upon us from behind. Then bear in mind the absolute impossibility that he could single-handed have inflicted this outrage upon a man quite as strong as himself. Finally, there is this question of the instrument with which these injuries were inflicted."

"What could it be but a scourge or flexible whip of some sort?"

"Have you examined the marks?" I asked.

"I have seen them. So has the doctor."

"But I have examined them very carefully with a lens. They have peculiarities."

"What are they, Mr. Holmes?"

I stepped to my bureau and brought out an enlarged photograph. "This is my method in such cases," I explained.

"You certainly do things thoroughly, Mr. Holmes."

"I should hardly be what I am if I did not. Now let us consider this weal which extends round the right shoulder. Do you observe nothing remarkable?"

"I can't say I do."

"Surely it is evident that it is unequal in its intensity. There is a dot of extravasated blood here, and another there. There are similar indications in this other weal down here. What can that mean?"

"I have no idea. Have you?"

"Perhaps I have. Perhaps I haven't. I may be able to say more soon. Anything which will define what made that mark will bring us a long way towards the criminal."

"It is, of course, an absurd idea," said the policeman, "but if a red-hot net of wire had been laid across the back, then these better marked points would represent where the meshes crossed each other."

"A most ingenious comparison. Or shall we say a very stiff cat-o'-nine-tails with small hard knots upon it?"

"By Jove, Mr. Holmes, I think you have hit it."

"Or there may be some very different cause, Mr. Bardle. But your case is far too weak for an arrest. Besides, we have those last words - the 'Lion's Mane.'"

"I have wondered whether Ian -"

"Yes, I have considered that. If the second word had borne any resemblance to Murdoch - but it did not. He gave it almost in a shriek. I am sure that it was 'Mane.'"

"Have you no alternative, Mr. Holmes?"

"Perhaps I have. But I do not care to discuss it until there is something more solid to discuss."

"And when will that be?"

"In an hour - possibly less."

The inspector rubbed his chin and looked at me with dubious eyes.

"I wish I could see what was in your mind, Mr. Holmes. Perhaps it's those fishing-boats."

"No, no, they were too far out."

"Well, then, is it Bellamy and that big son of his? They were not too sweet upon Mr. McPherson. Could they have done him a mischief?"

"No, no, you won't draw me until I am ready," said I with a smile.

"Now, Inspector, we each have our own work to do. Perhaps if you were to meet me here at midday -"

So far we had got when there came the tremendous interruption which was the beginning of the end.

My outer door was flung open, there were blundering footsteps in the passage, and Ian Murdoch staggered into the room, pallid, dishevelled, his clothes in wild disorder, clawing with his bony hands at the furniture to hold himself erect. "Brandy! Brandy!" he gasped, and fell groaning upon the sofa.

He was not alone. Behind him came Stackhurst, hatless and panting, almost as distrait as his companion.

"Yes, yes, brandy!" he cried. "The man is at his last gasp. It was all I could do to bring him here. He fainted twice upon the way."

Half a tumbler of the raw spirit brought about a wondrous change. He pushed himself up on one arm and swung his coat from his shoulders. "For God's sake oil, opium, morphia!" he cried. "Anything to ease this infernal agony!"

The inspector and I cried out at the sight. There, crisscrossed upon the man's naked shoulder, was the same strange reticulated pattern of red, inflamed lines which had been the death-mark of Fitzroy McPherson.

The pain was evidently terrible and was more than local, for the sufferer's breathing would stop for a time, his face would turn black, and then with loud gasps he would clap his hand to his heart, while his brow dropped beads of sweat. At any moment he might die. More and more brandy was poured down his throat, each fresh dose bringing him back to life. Pads of cotton-wool soaked in salad-oil seemed to take the agony from the strange wounds. At last his head fell heavily upon the cushion. Exhausted Nature had taken refuge in its last storehouse of vitality. It was half a sleep and half a faint, but at least it was ease from pain.

To question him had been impossible, but the moment we were assured of his condition Stackhurst turned upon me.

"My God!" he cried, "what is it, Holmes? What is it?"

"Where did you find him?"

"Down on the beach. Exactly where poor McPherson met his end. If this man's heart had been weak as McPherson's was, he would not be here now. More than once I thought he was gone as I brought him up. It was too far to The Gables, so I made for you."

"Did you see him on the beach?"

"I was walking on the cliff when I heard his cry. He was at the edge of the water, reeling about like a drunken man. I ran down, threw some clothes about him, and brought him up. For heaven's sake, Holmes, use all the powers you have and spare no pains to lift the curse from this place, for life is becoming unendurable. Can you, with all your world-wide reputation, do nothing for us?"

"I think I can, Stackhurst. Come with me now! And you, Inspector, come along! We will see if we cannot deliver this murderer into your hands."

Leaving the unconscious man in the charge of my housekeeper, we all three went down to the deadly lagoon. On the shingle there was piled a little heap of towels and clothes left by the stricken man. Slowly I walked round the edge of the water, my comrades in Indian file behind me. Most of the pool was quite shallow, but under the cliff where the beach was hollowed out it was four or five feet deep. It was to this part that a swimmer would naturally go, for it formed a beautiful pellucid green pool as clear as crystal. A line of rocks lay above it at the base of the cliff, and along this I led the way, peering eagerly into the depths beneath me. I had reached the deepest and stillest pool when my eyes caught that for which they were searching, and I burst into a shout of triumph.

"Cyanea!" I cried. "Cyanea! Behold the Lion's Mane!"

The strange object at which I pointed did indeed look like a tangled mass torn from the mane of a lion. It lay upon a rocky shelf some three feet under the water, a curious waving, vibrating, hairy creature with streaks of silver among its yellow tresses. It pulsated with a slow, heavy dilation and contraction.

"It has done mischief enough. Its day is over!" I cried. "Help me, Stackhurst! Let us end the murderer forever."

There was a big boulder just above the ledge, and we pushed it until it fell with a tremendous splash into the water. When the ripples had cleared we saw that it had settled upon the ledge below. One flapping edge of yellow membrane showed that our victim was beneath it. A thick oily scum oozed out from below the stone and stained the water round, rising slowly to the surface.

"Well, this gets me!" cried the inspector. "What was it, Mr. Holmes? I'm born and bred in these parts, but I never saw such a thing. It don't belong to Sussex."

"Just as well for Sussex," I remarked. "It may have been the southwest gale that brought it up. Come back to my house, both of you, and I will give you the terrible experience of one who has good reason to remember his own meeting with the same peril of the seas."

When we reached my study we found that Murdoch was so far recovered that he could sit up. He was dazed in mind, and every now and then was shaken by a paroxysm of pain. In broken words he explained that he had no notion what had occurred to him, save that terrific pangs had suddenly shot through him, and that it had taken all his fortitude to reach the bank.

"Here is a book," I said, taking up the little volume, "which first brought light into what might have been forever dark. It is Out of Doors, by the famous observer, J.G. Wood. Wood himself very nearly perished from contact with this vile creature, so he wrote with a very full knowledge. Cyanea capillata is the miscreant's full name, and he can be as dangerous to life as, and far more painful than, the bite of the cobra. Let me briefly give this extract."

"If the bather should see a loose roundish mass of tawny membranes and fibres, something like very large handfuls of lion's mane and silver paper, let him beware, for this is the fearful stinger, Cyanea capillata."

Could our sinister acquaintance be more clearly described?

"He goes on to tell of his own encounter with one when swimming off the coast of Kent. He found that the creature radiated almost invisible filaments to the distance of fifty feet, and that anyone within that circumference from the deadly centre was in danger of death. Even at a distance the effect upon Wood was almost fatal."

"The multitudinous threads caused light scarlet lines upon the skin which on closer examination resolved into minute dots or pustules, each dot charged as it were with a red-hot needle making its way through the nerves."

"The local pain was, as he explains, the least part of the exquisite torment."

"Pangs shot through the chest, causing me to fall as if struck by a bullet. The pulsation would cease, and then the heart would give six or seven leaps as if it would force its way through the chest."

"It nearly killed him, although he had only been exposed to it in the disturbed ocean and not in the narrow calm waters of a bathing-pool. He says that he could hardly recognize himself afterwards, so white, wrinkled and shrivelled was his face. He gulped down brandy, a whole bottleful, and it seems to have saved his life. There is the book, Inspector. I leave it with you, and you cannot doubt that it contains a full explanation of the tragedy of poor McPherson."

"And incidentally exonerates me," remarked Ian Murdoch with a wry smile. "I do not blame you, Inspector, nor you, Mr. Holmes, for your suspicions were natural. I feel that on the very eve of my arrest I have only cleared myself by sharing the fate of my poor friend."

"No, Mr. Murdoch. I was already upon the track, and had I been out as early as I intended I might well have saved you from this terrific experience."

"But how did you know, Mr. Holmes?"

"I am an omnivorous reader with a strangely retentive memory for trifles. That phrase 'the Lion's Mane' haunted my mind. I knew that I had seen it somewhere in an unexpected context. You have seen that it does describe the creature. I have no doubt that it was floating on the water when McPherson saw it, and that this phrase was the only one by which he could convey to us a warning as to the creature which had been his death."

"Then I, at least, am cleared," said Murdoch, rising slowly to his feet. "There are one or two words of explanation which I should give, for I know the direction in which your inquiries have run. It is true that I loved this lady, but from the day when she chose my friend McPherson my one desire was to help her to happiness. I was well content to stand aside and act as their go-between. Often I carried their messages, and it was because I was in their confidence and because she was so dear to me that I hastened to tell her of my friend's death, lest someone should forestall me in a more sudden and heartless manner. She would not tell you, sir, of our relations lest you should disapprove and I might suffer. But with your leave I must try to get back to The Gables, for my bed will be very welcome."

Stackhurst held out his hand. "Our nerves have all been at concert-pitch," said he. "Forgive what is past, Murdoch. We shall understand each other better in the future." They passed out together with their arms linked in friendly fashion. The inspector remained, staring at me in silence with his ox-like eyes.

"Well, you've done it!" he cried at last. "I had read of you, but I never believed it. It's wonderful!"

I was forced to shake my head. To accept such praise was to lower one's own standards.

"I was slow at the outset - culpably slow. Had the body been found in the water I could hardly have missed it. It was the towel which misled me. The poor fellow had never thought to dry himself, and so I in turn was led to believe that he had never been in the water. Why, then, should the attack of any water creature suggest itself to me? That was where I went astray. Well, well, Inspector, I often ventured to chaff you gentlemen of the police force, but Cyanea capillata very nearly avenged Scotland Yard."

THE ADVENTURE OF THE VEILED LODGER

When one considers that Mr. Sherlock Holmes was in active practice for twenty-three years, and that during seventeen of these I was allowed to cooperate with him and to keep notes of his doings, it will be clear that I have a mass of material at my command. The problem has always been not to find but to choose. There is the long row of year-books which fill a shelf and there are the dispatch-cases filled with documents, a perfect quarry for the student not only of crime but of the social and official scandals of the late Victorian era. Concerning these latter, I may say that the writers of agonized letters, who beg that the honour of their families or the reputation of famous forebears may not be touched, have nothing to fear. The discretion and high sense of professional honour which have always distinguished my friend are still at work in the choice of these memoirs, and no confidence will be abused. I deprecate, however, in the strongest way the attempts which have been made lately to get at and to destroy these papers. The source of these outrages is known, and if they are repeated I have Mr. Holmes's authority for saying that the whole story concerning the politician, the lighthouse, and the trained cormorant will be given to the public. There is at least one reader who will understand.

It is not reasonable to suppose that every one of these cases gave Holmes the opportunity of showing those curious gifts of instinct and observation which I have endeavoured to set forth in these memoirs. Sometimes he had with much effort to pick the fruit, sometimes it fell easily into his lap. But the most terrible human tragedies were often involved in those cases which brought him the fewest personal opportunities, and it is one of these which I now desire to record. In telling it, I have made a slight change of name and place, but otherwise the facts are as stated.

One forenoon - it was late in 1896 - I received a hurried note from Holmes asking for my attendance. When I arrived I found him seated in a smoke-laden atmosphere, with an elderly, motherly woman of the buxom landlady type in the corresponding chair in front of him.

"This is Mrs. Merrilow, of South Brixton," said my friend with a wave of the hand. "Mrs. Merrilow does not object to tobacco, Watson, if you wish to indulge your filthy habits. Mrs. Merrilow has an interesting story to tell which may well lead to further developments in which your presence may be useful."

"Anything I can do -"

"You will understand, Mrs. Merrilow, that if I come to Mrs. Ronder I should prefer to have a witness. You will make her understand that before we arrive."

"Lord bless you, Mr. Holmes," said our visitor, "she is that anxious to see you that you might bring the whole parish at your heels!"

"Then we shall come early in the afternoon. Let us see that we have our facts correct before we start. If we go over them it will help Dr. Watson to understand the situation. You say that Mrs. Ronder has been your lodger for seven years and that you have only once seen her face."

"And I wish to God I had not!" said Mrs. Merrilow.

"It was, I understand, terribly mutilated."

"Well, Mr. Holmes, you would hardly say it was a face at all. That's how it looked. Our milkman got a glimpse of her once peeping out of the upper window, and he dropped his tin and the milk all over the front garden. That is the kind of face it is. When I saw her - I happened on her unawares - she covered up quick, and then she said, 'Now, Mrs. Merrilow, you know at last why it is that I never raise my veil.'"

"Do you know anything about her history?"

"Nothing at all."

"Did she give references when she came?"

"No, sir, but she gave hard cash, and plenty of it. A quarter's rent right down on the table in advance and no arguing about terms. In these times a poor woman like me can't afford to turn down a chance like that."

"Did she give any reason for choosing your house?"

"Mine stands well back from the road and is more private than most. Then, again, I only take the one, and I have no family of my own. I reckon she had tried others and found that mine suited her best. It's privacy she is after, and she is ready to pay for it."

"You say that she never showed her face from first to last save on the one accidental occasion. Well, it is a very remarkable story, most remarkable, and I don't wonder that you want it examined."

"I don't, Mr. Holmes. I am quite satisfied so long as I get my rent. You could not have a quieter lodger, or one who gives less trouble."

"Then what has brought matters to a head?"

"Her health, Mr. Holmes. She seems to be wasting away. And there's something terrible on her mind. 'Murder!' she cries. 'Murder!' And once I heard her: 'You cruel beast! You monster!' she cried. It was in the night, and it fair rang through the house and sent the shivers through me. So I went to her in the morning. 'Mrs. Ronder,' I says, 'if you have anything that is troubling your soul, there's the clergy,' I says, 'and there's the police. Between them you should get some help.' 'For God's sake, not the police!' says she, 'and the clergy can't change what is past. And yet,' she says, 'it would ease my mind if someone knew the truth before I died.' 'Well,' says I, 'if you won't have the regulars, there is this detective man what we read about' -beggin' your pardon, Mr. Holmes. And she, she fair jumped at it. 'That's the man,' says she. 'I wonder I never thought of it before. Bring him here, Mrs. Merrilow, and if he won't come, tell him I am the wife of Ronder's wild beast show. Say that, and give him the name Abbas Parva. Here it is as she wrote it, Abbas Parva. 'That will bring him if he's the man I think he is.'"

"And it will, too," remarked Holmes. "Very good, Mrs. Merrilow. I should like to have a little chat with Dr. Watson. That will carry us till lunch-time. About three o'clock you may expect to see us at your house in Brixton."

Our visitor had no sooner waddled out of the room - no other verb can describe Mrs. Merrilow's method of progression - than Sherlock Holmes threw himself with fierce energy upon the pile of commonplace books in the corner. For a few minutes there was a constant swish of the leaves, and then with a grunt of satisfaction he came upon what he sought. So excited was he that he did not rise, but sat upon the floor like some strange Buddha, with crossed legs, the huge books all round him, and one open upon his knees.

"The case worried me at the time, Watson. Here are my marginal notes to prove it. I confess that I could make nothing of it. And yet I was convinced that the coroner was wrong. Have you no recollection of the Abbas Parva tragedy?"

"None, Holmes."

"And yet you were with me then. But certainly my own impression was very superficial. For there was nothing to go by, and none of the parties had engaged my services. Perhaps you would care to read the papers?"

"Could you not give me the points?"

"That is very easily done. It will probably come back to your memory as I talk. Ronder, of course, was a household word. He was the rival of Wombwell, and of Sanger, one of the greatest showmen of his day. There is evidence, however, that he took to drink, and that both he and his show were on the down grade at the time of the great tragedy. The caravan had halted for the night at Abbas Parva, which is a small village in Berkshire, when this horror occurred. They were on their way to Wimbledon, travelling by road, and they were simply camping and not exhibiting, as the place is so small a one that it would not have paid them to open."

"They had among their exhibits a very fine North African lion. Sahara King was its name, and it was the habit, both of Ronder and his wife, to give exhibitions inside its cage. Here, you see, is a photograph of the performance by which you will perceive that Ronder was a huge porcine person and that his wife was a very magnificent woman. It was deposed at the inquest that there had been some signs that the lion was dangerous, but, as usual, familiarity begat contempt, and no notice was taken of the fact."

"It was usual for either Ronder or his wife to feed the lion at night. Sometimes one went, sometimes both, but they never allowed anyone else to do it, for they believed that so long as they were the food-carriers he would regard them as benefactors and would never molest them. On this particular night, seven years ago, they both went, and a very terrible happening followed, the details of which have never been made clear."

"It seems that the whole camp was roused near midnight by the roars of the animal and the screams of the woman. The different grooms and employees rushed from their tents, carrying lanterns, and by their light an awful sight was revealed. Ronder lay, with the back of his head crushed in and deep claw-marks across his scalp, some ten yards from the cage, which was open. Close to the door of the cage lay Mrs. Ronder upon her back, with the creature squatting and snarling above her. It had torn her face in such a fashion that it was never thought that she could live. Several of the circus men, headed by Leonardo, the strong man, and Griggs, the clown, drove the creature off with poles, upon which it sprang back into the cage and was at once locked in. How it had got loose was a mystery. It was conjectured that the pair intended to enter the cage, but that when the door was loosed the creature bounded out upon them. There was no other point of interest in the evidence save that the woman in a delirium of agony kept screaming, 'Coward! Coward!' as she was carried back to the van in which they lived. It was six months before she was fit to give evidence, but the inquest was duly held, with the obvious verdict of death from misadventure."

"What alternative could be conceived?" said I.

"You may well say so. And yet there were one or two points which worried young Edmunds, of the Berkshire Constabulary. A smart lad that! He was sent later to Allahabad. That was how I came into the matter, for he dropped in and smoked a pipe or two over it."

"A thin, yellow-haired man?"

"Exactly. I was sure you would pick up the trail presently."

"But what worried him?"

"Well, we were both worried. It was so deucedly difficult to reconstruct the affair. Look at it from the lion's point of view. He is liberated. What does he do? He takes half a dozen bounds forward, which brings him to Ronder. Ronder turns to fly - the claw-marks were on the back of his head - but the lion strikes him down. Then, instead of bounding on and escaping, he returns to the woman, who was close to the cage, and he knocks her over and chews her face up. Then, again, those cries of hers would seem to imply that her husband had in some way failed her. What could the poor devil have done to help her? You see the difficulty?"

"Quite."

"And then there was another thing. It comes back to me now as I think it over. There was some evidence that just at the time the lion roared and the woman screamed, a man began shouting in terror."

"This man Ronder, no doubt."

"Well, if his skull was smashed in you would hardly expect to hear from him again. There were at least two witnesses who spoke of the cries of a man being mingled with those of a woman."

"I should think the whole camp was crying out by then. As to the other points, I think I could suggest a solution."

"I should be glad to consider it."

"The two were together, ten yards from the cage, when the lion got loose. The man turned and was struck down. The woman conceived the idea of getting into the cage and shutting the door. It was her only refuge. She made for it, and just as she reached it the beast bounded after her and knocked her over. She was angry with her husband for having encouraged the beast's rage by turning. If they had faced it they might have cowed it. Hence her cries of 'Coward!'"

"Brilliant, Watson! Only one flaw in your diamond."

"What is the flaw, Holmes?"

"If they were both ten paces from the cage, how came the beast to get loose?"

"Is it possible that they had some enemy who loosed it?"

"And why should it attack them savagely when it was in the habit of playing with them, and doing tricks with them inside the cage?"

"Possibly the same enemy had done something to enrage it."

Holmes looked thoughtful and remained in silence for some moments.

"Well, Watson, there is this to be said for your theory. Ronder was a man of many enemies. Edmunds told me that in his cups he was horrible. A huge bully of a man, he cursed and slashed at everyone who came in his way. I expect those cries about a monster, of which our visitor has spoken, were nocturnal reminiscences of the dear departed. However, our speculations are futile until we have all the facts. There is a cold partridge on the sideboard, Watson, and a bottle of Montrachet. Let us renew our energies before we make a fresh call upon them."

When our hansom deposited us at the house of Mrs. Merrilow, we found that plump lady blocking up the open door of her humble but retired abode. It was very clear that her chief preoccupation was lest she should lose a valuable lodger, and she implored us, before showing us up, to say and do nothing which could lead to so undesirable an end. Then, having reassured her, we followed her up the straight, badly carpeted staircase and were shown into the room of the mysterious lodger.

It was a close, musty, ill-ventilated place, as might be expected, since its inmate seldom left it. From keeping beasts in a cage, the woman seemed, by some retribution of fate, to have become herself a beast in a cage. She sat now in a broken armchair in the shadowy corner of the room. Long years of inaction had coarsened the lines of her figure, but at some period it must have been beautiful, and was still full and voluptuous. A thick dark veil covered her face, but it was cut off close at her upper lip and disclosed a perfectly shaped mouth and a delicately rounded chin. I could well conceive that she had indeed been a very remarkable woman. Her voice, too, was well modulated and pleasing.

"My name is not unfamiliar to you, Mr. Holmes," said she. "I thought that it would bring you."

"That is so, madam, though I do not know how you are aware that I was interested in your case."

"I learned it when I had recovered my health and was examined by Mr. Edmunds, the county detective. I fear I lied to him. Perhaps it would have been wiser had I told the truth."

"It is usually wiser to tell the truth. But why did you lie to him?"

"Because the fate of someone else depended upon it. I know that he was a very worthless being, and yet I would not have his destruction upon my conscience. We had been so close - so close!"

"But has this impediment been removed?"

"Yes, sir. The person that I allude to is dead."

"Then why should you not now tell the police anything you know?"

"Because there is another person to be considered. That other person is myself. I could not stand the scandal and publicity which would come from a police examination. I have not long to live, but I wish to die undisturbed. And yet I wanted to find one man of judgment to whom I could tell my terrible story, so that when I am gone all might be understood."

"You compliment me, madam. At the same time, I am a responsible person. I do not promise you that when you have spoken I may not myself think it my duty to refer the case to the police."

"I think not, Mr. Holmes. I know your character and methods too well, for I have followed your work for some years. Reading is the only pleasure which fate has left me, and I miss little which passes in the world. But in any case, I will take my chance of the use which you may make of my tragedy. It will ease my mind to tell it."

"My friend and I would be glad to hear it."

The woman rose and took from a drawer the photograph of a man. He was clearly a professional acrobat, a man of magnificent physique, taken with his huge arms folded across his swollen chest and a smile breaking from under his heavy moustache - the self-satisfied smile of the man of many conquests.

"That is Leonardo," she said.

"Leonardo, the strong man, who gave evidence?"

"The same. And this - this is my husband."

It was a dreadful face - a human pig, or rather a human wild boar, for it was formidable in its bestiality. One could imagine that vile mouth champing and foaming in its rage, and one could conceive those small, vicious eyes darting pure malignancy as they looked forth upon the world. Ruffian, bully, beast - it was all written on that heavy-jowled face.

"Those two pictures will help you, gentlemen, to understand the story. I was a poor circus girl brought up on the sawdust, and doing springs through the hoop before I was ten. When I became a woman this man loved me, if such lust as his can be called love, and in an evil moment I became his wife. From that day I was in hell, and he the devil who tormented me. There was no one in the show who did not know of his treatment. He deserted me for others. He tied me down and lashed me with his riding whip when I complained. They all pitied me and they all loathed him, but what could they do? They feared him, one and all. For he was terrible at all times, and murderous when he was drunk. Again and again he was had up for assault, and for cruelty to the beasts, but he had plenty of money and the fines were nothing to him. The best men all left us, and the show began to go downhill. It was only Leonardo and I who kept it up - with little Jimmy Griggs, the clown. Poor devil, he had not much to be funny about, but he did what he could to hold things together."

"Then Leonardo came more and more into my life. You see what he was like. I know now the poor spirit that was hidden in that splendid body, but compared to my husband he seemed like the angel Gabriel. He pitied me and helped me, till at last our intimacy turned to love - deep, deep, passionate love, such love as I had dreamed of but never hoped to feel. My husband suspected it, but I think that he was a coward as well as a bully, and that Leonardo was the one man that he was afraid of. He took revenge in his own way by torturing me more than ever. One night my cries brought Leonardo to the door of our van. We were near tragedy that night, and soon my lover and I understood that it could not be avoided. My husband was not fit to live. We planned that he should die."

"Leonardo had a clever, scheming brain. It was he who planned it. I do not say that to blame him, for I was ready to go with him every inch of the way. But I should never have had the wit to think of such a plan. We made a club - Leonardo made it - and in the leaden head he fastened five long steel nails, the points outward, with just such a spread as the lion's paw. This was to give my husband his death-blow, and yet to leave the evidence that it was the lion which we would loose who had done the deed."

"It was a pitch-dark night when my husband and I went down, as was our custom, to feed the beast. We carried with us the raw meat in a zinc pail. Leonardo was waiting at the corner of the big van which we should have to pass before we reached the cage. He was too slow, and we walked past him before he could strike, but he followed us on tiptoe and I heard the crash as the club smashed my husband's skull. My heart leaped with joy at the sound. I sprang forward, and I undid the catch which held the door of the great lion's cage."

"And then the terrible thing happened. You may have heard how quick these creatures are to scent human blood, and how it excites them. Some strange instinct had told the creature in one instant that a human being had been slain. As I slipped the bars it bounded out and was on me in an instant. Leonardo could have saved me. If he had rushed forward and struck the beast with his club he might have cowed it. But the man lost his nerve. I heard him shout in his terror, and then I saw him turn and fly. At the same instant the teeth of the lion met in my face. Its hot, filthy breath had already poisoned me and I was hardly conscious of pain. With the palms of my hands I tried to push the great steaming, blood-stained jaws away from me, and I screamed for help. I was conscious that the camp was stirring, and then dimly I remembered a group of men. Leonardo, Griggs, and others, dragging me from under the creature's paws. That was my last memory, Mr. Holmes, for many a weary month. When I came to myself and saw myself in the mirror, I cursed that lion - oh, how I cursed him! - not because he had torn away my beauty but because he had not torn away my life. I had but one desire, Mr. Holmes, and I had enough money to gratify it. It was that I should cover myself so that my poor face should be seen by none, and that I should dwell where none whom I had ever known should find me. That was all that was left to me to do - and that is what I have done. A poor wounded beast that has crawled into its hole to die - that is the end of Eugenia Ronder."

We sat in silence for some time after the unhappy woman had told her story. Then Holmes stretched out his long arm and patted her hand with such a show of sympathy as I had seldom known him to exhibit.

"Poor girl!" he said. "Poor girl! The ways of fate are indeed hard to understand. If there is not some compensation hereafter, then the world is a cruel jest. But what of this man Leonardo?"

"I never saw him or heard from him again. Perhaps I have been wrong to feel so bitterly against him. He might as soon have loved one of the freaks whom we carried round the country as the thing which the lion had left. But a woman's love is not so easily set aside. He had left me under the beast's claws, he had deserted me in my need, and yet I could not bring myself to give him to the gallows. For myself, I cared nothing what became of me. What could be more dreadful than my actual life? But I stood between Leonardo and his fate."

"And he is dead?"

"He was drowned last month when bathing near Margate. I saw his death in the paper."

"And what did he do with this five-clawed club, which is the most singular and ingenious part of all your story?"

"I cannot tell, Mr. Holmes. There is a chalk-pit by the camp, with a deep green pool at the base of it. Perhaps in the depths of that pool -"

"Well, well, it is of little consequence now. The case is closed."

"Yes," said the woman, "the case is closed."

We had risen to go, but there was something in the woman's voice which arrested Holmes's attention. He turned swiftly upon her.

"Your life is not your own," he said. "Keep your hands off it."

"What use is it to anyone?"

"How can you tell? The example of patient suffering is in itself the most precious of all lessons to an impatient world."

The woman's answer was a terrible one. She raised her veil and stepped forward into the light.

"I wonder if you would bear it," she said.

It was horrible. No words can describe the framework of a face when the face itself is gone. Two living and beautiful brown eyes looking sadly out from that grisly ruin did but make the view more awful. Holmes held up his hand in a gesture of pity and protest, and together we left the room.

Two days later, when I called upon my friend, he pointed with some pride to a small blue bottle upon his mantelpiece. I picked it up. There was a red poison label. A pleasant almondy odour rose when I opened it.

"Prussic acid?" said 1.

"Exactly. It came by post. 'I send you my temptation. I will follow your advice.' That was the message. I think, Watson, we can guess the name of the brave woman who sent it."

THE ADVENTURE OF SHOSCOMBE OLD PLACE

Sherlock Holmes had been bending for a long time over a low-power microscope. Now he straightened himself up and looked round at me in triumph.

"It is glue, Watson," said he. "Unquestionably it is glue. Have a look at these scattered objects in the field!"

I stooped to the eyepiece and focused for my vision.

"Those hairs are threads from a tweed coat. The irregular gray masses are dust. There are epithelial scales on the left. Those brown blobs in the centre are undoubtedly glue."

"Well," I said, laughing, "I am prepared to take your word for it. Does anything depend upon it?"

"It is a very fine demonstration," he answered. "In the St. Pancras case you may remember that a cap was found beside the dead policeman. The accused man denies that it is his. But he is a picture-frame maker who habitually handles glue."

"Is it one of your cases?"

"No; my friend, Merivale, of the Yard, asked me to look into the case. Since I ran down that coiner by the zinc and copper filings in the seam of his cuff they have begun to realize the importance of the microscope." He looked impatiently at his watch. "I had a new client calling, but he is overdue. By the way, Watson, you know something of racing?"

"I ought to. I pay for it with about half my wound pension."

"Then I'll make you my 'Handy Guide to the Turf.' What about Sir Robert Norberton? Does the name recall anything?"

"Well, I should say so. He lives at Shoscombe Old Place, and I know it well, for my summer quarters were down there once. Norberton nearly came within your province once."

"How was that?"

"It was when he horsewhipped Sam Brewer, the well-known Curzon Street money-lender, on Newmarket Heath. He nearly killed the man."

"Ah, he sounds interesting! Does he often indulge in that way?"

"Well, he has the name of being a dangerous man. He is about the most daredevil rider in England - second in the Grand National a few years back. He is one of those men who have overshot their true generation. He should have been a buck in the days of the Regency - a boxer, an athlete, a plunger on the turf, a lover of fair ladies, and, by all account, so far down Queer Street that he may never find his way back again."

"Capital, Watson! A thumb-nail sketch. I seem to know the man. Now, can you give me some idea of Shoscombe Old Place?"

"Only that it is in the centre of Shoscombe Park, and that the famous Shoscombe stud and training quarters are to be found there."

"And the head trainer," said Holmes, "is John Mason. You need not look surprised at my knowledge, Watson, for this is a letter from him which I am unfolding. But let us have some more about Shoscombe. I seem to have struck a rich vein."

"There are the Shoscombe spaniels," said I. "You hear of them at every dog show. The most exclusive breed in England. They are the special pride of the lady of Shoscombe Old Place."

"Sir Robert Norberton's wife, I presume!"

"Sir Robert has never married. Just as well, I think, considering his prospects. He lives with his widowed sister, Lady Beatrice Falder."

"You mean that she lives with him?"

"No, no. The place belonged to her late husband, Sir James. Norberton has no claim on it at all. It is only a life interest and reverts to her husband's brother. Meantime, she draws the rents every year."

"And brother Robert, I suppose, spends the said rents?"

"That is about the size of it. He is a devil of a fellow and must lead her a most uneasy life. Yet I have heard that she is devoted to him. But what is amiss at Shoscombe?"

"Ah, that is just what I want to know. And here, I expect, is the man who can tell us."

The door had opened and the page had shown in a tall, clean-shaven man with the firm, austere expression which is only seen upon those who have to control horses or boys. Mr. John Mason had many of both under his sway, and he looked equal to the task. He bowed with cold self-possession and seated himself upon the chair to which Holmes had waved him.

"You had my note, Mr. Holmes?"

"Yes, but it explained nothing."

"It was too delicate a thing for me to put the details on paper. And too complicated. It was only face to face I could do it."

"Well, we are at your disposal."

"First of all, Mr. Holmes, I think that my employer, Sir Robert, has gone mad."

Holmes raised his eyebrows. "This is Baker Street, not Harley Street," said he. "But why do you say so?"

"Well, sir, when a man does one queer thing, or two queer things, there may be a meaning to it, but when everything he does is queer, then you begin to wonder. I believe Shoscombe Prince and the Derby have turned his brain."

"That is a colt you are running?"

"The best in England, Mr. Holmes. I should know, if anyone does. Now, I'll be plain with you, for I know you are gentlemen of honour and that it won't go beyond the room. Sir Robert has got to win this Derby. He's up to the neck, and it's his last chance. Everything he could raise or borrow is on the horse -and at fine odds, too! You can get forties now, but it was nearer the hundred when he began to back him."

"But how is that if the horse is so good?"

"The public don't know how good he is. Sir Robert has been too clever for the touts. He has the Prince's half-brother out for spins. You can't tell 'em apart. But there are two lengths in a furlong between them when it comes to a gallop. He thinks of nothing but the horse and the race. His whole life is on it. He's holding off the Jews till then. If the Prince fails him he is done."

"It seems a rather desperate gamble, but where does the madness come in?"

"Well, first of all, you have only to look at him. I don't believe he sleeps at night. He is down at the stables at all hours. His eyes are wild. It has all been too much for his nerves. Then there is his conduct to Lady Beatrice!"

"Ah! What is that?"

"They have always been the best of friends. They had the same tastes, the two of them, and she loved the horses as much as he did. Every day at the same hour she would drive down to see them - and, above all, she loved the Prince. He would prick up his ears when he heard the wheels on the gravel, and he would trot out each morning to the carriage to get his lump of sugar. But that's all over now."

"Why?"

"Well, she seems to have lost all interest in the horses. For a week now she has driven past the stables with never so much as 'Good-morning'!"

"You think there has been a quarrel?"

"And a bitter, savage, spiteful quarrel at that. Why else would he give away her pet spaniel that she loved as if he were her child? He gave it a few days ago to old Barnes, what keeps the Green Dragon, three miles off, at Crendall."

"That certainly did seem strange."

"Of course, with her weak heart and dropsy one couldn't expect that she could get about with him, but he spent two hours every evening in her room. He might well do what he could, for she has been a rare good friend to him. But that's all over, too. He never goes near her. And she takes it to heart. She is brooding and sulky and drinking, Mr. Holmes - drinking like a fish."

"Did she drink before this estrangement?"

"Well, she took her glass, but now it is often a whole bottle of an evening. So Stephens, the butler, told me. It's all changed, Mr. Holmes, and there is something damned rotten about it. But then, again, what is master doing down at the old church crypt at night? And who is the man that meets him there?"

Holmes rubbed his hands.

"Go on, Mr. Mason. You get more and more interesting."

"It was the butler who saw him go. Twelve o'clock at night and raining hard. So next night I was up at the house and, sure enough, master was off again. Stephens and I went after him, but it was jumpy work, for it would have been a bad job if he had seen us. He's a terrible man with his fists if he gets started, and no respecter of persons. So we were shy of getting too near, but we marked him down all light. It was the haunted crypt that he was making for, and there was a man waiting for him there."

"What is this haunted cryp?"

"Well, sir, there is an old ruined chapel in the park. It is so old that nobody could fix its date. And under it there's a crypt which has a bad name among us. It's a dark, damp, lonely place by day, but there are few in that county that would have the nerve to go near it at night. But master's not afraid. He never feared anything in his life. But what is he doing there in the night-time?"

"Wait a bit!" said Holmes. "You say there is another man there. It must be one of your own stablemen, or someone from the house! Surely you have only to spot who it is and question him?"

"It's no one I know."

"How can you say that?"

"Because I have seen him, Mr. Holmes. It was on that second night. Sir Robert turned and passed us - me and Stephens, quaking in the bushes like two bunny-rabbits, for there was a bit of moon that night. But we could hear the other moving about behind. We were not afraid of him. So we up when Sir Robert was gone and pretended we were just having a walk like in the moonlight, and so we came right on him as casual and innocent as you please. 'Hullo, mate! who may you be?' says I. I guess he had not heard us coming, so he looked over his shoulder with a face as if he had seen the devil coming out of hell. He let out a yell, and away he went as hard as he could lick it in the darkness. He could run! - I'll give him that. In a minute he was out of sight and hearing, and who he was, or what he was, we never found."

"But you saw him clearly in the moonlight?"

"Yes, I would swear to his yellow face - a mean dog, I should say. What could he have in common with Sir Robert?"

Holmes sat for some time lost in thought.

"Who keeps Lady Beatrice Falder company?" he asked at last.

"There is her maid, Carrie Evans. She has been with her this five years."

"And is, no doubt, devoted?"

Mr. Mason shuffled uncomfortably.

"She's devoted enough," he answered at last. "But I won't say to whom."

"Ah!" said Holmes.

"I can't tell tales out of school."

"I quite understand, Mr. Mason. Of course, the situation is clear enough. From Dr. Watson's description of Sir Robert I can realize that no woman is safe from him. Don't you think the quarrel between brother and sister may lie there?"

"Well, the scandal has been pretty clear for a long time."

"But she may not have seen it before. Let us suppose that she has suddenly found it out. She wants to get rid of the woman. Her brother will not permit it. The invalid, with her weak heart and inability to get about, has no means of enforcing her will. The hated maid is still tied to her. The lady refuses to speak, sulks, takes to drink. Sir Robert in his anger takes her pet spaniel away from her. Does not all this hang together?"

"Well, it might do - so far as it goes."

"Exactly! As far as it goes. How would all that bear upon the visits by night to the old crypt? We can't fit that into our plot."

"No, sir, and there is something more that I can't fit in. Why should Sir Robert want to dig up a dead body?"

Holmes sat up abruptly.

"We only found it out yesterday - after I had written to you. Yesterday Sir Robert had gone to London, so Stephens and I went down to the crypt. It was all in order, sir, except that in one corner was a bit of a human body."

"You informed the police, I suppose?"

Our visitor smiled grimly.

"Well, sir, I think it would hardly interest them. It was just the head and a few bones of a mummy. It may have been a thousand years old. But it wasn't there before. That I'll swear, and so will Stephens. It had been stowed away in a corner and covered over with a board, but that corner had always been empty before."

"What did you do with it?"

"Well, we just left it there."

"That was wise. You say Sir Robert was away yesterday. Has he returned?"

"We expect him back to-day."

"When did Sir Robert give away his sister's dog?"

"It was just a week ago to-day. The creature was howling outside the old wellhouse, and Sir Robert was in one of his tantrums that morning. He caught it up, and I thought he would have killed it. Then he gave it to Sandy Bain, the jockey, and told him to take the dog to old Barnes at the Green Dragon, for he never wished to see it again."

Holmes sat for some time in silent thought. He had lit the oldest and foulest of his pipes.

"I am not clear yet what you want me to do in this matter, Mr. Mason," he said at last. "Can't you make it more definite?"

"Perhaps this will make it more definite, Mr. Holmes," said our vistor.

He took a paper from his pocket, and, unwrapping it carefully, he exposed a charred fragment of bone.

Holmes examined it with interest.

"Where did you get it?"

"There is a central heating furnace in the cellar under Lady Beatrice's room. It's been off for some time, but Sir Robert complained of cold and had it on again.

"Harvey runs it - he's one of my lads. This very morning he came to me with this which he found raking out the cinders. He didn't like the look of it."

"Nor do I," said Holmes. "What do you make of it, Watson?"

It was burned to a black cinder, but there could be no question as to its anatomical significance.

"It's the upper condyle of a human femur," said I.

"Exactly!" Holmes had become very serious. "When does this lad tend to the furnace?"

"He makes it up every evening and then leaves it."

"Then anyone could visit it during the night?"

"Yes, sir."

"Can you enter it from outside?"

"There is one door from outside. There is another which leads up by a stair to the passage in which Lady Beatrice's room is situated."

"These are deep waters, Mr. Mason; deep and rather dirty. You say that Sir Robert was not at home last night?"

"No, sir."

"Then, whoever was burning bones, it was not he."

"That's true sir."

"What is the name of that inn you spoke of?"

"The Green Dragon."

"Is there good fishing in that part of Berkshire?" The honest trainer showed very clearly upon his face that he was convinced that yet another lunatic had come into his harassed life.

"Well, sir, I've heard there are trout in the mill-stream and pike in the Hall lake."

"That's good enough. Watson and I are famous fishermen - are we not, Watson? You may address us in future at the Green Dragon. We should reach it to-night. I need not say that we don't want to see you, Mr. Mason, but a note will reach us, and no doubt I could find you if I want you. When we have gone a little farther into the matter I will let you have a considered opinion."

Thus it was that on a bright May evening Holmes and I found ourselves alone in a first-class carriage and bound for the little "halt-on-demand" station of Shoscombe. The rack above us was covered with a formidable litter of rods, reels, and baskets. On reaching our destination a short drive took us to an old-fashioned tavern, where a sporting host, Josiah Barnes, entered eagerly into our plans for the extirpation of the fish of the neighbourhood.

"What about the Hall lake and the chance of a pike?" said Holmes.

The face of the innkeeper clouded.

"That wouldn't do, sir. You might chance to find yourself in the lake before you were through."

"How's that, then?"

"It's Sir Robert, sir. He's terrible jealous of touts. If you two strangers were as near his training quarters as that he'd be after you as sure as fate. He ain't taking no chances, Sir Robert ain't."

"I've heard he has a horse entered for the Derby."

"Yes, and a good colt, too. He carries all our money for the race, and all Sir Robert's into the bargain. By the way" - he looked at us with thoughtful eyes - "I suppose you ain't on the turf yourselves?"

"No, indeed. Just two weary Londoners who badly need some good Berkshire air."

"Well, you are in the right place for that. There is a deal of it lying about. But mind what I have told you about Sir Robert. He's the sort that strikes first and speaks afterwards. Keep clear of the park."

"Surely, Mr. Barnes! We certainly shall. By the way, that was a most beautiful spaniel that was whining in the hall."

"I should say it was. That was the real Shoscombe breed. There ain't a better in England."

"I am a dog-fancier myself," said Holmes. "Now, if it is a fair question, what would a prize dog like that cost?"

"More than I could pay, sir. It was Sir Robert himself who gave me this one. That's why I have to keep it on a lead. It would be off to the Hall in a jiffy if I gave it its head."

"We are getting some cards in our hand, Watson," said Holmes when the landlord had left us. "It's not an easy one to play, but we may see our way in a day or two. By the way, Sir Robert is still in London, I hear. We might, perhaps, enter the sacred domain to-night without fear of bodily assault. There are one or two points on which I should like reassurance."

"Have you any theory, Holmes?"

"Only this, Watson, that something happened a week or so ago which has cut deep into the life of the Shoscombe household. What is that something? We can only guess at it from its effects. They seem to be of a curiously mixed character. But that should surely help us. It is only the colourless, uneventful case which is hopeless.

"Let us consider our data. The brother no longer visits the beloved invalid sister. He gives away her favourite dog. Her dog, Watson! Does that suggest nothing to you?"

"Nothing but the brother's spite."

"Well, it might be so. Or - well, there is an alternative. Now to continue our review of the situation from the time that the quarrel, if there is a quarrel, began. The lady keeps her room, alters her habits, is not seen save when she drives out with her maid, refuses to stop at the stables to greet her favourite horse and apparently takes to drink. That covers the case, does it not?"

"Save for the business in the crypt."

"That is another line of thought. There are two, and I beg you will not tangle them. Line A, which concerns Lady Beatrice, has a vaguely sinister flavour, has it not?"

"I can make nothing of it."

"Well, now, let us take up line B, which concerns Sir Robert. He is mad keen upon winning the Derby. He is in the hands of the Jews, and may at any moment be sold up and his racing stables seized by his creditors. He is a daring and desperate man. He derives his income from his sister. His sister's maid is his willing tool. So far we seem to be on fairly safe ground, do we not?"

"But the crypt?"

"Ah, yes, the crypt! Let us suppose, Watson - it is merely a scandalous supposition, a hypothesis put forward for argument's sake - that Sir Robert has done away with his sister."

"My dear Holmes, it is out of the question."

"Very possibly, Watson. Sir Robert is a man of an honourable stock. But you do occasionally find a carrion crow among the eagles. Let us for a moment argue upon this supposition. He could not fly the country until he had realized his fortune, and that fortune could only be realized by bringing off this coup with Shoscombe Prince. Therefore, he has still to stand his ground. To do this he would have to dispose of the body of his victim, and he would also have to find a substitute who would impersonate her. With the maid as his confidante that would not be impossible. The woman's body might be conveyed to the crypt, which is a place so seldom visited, and it might be secretly destroyed at night in the furnace, leaving behind it such evidence as we have already seen. What say you to that, Watson?"

"Well, it is all possible if you grant the original monstrous supposition."

"I think that there is a small experiment which we may try to-morrow, Watson, in order to throw some light on the matter. Meanwhile, if we mean to keep up our characters, I suggest that we have our host in for a glass of his own wine and hold some high converse upon eels and dace, which seems to be the straight road to his affections. We may chance to come upon some useful local gossip in the process."

In the morning Holmes discovered that we had come without our spoon-bait for jack, which absolved us from fishing for the day. About eleven o'clock we started for a walk, and he obtained leave to take the black spaniel with us.

"This is the place," said he as we came to two high park gates with heraldic griffins towering above them. "About midday, Mr. Barnes informs me, the old lady takes a drive, and the carriage must slow down while the gates are opened. When it comes through, and before it gathers speed, I want you, Watson, to stop the coachman with some question. Never mind me. I shall stand behind this holly-bush and see what I can see."

It was not a long vigil. Within a quarter of an hour we saw the big open yellow barouche coming down the long avenue, with two splendid, high-stepping gray carriage horses in the shafts. Holmes crouched behind his bush with the dog. I stood unconnectedly swinging a cane in the roadway. A keeper ran out and the gates swung open.

The carriage had slowed to a walk, and I was able to get a good look at the occupants. A highly coloured young woman with flaxen hair and impudent eyes sat on the left. At her right was an elderly person with rounded back and a huddle of shawls about her face and shoulders which proclaimed the invalid. When the horses reached the highroad I held up my hand with an authoritative gesture, and as the coachman pulled up I inquired if Sir Robert was at Shoscombe Old Place.

At the same moment Holmes stepped out and released the spaniel. With a joyous cry it dashed forward to the carriage and sprang upon the step. Then in a moment its eager greeting changed to furious rage, and it snapped at the black skirt above it.

"Drive on! Drive on!" shrieked a harsh voice. The coachman lashed the horses, and we were left standing in the roadway.

"Well, Watson, that's done it," said Holmes as he fastened the lead to the neck of the excited spaniel. "He thought it was his mistress, and he found it was a stranger. Dogs don't make mistakes."

"But it was the voice of a man!" I cried.

"Exactly! We have added one card to our hand, Watson, but it needs careful playing, all the same."

My companion seemed to have no further plans for the day, and we did actually use our fishing tackle in the mill-stream with the result that we had a dish of trout for our supper. It was only after that meal that Holmes showed signs of renewed activity. Once more we found ourselves upon the same road as in the morning, which led us to the park gates. A tall, dark figure was awaiting us there, who proved to be our London acquaintance, Mr. John Mason, the trainer.

"Good-evening, gentlemen," said he. "I got your note, Mr. Holmes. Sir Robert has not returned yet, but I hear that he is expected to-night."

"How far is this crypt from the house?" asked Holmes.

"A good quarter of a mile."

"Then I think we can disregard him altogether."

"I can't afford to do that, Mr. Holmes. The moment he arrives he will want to see me to get the last news of Shoscombe Prince."

"I see! In that case we must work without you, Mr. Mason. You can show us the crypt and then leave us."

It was pitch-dark and without a moon, but Mason led us over the grass-lands until a dark mass loomed up in front of us which proved to be the ancient chapel. We entered the broken gap which was once the porch, and our guide, stumbling among heaps of loose masonry, picked his way to the corner of the building, where a steep stair led down into the crypt. Striking a match, he illuminated the melancholy place - dismal and evil-smelling, with ancient crumbling walls of rough-hewn stone, and piles of coffins, some of lead and some of stone, extending upon one side right up to the arched and groined roof which lost itself in the shadows above our heads. Holmes had lit his lantern, which shot a tiny tunnel of vivid yellow light upon the mournful scene. Its rays were reflected back from the coffin-plates, many of them adorned with the griffin and coronet of this old family which carried its honours even to the gate of Death.

"You spoke of some bones, Mr. Mason. Could you show them before you go?"

"They are here in this corner." The trainer strode across and then stood in silent surprise as our light was turned upon the place. "They are gone," said he.

"So I expected," said Holmes, chuckling. "I fancy the ashes of them might even now be found in that oven which had already consumed a part."

"But why in the world would anyone want to burn the bones of a man who has been dead a thousand years?" asked John Mason.

"That is what we are here to find out," said Holmes. "It may mean a long search, and we need not detain you. I fancy that we shall get our solution before morning."

When John Mason had left us, Holmes set to work making a very careful examination of the graves, ranging from a very ancient one, which appeared to be Saxon, in the centre, through a long line of Norman Hugos and Odos, until we reached the Sir William and Sir Denis Falder of the eighteenth century. It was an hour or more before Holmes came to a leaden coffin standing on end before the entrance to the vault. I heard his little cry of satisfaction and was aware from his hurried but purposeful movements that he had reached a goal. With his lens he was eagerly examining the edges of the heavy lid. Then he drew from his pocket a short jemmy, a box-opener, which he thrust into a chink, levering back the whole front, which seemed to be secured by only a couple of clamps. There was a rending, tearing sound as it gave way, but it had hardly hinged back and partly revealed the contents before we had an unforeseen interruption.

Someone was walking in the chapel above. It was the firm, rapid step of one who came with a definite purpose and knew well the ground upon which he walked. A light streamed down the stairs, and an instant later the man who bore it was framed in the Gothic archway. He was a terrible figure, huge in stature and fierce in manner. A large stable-lantern which he held in front of him shone upward upon a strong, heavily moustached face and angry eyes, which glared round him into every recess of the vault, finally fixing themselves with a deadly stare upon my companion and myself.

"Who the devil are you?" he thundered. "And what are you doing upon my property?" Then, as Holmes returned no answer he took a couple of steps forward and raised a heavy stick which he carried. "Do you hear me?" he cried. "Who are you? What are you doing here?" His cudgel quivered in the air.

But instead of shrinking Holmes advanced to meet him.

"I also have a question to ask you, Sir Robert," he said in his sternest tone. "Who is this? And what is it doing here?"

He turned and tore open the coffin-lid behind him. In the glare of the lantern I saw a body swathed in a sheet from head to foot with dreadful, witch-like features, all nose and chin, projecting at one end, the dim, glazed eyes staring from a discoloured and crumbling face.

The baronet had staggered back with a cry and supported himself against a stone sarcophagus.

"How came you to know of this?" he cried. And then, with some return of his truculent manner: "What business is it of yours?"

"My name is Sherlock Holmes," said my companion. "Possibly it is familiar to you. In any case, my business is that of every other good citizen - to uphold the law. It seems to me that you have much to answer for."

Sir Robert glared for a moment, but Holmes's quiet voice and cool, assured manner had their effect.

"Fore God, Mr. Holmes, it's all right," said he. "Appearances are against me, I'll admit, but I could act no otherwise."

"I should be happy to think so, but I fear your explanations must be before the police."

Sir Robert shrugged his broad shoulders.

"Well, if it must be, it must. Come up to the house and you can judge for yourself how the matter stands."

A quarter of an hour later we found ourselves in what I judge, from the lines of polished barrels behind glass covers, to be the gun-room of the old house. It was comfortably furnished, and here Sir Robert left us for a few moments. When he returned he had two companions with him; the one, the florid young woman whom we had seen in the carriage; the other, a small rat-faced man with a disagreeably furtive manner. These two wore an appearance of utter bewilderment, which showed that the baronet had not yet had time to explain to them the turn events had taken.

"There," said Sir Robert with a wave of his hand, "are Mr. and Mrs. Norlett. Mrs. Norlett, under her maiden name of Evans, has for some years been my sister's confidential maid. I have brought them here because I feel that my best course is to explain the true position to you, and they are the two people upon earth who can substantiate what I say."

"Is this necessary, Sir Robert? Have you thought what you are doing?" cried the woman.

"As to me, I entirely disclaim all responsibility," said her husband.

Sir Robert gave him a glance of contempt. "I will take all responsibility," said he. "Now, Mr. Holmes, listen to a plain statement of the facts."

"You have clearly gone pretty deeply into my affairs or I should not have found you where I did. Therefore, you know already, in all probability, that I am running a dark horse for the Derby and that everything depends upon my success. If I win, all is easy. If I lose - well, I dare not think of that!"

"I understand the position," said Holmes.

"I am dependent upon my sister, Lady Beatrice, for everything. But it is well known that her interest in the estate is for her own life only. For myself, I am deeply in the hands of the Jews. I have always known that if my sister were to die my creditors would be on to my estate like a flock of vultures. Everything would be seized - my stables, my horses - everything. Well, Mr. Holmes, my sister did die just a week ago."

"And you told no one!"

"What could I do? Absolute ruin faced me. If I could stave things off for three weeks all would be well. Her maid's husband - this man here - is an actor. It came into our heads - it came into my head - that he could for that short period personate my sister. It was but a case of appearing daily in the carriage, for no one need enter her room save the maid. It was not difficult to arrange. My sister died of the dropsy which had long afflicted her."

"That will be for a coroner to decide."

"Her doctor would certify that for months her symptoms have threatened such an end."

"Well, what did you do?"

"The body could not remain there. On the first night Norlett and I carried it out to the old well-house, which is now never used. We were followed, however, by her pet spaniel, which yapped continually at the door, so I felt some safer place was needed. I got rid of the spaniel, and we carried the body to the crypt of the church. There was no indignity or irreverence, Mr. Holmes. I do not feel that I have wronged the dead."

"Your conduct seems to me inexcusable, Sir Robert."

The baronet shook his head impatiently. "It is easy to preach," said he. "Perhaps you would have felt differently if you had been in my position. One cannot see all one's hopes and all one's plans shattered at the last moment and make no effort to save them. It seemed to me that it would be no unworthy resting-place if we put her for the time in one of the coffins of her husband's ancestors lying in what is still consecrated ground. We opened such a coffin, removed the contents, and placed her as you have seen her. As to the old relics which we took out, we could not leave them on the floor of the crypt. Norlett and I removed them, and he descended at night and burned them in the central furnace. There is my story, Mr. Holmes, though how you forced my hand so that I have to tell it is more than I can say."

Holmes sat for some time lost in thought.

"There is one flaw in your narrative, Sir Robert," he said at last. "Your bets on the race, and therefore your hopes for the future, would hold good even if your creditors seized your estate."

"The horse would be part of the estate. What do they care for my bets? As likely as not they would not run him at all. My chief creditor is, unhappily, my most bitter enemy - a rascally fellow, Sam Brewer, whom I was once compelled to horsewhip on Newmarket Heath. Do you suppose that he would try to save me?"

"Well, Sir Robert," said Holmes, rising, "this matter must, of course, be referred to the police. It was my duty to bring the facts to light, and there I must leave it. As to the morality or decency of your conduct, it is not for me to express an opinion. It is nearly midnight, Watson, and I think we may make our way back to our humble abode."

It is generally known now that this singular episode ended upon a happier note than Sir Robert's actions deserved. Shoscombe Prince did win the Derby, the sporting owner did net eighty thousand pounds in bets, and the creditors did hold their hand until the race was over, when they were paid in full, and enough was left to reestablish Sir Robert in a fair position in life. Both police and coroner took a lenient view of the transaction, and beyond a mild censure for the delay in registering the lady's decease, the lucky owner got away scatheless from this strange incident in a career which has now outlived its shadows and promises to end in an honoured old age.

THE ADVENTURE OF THE RETIRED COLOURMAN

Sherlock Holmes was in a melancholy and philosophic mood that morning. His alert practical nature was subject to such reactions.

"Did you see him?" he asked.

"You mean the old fellow who has just gone out?"

"Precisely."

"Yes, I met him at the door."

"What did you think of him?"

"A pathetic, futile, broken creature."

"Exactly, Watson. Pathetic and futile. But is not all life pathetic and futile? Is not his story a microcosm of the whole? We reach. We grasp. And what is left in our hands at the end? A shadow. Or worse than a shadow - misery."

"Is he one of your clients?"

"Well, I suppose I may call him so. He has been sent on by the Yard. Just as medical men occasionally send their incurables to a quack. They argue that they can do nothing more, and that whatever happens the patient can be no worse than he is."

"What is the matter?"

Holmes took a rather soiled card from the table. "Josiah Amberley. He says he was junior partner of Brickfall and Amberley, who are manufacturers of artistic materials. You will see their names upon paint-boxes. He made his little pile, retired from business at the age of sixty-one, bought a house at Lewisham and settled down to rest after a life of ceaseless grind. One would think his future was tolerably assured."

"Yes, indeed."

Holmes glanced over some notes which he had scribbled upon the back of an envelope.

"Retired in 1896, Watson. Early in 1897 he married a woman twenty years younger than himself - a good-looking woman, too. if the photograph does not flatter. A competence, a wife, leisure - it seemed a straight road which lay before him. And yet within two years he is, as you have seen, as broken and miserable a creature as crawls beneath the sun."

"But what has happened?"

"The old story, Watson. A treacherous friend and a fickle wife. It would appear that Amberley has one hobby in life, and it is chess. Not far from him at Lewisham there lives a young doctor who is also a chess-player. I have noted his name as Dr. Ray Ernest. Ernest was frequently in the house, and an intimacy between him and Mrs. Amberley was a natural sequence, for you must admit that our unfortunate client has few outward graces, whatever his inner virtues may be. The couple went off together last week - destination untraced. What is more, the faithless spouse carried off the old man's deed-box as her personal luggage with a good part of his life's savings within. Can we find the lady? Can we save the money? A commonplace problem so far as it has developed, and yet a vital one for Josiah Amberley."

"What will you do about it?"

"Well, the immediate question, my dear Watson, happens to be, What will you do? - if you will be good enough to understudy me. You know that I am preoccupied with this case of the two Coptic Patriarchs, which should come to a head to-day. I really have not time to go out to Lewisham, and yet evidence taken on the spot has a special value. The old fellow was quite insistent that I should go, but I explained my difficulty. He is prepared to meet a representative."

"By all means," I answered. "I confess I don't see that I can be of much service, but I am willing to do my best." And so it was that on a summer afternoon I set forth to Lewisham, little dreaming that within a week the affair in which I was engaging would be the eager debate of all England.

It was late that evening before I returned to Baker Street and gave an account of my mission. Holmes lay with his gaunt figure stretched in his deep chair, his pipe curling forth slow wreaths of acrid tobacco, while his eyelids drooped over his eyes so lazily that he might almost have been asleep were it not that at any halt or questionable passage of my narrative they half lifted, and two gray eyes, as bright and keen as rapiers, transfixed me with their searching glance.

"The Haven is the name of Mr. Josiah Amberley's house," I explained. "I think it would interest you, Holmes. It is like some penurious patrician who has sunk into the company of his inferiors. You know that particular quarter, the monotonous brick streets, the weary suburban highways. Right in the middle of them, a little island of ancient culture and comfort, lies this old home, surrounded by a high sun-baked wall mottled with lichens and topped with moss, the sort of wall -"

"Cut out the poetry, Watson," said Holmes severely. "I note that it was a high brick wall."

"Exactly. I should not have known which was The Haven had I not asked a lounger who was smoking in the street. I have a reason for mentioning him. He was a tall, dark, heavily moustached, rather military-looking man. He nodded in answer to my inquiry and gave me a curiously questioning glance, which came back to my memory a little later."

"I had hardly entered the gateway before I saw Mr. Amberley coming down the drive. I only had a glimpse of him this morning, and he certainly gave me the impression of a strange creature, but when I saw him in full light his appearance was even more abnormal."

"I have, of course, studied it, and yet I should be interested to have your impression," said Holmes.

"He seemed to me like a man who was literally bowed down by care. His back was curved as though he carried a heavy burden. Yet he was not the weakling that I had at first imagined, for his shoulders and chest have the framework of a giant, though his figure tapers away into a pair of spindled legs."

"Left shoe wrinkled, right one smooth."

"I did not observe that."

"No, you wouldn't. I spotted his artificial limb. But proceed."

"I was struck by the snaky locks of grizzled hair which curled from under his old straw hat, and his face with its fierce, eager expression and the deeply lined features."

"Very good, Watson. What did he say?"

"He began pouring out the story of his grievances. We walked down the drive together, and of course I took a good look round. I have never seen a worse-kept place. The garden was all running to seed, giving me an impression of wild neglect in which the plants had been allowed to find the way of Nature rather than of art. How any decent woman could have tolerated such a state of things, I don't know. The house, too, was slatternly to the last degree, but the poor man seemed himself to be aware of it and to be trying to remedy it, for a great pot of green paint stood in the centre of the hall, and he was carrying a thick brush in his left hand. He had been working on the woodwork."

"He took me into his dingy sanctum, and we had a long chat. Of course, he was disappointed that you had not come yourself. 'I hardly expected,' he said, 'that so humble an individual as myself, especially after my heavy financial loss, could obtain the complete attention of so famous a man as Mr. Sherlock Holmes.'"

"I assured him that the financial question did not arise. 'No of course, it is art for art's sake with him,' said he, 'but even on the artistic side of crime he might have found something here to study. And human nature, Dr. Watson - the black ingratitude of it all! When did I ever refuse one of her requests? Was ever a woman so pampered? And that young man - he might have been my own son. He had the run of my house. And yet see how they have treated me! Oh, Dr. Watson, it is a dreadful, dreadful world'!"

"That was the burden of his song for an hour or more. He had, it seems, no suspicion of an intrigue. They lived alone save for a woman who comes in by the day and leaves every evening at six. On that particular evening old Amberley, wishing to give his wife a treat, had taken two upper circle seats at the Haymarket Theatre. At the last moment she had complained of a headache and had refused to go. He had gone alone. There seemed to be no doubt about the fact, for he produced the unused ticket which he had taken for his wife."

"That is remarkable - most remarkable," said Holmes, whose interest in the case seemed to be rising. "Pray continue, Watson. I find your narrative most arresting. Did you personally examine this ticket? You did not, perchance, take the number?"

"It so happens that I did," I answered with some pride. "It chanced to be my old school number, thirty-one, and so is stuck in my head."

"Excellent, Watson! His seat, then, was either thirty or thirty-two."

"Quite so," I answered with some mystification. "And on B row."

"That is most satisfactory. What else did he tell you?"

"He showed me his strong-room, as he called it. It really is a strong-room - like a bank -with iron door and shutter - burglarproof, as he claimed. However, the woman seems to have had a duplicate key, and between them they had carried off some seven thousand pounds' worth of cash and securities."

"Securities! How could they dispose of those?"

"He said that he had given the police a list and that he hoped they would be unsaleable. He had got back from the theatre about midnight and found the place plundered, the door and window open, and the fugitives gone. There was no letter or message, nor has he heard a word since. He at once gave the alarm to the police."

Holmes brooded for some minutes.

"You say he was painting. What was he painting?"

"Well, he was painting the passage. But he had already painted the door and woodwork of this room I spoke of."

"Does it not strike you as a strange occupation in the circumstances?"

"'One must do something to ease an aching heart.' That was his own explanation. It was eccentric, no doubt, but he is clearly an eccentric man. He tore up one of his wife's photographs in my presence - tore it up furiously in a tempest of passion. 'I never wish to see her damned face again,' he shrieked."

"Anything more, Watson?"

"Yes, one thing which struck me more than anything else. I had driven to the Blackheath Station and had caught my train there when, just as it was starting, I saw a man dart into the carriage next to my own. You know that I have a quick eye for faces, Holmes. It was undoubtedly the tall, dark man whom I had addressed in the street. I saw him once more at London Bridge, and then I lost him in the crowd. But I am convinced that he was following me."

"No doubt! No doubt!" said Holmes. "A tall, dark, heavily moustached man, you say, with gray-tinted sun-glasses?"

"Holmes, you are a wizard. I did not say so, but he had gray-tinted sun-glasses."

"And a Masonic tie-pin?"

"Holmes!"

"Quite simple, my dear Watson. But let us get down to what is practical. I must admit to you that the case, which seemed to me to be so absurdly simple as to be hardly worth my notice, is rapidly assuming a very different aspect. It is true that though in your mission you have missed everything of importance, yet even those things which have obtruded themselves upon your notice give rise to serious thought."

"What have I missed?"

"Don't be hurt, my dear fellow. You know that I am quite impersonal. No one else would have done better. Some possibly not so well. But clearly you have missed some vital points. What is the opinion of the neighbours about this man Amberley and his wife? That surely is of importance. What of Dr. Ernest? Was he the gay Lothario one would expect? With your natural advantages, Watson, every lady is your helper and accomplice. What about the girl at the post-office, or the wife of the greengrocer? I can picture you whispering soft nothings with the young lady at the Blue Anchor, and receiving hard somethings in exchange. All this you have left undone."

"It can still be done."

"It has been done. Thanks to the telephone and the help of the Yard, I can usually get my essentials without leaving this room. As a matter of fact, my information confirms the man's story. He has the local repute of being a miser as well as a harsh and exacting husband. That he had a large sum of money in that strong-room of his is certain. So also is it that young Dr. Ernest, an unmarried man, played chess with Amberley, and probably played the fool with his wife. All this seems plain sailing, and one would think that there was no more to be said - and yet! -and yet!"

"Where lies the difficulty?"

"In my imagination, perhaps. Well, leave it there, Watson. Let us escape from this weary workaday world by the side door of music. Carina sings to-night at the Albert Hall, and we still have time to dress, dine, and enjoy."

In the morning I was up betimes, but some toast crumbs and two empty eggshells told me that my companion was earlier still. I found a scribbled note upon the table.

DEAR Watson:

There are one or two points of contact which I should wish to establish with Mr. Josiah Amberley. When I have done so we can dismiss the case - or not. I would only ask you to be on hand about three o'clock, as I conceive it possible that I may want you.

S.H.

I saw nothing of Holmes all day, but at the hour named he returned, grave, preoccupied, and aloof. At such times it was wiser to leave him to himself.

"Has Amberley been here yet?"

"No."

"Ah! I am expecting him."

He was not disappointed, for presently the old fellow arrived with a very worried and puzzled expression upon his austere face.

"I've had a telegram, Mr. Holmes. I can make nothing of it." He handed it over, and Holmes read it aloud.

"Come at once without fail. Can give you information as to your recent loss."

"ELMAN"

"The Vicarage"

"Dispatched at 2:10 from Little Purlington," said Holmes. "Little Purlington is in Essex, I believe, not far from Frinton. Well, of course you will start at once. This is evidently from a responsible person, the vicar of the place. Where is my Crockford? Yes, here we have him: 'J.C.

Elman, M.A., Living of Moosmoor cum Little Purlington.' Look up the trains, Watson."

"There is one at 5:20 from Liverpool Street."

"Excellent. You had best go with him, Watson. He may need help or advice. Clearly we have come to a crisis in this affair."

But our client seemed by no means eager to start.

"It's perfectly absurd, Mr. Holmes," he said. "What can this man possibly know of what has occurred? It is waste of time and money."

"He would not have telegraphed to you if he did not know something. Wire at once that you are coming."

"I don't think I shall go."

Holmes assumed his sternest aspect.

"It would make the worst possible impression both on the police and upon myself, Mr. Amberley, if when so obvious a clue arose you should refuse to follow it up. We should feel that you were not really in earnest in this investigation."

Our client seemed horrified at the suggestion.

"Why, of course I shall go if you look at it in that way," said he. "On the face of it, it seems absurd to suppose that this parson knows anything, but if you think -"

"I do think," said Holmes with emphasis, and so we were launched upon our journey. Holmes took me aside before we left the room and gave me one word of counsel, which showed that he considered the matter to be of importance. "Whatever you do, see that he really does go," said he. "Should he break away or return, get to the nearest telephone exchange and send the single word 'Bolted.' I will arrange here that it shall reach me wherever I am."

Little Purlington is not an easy place to reach, for it is on a branch line. My remembrance of the journey is not a pleasant one, for the weather was hot, the train slow, and my companion sullen and silent, hardly talking at all save to make an occasional sardonic remark as to the futility of our proceedings. When we at last reached the little station it was a two-mile drive before we came to the Vicarage, where a big, solemn, rather pompous clergyman received us in his study. Our telegram lay before him.

SIR ARTHUR CONAN DOYLE

"Well, gentlemen," he asked, "what can I do for you?"

"We came," I explained, "in answer to your wire."

"My wire! I sent no wire."

"I mean the wire which you sent to Mr. Josiah Amberley about his wife and his money."

"If this is a joke, sir, it is a very questionable one," said the vicar angrily. "I have never heard of the gentleman you name, and I have not sent a wire to anyone."

Our client and I looked at each other in amazement.

"Perhaps there is some mistake," said I; "are there perhaps two vicarages? Here is the wire itself, signed Elman and dated from the Vicarage."

"There is only one vicarage, sir, and only one vicar, and this wire is a scandalous forgery, the origin of which shall certainly be investigated by the police. Meanwhile, I can see no possible object in prolonging this interview."

So Mr. Amberley and I found ourselves on the roadside in what seemed to me to be the most primitive village in England. We made for the telegraph office, but it was already closed. There was a telephone, however, at the little Railway Arms, and by it I got into touch with Holmes, who shared in our amazement at the result of our journey.

"Most singular!" said the distant voice. "Most remarkable! I much fear, my dear Watson, that there is no return train to-night. I have unwittingly condemned you to the horrors of a country inn. However, there is always Nature, Watson - Nature and Josiah Amberley - you can be in close commune with both." I heard his dry chuckle as he turned away.

It was soon apparent to me that my companion's reputation as a miser was not undeserved. He had grumbled at the expense of the journey, had insisted upon travelling third-class, and was now clamorous in his objections to the hotel bill. Next morning, when we did at last arrive in London, it was hard to say which of us was in the worse humour.

"You had best take Baker Street as we pass," said I. "Mr. Holmes may have some fresh instructions."

"If they are not worth more than the last ones they are not of much use," said Amberley with a malevolent scowl. None the less, he kept me company. I had already warned Holmes by telegram of the hour of our arrival, but we found a message waiting that he was at Lewisham and would expect us there. That was a surprise, but an even greater one was to find that he was not alone in the sitting-room of our client. A stern-looking, impassive man sat beside him, a dark man with gray-tinted glasses and a large Masonic pin projecting from his tie.

"This is my friend Mr. Barker," said Holmes. "He has been interesting himself also in your business, Mr. Josiah Amberley, though we have been working independently. But we both have the same question to ask you!"

Mr. Amberley sat down heavily. He sensed impending danger. I read it in his straining eyes and his twitching features.

"What is the question, Mr. Holmes?"

"Only this: What did you do with the bodies?"

The man sprang to his feet with a hoarse scream. He clawed into the air with his bony hands. His mouth was open, and for the instant he looked like some horrible bird of prey. In a flash we got a glimpse of the real Josiah Amberley, a misshapen demon with a soul as distorted as his body. As he fell back into his chair he clapped his hand to his lips as if to stifle a cough. Holmes sprang at his throat like a tiger and twisted his face towards the ground. A white pellet fell from between his gasping lips.

"No short cuts, Josiah Amberley. Things must be done decently and in order. What about it, Barker?"

"I have a cab at the door," said our taciturn companion.

"It is only a few hundred yards to the station. We will go together. You can stay here, Watson. I shall be back within half an hour."

The old colourman had the strength of a lion in that great trunk of his, but he was helpless in the hands of the two experienced man-handlers. Wriggling and twisting he was dragged to the waiting cab, and I was left to my solitary vigil in the ill-omened house. In less time than he had named, however, Holmes was back, in company with a smart young police inspector.

"I've left Barker to look after the formalities," said Holmes. "You had not met Barker, Watson. He is my hated rival upon the Surrey shore.

When you said a tall dark man it was not difficult for me to complete the picture. He has several good cases to his credit, has he not, Inspector?"

"He has certainly interfered several times," the inspector answered with reserve.

"His methods are irregular, no doubt, like my own. The irregulars are useful sometimes, you know. You, for example, with your compulsory warning about whatever he said being used against him, could never have bluffed this rascal into what is virtually a confession."

"Perhaps not. But we get there all the same, Mr. Holmes. Don't imagine that we had not formed our own views of this case, and that we would not have laid our hands on our man. You will excuse us for feeling sore when you jump in with methods which we cannot use, and so rob us of the credit."

"There shall be no such robbery, MacKinnon. I assure you that I efface myself from now onward, and as to Barker, he has done nothing save what I told him."

The inspector seemed considerably relieved.

"That is very handsome of you, Mr. Holmes. Praise or blame can matter little to you, but it is very different to us when the newspapers begin to ask questions."

"Quite so. But they are pretty sure to ask questions anyhow, so it would be as well to have answers. What will you say, for example, when the intelligent and enterprising reporter asks you what the exact points were which aroused your suspicion, and finally gave you a certain conviction as to the real facts?"

The inspector looked puzzled.

"We don't seem to have got any real facts yet, Mr. Holmes. You say that the prisoner, in the presence of three witnesses, practically confessed by trying to commit suicide, that he had murdered his wife and her lover. What other facts have you?"

"Have you arranged for a search?"

"There are three constables on their way."

"Then you will soon get the clearest fact of all. The bodies cannot be far away. Try the cellars and the garden. It should not take long to dig up the likely places. This house is older than the water-pipes. There must be a disused well somewhere. Try your luck there."

"But how did you know of it, and how was it done?"

"I'll show you first how it was done, and then I will give the explanation which is due to you, and even more to my longsuffering friend here, who has been invaluable throughout. But, first, I would give you an insight into this man's mentality. It is a very unusual one - so much so that I think his destination is more likely to be Broadmoor than the scaffold. He has, to a high degree, the sort of mind which one associates with the mediaeval Italian nature rather than with the modern Briton. He was a miserable miser who made his wife so wretched by his niggardly ways that she was a ready prey for any adventurer. Such a one came upon the scene in the person of this chess-playing doctor. Amberley excelled at chess - one mark, Watson, of a scheming mind. Like all misers, he was a jealous man, and his jealousy became a frantic mania. Rightly or wrongly, he suspected an intrigue. He determined to have his revenge, and he planned it with diabolical cleverness. Come here!"

Holmes led us along the passage with as much certainty as if he had lived in the house and halted at the open door of the strong-room.

"Pooh! What an awful smell of paint!" cried the inspector.

"That was our first clue," said Holmes. "You can thank Dr. Watson's observation for that, though he failed to draw the inference. It set my foot upon the trail. Why should this man at such a time be filling his house with strong odours? Obviously, to cover some other smell which he wished to conceal - some guilty smell which would suggest suspicions. Then came the idea of a room such as you see here with iron door and shutter - a hermetically sealed room. Put those two facts together, and whither do they lead? I could only determine that by examining the house myself. I was already certain that the case was serious, for I had examined the box-office chart at the Haymarket Theatre - another of Dr. Watson's bull's-eyes - and ascertained that neither B thirty nor thirty-two of the upper circle had been occupied that night. Therefore, Amberley had not been to the theatre, and his alibi fell to the ground. He made a bad slip when he allowed my astute friend to notice the number of the seat taken for his wife. The question now arose how I might be able to examine the house. I sent an agent to the most impossible village I could think of, and summoned my man to it at such an hour that he could not possibly get back. To prevent any miscarriage, Dr. Watson accompanied him. The good vicar's name I took, of course, out of my Crockford. Do I make it all clear to you?"

"It is masterly," said the inspector in an awed voice.

"There being no fear of interruption I proceeded to burgle the house. Burglary has always been an alternative profession had I cared to adopt it, and I have little doubt that I should have come to the front. Observe what I found. You see the gas-pipe along the skirting here. Very good. It rises in the angle of the wall, and there is a tap here in the corner. The pipe runs out into the strong-room, as you can see, and ends in that plaster rose in the centre of the ceiling, where it is concealed by the ornamentation. That end is wide open. At any moment by turning the outside tap the room could be flooded with gas. With door and shutter closed and the tap full on I would not give two minutes of conscious sensation to anyone shut up in that little chamber. By what devilish device he decoyed them there I do not know, but once inside the door they were at his mercy."

The inspector examined the pipe with interest. "One of our officers mentioned the smell of gas," said he, "but of course the window and door were open then, and the paint - or some of it - was already about. He had begun the work of painting the day before, according to his story. But what next, Mr. Holmes?"

"Well, then came an incident which was rather unexpected to myself. I was slipping through the pantry window in the early dawn when I felt a hand inside my collar, and a voice said: 'Now, you rascal, what are you doing in there?' When I could twist my head round I looked into the tinted spectacles of my friend and rival, Mr. Barker. It was a curious foregathering and set us both smiling. It seems that he had been engaged by Dr. Ray Ernest's family to make some investigations and had come to the same conclusion as to foul play. He had watched the house for some days and had spotted Dr. Watson as one of the obviously suspicious characters who had called there. He could hardly arrest Watson, but when he saw a man actually climbing out of the pantry window there came a limit to his restraint. Of course, I told him how matters stood and we continued the case together."

"Why him? Why not us?"

"Because it was in my mind to put that little test which answered so admirably. I fear you would not have gone so far."

The inspector smiled.

"Well, maybe not. I understand that I have your word, Mr. Holmes, that you step right out of the case now and that you turn all your results over to us."

"Certainly, that is always my custom."

"Well, in the name of the force I thank you. It seems a clear case, as you put it, and there can't be much difficulty over the bodies."

"I'll show you a grim little bit of evidence," said Holmes, "and I am sure Amberley himself never observed it. You'll get results, Inspector, by always putting yourself in the other fellow's place, and thinking what you would do yourself. It takes some imagination, but it pays. Now, we will suppose that you were shut up in this little room, had not two minutes to live, but wanted to get even with the fiend who was probably mocking at you from the other side of the door. What would you do?"

"Write a message."

"Exactly. You would like to tell people how you died. No use writing on paper. That would be seen. If you wrote on the wall someone might rest upon it. Now, look here! Just above the skirting is scribbled with a purple indelible pencil: 'We we -' That's all.

"What do you make of that?"

"Well, it's only a foot above the ground. The poor devil was on the floor dying when he wrote it. He lost his senses before he could finish."

"He was writing, 'We were murdered.'"

"That's how I read it. If you find an indelible pencil on the body -"

"We'll look out for it, you may be sure. But those securities? Clearly there was no robbery at all. And yet he did possess those bonds. We verified that."

"You may be sure he has them hidden in a safe place. When the whole elopement had passed into history, he would suddenly discover them and announce that the guilty couple had relented and sent back the plunder or had dropped it on the way."

"You certainly seem to have met every difficulty," said the inspector. "Of course, he was bound to call us in, but why he should have gone to you I can't understand."

"Pure swank!" Holmes answered. "He felt so clever and so sure of himself that he imagined no one could touch him. He could say to any suspicious neighbour, 'Look at the steps I have taken. I have consulted not only the police but even Sherlock Holmes.'"

The inspector laughed.

"We must forgive you your 'even,' Mr. Holmes," said he "it's as workmanlike a job as I can remember."

A couple of days later my friend tossed across to me a copy of the bi-weekly North Surrey Observer. Under a series of flaming headlines, which began with "The Haven Horror" and ended with "Brilliant Police Investigation," there was a packed column of print which gave the first consecutive account of the affair. The concluding paragraph is typical of the whole. It ran thus:

The remarkable acumen by which Inspector MacKinnon deduced from the smell of paint that some other smell, that of gas, for example, might be concealed; the bold deduction that the strong-room might also be the death-chamber, and the subsequent inquiry which led to the discovery of the bodies in a disused well, cleverly concealed by a dog kennel, should live in the history of crime as a standing example of the intelligence of our professional detectives.

"Well, well, MacKinnon is a good fellow," said Holmes with a tolerant smile. "You can file it in our archives, Watson. Some day the true story may be told."

The Parasite

THE PARASITE

I

March 24. The spring is fairly with us now. Outside my laboratory window the great chestnut-tree is all covered with the big, glutinous, gummy buds, some of which have already begun to break into little green shuttlecocks. As you walk down the lanes you are conscious of the rich, silent forces of nature working all around you. The wet earth smells fruitful and luscious. Green shoots are peeping out everywhere. The twigs are stiff with their sap; and the moist, heavy English air is laden with a faintly resinous perfume. Buds in the hedges, lambs beneath them - everywhere the work of reproduction going forward!

I can see it without, and I can feel it within. We also have our spring when the little arterioles dilate, the lymph flows in a brisker stream, the glands work harder, winnowing and straining. Every year nature readjusts the whole machine. I can feel the ferment in my blood at this very moment, and as the cool sunshine pours through my window I could dance about in it like a gnat. So I should, only that Charles Sadler would rush upstairs to know what was the matter. Besides, I must remember that I am Professor Gilroy. An old professor may afford to be natural, but when fortune has given one of the first chairs in the university to a man of four-and-thirty he must try and act the part consistently.

What a fellow Wilson is! If I could only throw the same enthusiasm into physiology that he does into psychology, I should become a Claude Bernard at the least. His whole life and soul and energy work to one end. He drops to sleep collating his results of the past day, and he wakes to plan his researches for the coming one. And yet, outside the narrow circle who follow his proceedings, he gets so little credit for it. Physiology is a recognized science. If I add even a brick to the edifice, everyone sees and applauds it. But Wilson is trying to dig the foundations for a science of the future. His work is underground and does not show. Yet he goes on uncomplainingly, corresponding with a hundred semi-maniacs in the hope of finding one reliable witness, sifting a hundred lies on the chance of gaining one little speck of truth, collating old books, devouring new ones, experimenting, lecturing, trying to light up in others the fiery interest which is consuming him. I am filled with wonder and admiration when I think of him, and yet, when he asks me to associate myself with his researches, I am compelled to tell him that, in their present state, they offer little attraction to a man who is devoted to exact science. If he could show me something positive and objective, I might then be tempted to approach the question from its physiological side. So long as half his subjects are tainted with charlatanerie and the other half with hysteria, we physiologists must content ourselves with the body and leave the mind to our descendants.

No doubt I am a materialist. Agatha says that I am a rank one. I tell her that is an excellent reason for shortening our engagement, since I am in such urgent need of her spirituality. And yet I may claim to be a curious example of the effect of education upon temperament, for by nature I am, unless I deceive myself, a highly psychic man. I was a nervous, sensitive boy, a dreamer, a somnambulist, full of impressions and intuitions. My black hair, my dark eyes, my thin, olive face, my tapering fingers, are all characteristic of my real temperament, and cause experts like Wilson to claim me as their own. But my brain is soaked with exact knowledge. I have trained myself to deal only with fact and with proof. Surmise and fancy have no place in my scheme of thought. Show me what I can see with my microscope, cut with my scalpel, weigh in my balance, and I will devote a lifetime to its investigation. But when you ask me to study feelings, impressions, suggestions, you ask me to do what is distasteful and even demoralizing. A departure from pure reason affects me like an evil smell or a musical discord.

Which is a very sufficient reason why I am a little loath to go to Professor Wilson's tonight. Still I feel that I could hardly get out of the invitation without positive rudeness; and, now that Mrs. Marden and Agatha are going, of course I would not if I could. But I had rather meet them anywhere else. I know that Wilson would draw me into this nebulous semi-science of his if he could. In his enthusiasm he is perfectly impervious to hints or remonstrances. Nothing short of a positive quarrel will make him realize my aversion to the whole business. I have no doubt that he has some new mesmerist or clairvoyant or medium or trickster of some sort whom he is going to exhibit to us, for even his entertainments bear upon his hobby. Well, it will be a treat for Agatha, at any rate. She is interested in it, as woman usually is in whatever is vague and mystical and indefinite.

10.50 P.M. This diary-keeping of mine is, I fancy, the outcome of that scientific habit of mind about which I wrote this morning. I like to register impressions while they are fresh. Once a day at least I endeavor to define my own mental position. It is a useful piece of self-analysis, and has, I fancy, a steadying effect upon the character. Frankly, I must confess that my own needs what stiffening I can give it. I fear that, after all, much of my neurotic temperament survives, and that I am far from that cool, calm precision which characterizes Murdoch or Pratt-Haldane. Otherwise, why should the tomfoolery which I have witnessed this evening have set my nerves thrilling so that even now I am all unstrung? My only comfort is that neither Wilson nor Miss Penclosa nor even Agatha could have possibly known my weakness.

And what in the world was there to excite me? Nothing, or so little that it will seem ludicrous when I set it down.

The Mardens got to Wilson's before me. In fact, I was one of the last to arrive and found the room crowded. I had hardly time to say a word to Mrs. Marden and to Agatha, who was looking charming in white and pink, with glittering wheat-ears in her hair, when Wilson came twitching at my sleeve.

"You want something positive, Gilroy," said he, drawing me apart into a corner. "My dear fellow, I have a phenomenon - a phenomenon!"

I should have been more impressed had I not heard the same before. His sanguine spirit turns every fire-fly into a star.

"No possible question about the bona fides this time," said he, in answer, perhaps, to some little gleam of amusement in my eyes. "My wife has known her for many years. They both come from Trinidad, you know.

Miss Penclosa has only been in England a month or two, and knows no one outside the university circle, but I assure you that the things she has told us suffice in themselves to establish clairvoyance upon an absolutely scientific basis. There is nothing like her, amateur or professional. Come and be introduced!"

I like none of these mystery-mongers, but the amateur least of all. With the paid performer you may pounce upon him and expose him the instant that you have seen through his trick. He is there to deceive you, and you are there to find him out. But what are you to do with the friend of your host's wife? Are you to turn on a light suddenly and expose her slapping a surreptitious banjo? Or are you to hurl cochineal over her evening frock when she steals round with her phosphorus bottle and her supernatural platitude? There would be a scene, and you would be looked upon as a brute. So you have your choice of being that or a dupe. I was in no very good humor as I followed Wilson to the lady.

Any one less like my idea of a West Indian could not be imagined. She was a small, frail creature, well over forty, I should say, with a pale, peaky face, and hair of a very light shade of chestnut. Her presence was insignificant and her manner retiring. In any group of ten women she would have been the last whom one would have picked out. Her eyes were perhaps her most remarkable, and also, I am compelled to say, her least pleasant, feature. They were gray in color, - gray with a shade of green, - and their expression struck me as being decidedly furtive. I wonder if furtive is the word, or should I have said fierce? On second thoughts, feline would have expressed it better. A crutch leaning against the wall told me what was painfully evident when she rose: that one of her legs was crippled.

So I was introduced to Miss Penclosa, and it did not escape me that as my name was mentioned she glanced across at Agatha. Wilson had evidently been talking. And presently, no doubt, thought I, she will inform me by occult means that I am engaged to a young lady with wheat-ears in her hair. I wondered how much more Wilson had been telling her about me.

"Professor Gilroy is a terrible sceptic," said he; "I hope, Miss Penclosa, that you will be able to convert him."

She looked keenly up at me.

"Professor Gilroy is quite right to be sceptical if he has not seen anything convincing," said she. "I should have thought," she added, "that you would yourself have been an excellent subject."

"For what, may I ask?" said I.

"Well, for mesmerism, for example."

"My experience has been that mesmerists go for their subjects to those who are mentally unsound. All their results are vitiated, as it seems to me, by the fact that they are dealing with abnormal organisms."

"Which of these ladies would you say possessed a normal organism?" she asked. "I should like you to select the one who seems to you to have the best balanced mind. Should we say the girl in pink and white? - Miss Agatha Marden, I think the name is."

"Yes, I should attach weight to any results from her."

"I have never tried how far she is impressionable. Of course some people respond much more rapidly than others. May I ask how far your scepticism extends? I suppose that you admit the mesmeric sleep and the power of suggestion."

"I admit nothing, Miss Penclosa."

"Dear me, I thought science had got further than that. Of course I know nothing about the scientific side of it. I only know what I can do. You see the girl in red, for example, over near the Japanese jar. I shall will that she come across to us."

She bent forward as she spoke and dropped her fan upon the floor. The girl whisked round and came straight toward us, with an enquiring look upon her face, as if someone had called her.

"What do you think of that, Gilroy?" cried Wilson, in a kind of ecstasy.

I did not dare to tell him what I thought of it. To me it was the most barefaced, shameless piece of imposture that I had ever witnessed. The collusion and the signal had really been too obvious.

"Professor Gilroy is not satisfied," said she, glancing up at me with her strange little eyes. "My poor fan is to get the credit of that experiment. Well, we must try something else. Miss Marden, would you have any objection to my putting you off?"

"Oh, I should love it!" cried Agatha.

By this time all the company had gathered round us in a circle, the shirt-fronted men, and the white-throated women, some awed, some critical, as though it were something between a religious ceremony and a conjurer's entertainment. A red velvet arm-chair had been pushed into the centre, and Agatha lay back in it, a little flushed and trembling slightly from excitement. I could see it from the vibration of the wheat-ears. Miss Penclosa rose from her seat and stood over her, leaning upon her crutch.

And there was a change in the woman. She no longer seemed small or insignificant. Twenty years were gone from her age. Her eyes were shining, a tinge of color had come into her sallow cheeks, her whole figure had expanded. So I have seen a dull-eyed, listless lad change in an instant into briskness and life when given a task of which he felt himself master. She looked down at Agatha with an expression which I resented from the bottom of my soul - the expression with which a Roman empress might have looked at her kneeling slave. Then with a quick, commanding gesture she tossed up her arms and swept them slowly down in front of her.

I was watching Agatha narrowly. During three passes she seemed to be simply amused. At the fourth I observed a slight glazing of her eyes, accompanied by some dilation of her pupils. At the sixth there was a momentary rigor. At the seventh her lids began to droop. At the tenth her eyes were closed, and her breathing was slower and fuller than usual. I tried as I watched to preserve my scientific calm, but a foolish, causeless agitation convulsed me. I trust that I hid it, but I felt as a child feels in the dark. I could not have believed that I was still open to such weakness.

"She is in the trance," said Miss Penclosa.

"She is sleeping!" I cried.

"Wake her, then!"

I pulled her by the arm and shouted in her ear. She might have been dead for all the impression that I could make. Her body was there on the velvet chair. Her organs were acting - her heart, her lungs. But her soul! It had slipped from beyond our ken. Whither had it gone? What power had dispossessed it? I was puzzled and disconcerted.

"So much for the mesmeric sleep," said Miss Penclosa. "As regards suggestion, whatever I may suggest Miss Marden will infallibly do, whether it be now or after she has awakened from her trance. Do you demand proof of it?"

"Certainly," said I.

"You shall have it." I saw a smile pass over her face, as though an amusing thought had struck her. She stooped and whispered earnestly into her subject's ear. Agatha, who had been so deaf to me, nodded her head as she listened.

"Awake!" cried Miss Penclosa, with a sharp tap of her crutch upon the floor. The eyes opened, the glazing cleared slowly away, and the soul looked out once more after its strange eclipse.

We went away early. Agatha was none the worse for her strange excursion, but I was nervous and unstrung, unable to listen to or answer the stream of comments which Wilson was pouring out for my benefit. As I bade her good-night Miss Penclosa slipped a piece of paper into my hand.

"Pray forgive me," said she, "if I take means to overcome your scepticism. Open this note at ten o'clock tomorrow morning. It is a little private test."

I can't imagine what she means, but there is the note, and it shall be opened as she directs. My head is aching, and I have written enough for tonight. Tomorrow I dare say that what seems so inexplicable will take quite another complexion. I shall not surrender my convictions without a struggle.

March 25. I am amazed, confounded. It is clear that I must reconsider my opinion upon this matter. But first let me place on record what has occurred.

I had finished breakfast, and was looking over some diagrams with which my lecture is to be illustrated, when my housekeeper entered to tell me that Agatha was in my study and wished to see me immediately. I glanced at the clock and saw with sun rise that it was only half-past nine.

When I entered the room, she was standing on the hearth-rug facing me. Something in her pose chilled me and checked the words which were rising to my lips. Her veil was half down, but I could see that she was pale and that her expression was constrained.

"Austin," she said, "I have come to tell you that our engagement is at an end."

I staggered. I believe that I literally did stagger. I know that I found myself leaning against the bookcase for support.

"But - but - " I stammered. "This is very sudden, Agatha."

"Yes, Austin, I have come here to tell you that our engagement is at an end."

"But surely," I cried, "you will give me some reason! This is unlike you, Agatha. Tell me how I have been unfortunate enough to offend you."

"It is all over, Austin."

"But why? You must be under some delusion, Agatha. Perhaps you have been told some falsehood about me. Or you may have misunderstood something that I have said to you. Only let me know what it is, and a word may set it all right."

"We must consider it all at an end."

"But you left me last night without a hint at any disagreement. What could have occurred in the interval to change you so? It must have been something that happened last night. You have been thinking it over and you have disapproved of my conduct. Was it the mesmerism? Did you blame me for letting that woman exercise her power over you? You know that at the least sign I should have interfered."

"It is useless, Austin. All is over."

Her voice was cold and measured; her manner strangely formal and hard. It seemed to me that she was absolutely resolved not to be drawn into any argument or explanation. As for me, I was shaking with agitation, and I turned my face aside, so ashamed was I that she should see my want of control.

"You must know what this means to me!" I cried. "It is the blasting of all my hopes and the ruin of my life! You surely will not inflict such a punishment upon me unheard. You will let me know what is the matter. Consider how impossible it would be for me, under any circumstances, to treat you so. For God's sake, Agatha, let me know what I have done!"

She walked past me without a word and opened the door.

"It is quite useless, Austin," said she. "You must consider our engagement at an end." An instant later she was gone, and, before I could recover myself sufficiently to follow her, I heard the hall-door close behind her.

I rushed into my room to change my coat, with the idea of hurrying round to Mrs. Marden's to learn from her what the cause of my misfortune might be. So shaken was I that I could hardly lace my boots. Never shall I forget those horrible ten minutes. I had just pulled on my overcoat when the clock upon the mantel-piece struck ten.

Ten! I associated the idea with Miss Penclosa's note. It was lying before me on the table, and I tore it open. It was scribbled in pencil in a peculiarly angular handwriting.

"MY DEAR PROFESSOR GILROY [it said]:

Pray excuse the personal nature of the test which I am giving you. Professor Wilson happened to mention the relations between you and my subject of this evening, and it struck me that nothing could be more convincing to you than if I were to suggest to Miss Marden that she should call upon you at half-past nine tomorrow morning and suspend your engagement for half an hour or so. Science is so exacting that it is difficult to give a satisfying test, but I am convinced that this at least will be an action which she would be most unlikely to do of her own free will. Forget anything that she may have said, as she has really nothing whatever to do with it, and will certainly not recollect anything about it. I write this note to shorten your anxiety, and to beg you to forgive me for the momentary unhappiness which my suggestion must have caused you.

Yours faithfully;

"HELEN PENCLOSA"

Really, when I had read the note, I was too relieved to be angry. It was a liberty. Certainly it was a very great liberty indeed on the part of a lady whom I had only met once. But, after all, I had challenged her by my scepticism. It may have been, as she said, a little difficult to devise a test which would satisfy me.

And she had done that. There could be no question at all upon the point. For me hypnotic suggestion was finally established. It took its place from now onward as one of the facts of life. That Agatha, who of all women of my acquaintance has the best balanced mind, had been reduced to a condition of automatism appeared to be certain. A person at a distance had worked her as an engineer on the shore might guide a Brennan torpedo. A second soul had stepped in, as it were, had pushed her own aside, and had seized her nervous mechanism, saying: "I will work this for half an hour." And Agatha must have been unconscious as she came and as she returned. Could she make her way in safety through the streets in such a state? I put on my hat and hurried round to see if all was well with her.

Yes. She was at home. I was shown into the drawing-room and found her sitting with a book upon her lap.

"You are an early visitor, Austin," said she, smiling.

"And you have been an even earlier one," I answered.

She looked puzzled. "What do you mean?" she asked.

"You have not been out today?"

"No, certainly not."

"Agatha," said I seriously, "would you mind telling me exactly what you have done this morning?"

She laughed at my earnestness.

"You've got on your professional look, Austin. See what comes of being engaged to a man of science. However, I will tell you, though I can't imagine what you want to know for. I got up at eight. I breakfasted at half-past. I came into this room at ten minutes past nine and began to read the 'Memoirs of Mme. de Remusat.' In a few minutes I did the French lady the bad compliment of dropping to sleep over her pages, and I did you, sir, the very flattering one of dreaming about you. It is only a few minutes since I woke up."

"And found yourself where you had been before?"

"Why, where else should I find myself?"

"Would you mind telling me, Agatha, what it was that you dreamed about me? It really is not mere curiosity on my part."

"I merely had a vague impression that you came into it. I cannot recall any thing definite."

"If you have not been out today, Agatha, how is it that your shoes are dusty?"

A pained look came over her face.

"Really, Austin, I do not know what is the matter with you this morning. One would almost think that you doubted my word. If my boots are dusty, it must be, of course, that I have put on a pair which the maid had not cleaned."

It was perfectly evident that she knew nothing whatever about the matter, and I reflected that, after all, perhaps it was better that I should not enlighten her. It might frighten her, and could serve no good purpose that I could see. I said no more about it, therefore, and left shortly afterward to give my lecture.

But I am immensely impressed. My horizon of scientific possibilities has suddenly been enormously extended. I no longer wonder at Wilson's demonic energy and enthusiasm. Who would not work hard who had a vast virgin field ready to his hand? Why, I have known the novel shape of a nucleolus, or a trifling peculiarity of striped muscular fibre seen under a 300-diameter lens, fill me with exultation. How petty do such researches seem when compared with this one which strikes at the very roots of life and the nature of the soul! I had always looked upon spirit as a product of matter. The brain, I thought, secreted the mind, as the liver does the bile. But how can this be when I see mind working from a distance and playing upon matter as a musician might upon a violin? The body does not give rise to the soul, then, but is rather the rough instrument by which the spirit manifests itself. The windmill does not give rise to the wind, but only indicates it. It was opposed to my whole habit of thought, and yet it was undeniably possible and worthy of investigation.

And why should I not investigate it? I see that under yesterday's date I said: "If I could see something positive and objective, I might be tempted to approach it from the physiological aspect." Well, I have got my test. I shall be as good as my word. The investigation would, I am sure, be of immense interest. Some of my colleagues might look askance at it, for science is full of unreasoning prejudices, but if Wilson has the courage of his convictions, I can afford to have it also. I shall go to him tomorrow morning - to him and to Miss Penclosa. If she can show us so much, it is probable that she can show us more.

II

March 26. Wilson was, as I had anticipated, very exultant over my conversion, and Miss Penclosa was also demurely pleased at the result of her experiment. Strange what a silent, colorless creature she is save only when she exercises her power! Even talking about it gives her color and life. She seems to take a singular interest in me. I cannot help observing how her eyes follow me about the room.

We had the most interesting conversation about her own powers. It is just as well to put her views on record, though they cannot, of course, claim any scientific weight.

"You are on the very fringe of the subject," said she, when I had expressed wonder at the remarkable instance of suggestion which she had shown me. "I had no direct influence upon Miss Marden when she came round to you. I was not even thinking of her that morning. What I did was to set her mind as I might set the alarum of a clock so that at the hour named it would go off of its own accord. If six months instead of twelve hours had been suggested, it would have been the same."

"And if the suggestion had been to assassinate me?"

"She would most inevitably have done so."

"But this is a terrible power!" I cried.

"It is, as you say, a terrible power," she answered gravely, "and the more you know of it the more terrible will it seem to you."

"May I ask," said I, "what you meant when you said that this matter of suggestion is only at the fringe of it? What do you consider the essential?"

"I had rather not tell you."

I was surprised at the decision of her answer.

"You understand," said I, "that it is not out of curiosity I ask, but in the hope that I may find some scientific explanation for the facts with which you furnish me."

"Frankly, Professor Gilroy," said she, "I am not at all interested in science, nor do I care whether it can or cannot classify these powers."

"But I was hoping - "

"Ah, that is quite another thing. If you make it a personal matter," said she, with the pleasantest of smiles, "I shall be only too happy to tell you anything you wish to know. Let me see; what was it you asked me? Oh, about the further powers. Professor Wilson won't believe in them, but they are quite true all the same. For example, it is possible for an operator to gain complete command over his subject - presuming that the latter is a good one. Without any previous suggestion he may make him do whatever he likes."

"Without the subject's knowledge?"

"That depends. If the force were strongly exerted, he would know no more about it than Miss Marden did when she came round and frightened you so. Or, if the influence was less powerful, he might be conscious of what he was doing, but be quite unable to prevent himself from doing it."

"Would he have lost his own will power, then?"

"It would be over-ridden by another stronger one."

"Have you ever exercised this power yourself?"

"Several times."

"Is your own will so strong, then?"

"Well, it does not entirely depend upon that. Many have strong wills which are not detachable from themselves. The thing is to have the gift of projecting it into another person and superseding his own. I find that the power varies with my own strength and health."

"Practically, you send your soul into another person's body."

"Well, you might put it that way."

"And what does your own body do?"

"It merely feels lethargic."

"Well, but is there no danger to your own health?" I asked.

"There might be a little. You have to be careful never to let your own consciousness absolutely go; otherwise, you might experience some difficulty in finding your way back again. You must always preserve the connection, as it were. I am afraid I express myself very badly, Professor Gilroy, but of course I don't know how to put these things in a scientific way. I am just giving you my own experiences and my own explanations."

Well, I read this over now at my leisure, and I marvel at myself! Is this Austin Gilroy, the man who has won his way to the front by his hard reasoning power and by his devotion to fact? Here I am gravely retailing the gossip of a woman who tells me how her soul may be projected from her body, and how, while she lies in a lethargy, she can control the actions of people at a distance. Do I accept it? Certainly not. She must prove and re-prove before I yield a point. But if I am still a sceptic, I have at least ceased to be a scoffer. We are to have a sitting this evening, and she is to try if she can produce any mesmeric effect upon me. If she can, it will make an excellent starting-point for our investigation. No one can accuse me, at any rate, of complicity. If she cannot, we must try and find some subject who will be like Caesar's wife. Wilson is perfectly impervious.

10 P.M. I believe that I am on the threshold of an epoch-making investigation. To have the power of examining these phenomena from inside - to have an organism which will respond, and at the same time a brain which will appreciate and criticise - that is surely a unique advantage. I am quite sure that Wilson would give five years of his life to be as susceptible as I have proved myself to be.

There was no one present except Wilson and his wife. I was seated with my head leaning back, and Miss Penclosa, standing in front and a little to the left, used the same long, sweeping strokes as with Agatha. At each of them a warm current of air seemed to strike me, and to suffuse a thrill and glow all through me from head to foot. My eyes were fixed upon Miss Penclosa's face, but as I gazed the features seemed to blur and to fade away. I was conscious only of her own eyes looking down at me, gray, deep, inscrutable. Larger they grew and larger, until they changed suddenly into two mountain lakes toward which I seemed to be falling with horrible rapidity. I shuddered, and as I did so some deeper stratum of thought told me that the shudder represented the rigor which I had observed in Agatha. An instant later I struck the surface of the lakes, now joined into one, and down I went beneath the water with a fullness in my head and a buzzing in my ears. Down I went, down, down, and then with a swoop up again until I could see the light streaming brightly through the green water. I was almost at the surface when the word "Awake!" rang through my head, and, with a start, I found myself back in the arm-chair, with Miss Penclosa leaning on her crutch, and Wilson, his note book in his hand, peeping over her shoulder. No heaviness or weariness was left behind. On the contrary, though it is only an hour or so since the experiment, I feel so wakeful that I am more inclined for my study than my bedroom. I see quite a vista of interesting experiments extending before us, and am all impatience to begin upon them.

March 27. A blank day, as Miss Penclosa goes with Wilson and his wife to the Suttons'. Have begun Binet and Ferre's "Animal Magnetism." What strange, deep waters these are! Results, results, results - and the cause an absolute mystery. It is stimulating to the imagination, but I must be on my guard against that. Let us have no inferences nor deductions, and nothing but solid facts. I KNOW that the mesmeric trance is true; I KNOW that mesmeric suggestion is true; I KNOW that I am myself sensitive to this force. That is my present position. I have a large new note-book which shall be devoted entirely to scientific detail.

Long talk with Agatha and Mrs. Marden in the evening about our marriage. We think that the summer vac. (the beginning of it) would be the best time for the wedding. Why should we delay? I grudge even those few months. Still, as Mrs. Marden says, there are a good many things to be arranged.

March 28. Mesmerized again by Miss Penclosa. Experience much the same as before, save that insensibility came on more quickly. See Note-book A for temperature of room, barometric pressure, pulse, and respiration as taken by Professor Wilson.

March 29. Mesmerized again. Details in Note-book A.

March 30. Sunday, and a blank day. I grudge any interruption of our experiments. At present they merely embrace the physical signs which go with slight, with complete, and with extreme insensibility. Afterward we hope to pass on to the phenomena of suggestion and of lucidity. Professors have demonstrated these things upon women at Nancy and at the Salpetriere. It will be more convincing when a woman demonstrates it upon a professor, with a second professor as a witness. And that I should be the subject - I, the sceptic, the materialist! At least, I have shown that my devotion to science is greater than to my own personal consistency. The eating of our own words is the greatest sacrifice which truth ever requires of us.

My neighbor, Charles Sadler, the handsome young demonstrator of anatomy, came in this evening to return a volume of Virchow's "Archives" which I had lent him. I call him young, but, as a matter of fact, he is a year older than I am.

"I understand, Gilroy," said he, "that you are being experimented upon by Miss Penclosa."

"Well," he went on, when I had acknowledged it, "if I were you, I should not let it go any further. You will think me very impertinent, no doubt, but, none the less, I feel it to be my duty to advise you to have no more to do with her."

Of course I asked him why.

"I am so placed that I cannot enter into particulars as freely as I could wish," said he. "Miss Penclosa is the friend of my friend, and my position is a delicate one. I can only say this: that I have myself been the subject of some of the woman's experiments, and that they have left a most unpleasant impression upon my mind."

He could hardly expect me to be satisfied with that, and I tried hard to get something more definite out of him, but without success. Is it conceivable that he could be jealous at my having superseded him? Or is he one of those men of science who feel personally injured when facts run counter to their preconceived opinions? He cannot seriously suppose that because he has some vague grievance I am, therefore, to abandon a series of experiments which promise to be so fruitful of results. He appeared to be annoyed at the light way in which I treated his shadowy warnings, and we parted with some little coldness on both sides.

March 31. Mesmerized by Miss P.

April 1. Mesmerized by Miss P. (Note-book A.)

April 2. Mesmerized by Miss P. (Sphygmographic chart taken by Professor Wilson.)

April 3. It is possible that this course of mesmerism may be a little trying to the general constitution. Agatha says that I am thinner and

SIR ARTHUR CONAN DOYLE

darker under the eyes. I am conscious of a nervous irritability which I had not observed in myself before. The least noise, for example, makes me start, and the stupidity of a student causes me exasperation instead of amusement. Agatha wishes me to stop, but I tell her that every course of study is trying, and that one can never attain a result without paying some price for it. When she sees the sensation which my forthcoming paper on "The Relation between Mind and Matter" may make, she will understand that it is worth a little nervous wear and tear. I should not be surprised if I got my F.R.S. over it.

Mesmerized again in the evening. The effect is produced more rapidly now, and the subjective visions are less marked. I keep full notes of each sitting. Wilson is leaving for town for a week or ten days, but we shall not interrupt the experiments, which depend for their value as much upon my sensations as on his observations.

April 4. I must be carefully on my guard. A complication has crept into our experiments which I had not reckoned upon. In my eagerness for scientific facts I have been foolishly blind to the human relations between Miss Penclosa and myself. I can write here what I would not breathe to a living soul. The unhappy woman appears to have formed an attachment for me.

I should not say such a thing, even in the privacy of my own intimate journal, if it had not come to such a pass that it is impossible to ignore it. For some time, - that is, for the last week, - there have been signs which I have brushed aside and refused to think of. Her brightness when I come, her dejection when I go, her eagerness that I should come often, the expression of her eyes, the tone of her voice - I tried to think that they meant nothing, and were, perhaps, only her ardent West Indian manner. But last night, as I awoke from the mesmeric sleep, I put out my hand, unconsciously, involuntarily, and clasped hers. When I came fully to myself, we were sitting with them locked, she looking up at me with an expectant smile. And the horrible thing was that I felt impelled to say what she expected me to say. What a false wretch I should have been! How I should have loathed myself to-day had I yielded to the temptation of that moment! But, thank God, I was strong enough to spring up and hurry from the room. I was rude, I fear, but I could not, no, I COULD not, trust myself another moment. I, a gentleman, a man of honor, engaged to one of the sweetest girls in England - and yet in a moment of reasonless passion I nearly professed love for this woman whom I hardly know. She is far older than myself and a cripple. It is monstrous, odious; and yet the impulse was so strong that, had I stayed another minute in her presence, I should have committed myself. What was it? I have to teach others the workings of our organism, and what do I know of it myself? Was it the sudden upcropping of some lower stratum in my nature - a brutal primitive instinct suddenly asserting itself? I could almost believe the tales of obsession by evil spirits, so overmastering was the feeling.

Well, the incident places me in a most unfortunate position. On the one hand, I am very loath to abandon a series of experiments which have already gone so far, and which promise such brilliant results. On the other, if this unhappy woman has conceived a passion for me - But surely even now I must have made some hideous mistake. She, with her age and her deformity! It is impossible. And then she knew about Agatha. She understood how I was placed. She only smiled out of amusement, perhaps, when in my dazed state I seized her hand. It was my half-mesmerized brain which gave it a meaning, and sprang with such bestial swiftness to meet it. I wish I could persuade myself that it was indeed so. On the whole, perhaps, my wisest plan would be to postpone our other experiments until Wilson's return. I have written a note to Miss Penclosa, therefore, making no allusion to last night, but saying that a press of work would cause me to interrupt our sittings for a few days. She has answered, formally enough, to say that if I should change my mind I should find her at home at the usual hour.

10 P.M. Well, well, what a thing of straw I am! I am coming to know myself better of late, and the more I know the lower I fall in my own estimation. Surely I was not always so weak as this. At four o'clock I should have smiled had any one told me that I should go to Miss Penclosa's tonight, and yet, at eight, I was at Wilson's door as usual. I don't know how it occurred. The influence of habit, I suppose. Perhaps there is a mesmeric craze as there is an opium craze, and I am a victim to it. I only know that as I worked in my study I became more and more uneasy. I fidgeted. I worried. I could not concentrate my mind upon the

papers in front of me. And then, at last, almost before I knew what I was doing, I seized my hat and hurried round to keep my usual appointment.

We had an interesting evening. Mrs. Wilson was present during most of the time, which prevented the embarrassment which one at least of us must have felt. Miss Penclosa's manner was quite the same as usual, and she expressed no surprise at my having come in spite of my note. There was nothing in her bearing to show that yesterday's incident had made any impression upon her, and so I am inclined to hope that I overrated it.

April 6 (evening). No, no, no, I did not overrate it. I can no longer attempt to conceal from myself that this woman has conceived a passion for me. It is monstrous, but it is true. Again, tonight, I awoke from the mesmeric trance to find my hand in hers, and to suffer that odious feeling which urges me to throw away my honor, my career, everything, for the sake of this creature who, as I can plainly see when I am away from her influence, possesses no single charm upon earth. But when I am near her, I do not feel this. She rouses something in me, something evil, something I had rather not think of. She paralyzes my better nature, too, at the moment when she stimulates my worse. Decidedly it is not good for me to be near her.

Last night was worse than before. Instead of flying I actually sat for some time with my hand in hers talking over the most intimate subjects with her. We spoke of Agatha, among other things. What could I have been dreaming of? Miss Penclosa said that she was conventional, and I agreed with her. She spoke once or twice in a disparaging way of her, and I did not protest. What a creature I have been!

Weak as I have proved myself to be, I am still strong enough to bring this sort of thing to an end. It shall not happen again. I have sense enough to fly when I cannot fight. From this Sunday night onward I shall never sit with Miss Penclosa again. Never! Let the experiments go, let the research come to an end; anything is better than facing this monstrous temptation which drags me so low. I have said nothing to Miss Penclosa, but I shall simply stay away. She can tell the reason without any words of mine.

April 7. Have stayed away as I said. It is a pity to ruin such an interesting investigation, but it would be a greater pity still to ruin my life, and I KNOW that I cannot trust myself with that woman.

11 P.M. God help me! What is the matter with me? Am I going mad? Let me try and be calm and reason with myself. First of all I shall set down exactly what occurred.

It was nearly eight when I wrote the lines with which this day begins. Feeling strangely restless and uneasy, I left my rooms and walked round to spend the evening with Agatha and her mother. They both remarked that I was pale and haggard. About nine Professor Pratt-Haldane came in, and we played a game of whist. I tried hard to concentrate my attention upon the cards, but the feeling of restlessness grew and grew until I found it impossible to struggle against it. I simply COULD not sit still at the table. At last, in the very middle of a hand, I threw my cards down and, with some sort of an incoherent apology about having an appointment, I rushed from the room. As if in a dream I have a vague recollection of tearing through the hall, snatching my hat from the stand, and slamming the door behind me. As in a dream, too, I have the impression of the double line of gas-lamps, and my bespattered boots tell me that I must have run down the middle of the road. It was all misty and strange and unnatural. I came to Wilson's house; I saw Mrs. Wilson and I saw Miss Penclosa. I hardly recall what we talked about, but I do remember that Miss P. shook the head of her crutch at me in a playful way, and accused me of being late and of losing interest in our experiments. There was no mesmerism, but I stayed some time and have only just returned.

My brain is quite clear again now, and I can think over what has occurred. It is absurd to suppose that it is merely weakness and force of habit. I tried to explain it in that way the other night, but it will no longer suffice. It is something much deeper and more terrible than that. Why, when I was at the Mardens' whist-table, I was dragged away as if the noose of a rope had been cast round me. I can no longer disguise it from myself. The woman has her grip upon me. I am in her clutch. But I must keep my head and reason it out and see what is best to be done.

But what a blind fool I have been! In my enthusiasm over my research I have walked straight into the pit, although it lay gaping before me. Did she not herself warn me? Did she not tell me, as I can read in my own journal, that when she has acquired power over a subject she can make him do her will? And she has acquired that power over me. I am for the moment at the beck and call of this creature with the crutch. I must come when she wills it. I must do as she wills. Worst of all, I must feel as she wills. I loathe her and fear her, yet, while I am under the spell, she can doubtless make me love her.

There is some consolation in the thought, then, that those odious impulses for which I have blamed myself do not really come from me at all. They are all transferred from her, little as I could have guessed it at the time. I feel cleaner and lighter for the thought.

April 8. Yes, now, in broad daylight, writing coolly and with time for reflection, I am compelled to confirm everything which I wrote in my journal last night. I am in a horrible position, but, above all, I must not lose my head. I must pit my intellect against her powers. After all, I am no silly puppet, to dance at the end of a string. I have energy, brains, courage. For all her devil's tricks I may beat her yet. May! I MUST, or what is to become of me?

Let me try to reason it out! This woman, by her own explanation, can dominate my nervous organism. She can project herself into my body and take command of it. She has a parasite soul; yes, she is a parasite, a monstrous parasite. She creeps into my frame as the hermit crab does into the whelk's shell. I am powerless. What can I do? I am dealing with forces of which I know nothing. And I can tell no one of my trouble. They would set me down as a madman. Certainly, if it got noised abroad, the university would say that they had no need of a devil-ridden professor. And Agatha! No, no, I must face it alone.

III

I read over my notes of what the woman said when she spoke about her powers. There is one point which fills me with dismay. She implies that when the influence is slight the subject knows what he is doing, but cannot control himself, whereas when it is strongly exerted he is absolutely unconscious. Now, I have always known what I did, though less so last night than on the previous occasions. That seems to mean that she has never yet exerted her full powers upon me. Was ever a man so placed before?

Yes, perhaps there was, and very near me, too. Charles Sadler must know something of this! His vague words of warning take a meaning now. Oh, if I had only listened to him then, before I helped by these repeated sittings to forge the links of the chain which binds me! But I will see him today. I will apologize to him for having treated his warning so lightly. I will see if he can advise me.

4 P.M. No, he cannot. I have talked with him, and he showed such surprise at the first words in which I tried to express my unspeakable secret that I went no further. As far as I can gather (by hints and inferences rather than by any statement), his own experience was limited to some words or looks such as I have myself endured. His abandonment of Miss Penclosa is in itself a sign that he was never really in her toils. Oh, if he only knew his escape! He has to thank his phlegmatic Saxon temperament for it. I am black and Celtic, and this hag's clutch is deep in my nerves. Shall I ever get it out? Shall I ever be the same man that I was just one short fortnight ago?

Let me consider what I had better do. I cannot leave the university in the middle of the term. If I were free, my course would be obvious. I should start at once and travel in Persia. But would she allow me to start? And could her influence not reach me in Persia, and bring me back to within touch of her crutch? I can only find out the limits of this hellish power by my own bitter experience. I will fight and fight and fight - and what can I do more?

I know very well that about eight o'clock tonight that craving for her society, that irresistible restlessness, will come upon me. How shall I overcome it? What shall I do? I must make it impossible for me to leave the room. I shall lock the door and throw the key out of the window. But, then, what am I to do in the morning? Never mind about the morning. I must at all costs break this chain which holds me.

April 9. Victory! I have done splendidly! At seven o'clock last night I took a hasty dinner, and then locked myself up in my bedroom and dropped the key into the garden. I chose a cheery novel, and lay in bed for three hours trying to read it, but really in a horrible state of trepidation, expecting every instant that I should become conscious of the impulse. Nothing of the sort occurred, however, and I awoke this morning with the feeling that a black nightmare had been lifted off me. Perhaps the creature realized what I had done, and understood that it was useless to try to influence me. At any rate, I have beaten her once, and if I can do it once, I can do it again.

It was most awkward about the key in the morning. Luckily, there was an under-gardener below, and I asked him to throw it up. No doubt he thought I had just dropped it. I will have doors and windows screwed up and six stout men to hold me down in my bed before I will surrender myself to be hag-ridden in this way.

I had a note from Mrs. Marden this afternoon asking me to go round and see her. I intended to do so in any case, but had not excepted to find bad news waiting for me. It seems that the Armstrongs, from whom Agatha has expectations, are due home from Adelaide in the Aurora, and that they have written to Mrs. Marden and her to meet them in town. They will probably be away for a month or six weeks, and, as the Aurora is due on Wednesday, they must go at once - tomorrow, if they are ready in time. My consolation is that when we meet again there will be no more parting between Agatha and me.

"I want you to do one thing, Agatha," said I, when we were alone together. "If you should happen to meet Miss Penclosa, either in town or here, you must promise me never again to allow her to mesmerize you."

Agatha opened her eyes.

"Why, it was only the other day that you were saying how interesting it all was, and how determined you were to finish your experiments."

"I know, but I have changed my mind since then."

"And you won't have it any more?"

"No."

"I am so glad, Austin. You can't think how pale and worn you have been lately. It was really our principal objection to going to London now that we did not wish to leave you when you were so pulled down. And your manner has been so strange occasionally - especially that night when you left poor Professor Pratt-Haldane to play dummy. I am convinced that these experiments are very bad for your nerves."

"I think so, too, dear."

"And for Miss Penclosa's nerves as well. You have heard that she is ill?"

"No."

"Mrs. Wilson told us so last night. She described it as a nervous fever. Professor Wilson is coming back this week, and of course Mrs. Wilson is very anxious that Miss Penclosa should be well again then, for he has quite a programme of experiments which he is anxious to carry out."

I was glad to have Agatha's promise, for it was enough that this woman should have one of us in her clutch. On the other hand, I was disturbed to hear about Miss Penclosa's illness. It rather discounts the victory which I appeared to win last night. I remember that she said that loss of health interfered with her power. That may be why I was able to hold my own so easily. Well, well, I must take the same precautions tonight and see what comes of it. I am childishly frightened when I think of her.

April 10. All went very well last night. I was amused at the gardener's face when I had again to hail him this morning and to ask him to throw up my key. I shall get a name among the servants if this sort of thing goes on. But the great point is that I stayed in my room without the slightest inclination to leave it. I do believe that I am shaking myself clear of this incredible bond - or is it only that the woman's power is in abeyance until she recovers her strength? I can but pray for the best.

The Mardens left this morning, and the brightness seems to have gone out of the spring sunshine. And yet it is very beautiful also as it gleams on the green chestnuts opposite my windows, and gives a touch of gayety to the heavy, lichen-mottled walls of the old colleges. How sweet and gentle and soothing is Nature! Who would think that there lurked in her also such vile forces, such odious possibilities! For of course I understand that this dreadful thing which has sprung out at me is neither supernatural nor even preternatural. No, it is a natural force which this woman can use and society is ignorant of. The mere fact that it ebbs with her strength shows how entirely it is subject to physical laws. If I had time, I might probe it to the bottom and lay my hands upon its antidote. But you cannot tame the tiger when you are beneath his claws. You can but try to writhe away from him. Ah, when I look in the glass and see my own dark eyes and clear-cut Spanish face, I long for a vitriol splash or a bout of the small-pox. One or the other might have saved me from this calamity.

I am inclined to think that I may have trouble tonight. There are two things which make me fear so. One is that I met Mrs. Wilson in the street, and that she tells me that Miss Penclosa is better, though still weak. I find myself wishing in my heart that the illness had been her last. The other is that Professor Wilson comes back in a day or two, and his presence would act as a constraint upon her. I should not fear our interviews if a third person were present. For both these reasons I have a presentiment of trouble tonight, and I shall take the same precautions as before.

April 10. No, thank God, all went well last night. I really could not face the gardener again. I locked my door and thrust the key underneath it, so that I had to ask the maid to let me out in the morning. But the precaution was really not needed, for I never had any inclination to go out at all. Three evenings in succession at home! I am surely near the end of my troubles, for Wilson will be home again either today or tomorrow. Shall I tell him of what I have gone through or not? I am convinced that I should not have the slightest sympathy from him. He would look upon me as an interesting case, and read a paper about me at the next meeting of the Psychical Society, in which he would gravely discuss the possibility of my being a deliberate liar, and weigh it against the chances of my being in an early stage of lunacy. No, I shall get no comfort out of Wilson.

I am feeling wonderfully fit and well. I don't think I ever lectured with greater spirit. Oh, if I could only get this shadow off my life, how happy I should be! Young, fairly wealthy, in the front rank of my profession, engaged to a beautiful and charming girl - have I not everything which a man could ask for? Only one thing to trouble me, but what a thing it is!

Midnight. I shall go mad. Yes, that will be the end of it. I shall go mad. I am not far from it now. My head throbs as I rest it on my hot hand. I am quivering all over like a scared horse. Oh, what a night I have had! And yet I have some cause to be satisfied also.

At the risk of becoming the laughing-stock of my own servant, I again slipped my key under the door, imprisoning myself for the night. Then, finding it too early to go to bed, I lay down with my clothes on and began to read one of Dumas's novels. Suddenly I was gripped -

gripped and dragged from the couch. It is only thus that I can describe the overpowering nature of the force which pounced upon me. I clawed at the coverlet. I clung to the wood-work. I believe that I screamed out in my frenzy. It was all useless, hopeless. I MUST go. There was no way out of it. It was only at the outset that I resisted. The force soon became too overmastering for that. I thank goodness that there were no watchers there to interfere with me. I could not have answered for myself if there had been. And, besides the determination to get out, there came to me, also, the keenest and coolest judgment in choosing my means. I lit a candle and endeavored, kneeling in front of the door, to pull the key through with the feather-end of a quill pen. It was just too short and pushed it further away. Then with quiet persistence I got a paper-knife out of one of the drawers, and with that I managed to draw the key back. I opened the door, stepped into my study, took a photograph of myself from the bureau, wrote something across it, placed it in the inside pocket of my coat, and then started off for Wilson's.

It was all wonderfully clear, and yet disassociated from the rest of my life, as the incidents of even the most vivid dream might be. A peculiar double consciousness possessed me. There was the predominant alien will, which was bent upon drawing me to the side of its owner, and there was the feebler protesting personality, which I recognized as being myself, tugging feebly at the overmastering impulse as a led terrier might at its chain. I can remember recognizing these two conflicting forces, but I recall nothing of my walk, nor of how I was admitted to the house.

Very vivid, however, is my recollection of how I met Miss Penclosa. She was reclining on the sofa in the little boudoir in which our experiments had usually been carried out. Her head was rested on her hand, and a tiger-skin rug had been partly drawn over her. She looked up expectantly as I entered, and, as the lamp-light fell upon her face, I could see that she was very pale and thin, with dark hollows under her eyes. She smiled at me, and pointed to a stool beside her. It was with her left hand that she pointed, and I, running eagerly forward, seized it, - I loathe myself as I think of it, - and pressed it passionately to my lips. Then, seating myself upon the stool, and still retaining her hand, I gave her the photograph which I had brought with me, and talked and talked and talked - of my love for her, of my grief over her illness, of my joy at her recovery, of the misery it was to me to be absent a single evening from her side. She lay quietly looking down at me with imperious eyes and her provocative smile. Once I remember that she passed her hand over my hair as one caresses a dog; and it gave me pleasure - the caress. I thrilled under it. I was her slave, body and soul, and for the moment I rejoiced in my slavery.

And then came the blessed change. Never tell me that there is not a Providence! I was on the brink of perdition. My feet were on the edge. Was it a coincidence that at that very instant help should come? No, no, no; there is a Providence, and its hand has drawn me back. There is something in the universe stronger than this devil woman with her tricks. Ah, what a balm to my heart it is to think so!

As I looked up at her I was conscious of a change in her. Her face, which had been pale before, was now ghastly. Her eyes were dull, and the lids drooped heavily over them. Above all, the look of serene confidence had gone from her features. Her mouth had weakened. Her forehead had puckered. She was frightened and undecided. And as I watched the change my own spirit fluttered and struggled, trying hard to tear itself from the grip which held it - a grip which, from moment to moment, grew less secure.

"Austin," she whispered, "I have tried to do too much. I was not strong enough. I have not recovered yet from my illness. But I could not live longer without seeing you. You won't leave me, Austin? This is only a passing weakness. If you will only give me five minutes, I shall be myself again. Give me the small decanter from the table in the window."

But I had regained my soul. With her waning strength the influence had cleared away from me and left me free. And I was aggressive - bitterly, fiercely aggressive. For once at least I could make this woman understand what my real feelings toward her were. My soul was filled with a hatred as bestial as the love against which it was a reaction. It was the savage, murderous passion of the revolted serf. I could have taken the crutch from her side and beaten her face in with it. She threw her hands up, as if to avoid a blow, and cowered away from me into the corner of the settee.

"The brandy!" she gasped. "The brandy!"

I took the decanter and poured it over the roots of a palm in the window. Then I snatched the photograph from her hand and tore it into a hundred pieces.

"You vile woman," I said, "if I did my duty to society, you would never leave this room alive!"

"I love you, Austin; I love you!" she wailed.

"Yes," I cried, "and Charles Sadler before. And how many others before that?"

"Charles Sadler!" she gasped. "He has spoken to you? So, Charles Sadler, Charles Sadler!" Her voice came through her white lips like a snake's hiss.

"Yes, I know you, and others shall know you, too. You shameless creature! You knew how I stood. And yet you used your vile power to bring me to your side. You may, perhaps, do so again, but at least you will remember that you have heard me say that I love Miss Marden from the bottom of my soul, and that I loathe you, abhor you!"

"The very sight of you and the sound of your voice fill me with horror and disgust. The thought of you is repulsive. That is how I feel toward you, and if it pleases you by your tricks to draw me again to your side as you have done tonight, you will at least, I should think, have little satisfaction in trying to make a lover out of a man who has told you his real opinion of you. You may put what words you will into my mouth, but you cannot help remembering - "

I stopped, for the woman's head had fallen back, and she had fainted. She could not bear to hear what I had to say to her! What a glow of satisfaction it gives me to think that, come what may, in the future she can never misunderstand my true feelings toward her. But what will occur in the future? What will she do next? I dare not think of it. Oh, if only I could hope that she will leave me alone! But when I think of what I said to her - Never mind; I have been stronger than she for once.

April 11. I hardly slept last night, and found myself in the morning so unstrung and feverish that I was compelled to ask Pratt-Haldane to do my lecture for me. It is the first that I have ever missed. I rose at mid-day, but my head is aching, my hands quivering, and my nerves in a pitiable state.

Who should come round this evening but Wilson. He has just come back from London, where he has lectured, read papers, convened meetings, exposed a medium, conducted a series of experiments on thought transference, entertained Professor Richet of Paris, spent hours gazing into a crystal, and obtained some evidence as to the passage of matter through matter. All this he poured into my ears in a single gust.

"But you!" he cried at last. "You are not looking well. And Miss Penclosa is quite prostrated today. How about the experiments?"

"I have abandoned them."

"Tut, tut! Why?"

"The subject seems to me to be a dangerous one."

Out came his big brown note-book.

"This is of great interest," said he. "What are your grounds for saying that it is a dangerous one? Please give your facts in chronological order, with approximate dates and names of reliable witnesses with their permanent addresses."

"First of all," I asked, "would you tell me whether you have collected any cases where the mesmerist has gained a command over the subject and has used it for evil purposes?"

"Dozens!" he cried exultantly. "Crime by suggestion - "

"I don't mean suggestion. I mean where a sudden impulse comes from a person at a distance - an uncontrollable impulse."

"Obsession!" he shrieked, in an ecstasy of delight. "It is the rarest condition. We have eight cases, five well attested. You don't mean to say-" His exultation made him hardly articulate.

"No, I don't," said I. "Good-evening! You will excuse me, but I am not very well tonight." And so at last I got rid of him, still brandishing his pencil and his note-book. My troubles may be bad to hear, but at least it is better to hug them to myself than to have myself exhibited by Wilson, like a freak at a fair. He has lost sight of human beings. Everything to him is a case and a phenomenon. I will die before I speak to him again upon the matter.

April 12. Yesterday was a blessed day of quiet, and I enjoyed an uneventful night. Wilson's presence is a great consolation. What can the woman do now? Surely, when she has heard me say what I have said, she will conceive the same disgust for me which I have for her. She could not, no, she COULD not, desire to have a lover who had insulted her so. No, I believe I am free from her love - but how about her hate? Might she not use these powers of hers for revenge? Tut! why should I frighten myself over shadows? She will forget about me, and I shall forget about her, and all will be well.

April 13. My nerves have quite recovered their tone. I really believe that I have conquered the creature. But I must confess to living in some suspense. She is well again, for I hear that she was driving with Mrs. Wilson in the High Street in the afternoon.

April 14. I do wish I could get away from the place altogether. I shall fly to Agatha's side the very day that the term closes. I suppose it is pitiably weak of me, but this woman gets upon my nerves most terribly. I have seen her again, and I have spoken with her.

It was just after lunch, and I was smoking a cigarette in my study, when I heard the step of my servant Murray in the passage. I was languidly conscious that a second step was audible behind, and had hardly troubled myself to speculate who it might be, when suddenly a slight noise brought me out of my chair with my skin creeping with apprehension. I had never particularly observed before what sort of sound the tapping of a crutch was, but my quivering nerves told me that I heard it now in the sharp wooden clack which alternated with the muffled thud of the foot fall. Another instant and my servant had shown her in.

I did not attempt the usual conventions of society, nor did she. I simply stood with the smouldering cigarette in my hand, and gazed at her. She in her turn looked silently at me, and at her look I remembered how in these very pages I had tried to define the expression of her eyes, whether they were furtive or fierce. To-day they were fierce - coldly and inexorably so.

"Well," said she at last, "are you still of the same mind as when I saw you last?"

"I have always been of the same mind."

"Let us understand each other, Professor Gilroy," said she slowly. "I am not a very safe person to trifle with, as you should realize by now. It was you who asked me to enter into a series of experiments with you, it was you who won my affections, it was you who professed your love for me, it was you who brought me your own photograph with words of affection upon it, and, finally, it was you who on the very same evening thought fit to insult me most outrageously, addressing me as no man has ever dared to speak to me yet. Tell me that those words came from you in a moment of passion and I am prepared to forget and to forgive them. You did not mean what you said, Austin? You do not really hate me?"

I might have pitied this deformed woman - such a longing for love broke suddenly through the menace of her eyes. But then I thought of what I had gone through, and my heart set like flint.

"If ever you heard me speak of love," said I, "you know very well that it was your voice which spoke, and not mine. The only words of truth which I have ever been able to say to you are those which you heard when last we met."

"I know. Someone has set you against me. It was he!" She tapped with her crutch upon the floor. "Well, you know very well that I could bring you this instant crouching like a spaniel to my feet. You will not find me again in my hour of weakness, when you can insult me with impunity. Have a care what you are doing, Professor Gilroy. You stand in a terrible position. You have not yet realized the hold which I have upon you."

I shrugged my shoulders and turned away.

"Well," said she, after a pause, "if you despise my love, I must see what can be done with fear. You smile, but the day will come when you will come screaming to me for pardon. Yes, you will grovel on the ground before me, proud as you are, and you will curse the day that ever you turned me from your best friend into your most bitter enemy. Have a care, Professor Gilroy!" I saw a white hand shaking in the air, and a face which was scarcely human, so convulsed was it with passion. An instant later she was gone, and I heard the quick hobble and tap receding down the passage.

But she has left a weight upon my heart. Vague presentiments of coming misfortune lie heavy upon me. I try in vain to persuade myself that these are only words of empty anger. I can remember those relentless eyes too clearly to think so. What shall I do - ah, what shall I do? I am no longer master of my own soul. At any moment this loathsome parasite may creep into me, and then - I must tell someone my hideous secret - I must tell it or go mad. If I had someone to sympathize and advise! Wilson is out of the question. Charles Sadler would understand me only so far as his own experience carries him. Pratt-Haldane! He is a well-balanced man, a man of great common-sense and resource. I will go to him. I will tell him everything. God grant that he may be able to advise me!

IV

6.45 P.M. No, it is useless. There is no human help for me; I must fight this out single-handed. Two courses lie before me. I might become this woman's lover. Or I must endure such persecutions as she can inflict upon me. Even if none come, I shall live in a hell of apprehension. But she may torture me, she may drive me mad, she may kill me: I will never, never, never give in. What can she inflict which would be worse than the loss of Agatha, and the knowledge that I am a perjured liar, and have forfeited the name of gentleman?

Pratt-Haldane was most amiable, and listened with all politeness to my story. But when I looked at his heavy set features, his slow eyes, and the ponderous study furniture which surrounded him, I could hardly tell him what I had come to say. It was all so substantial, so material. And, besides, what would I myself have said a short month ago if one of my colleagues had come to me with a story of demonic possession? Perhaps. I should have been less patient than he was. As it was, he took notes of my statement, asked me how much tea I drank, how many hours I slept, whether I had been overworking much, had I had sudden pains in the head, evil dreams, singing in the ears, flashes before the eyes - all questions which pointed to his belief that brain congestion was at the bottom of my trouble. Finally he dismissed me with a great many platitudes about open-air exercise, and avoidance of nervous excitement. His prescription, which was for chloral and bromide, I rolled up and threw into the gutter.

No, I can look for no help from any human being. If I consult any more, they may put their heads together and I may find myself in an asylum. I can but grip my courage with both hands, and pray that an honest man may not be abandoned.

April 10. It is the sweetest spring within the memory of man. So green, so mild, so beautiful! Ah, what a contrast between nature without and my own soul so torn with doubt and terror! It has been an uneventful day, but I know that I am on the edge of an abyss. I know it, and yet I go on with the routine of my life. The one bright spot is that Agatha is happy and well and out of all danger. If this creature had a hand on each of us, what might she not do?

April 16. The woman is ingenious in her torments. She knows how fond I am of my work, and how highly my lectures are thought of. So it is from that point that she now attacks me. It will end, I can see, in my losing my professorship, but I will fight to the finish. She shall not drive me out of it without a struggle.

I was not conscious of any change during my lecture this morning save that for a minute or two I had a dizziness and swimminess which rapidly passed away. On the contrary, I congratulated myself upon having made my subject (the functions of the red corpuscles) both interesting and clear. I was surprised, therefore, when a student came into my laboratory immediately after the lecture, and complained of being puzzled by the discrepancy between my statements and those in the text books. He showed me his note-book, in which I was reported as having in one portion of the lecture championed the most outrageous and unscientific heresies. Of course I denied it, and declared that he had misunderstood me, but on comparing his notes with those of his companions, it became clear that he was right, and that I really had made some most preposterous statements. Of course I shall explain it away as being the result of a moment of aberration, but I feel only too sure that it will be the first of a series. It is but a month now to the end of the session, and I pray that I may be able to hold out until then.

April 26. Ten days have elapsed since I have had the heart to make any entry in my journal. Why should I record my own humiliation and degradation? I had vowed never to open it again. And yet the force of habit is strong, and here I find myself taking up once more the record of my own dreadful experiences - in much the same spirit in which a suicide has been known to take notes of the effects of the poison which killed him.

Well, the crash which I had foreseen has come - and that no further back than yesterday. The university authorities have taken my lectureship from me. It has been done in the most delicate way, purporting to be a temporary measure to relieve me from the effects of overwork, and to give me the opportunity of recovering my health. None the less, it has been done, and I am no longer Professor Gilroy. The laboratory is still in my charge, but I have little doubt that that also will soon go.

The fact is that my lectures had become the laughing-stock of the university. My class was crowded with students who came to see and hear what the eccentric professor would do or say next. I cannot go into the detail of my humiliation. Oh, that devilish woman! There is no depth of buffoonery and imbecility to which she has not forced me. I would begin my lecture clearly and well, but always with the sense of a coming eclipse. Then as I felt the influence I would struggle against it, striving with clenched hands and beads of sweat upon my brow to get the better of it, while the students, hearing my incoherent words and watching my contortions, would roar with laughter at the antics of their professor. And then, when she had once fairly mastered me, out would come the most outrageous things - silly jokes, sentiments as though I were proposing a toast, snatches of ballads, personal abuse even against some member of my class. And then in a moment my brain would clear again, and my lecture would proceed decorously to the end. No wonder that my conduct has been the talk of the colleges. No wonder that the University Senate has been compelled to take official notice of such a scandal. Oh, that devilish woman!

And the most dreadful part of it all is my own loneliness. Here I sit in a commonplace English bow-window, looking out upon a commonplace English street with its garish buses and its lounging policeman, and behind me there hangs a shadow which is out of all keeping with the age and place. In the home of knowledge I am weighed down and tortured by a power of which science knows nothing. No magistrate would listen to me. No paper would discuss my case. No doctor would believe my symptoms. My own most intimate friends would only look upon it as a sign of brain derangement. I am out of all touch with my kind. Oh, that devilish woman! Let her have a care! She may push me too far. When the law cannot help a man, he may make a law for himself.

She met me in the High Street yesterday evening and spoke to me. It was as well for her, perhaps, that it was not between the hedges of a lonely country road. She asked me with her cold smile whether I had been chastened yet. I did not deign to answer her. "We must try another turn of the screw;" said she. Have a care, my lady, have a care! I had her at my mercy once. Perhaps another chance may come.

April 28. The suspension of my lectureship has had the effect also of taking away her means of annoying me, and so I have enjoyed two blessed days of peace. After all, there is no reason to despair. Sympathy pours in to me from all sides, and everyone agrees that it is my devotion to science and the arduous nature of my researches which have shaken my nervous system. I have had the kindest message from the council advising me to travel abroad, and expressing the confident hope that I may be able to resume all my duties by the beginning of the summer term. Nothing could be more flattering than their allusions to my career and to my services to the university. It is only in misfortune that one can test one's own popularity. This creature may weary of tormenting me, and then all may yet be well. May God grant it!

April 29. Our sleepy little town has had a small sensation. The only knowledge of crime which we ever have is when a rowdy undergraduate breaks a few lamps or comes to blows with a policeman. Last night, however, there was an attempt made to break-into the branch of the Bank of England, and we are all in a flutter in consequence.

Parkenson, the manager, is an intimate friend of mine, and I found him very much excited when I walked round there after breakfast. Had the thieves broken into the counting-house, they would still have had the safes to reckon with, so that the defence was considerably stronger than the attack. Indeed, the latter does not appear to have ever been very formidable. Two of the lower windows have marks as if a chisel or some such instrument had been pushed under them to force them open. The police should have a good clue, for the wood-work had been done with green paint only the day before, and from the smears it is evident that some of it has found its way on to the criminal's hands or clothes.

4.30 P.M. Ah, that accursed woman! That thrice accursed woman! Never mind! She shall not beat me! No, she shall not! But, oh, the she-devil! She has taken my professorship. Now she would take my honor. Is there nothing I can do against her, nothing save - Ah, but, hard pushed as I am, I cannot bring myself to think of that!

It was about an hour ago that I went into my bedroom, and was brushing my hair before the glass, when suddenly my eyes lit upon something which left me so sick and cold that I sat down upon the edge of the bed and began to cry. It is many a long year since I shed tears, but all my nerve was gone, and I could but sob and sob in impotent grief and anger. There was my house jacket, the coat I usually wear after dinner, hanging on its peg by the wardrobe, with the right sleeve thickly crusted from wrist to elbow with daubs of green paint.

So this was what she meant by another turn of the screw! She had made a public imbecile of me. Now she would brand me as a criminal. This time she has failed. But how about the next? I dare not think of it - and of Agatha and my poor old mother! I wish that I were dead!

Yes, this is the other turn of the screw. And this is also what she meant, no doubt, when she said that I had not realized yet the power she has over me. I look back at my account of my conversation with her, and I see how she declared that with a slight exertion of her will her subject would be conscious, and with a stronger one unconscious. Last night I was unconscious. I could have sworn that I slept soundly in my bed without so much as a dream. And yet those stains tell me that I dressed, made my way out, attempted to open the bank windows, and returned. Was I observed? Is it possible that some one saw me do it and followed me home? Ah, what a hell my life has become! I have no peace, no rest. But my patience is nearing its end.

10 P.M. I have cleaned my coat with turpentine. I do not think that anyone could have seen me. It was with my screw-driver that I made the marks. I found it all crusted with paint, and I have cleaned it. My head aches as if it would burst, and I have taken five grains of antipyrine. If it were not for Agatha, I should have taken fifty and had an end of it.

May 3. Three quiet days. This hell fiend is like a cat with a mouse. She lets me loose only to pounce upon me again. I am never so frightened as when everything is still. My physical state is deplorable - perpetual hiccough and ptosis of the left eyelid.

I have heard from the Mardens that they will be back the day after tomorrow. I do not know whether I am glad or sorry. They were safe in London. Once here they may be drawn into the miserable network in which I am myself struggling. And I must tell them of it. I cannot marry Agatha so long as I know that I am not responsible for my own actions. Yes, I must tell them, even if it brings everything to an end between us.

Tonight is the university ball, and I must go. God knows I never felt less in the humor for festivity, but I must not have it said that I am unfit to appear in public. If I am seen there, and have speech with some of the elders of the university it will go a long way toward showing them that it would be unjust to take my chair away from me.

10 P.M. I have been to the ball. Charles Sadler and I went together, but I have come away before him. I shall wait up for him, however, for, indeed, I fear to go to sleep these nights. He is a cheery, practical fellow, and a chat with him will steady my nerves. On the whole, the evening was a great success. I talked to everyone who has influence, and I think that I made them realize that my chair is not vacant quite yet. The creature was at the ball - unable to dance, of course, but sitting with Mrs. Wilson. Again and again her eyes rested upon me. They were almost the last things I saw before I left the room. Once, as I sat sideways to her, I watched her, and saw that her gaze was following someone else. It was Sadler, who was dancing at the time with the second Miss Thurston. To judge by her expression, it is well for him that he is not in her grip as I am. He does not know the escape he has had. I think I hear his step in the street now, and I will go down and let him in. If he will -

May 4. Why did I break off in this way last night? I never went down stairs, after all - at least, I have no recollection of doing so. But, on the other hand, I cannot remember going to bed. One of my hands is greatly swollen this morning, and yet I have no remembrance of injuring it yesterday. Otherwise, I am feeling all the better for last night's festivity. But I cannot understand how it is that I did not meet Charles Sadler when

I so fully intended to do so. Is it possible - My God, it is only too probable! Has she been leading me some devil's dance again? I will go down to Sadler and ask him.

Mid-day. The thing has come to a crisis. My life is not worth living. But, if I am to die, then she shall come also. I will not leave her behind, to drive some other man mad as she has me. No, I have come to the limit of my endurance. She has made me as desperate and dangerous a man as walks the earth. God knows I have never had the heart to hurt a fly, and yet, if I had my hands now upon that woman, she should never leave this room alive. I shall see her this very day, and she shall learn what she has to expect from me.

I went to Sadler and found him, to my surprise, in bed. As I entered he sat up and turned a face toward me which sickened me as I looked at it.

"Why, Sadler, what has happened?" I cried, but my heart turned cold as I said it.

"Gilroy," he answered, mumbling with his swollen lips, "I have for some weeks been under the impression that you are a madman. Now I know it, and that you are a dangerous one as well. If it were not that I am unwilling to make a scandal in the college, you would now be in the hands of the police."

"Do you mean - " I cried.

"I mean that as I opened the door last night you rushed out upon me, struck me with both your fists in the face, knocked me down, kicked me furiously in the side, and left me lying almost unconscious in the street. Look at your own hand bearing witness against you."

Yes, there it was, puffed up, with sponge-like knuckles, as after some terrific blow. What could I do? Though he put me down as a madman, I must tell him all. I sat by his bed and went over all my troubles from the beginning. I poured them out with quivering hands and burning words which might have carried conviction to the most sceptical. "She hates you and she hates me!" I cried. "She revenged herself last night on both of us at once. She saw me leave the ball, and she must have seen you also. She knew how long it would take you to reach home. Then she had but to use her wicked will. Ah, your bruised face is a small thing beside my bruised soul!"

He was struck by my story. That was evident. "Yes, yes, she watched me out of the room," he muttered. "She is capable of it. But is it possible that she has really reduced you to this? What do you intend to do?"

"To stop it!" I cried. "I am perfectly desperate; I shall give her fair warning today, and the next time will be the last."

"Do nothing rash," said he.

"Rash!" I cried. "The only rash thing is that I should postpone it another hour." With that I rushed to my room, and here I am on the eve of what may be the great crisis of my life. I shall start at once. I have gained one thing today, for I have made one man, at least, realize the truth of this monstrous experience of mine. And, if the worst should happen, this diary remains as a proof of the goad that has driven me.

Evening. When I came to Wilson's, I was shown up, and found that he was sitting with Miss Penclosa. For half an hour I had to endure his fussy talk about his recent research into the exact nature of the spiritualistic rap, while the creature and I sat in silence looking across the room at each other. I read a sinister amusement in her eyes, and she must have seen hatred and menace in mine. I had almost despaired of having speech with her when he was called from the room, and we were left for a few moments together.

"Well, Professor Gilroy - or is it Mr. Gilroy?" said she, with that bitter smile of hers. "How is your friend Mr. Charles Sadler after the ball?"

"You fiend!" I cried. "You have come to the end of your tricks now. I will have no more of them. Listen to what I say." I strode across and shook her roughly by the shoulder "As sure as there is a God in heaven, I swear that if you try another of your deviltries upon me I will have your life for it. Come what may, I will have your life. I have come to the end of what a man can endure."

"Accounts are not quite settled between us," said she, with a passion that equalled my own. "I can love, and I can hate. You had your choice. You chose to spurn the first; now you must test the other. It will take a little more to break your spirit, I see, but broken it shall be. Miss Marden comes back tomorrow, as I understand."

"What has that to do with you?" I cried. "It is a pollution that you should dare even to think of her. If I thought that you would harm her - "

She was frightened, I could see, though she tried to brazen it out. She read the black thought in my mind, and cowered away from me.

"She is fortunate in having such a champion," said she. "He actually dares to threaten a lonely woman. I must really congratulate Miss Marden upon her protector."

The words were bitter, but the voice and manner were more acid still.

"There is no use talking," said I. "I only came here to tell you, - and to tell you most solemnly, - that your next outrage upon me will be your last." With that, as I heard Wilson's step upon the stair, I walked from the room. Ay, she may look venomous and deadly, but, for all that, she is beginning to see now that she has as much to fear from me as I can have from her. Murder! It has an ugly sound. But you don't talk of murdering a snake or of murdering a tiger. Let her have a care now.

May 5. I met Agatha and her mother at the station at eleven o'clock. She is looking so bright, so happy, so beautiful. And she was so overjoyed to see me. What have I done to deserve such love? I went back home with them, and we lunched together. All the troubles seem in a moment to have been shredded back from my life. She tells me that I am looking pale and worried and ill. The dear child puts it down to my loneliness and the perfunctory attentions of a housekeeper. I pray that she may never know the truth! May the shadow, if shadow there must be, lie ever black across my life and leave hers in the sunshine. I have just come back from them, feeling a new man. With her by my side I think that I could show a bold face to anything which life might send.

5 P.M. Now, let me try to be accurate. Let me try to say exactly how it occurred. It is fresh in my mind, and I can set it down correctly, though it is not likely that the time will ever come when I shall forget the doings of today.

I had returned from the Mardens' after lunch, and was cutting some microscopic sections in my freezing microtome, when in an instant I lost consciousness in the sudden hateful fashion which has become only too familiar to me of late.

When my senses came back to me I was sitting in a small chamber, very different from the one in which I had been working. It was cosy and bright, with chintz-covered settees, colored hangings, and a thousand pretty little trifles upon the wall. A small ornamental clock ticked in front of me, and the hands pointed to half-past three. It was all quite familiar to me, and yet I stared about for a moment in a half-dazed way until my eyes fell upon a cabinet photograph of myself upon the top of the piano. On the other side stood one of Mrs. Marden. Then, of course, I remembered where I was. It was Agatha's boudoir.

But how came I there, and what did I want? A horrible sinking came to my heart. Had I been sent here on some devilish errand? Had that errand already been done? Surely it must; otherwise, why should I be allowed to come back to consciousness? Oh, the agony of that moment! What had I done? I sprang to my feet in my despair, and as I did so a small glass bottle fell from my knees on to the carpet.

It was unbroken, and I picked it up. Outside was written "Sulphuric Acid. Fort." When I drew the round glass stopper, a thick fume rose slowly up, and a pungent, choking smell pervaded the room. I recognized it as one which I kept for chemical testing in my chambers. But why had I brought a bottle of vitriol into Agatha's chamber? Was it not this thick, reeking liquid with which jealous women had been known to mar the beauty of their rivals? My heart stood still as I held the bottle to the light. Thank God, it was full! No mischief had been done as yet. But had Agatha come in a minute sooner, was it not certain that the hellish parasite within me would have dashed the stuff into her - Ah, it will not bear to be thought of! But it must have been for that. Why else should I have brought it? At the thought of what I might have done my worn nerves broke down, and I sat shivering and twitching, the pitiable wreck of a man.

It was the sound of Agatha's voice and the rustle of her dress which restored me. I looked up, and saw her blue eyes, so full of tenderness and pity, gazing down at me.

"We must take you away to the country, Austin," she said. "You want rest and quiet. You look wretchedly ill."

"Oh, it is nothing!" said I, trying to smile. "It was only a momentary weakness. I am all right again now."

"I am so sorry to keep you waiting. Poor boy, you must have been here quite half an hour! The vicar was in the drawing-room, and, as I knew that you did not care for him, I thought it better that Jane should show you up here. I thought the man would never go!"

"Thank God he stayed! Thank God he stayed!" I cried hysterically.

"Why, what is the matter with you, Austin?" she asked, holding my arm as I staggered up from the chair. "Why are you glad that the vicar stayed? And what is this little bottle in your hand?"

"Nothing," I cried, thrusting it into my pocket. "But I must go. I have something important to do."

"How stern you look, Austin! I have never seen your face like that. You are angry?"

"Yes, I am angry."

"But not with me?"

"No, no, my darling! You would not understand."

"But you have not told me why you came."

"I came to ask you whether you would always love me - no matter what I did, or what shadow might fall on my name. Would you believe in me and trust me however black appearances might be against me?"

"You know that I would, Austin."

"Yes, I know that you would. What I do I shall do for you. I am driven to it. There is no other way out, my darling!" I kissed her and rushed from the room.

The time for indecision was at an end. As long as the creature threatened my own prospects and my honor there might be a question as to what I should do. But now, when Agatha - my innocent Agatha - was endangered, my duty lay before me like a turnpike road. I had no weapon, but I never paused for that. What weapon should I need, when I felt every muscle quivering with the strength of a frenzied man? I ran through the streets, so set upon what I had to do that I was only dimly conscious of the faces of friends whom I met - dimly conscious also that Professor Wilson met me, running with equal precipitance in the opposite direction. Breathless but resolute I reached the house and rang the bell. A white cheeked maid opened the door, and turned whiter yet when she saw the face that looked in at her.

"Show me up at once to Miss Penclosa," I demanded.

"Sir," she gasped, "Miss Penclosa died this afternoon at half-past three!"

Short Stories

THE MYSTERY OF SASASSA VALLEY

Do I know why Tom Donahue is called "Lucky Tom?" Yes; I do; and that is more than one in ten of those who call him so can say. I have knocked about a deal in my time, and seen some strange sights, but none stranger than the way in which Tom gained that sobriquet and his fortune with it. For I was with him at the time. - Tell it? Oh, certainly; but it is a longish story and a very strange one; so fill up your glass again, and light another cigar while I try to reel it off. Yes; a very strange one; beats some fairy stories I have heard; but it's true sir, every word of it. There are men alive at Cape Colony now who'll remember it and confirm what I say. Many a time has the tale been told round the fire in Boers' cabins from Orange State to Griqualand; yes, and out in the Bush and at the Diamond Fields too.

I'm roughish now sir; but I was entered at the Middle Temple once, and studied for the Bar. Tom - worse luck! - was one of my fellow-students; and a wildish time we had of it, until at last our finances ran short, and we were compelled to give up our so-called studies, and look about for some part of the world where two young fellows with strong arms and sound constitutions might make their mark. In those days the tide of emigration had scarcely begun to set in towards Africa, and so we thought our best chance would be down at Cape Colony. Well - to make a long story short - we set sail, and were deposited in Cape Town with less than five pounds in our pockets; and there we parted. We each tried our hands at many things, and had ups and downs; but when, at the end of three years, chance led each of us up-country and we met again, we were, I regret to say, in almost as bad a plight as when we started.

Well, this was not much of a commencement; and very disheartened we were, so disheartened that Tom spoke of going back to England and getting a clerkship. For you see we didn't know that we had played out all our small cards, and that the trumps were going to turn up. No; we thought our "hands" were bad all through. It was a very lonely part of the country that we were in, inhabited by a few scattered farmers, whose houses were stockaded and fenced in to defend them against the Kaffirs. Tom Donahue and I had a little hut right out in the Bush; but we were known to possess nothing, and to be handy with our revolvers, so we had little to fear. There we waited doing odd jobs, and hoping that something would turn up. Well, after we had been there about a month something did turn up upon a certain night, something which was the making of both of us; and it's about that night sir, that I'm going to tell you. I remember it well. The wind was howling past our cabin, and the rain threatened to burst in our rude window. We had a great wood-fire crackling and sputtering on the hearth, by which I was sitting mending a whip, while Tom was lying in his bunk groaning disconsolately at the chance which had led him to such a place.

"Cheer up, Tom - cheer up," said I. "No man ever knows what may be awaiting him."

"Ill-luck, ill-luck, Jack," he answered. "I always was an unlucky dog. Here have I been three years in this abominable country; and I see lads fresh from England jingling the money in their pockets, while I am as poor as when I landed. Ah, Jack, if you want to keep your head above water, old friend, you must try your fortune away from me."

"Nonsense, Tom; you're down in your luck tonight. But hark! Here's some one coming outside. Dick Wharton, by the tread; he'll rouse you, if any man can."

Even as I spoke the door was flung open, and honest Dick Wharton, with the water pouring from him, stepped in, his hearty red face looking through the haze like a harvest-moon. He shook himself, and after greeting us sat down by the fire to warm himself.

"Whereaway, Dick, on such a night as this?" said I. "You'll find the rheumatism a worse foe than the Kaffirs, unless you keep more regular hours."

Dick was looking unusually serious, almost frightened, one would say, if one did not know the man. "Had to go," he replied - "had to go. One of Madison's cattle has been straying down Sasassa Valley, and of course none of our blacks would go down that Valley at night; and if we lad waited till morning, the brute would have been in Kaffirland."

"Why wouldn't they go down Sasassa Valley at night?" asked Tom.

"Kaffirs, I suppose," said I.

"Ghosts," said Dick.

We both laughed.

"I suppose they didn't give such a matter-of-fact fellow as you a sight of their charms?" said Tom from the bunk.

"Yes," said Dick seriously - "yes; I saw what the niggers talk about; and I promise you, lads, I don't want ever to see it again."

Tom sat up in his bed. "Nonsense, Dick; you're joking, man! Come, tell us all about it. The legend first, and your own experience afterwards. - Pass him over the bottle, Jack."

"Well, as to the legend," began Dick " - it seems that the niggers have had it handed down to them that Sasassa Valley is haunted by a frightful fiend. Hunters and wanderers passing down the defile have seen its glowing eyes under the shadows of the cliff; and the story goes that whoever has chanced to encounter that baleful glare, has had his after-life blighted by the malignant power of this creature. Whether that be true or not," continued Dick ruefully, "I may have an opportunity of judging for myself."

"Go on, Dick - go on," cried Tom. "Let's hear about what you saw."

"Well, I was groping down the Valley, looking for that cow of Madison's, and I had, I suppose, got half-way down, where a black craggy cliff juts into the ravine on the right, when I halted to have a pull at my flask. I had my eye fixed at the time upon the projecting cliff I have mentioned, and noticed nothing unusual about it. I then put up my flask and took a step or two forward, when in a moment there burst apparently from the base of the rock, about eight feet from the ground and a hundred yards from me, a strange lurid glare, flickering and oscillating, gradually dying away and then reappearing again. - No, no; I've seen many a glow-worm and firefly - nothing of that sort. There it was burning away, and I suppose I gazed at it, trembling in every limb, for fully ten minutes. Then I took a step forwards, when instantly it vanished, vanished like a candle blown out. I stepped back again; but it was some time before I could find the exact spot and position from which it was visible. At last, there it was, the weird reddish light, flickering away as before. Then I screwed up my courage, and made for the rock; but the ground was so uneven that it was impossible to steer straight; and though I walked along the whole base of the cliff, I could see nothing. Then I made tracks for home; and I can tell you boys, that until you remarked it, I never knew it was raining, the whole way along. - But hullo! what's the matter with Tom?"

What indeed? Tom was now sitting with his legs over the side of the bunk, and his whole face betraying excitement so intense as to be almost painful. "The fiend would have two eyes. How many lights did you see, Dick? Speak out!"

"Only one."

"Hurrah!" cried Tom - "that's better!" Whereupon he kicked the blankets into the middle of the room, and began pacing up and down with long feverish strides. Suddenly he stopped opposite Dick, and laid his hand upon his shoulder: "I say Dick, could we get to Sasassa Valley before sunrise?"

"Scarcely," said Dick.

"Well, look here; we are old friends, Dick Wharton, you and I. Now, don't you tell any other man what you have told us, for a week. You'll promise that; won't you?"

I could see by the look on Dick's face as he acquiesced that he considered poor Tom to be mad; and indeed I was myself completely mystified by his conduct. I had, however, seen so many proofs of my friend's good sense and quickness of apprehension, that I thought it quite possible that Wharton's story had had a meaning in his eyes which I was too obtuse to take in.

All night Tom Donahue was greatly excited, and when Wharton left he begged him to remember his promise, and also elicited from him a description of the exact spot at which he had seen the apparition, as well as the hour at which it appeared. After his departure, which must have been about four in the morning, I turned into my bunk and watched Tom sitting by the fire splicing two sticks together, until I fell asleep. I suppose

I must have slept about two hours; but when I awoke, Tom was still sitting working away in almost the same position. He had fixed the one stick across the top of the other so as to form a rough T, and was now busy in fitting a smaller stick into the angle between them, by manipulating which, the cross one could be either cocked up or depressed to any extent. He had cut notches too in the perpendicular stick, so that by the aid of the small prop, the cross one could be kept in any position for an indefinite time.

"Look here, Jack!" he cried, whenever he saw that I was awake, "Come, and give me your opinion. Suppose I put this cross-stick pointing straight at a thing, and arranged this small one so as to keep it so, and left it, I could find that thing again if I wanted it - don't you think I could, Jack - don't you think so?" he continued nervously, clutching me by the arm.

"Well," I answered, "it would depend on how far off the thing was, and how accurately it was pointed. If it were any distance, I'd cut sights on your cross-stick; then a string tied to the end of it, and held in a plumb-line forwards, would lead you pretty near what you wanted. But surely, Tom, you don't intend to localise the ghost in that way?"

"You'll see tonight, old friend - you'll see tonight. I'll carry this to the Sasassa Valley. You get the loan of Madison's crowbar, and come with me; but mind you tell no man where you are going, or what you want it for."

All day Tom was walking up and down the room, or working hard at the apparatus. His eyes were glistening, his cheek hectic, and he had all the symptoms of high fever. "Heaven grant that Dick's diagnosis be not correct!" I thought, as I returned with the crowbar; and yet, as evening drew near, I found myself imperceptibly sharing the excitement.

About six o'clock Tom sprang to his feet and seized his sticks. "I can stand it no longer, Jack," he cried; "up with your crowbar, and hey for Sasassa Valley! Tonight's work, my lad, will either make us or mar us! Take your six-shooter, in case we meet the Kaffirs. I daren't take mine, Jack," he continued, putting his hands upon my shoulders - "I daren't take mine; for if my ill-luck sticks to me tonight, I don't know what I might not do with it."

Well, having filled our pockets with provisions, we set out, and as we took our wearisome way towards the Sasassa Valley, I frequently attempted to elicit from my companion some clue as to his intentions. But his only answer was: "Let us hurry on, Jack. Who knows how many have heard of Wharton's adventure by this time! Let us hurry on, or we may not be first in the field!"

Well sir, we struggled on through the hills for a matter of ten miles; till at last, after descending a crag, we saw opening out in front of us a ravine so sombre and dark that it might have been the gate of Hades itself; cliffs many hundred feet high shut in on every side the gloomy boulder-studded passage which led through the haunted defile into Kaffirland. The moon rising above the crags, threw into strong relief the rough irregular pinnacles of rock by which they were topped, while all below was dark as Erebus.

"The Sasassa Valley?" said I.

"Yes," said Tom.

I looked at him. He was calm now; the flush and feverishness had passed away; his actions were deliberate and slow. Yet there was a certain rigidity in his face and glitter in his eye which shewed that a crisis had come.

We entered the pass, stumbling along amid the great boulders. Suddenly I heard a short quick exclamation from Tom. "That's the crag!" he cried, pointing to a great mass looming before us in the darkness. "Now Jack, for any favour use your eyes! We're about a hundred yards from that cliff, I take it; so you move slowly towards one side, and I'll do the same towards the other. When you see anything, stop, and call out. Don't take more than twelve inches in a step, and keep your eye fixed on the cliff about eight feet from the ground. Are you ready?"

"Yes." I was even more excited than Tom by this time. What his intention or object was, I could not conjecture, beyond that he wanted to examine by daylight the part of the cliff from which the light came. Yet the influence of the romantic situation and of my companion's suppressed excitement was so great, that I could feel the blood coursing through my veins and count the pulses throbbing at my temples.

"Start!" cried Tom; and we moved off, he to the right, I to the left, each with our eyes fixed intently on the base of the crag. I had moved perhaps twenty feet, when in a moment it burst upon me. Through the growing darkness there shone a small ruddy glowing point, the light from which waned and increased, flickered and oscillated, each change producing a more weird effect than the last. The old Kaffir superstition came into my mind, and I felt a cold shudder pass over me. In my excitement, I stepped a pace backwards, when instantly the light went out, leaving utter darkness in its place; but when I advanced again, there was the ruddy glare glowing from the base of the cliff. "Tom, Tom!" I cried.

"Ay, ay!" I heard him exclaim, as he hurried over towards me.

"There it is - there, up against the cliff!"

Tom was at my elbow. "I see nothing," said he.

"Why, there, there, man, in front of you!" I stepped to the right as I spoke, when the light instantly vanished from my eyes.

But from Tom's ejaculations of delight it was clear that from my former position it was visible to him also. "Jack," he cried, as he turned and wrung my hand - "Jack, you and I can never complain of our luck again. Now heap up a few stones where we are standing. - That's right. Now we must fix my sign-post firmly in at the top. There! It would take a strong wind to blow that down; and we only need it to hold out till morning. O Jack, my boy, to think that only yesterday we were talking of becoming clerks, and you saying that no man knew what was awaiting him too! By Jove, Jack, it would make a good story!"

By this time we had firmly fixed the perpendicular stick in between two large stones; and Tom bent down and peered along the horizontal one. For fully a quarter of an hour he was alternately raising and depressing it, until at last, with a sigh of satisfaction, he fixed the prop into the angle, and stood up. "Look along, Jack," he said. "You have as straight an eye to take a sight as any man I know of."

I looked along. There, beyond the further sight was the ruddy scintillating speck, apparently at the end of the stick itself, so accurately had it been adjusted. "And now, my boy," said Tom, "let's have some supper, and a sleep. There's nothing more to be done tonight; but we'll need all our wits and strength tomorrow. Get some sticks, and kindle a fire here, and then we'll be able to keep an eye on our signal-post, and see that nothing happens to it during the night."

Well sir, we kindled a fire, and had supper with the Sasassa demon's eye rolling and glowing in front of us the whole night through. Not always in the same place though; for after supper, when I glanced along the sights to have another look at it, it was nowhere to be seen. The information did not, however, seem to disturb Tom in any way. He merely remarked: "It's the moon, not the thing, that has shifted;" and coiling himself up, went to sleep.

By early dawn we were both up, and gazing along our pointer at the cliff; but we could make out nothing save one dead monotonous slaty surface, rougher perhaps at the part we were examining than elsewhere, but otherwise presenting nothing remarkable.

"Now for your idea, Jack!" said Tom Donahue, unwinding a long thin cord from round his waist. "You fasten it, and guide me while I take the other end." So saying he walked off to the base of the cliff, holding one end of the cord, while I drew the other taut, and wound it round the middle of the horizontal stick, passing it through the sight at the end. By this means I could direct Tom to the right or left, until we had our string stretching from the point of attachment, through the sight, and on to the rock, which it struck about eight feet from the ground. Tom drew a chalk circle of about three feet diameter round the spot, and then called to me to come and join him. "We've managed this business together, Jack," he said, "and we'll find what we are to find, together." The circle he had drawn embraced a part of the rock smoother than the rest, save that about the centre there were a few rough protuberances or knobs. One of these Tom pointed to with a cry of delight. It was a roughish brownish mass about the size of a man's closed fist, and looking like a bit of dirty glass let into the wall of the cliff. "That's it!" he cried - "that's it!"

"That's what?"

"Why, man, a diamond, and such a one as there isn't a monarch in Europe but would envy Tom Donahue the possession of. Up with your crowbar, and we'll soon exorcise the demon of Sasassa Valley!"

I was so astounded that for a moment I stood speechless with surprise, gazing at the treasure which had so unexpectedly fallen into our hands.

"Here, hand me the crowbar," said Tom. "Now, by using this little round knob which projects from the cliff here, as a fulcrum, we may be able to lever it off. - Yes; there it goes. I never thought it could have come so easily. Now, Jack, the sooner we get back to our hut and then down to Cape Town, the better."

We wrapped up our treasure, and made our way across the hills, towards home. On the way, Tom told me how, while a law-student in the Middle Temple, he had come upon a dusty pamphlet in the library, by one Jans van Hounym, which told of an experience very similar to ours, which had befallen that worthy Duchman in the latter part of the seventeenth century, and which resulted in the discovery of a luminous diamond. This tale it was which had come into Tom's head as he listened to honest Dick Wharton's ghost-story; while the means which he had adopted to verify his supposition sprang from his own fertile Irish brain.

"We'll take it down to Cape Town," continued Tom, "and if we can't dispose of it with advantage there, it will be worth our while to ship for London with it. Let us go along to Madison's first, though; he knows something of these things, and can perhaps give us some idea of what we may consider a fair price for our treasure."

We turned off from the track accordingly, before reaching our hut, and kept along the narrow path leading to Madison's farm. He was at lunch when we entered; and in a minute we were seated at each side of him, enjoying South African hospitality.

"Well," he said, after the servants were gone, "what's in the wind now? I see you have something to say to me. What is it?"

Tom produced his packet, and solemnly untied the handkerchiefs which enveloped it. "There!" he said, putting his crystal on the table; "what would you say was a fair price for that?"

Madison took it up and examined it critically. "Well," he said, laying it down again, "in its crude state about twelve shillings per ton."

"Twelve shillings!" cried Tom, starting to his feet. "Don't you see what it is?"

"Rock-salt!"

"Rock fiddle; a diamond."

"Taste it!" said Madison.

Tom put it to his lips, dashed it down with a dreadful exclamation, and rushed out of the room.

I felt sad and disappointed enough myself; but presently remembering what Tom had said about the pistol, I, too, left the house, and made for the hut, leaving Madison open-mouthed with astonishment. When I got in, I found Tom lying in his bunk with his face to the wall, too dispirited apparently to answer my consolations. Anathematising Dick and Madison, the Sasassa demon, and everything else, I strolled out of the hut, and refreshed myself with a pipe after our wearisome adventure. I was about fifty yards away from the hut, when I heard issuing from it the sound which of all others I least expected to hear. Had it been a groan or an oath, I should have taken it as a matter of course; but the sound which caused me to stop and take the pipe out of my mouth was a hearty roar of laughter! Next moment, Tom himself emerged from the door, his whole face radiant with delight. "Game for another ten-mile walk, old fellow?"

"What! for another lump of rock-salt, at twelve shillings a ton?"

"'No more of that, Hal, an you love me,'" grinned Tom. "Now look here, Jack. What blessed fools we are to be so floored by a trifle! Just sit on this stump for five minutes, and I'll make it as clear as daylight. You've seen many a lump of rock-salt stuck in a crag, and so have I, though we did make such a mull of this one. Now, Jack, did any of the pieces you have ever seen shine in the darkness brighter than any fire-fly?"

"Well, I can't say they ever did."

"I'd venture to prophesy that if we waited until night, which we won't do, we would see that light still glimmering among the rocks. Therefore, Jack, when we took away this worthless salt, we took the wrong crystal. It is no very strange thing in these hills that a piece of rock-salt should be lying within a foot of a diamond. It caught our eyes, and we were excited, and so we made fools of ourselves, and left the real stone behind. Depend upon it, Jack, the Sasassa gem is lying within this magic circle of chalk upon the face of yonder cliff. Come, old fellow, light your pipe and stow your revolver, and we'll be off before that fellow Madison has time to put two and two together."

I don't know that I was very sanguine this time. I had begun in fact to look upon the diamond as a most unmitigated nuisance. However, rather than throw a damper on Tom's expectations, I announced myself eager to start. What a walk it was! Tom was always a good mountaineer, but his excitement seemed to lend him wings that day, while I scrambled along after him as best I could. When we got within half a mile he broke into the "double," and never pulled up until he reached the round white circle upon the cliff. Poor old Tom! when I came up, his mood had changed, and he was standing with his hands in his pockets, gazing vacantly before him with a rueful countenance.

"Look!" he said - "look!" and he pointed at the cliff. Not a sign of anything in the least resembling a diamond there. The circle included nothing but flat slate-coloured stone, with one large hole, where we had extracted the rock-salt, and one or two smaller depressions. No sign of the gem. "I've been over every inch of it," said poor Tom. "It's not there. Someone has been here and noticed the chalk, and taken it. Come home, Jack; I feel sick and tired. Oh! had any man ever luck like mine!"

I turned to go, but took one last look at the cliff first. Tom was already ten paces off.

"Honor!" I cried, "don't you see any change in that circle since yesterday?"

"What d'ye mean?" said Tom.

"Don't you miss a thing that was there before?"

"The rock-salt?" said Tom.

"No; but the little round knob that we used for a fulcrum. I suppose we must have wrenched it off in using the lever. Let's have a look at what it's made of."

Accordingly, at the foot of the cliff we searched about among the loose stones.

"Here you are, Jack! We've done it at last! We're made men!"

I turned round, and there was Tom radiant with delight, and with a little corner of black rock in his hand. At first sight it seemed to be merely a chip from the cliff; but near the base there was projecting from it an object which Tom was now exultingly pointing out. It looked at first something like a glass eye; but there was a depth and brilliancy about it such as glass never exhibited. There was no mistake this time; we had certainly got possession of a jewel of great value; and with light hearts we turned from the valley, bearing away with us the "fiend" which had so long reigned there.

There sir; I've spun my story out too long, and tired you perhaps. You see when I get talking of those rough old days, I kind of see the little cabin again, and the brook beside it, and the bush around, and seem to hear Tom's honest voice once more. There's little for me to say now. We prospered on the gem. Tom Donahue, as you know, has set up here, and is well known about town. I have done well, farming and ostrich-raising in Africa. We set old Dick Wharton up in business, and he is one of our nearest neighbours. If you should ever be coming up our way sir, you'll not forget to ask for Jack Turnbull - Jack Turnbull of Sasassa Farm.

THAT LITTLE SQUARE BOX

"All aboard?" said the captain.

"All aboard, sir!" said the mate.

"Then stand by to let her go."

It was nine o'clock on a Wednesday morning. The good ship Spartan was lying off Boston Quay with her cargo under hatches, her passengers shipped, and everything prepared for a start. The warning whistle had been sounded twice; the final bell had been rung. Her bowsprit was turned towards England, and the hiss of escaping steam showed that all was ready for her run of three thousand miles. She strained at the warps that held her like a greyhound at its leash,

I have the misfortune to be a very nervous man. A sedentary literary life has helped to increase the morbid love of solitude which, even in my boyhood, was one of my distinguishing characteristics. As I stood upon the quarter-deck of the Transatlantic steamer, I bitterly cursed the necessity which drove me back to the land of my forefathers. The shouts of the sailors, the rattle of the cordage, the farewells of my fellow-passengers, and the cheers of the mob, each and all jarred upon my sensitive nature. I felt sad too. An indescribable feeling, as of some impending calamity, seemed to haunt me. The sea was calm, and the breeze light. There was nothing to disturb the equanimity of the most confirmed of landsmen, yet I felt as if I stood upon the verge of a great though indefinable danger. I have noticed that such presentiments occur often in men of my peculiar temperament, and that they are not uncommonly fulfilled. There is a theory that it arises from a species of second-sight, a subtle spiritual communication with the future. I well remember that Herr Raumer, the eminent spiritualist, remarked on one occasion that I was the most sensitive subject as regards supernatural phenomena that he had ever encountered in the whole of his wide experience. Be that as it may, I certainly felt far from happy as I threaded my way among the weeping, cheering groups which dotted the white decks of the good ship Spartan. Had I known the experience which awaited me in the course of the next twelve hours I should even then at the last moment have sprung upon the shore, and made my escape from the accursed vessel.

"Time's up!" said the captain, closing his chronometer with a snap, and replacing it in his pocket. "Time's up!" said the mate. There was a last wail from the whistle, a rush of friends and relatives upon the land. One warp was loosened, the gangway was being pushed away, when there was a shout from the bridge, and two men appeared, running rapidly down the quay. They were waving their hands and making frantic gestures, apparently with the intention of stopping the ship. "Look sharp!" shouted the crowd.

"Hold hard!" cried the captain. "Ease her! stop her! Up with the gangway!" and the two men sprang aboard just as the second warp parted, and a convulsive throb of the engine shot us clear of the shore. There was a cheer from the deck, another from the quay, a mighty fluttering of handkerchiefs, and the great vessel ploughed its way out of the harbour, and steamed grandly away across the placid bay.

We were fairly started upon our fortnight's voyage. There was a general dive among the passengers in quest of berths and luggage, while a popping of corks in the saloon proved that more than one bereaved traveller was adopting artificial means for drowning the pangs of separation. I glanced round the deck and took a running inventory of my compagnons de voyage. They presented the usual types met with upon these occasions. There was no striking face among them. I speak as a connoisseur, for faces are a specialty of mine. I pounce upon a characteristic feature as a botanist does on a flower, and bear it away with me to analyse at my leisure, and classify and label it in my little anthropological museum. There was nothing worthy of me here. Twenty types of young America going to "Yurrup," a few respectable middle-aged couples as an antidote, a sprinkling of clergymen and professional men, young ladies, bagmen, British exclusives, and all the olla podrida of an ocean-going steamer. I turned away from them and gazed back at the receding shores of America, and, as a cloud of remembrances rose before me, my heart warmed towards the land of my adoption. A pile of portmanteaus and luggage chanced to be lying on one side of the deck, awaiting their turn to be taken below. With my usual love for solitude I walked behind these, and sitting on a coil of rope between them and the vessel's side, I indulged in a melancholy reverie.

I was aroused from this by a whisper behind me. "Here's a quiet place," said the voice. "Sit down, and we can talk it over in safety."

Glancing through a chink between two colossal chests, I saw that the passengers who had joined us at the last moment were standing at the other side of the pile. They had evidently failed to see me as I crouched in the shadow of the boxes. The one who had spoken was a tall and very thin man with a blue-black beard and a colourless face. His manner was nervous and excited. His companion was a short plethoric little fellow, with a brisk and resolute air. He had a cigar in his mouth, and a large ulster slung over his left arm. They both glanced round uneasily, as if to ascertain whether they were alone. "This is just the place," I heard the other say. They sat down on a bale of goods with their backs turned towards me, and I found myself, much against my will, playing the unpleasant part of eavesdropper to their conversation.

"Well, Muller," said the taller of the two, "we've got it aboard right enough."

"Yes," assented the man whom he had addressed as Muller, "it's safe aboard."

"It was rather a near go."

"It was that, Flannigan."

"It wouldn't have done to have missed the ship."

"No, it would have put our plans out."

"Ruined them entirely," said the little man, and puffed furiously at his cigar for some minutes.

"I've got it here," he said at last.

"Let me see it."

"Is no one looking?"

"No, they are nearly all below."

"We can't be too careful where so much is at stake," said Muller, as he uncoiled the ulster which hung over his arm, and disclosed a dark object which he laid upon the deck. One glance at it was enough to cause me to spring to my feet with an exclamation of horror. Luckily they were so engrossed in the matter on hand that neither of them observed me. Had they turned their heads they would infallibly have seen my pale face glaring at them over the pile of boxes.

From the first moment of their conversation a horrible misgiving had come over me. It seemed more than confirmed as I gazed at what lay before me. It was a little square box made of some dark wood, and ribbed with brass. I suppose it was about the size of a cubic foot. It reminded me of a pistol-case, only it was decidedly higher. There was an appendage to it, however, on which my eyes were riveted, and which suggested the pistol itself rather than its receptacle. This was a trigger-like arrangement upon the lid, to which a coil of string was attached. Beside this trigger there was a small square aperture through the wood. The tall man, Flannigan, as his companion called him, applied his eye to this, and peered in for several minutes with an expression of intense anxiety upon his face.

"It seems right enough," he said at last.

"I tried not to shake it," said his companion.

"Such delicate things need delicate treatment. Put in some of the needful, Muller."

The shorter man fumbled in his pocket for some time, and then produced a small paper packet. He opened this, and took out of it half a handful of whitish granules, which he poured down through the hole. A curious clicking noise followed from the inside of the box, and both the men smiled in a satisfied way.

"Nothing much wrong there," said Flannigan.

"Right as a trivet," answered his companion.

"Look out! here's some one coming. Take it down to our berth. It wouldn't do to have any one suspecting what our game is, or, worse still, have them fumbling with it, and letting it off by mistake."

"Well, it would come to the same, whoever let it off," said Muller.

"They'd be rather astonished if they pulled the trigger," said the taller, with a sinister laugh. "Ha, ha! fancy their faces! It's not a bad bit of workmanship, I flatter myself."

"No," said Muller. "I hear it is your own design, every bit of it, isn't it?"

"Yes, the spring and the sliding shutter are my own."

"We should take out a patent."

And the two men laughed again with a cold harsh laugh, as they took up the little brass-bound package, and concealed it in Muller's voluminous overcoat.

"Come down, and we'll stow it in our berth," said Flannigan. "We won't need it until tonight, and it will be safe there."

His companion assented, and the two went arm-in-arm along the deck and disappeared down the hatchway, bearing the mysterious little box away with them. The last words I heard were a muttered injunction from Flannigan to carry it carefully, and avoid knocking it against the bulwarks.

How long I remained sitting on that coil of rope I shall never know. The horror of the conversation I had just overheard was aggravated by the first sinking qualms of sea-sickness. The long roll of the Atlantic was beginning to assert itself over both ship and passengers. I felt prostrated in mind and in body, and fell into a state of collapse, from which I was finally aroused by the hearty voice of our worthy quartermaster.

"Do you mind moving out of that, sir?" he said. "We want to get this lumber cleared off the deck."

His bluff manner and ruddy healthy face seemed to be a positive insult to me in my present condition. Had I been a courageous or a muscular man I could have struck him. As it was, I treated the honest sailor to a melodramatic scowl which seemed to cause him no small astonishment, and strode past him to the other side of the deck. Solitude was what I wanted - solitude in which I could brood over the frightful crime which was being hatched before my very eyes. One of the quarter-boats was hanging rather low down upon the davits. An idea struck me, and climbing on the bulwarks, I stepped into the empty boat and lay down in the bottom of it. Stretched on my back, with nothing but the blue sky above me, and an occasional view of the mizen as the vessel rolled, I was at least alone with my sickness and my thoughts.

I tried to recall the words which had been spoken in the terrible dialogue I had overheard. Would they admit of any construction but the one which stared me in the face? My reason forced me to confess that they would not. I endeavoured to array the various facts which formed the chain of circumstantial evidence, and to find a flaw in it; but no, not a link was missing. There was the strange way in which our passengers had come aboard, enabling them to evade any examination of their luggage. The very name of "Flannigan" smacked of Fenianism, while "Muller" suggested nothing but socialism and murder. Then their mysterious manner; their remark that their plans would have been ruined had they missed the ship; their fear of being observed; last, but not least, the clenching evidence in the production of the little square box with the trigger, and their grim joke about the face of the man who should let it off by mistake - could these facts lead to any conclusion other than that they were the desperate emissaries of some body, political or otherwise, who intended to sacrifice themselves, their fellow-passengers, and the ship, in one great holocaust? The whitish granules which I had seen one of them pour into the box formed no doubt a fuse or train for exploding it. I had myself heard a sound come from it which might have emanated from some delicate piece of machinery. But what did they mean by their allusion to tonight? Could it be that they contemplated putting their horrible design into execution on the very first evening of our voyage? The mere thought of it sent a cold shudder over me, and made me for a moment superior even to the agonies of sea-sickness.

I have remarked that I am a physical coward. I am a moral one also. It is seldom that the two defects are united to such a degree in the one character. I have known many men who were most sensitive to bodily danger, and yet were distinguished for the independence and strength of their minds. In my own case, however, I regret to say that my quiet and retiring habits had fostered a nervous dread of doing anything remarkable or making myself conspicuous, which exceeded, if possible, my fear of personal peril. An ordinary mortal placed under the circumstances in which I now found myself would have gone at once to the Captain, confessed his fears, and put the matter into his hands. To me, however, constituted as I am, the idea was most repugnant. The thought of becoming the observed of all observers, cross-questioned by a stranger, and confronted with two desperate conspirators in the character of a denouncer, was hateful to me. Might it not by some remote possibility prove that I was mistaken? What would be my feelings if there should turn out to be no grounds for my accusation? No, I would procrastinate; I would keep my eye on the two desperadoes and dog them at every turn. Anything was better than the possibility of being wrong.

Then it struck me that even at that moment some new phase of the conspiracy might be developing itself. The nervous excitement seemed to have driven away my incipient attack of sickness, for I was able to stand up and lower myself from the boat without experiencing any return of it. I staggered along the deck with the intention of descending into the cabin and finding how my acquaintances of the morning were occupying themselves. Just as I had my hand on the companion-rail, I was astonished by receiving a hearty slap on the back, which nearly shot me down the steps with more haste than dignity.

"Is that you, Hammond?" said a voice which I seemed to recognise.

"God bless me," I said, as I turned round, "it can't be Dick Merton! Why, how are you, old man?"

This was an unexpected piece of luck in the midst of my perplexities. Dick was just the man I wanted; kindly and shrewd in his nature, and prompt in his actions, I should have no difficulty in telling him my suspicions, and could rely upon his sound sense to point out the best course to pursue. Since I was a little lad in the second form at Harrow, Dick had been my adviser and protector. He saw at a glance that something had gone wrong with me.

"Hullo!" he said, in his kindly way, "what's put you about, Hammond? You look as white as a sheet. Mal de mer, eh?"

"No, not that altogether," said I. "Walk up and down with me, Dick; I want to speak to you. Give me your arm."

Supporting myself on Dick's stalwart frame, I tottered along by his side; but it was some time before I could muster resolution to speak.

"Have a cigar," said he, breaking the silence.

"No, thanks," said I. "Dick, we shall be all corpses tonight."

"That's no reason against your having a cigar now," said Dick, in his cool way, but looking hard at me from under his shaggy eyebrows as he spoke. He evidently thought that my intellect was a little gone.

"No," I continued, "it's no laughing matter; and I speak in sober earnest, I assure you. I have discovered an infamous conspiracy, Dick, to destroy this ship and every soul that is in her;" and I then proceeded systematically, and in order, to lay before him the chain of evidence which I had collected. "There, Dick," I said, as I concluded, "what do you think of that? and, above all, what am I to do?"

To my astonishment he burst into a hearty fit of laughter.

"I'd be frightened," he said, "if any fellow but you had told me as much. You always had a way, Hammond, of discovering mares' nests. I like to see the old traits breaking out again. Do you remember at school how you swore there was a ghost in the long room, and how it turned out to be your own reflection in the mirror. Why, man," he continued, "what object would anyone have in destroying this ship? We have no great political guns aboard. On the contrary, the majority of the passengers are Americans. Besides, in this sober nineteenth century, the most wholesale murderers stop at including themselves among their victims. Depend upon it, you have misunderstood them, and have mistaken a photographic camera, or something equally innocent, for an infernal machine."

"Nothing of the sort, sir," said I, rather touchily "You will learn to your cost, I fear, that I have neither exaggerated nor misinterpreted a word. As to the box, I have certainly never before seen one like it. It contained delicate machinery; of that I am convinced, from the way in which the men handled it and spoke of it."

"You'd make out every packet of perishable goods to be a torpedo," said Dick, "if that is to be your only test."

"The man's name was Flannigan," I continued.

"I don't think that would go very far in a court of law," said Dick; "but come, I have finished my cigar. Suppose we go down together and split a bottle of claret. You can point out these two Orsinis to me if they are still in the cabin."

"All right," I answered; "I am determined not to lose sight of them all day. Don't look hard at them, though, for I don't want them to think that they are being watched."

"Trust me," said Dick; "I'll look as unconscious and guileless as a lamb;" and with that we passed down the companion and into the saloon.

A good many passengers were scattered about the great central table, some wrestling with refractory carpet bags and rug-straps, some having their luncheon, and a few reading and otherwise amusing themselves. The objects of our quest were not there. We passed down the room and peered into every berth, but there was no sign of them. "Heavens!" thought I, "perhaps at this very moment they are beneath our feet, in the hold or engine-room, preparing their diabolical contrivance!" It was better to know the worst than to remain in such suspense.

"Steward," said Dick, "are there any other gentlemen about?"

"There's two in the smoking-room, sir," answered the steward.

The smoking-room was a little snuggery, luxuriously fitted up, and adjoining the pantry. We pushed the door open and entered. A sigh of relief escaped from my bosom. The very first object on which my eye rested was the cadaverous face of Flannigan, with its hard-set mouth and unwinking eye. His companion sat opposite to him. They were both drinking, and a pile of cards lay upon the table. They were engaged in playing as we entered. I nudged Dick to show him that we had found our quarry, and we sat down beside them with as unconcerned an air as possible. The two conspirators seemed to take little notice of our presence. I watched them both narrowly. The game at which they were playing was "Napoleon." Both were adepts at it, and I could not help admiring the consummate nerve of men who, with such a secret at their hearts, could devote their minds to the manipulating of a long suit or the finessing of a queen. Money changed hands rapidly; but the run of luck seemed to be all against the taller of the two players. At last he threw down his cards on the table with an oath, and refused to go on.

"No, I'm hanged if I do," he said; "I haven't had more than two of a suit for five hands."

"Never mind," said his comrade, as he gathered up his winnings; "a few dollars one way or the other won't go very far after tonight's work."

I was astonished at the rascal's audacity, but took care to keep my eyes fixed abstractedly upon the ceiling, and drank my wine in as unconscious a manner as possible. I felt that Flannigan was looking towards me with his wolfish eyes to see if I had noticed the allusion. He whispered something to his companion which I failed to catch. It was a caution, I suppose, for the other answered rather angrily -

"Nonsense! Why shouldn't I say what I like? Over-caution is just what would ruin us."

"I believe you want it not to come off," said Flannigan.

"You believe nothing of the sort," said the other, speaking rapidly and loudly. "You know as well as I do that when I play for a stake I like to win it. But I won't have my words criticised and cut short by you or any other man. I have as much interest in our success as you have - more, I hope."

He was quite hot about it, and puffed furiously at his cigar for some minutes. The eyes of the other ruffian wandered alternately from Dick Merton to myself. I knew that I was in the presence of a desperate man, that a quiver of my lip might be the signal for him to plunge a weapon into my heart, but I betrayed more self-command than I should have given myself credit for under such trying circumstances. As to Dick, he was as immovable and apparently as unconscious as the Egyptian Sphinx.

There was silence for some time in the smoking-room, broken only by the crisp rattle of the cards, as the man Muller shuffled them up before replacing them in his pocket. He still seemed to be somewhat flushed and irritable. Throwing the end of his cigar into the spittoon, he glanced defiantly at his companion and turned towards me.

"Can you tell me, sir," he said, "when this ship will be heard of again?"

They were both looking at me; but though my face may have turned a trifle paler, my voice was as steady as ever as I answered -

"I presume, sir, that it will be heard of first when it enters Queenstown Harbour."

"Ha, ha!" laughed the angry little man, "I knew you would say that. Don't you kick me under the table, Flannigan, I won't stand it. I know what I am doing. You are wrong, sir," he continued, turning to me, "utterly wrong."

"Some passing ship, perhaps," suggested Dick.

"No, nor that either."

"The weather is fine," I said; "why should we not be heard of at our destination."

"I didn't say we shouldn't be heard of at our destination. Possibly we may not, and in any case that is not where we shall be heard of first."

"Where then?" asked Dick.

"That you shall never know. Suffice it that a rapid and mysterious agency will signal our whereabouts, and that before the day is out. Ha, ha!" and he chuckled once again.

"Come on deck!" growled his comrade; "you have drunk too much of that confounded brandy-and-water. It has loosened your tongue. Come away!" and taking him by the arm he half led him, half forced him out of the smoking-room, and we heard them stumbling up the companion together, and on to the deck.

"Well, what do you think now?" I gasped, as I turned towards Dick. He was as imperturbable as ever.

"Think!" he said; "why, I think what his companion thinks, that we have been listening to the ravings of a half-drunken man. The fellow stunk of brandy."

"Nonsense, Dick I you saw how the other tried to stop his tongue."

"Of course he did. He didn't want his friend to make a fool of himself before strangers. Maybe the short one is a lunatic, and the other his private keeper. It's quite possible."

"O Dick, Dick," I cried, "how can you be so blind! Don't you see that every word confirmed our previous suspicion?"

"Humbug, man!" said Dick; "you're working yourself into a state of nervous excitement. Why, what the devil do you make of all that nonsense about a mysterious agent which would signal our whereabouts?"

"I'll tell you what he meant, Dick," I said, bending forward and grasping my friend's arm. "He meant a sudden glare and a flash seen far out at sea by some lonely fisherman off the American coast. That's what he meant."

"I didn't think you were such a fool, Hammond," said Dick Merton testily. "If you try to fix a literal meaning on the twaddle that every drunken man talks, you will come to some queer conclusions. Let us follow their example, and go on deck. You need fresh air, I think. Depend upon it, your liver is out of order. A sea-voyage will do you a world of good."

"If ever I see the end of this one," I groaned, "I'll promise never to venture on another. They are laying the cloth, so it's hardly worth while my going up. I'll stay below and unpack my things."

"I hope dinner will find you in a more pleasant state of mind," said Dick; and he went out, leaving me to my thoughts until the clang of the great gong summoned us to the saloon.

My appetite, I need hardly say, had not been improved by the incidents which had occurred during the day. I sat down, however, mechanically at the table, and listened to the talk which was going on around me. There were nearly a hundred first-class passengers, and as the wine began to circulate, their voices combined with the clash of the dishes to form a perfect Babel. I found myself seated between a very stout and nervous old lady and a prim little clergyman; and as neither made any advances I retired into my shell, and spent my time in observing the appearance of my fellow-voyagers. I could see Dick in the dim distance dividing his attentions between a jointless fowl in front of him and a self-possessed young lady at his side. Captain Dowie was doing the honours at my end, while the surgeon of the vessel was seated at the other. I was glad to notice that Flannigan was placed almost opposite to me. As long as I had him before my eyes I knew that, for the time at least, we were safe. He was sitting with what was meant to be a sociable smile on his grim face. It did not escape me that he drank largely of wine - so largely that even before the dessert appeared his voice had become decidedly husky. His friend Muller was seated a few places lower down. He ate little, and appeared to be nervous and restless.

"Now, ladies," said our genial Captain, "I trust that you will consider yourselves at home aboard my vessel. I have no fears for the gentlemen. A bottle of champagne, steward. Here's to a fresh breeze and a quick passage! I trust our friends in America will hear of our safe arrival in eight days, or in nine at the very latest."

I looked up. Quick as was the glance which passed between Flannigan and his confederate, I was able to intercept it. There was an evil smile upon the former's thin lips.

The conversation rippled on. Politics, the sea, amusements, religion, each was in turn discussed. I remained a silent though an interested listener. It struck me that no harm could be done by introducing the subject which was ever in my mind. It could be managed in an off-hand way, and would at least have the effect of turning the Captain's thoughts in that direction. I could watch, too, what effect it would have upon the faces of the conspirators.

There was a sudden lull in the conversation. The ordinary subjects of interest appeared to be exhausted. The opportunity was a favourable one.

"May I ask, Captain," I said, bending forward and speaking very distinctly, "what you think of Fenian manifestoes?"

The Captain's ruddy face became a shade darker from honest indignation.

"They are poor cowardly things," he said, "as silly as they are wicked."

"The impotent threats of a set of anonymous scoundrels," said a pompous-looking old gentleman beside him.

"O Captain!" said the fat lady at my side, "you don't really think they would blow up a ship?"

"I have no doubt they would if they could. But I am very sure they shall never blow up mine."

"May I ask what precautions are taken against them?" asked an elderly man at the end of the table.

"All goods sent aboard the ship are strictly examined," said Captain Dowie.

"But suppose a man brought explosives aboard with him?" I suggested.

"They are too cowardly to risk their own lives in that way."

During this conversation Flannigan had not betrayed the slightest interest in what was going on. He raised his head now and looked at the Captain.

"Don't you think you are rather underrating them?" he said. "Every secret society has produced desperate men - why shouldn't the Fenians have them too? Many men think it a privilege to die in the service of a cause which seems right in their eyes, though others may think it wrong"

"Indiscriminate murder cannot be right in anybody's eyes," said the little clergyman.

"The bombardment of Paris was nothing else," said Flannigan; "yet the whole civilised world agreed to look on with folded arms, and change the ugly word 'murder' into the more euphonious one of 'war.' It seemed right enough to German eyes; why shouldn't dynamite seem so to the Fenian?"

"At any rate their empty vapourings have led to nothing as yet," said the Captain.

"Excuse me," returned Flannigan, "but is there not some room for doubt yet as to the fate of the Dotterel? I have met men in America who asserted from their own personal knowledge that there was a coal torpedo aboard that vessel."

"Then they lied," said the Captain. "It was proved conclusively at the court-martial to have arisen from an explosion of coal-gas - but we had better change the subject, or we may cause the ladies to have a restless night;" and the conversation once more drifted back into its original channel.

During this little discussion Flannigan had argued his point with a gentlemanly deference and a quiet power for which I had not given him credit. I could not help admiring a man who, on the eve of a desperate enterprise, could courteously argue upon a point which must touch him so nearly. He had, as I have already mentioned, partaken of a considerable quantity of wine; but though there was a slight flush upon his pale cheek, his manner was as reserved as ever. He did not join in the conversation again, but seemed to be lost in thought.

A whirl of conflicting ideas was battling in my own mind. What was I to do? Should I stand up now and denounce them before both passengers and Captain? Should I demand a few minutes' conversation with the latter in his own cabin, and reveal it all? For an instant I was half resolved to do it, but then the old constitutional timidity came back with redoubled force. After all there might be some mistake. Dick had heard the evidence and had refused to believe in it. I determined to let things go on their course. A strange reckless feeling came over me. Why should I help men who were blind to their own danger? Surely it was the duty of the officers to protect us, not ours to give warning to them. I drank off a couple of glasses of wine, and staggered upon deck with the determination of keeping my secret locked in my own bosom.

It was a glorious evening. Even in my excited state of mind I could not help leaning against the bulwarks and enjoying the refreshing breeze. Away to the westward a solitary sail stood out as a dark speck against the great sheet of flame left by the setting sun. I shuddered as I looked at it. It was grand but appalling. A single star was twinkling faintly above our mainmast, but a thousand seemed to gleam in the water below with every stroke of our propeller. The only blot in the fair scene was the great trail of smoke which stretched away behind us like a black slash upon a crimson curtain. It was hard to believe that the great peace which hung over all Nature could be marred by a poor miserable mortal.

"After all," I thought, as I gazed into the blue depths beneath me, "if the worst comes to the worst, it is better to die here than to linger in agony upon a sick-bed on land." A man's life seems a very paltry thing amid the great forces of Nature. All my philosophy could not prevent my shuddering, however, when I turned my head and saw two shadowy figures at the other side of the deck, which I had no difficulty in recognising. They seemed to be conversing earnestly, but I had no opportunity of overhearing what was said; so I contented myself with pacing up and down, and keeping a vigilant watch upon their movements.

It was a relief to me when Dick came on deck. Even an incredulous confidant is better than none at all.

"Well, old man," he said, giving me a facetious dig in the ribs, "we've not been blown up yet."

"No, not yet," said I; "but that's no proof that we are not going to be."

"Nonsense, man!" said Dick; "I can't conceive what has put this extraordinary idea into your head. I have been talking to one of your supposed assassins, and he seems a pleasant fellow enough; quite a sporting character, I should think, from the way he speaks."

"Dick," I said, "I am as certain that those men have an infernal machine, and that we are on the verge of eternity, as if I saw them putting the match to the fuse."

"Well, if you really think so," said Dick, half awed for the moment by the earnestness of my manner, "it is your duty to let the Captain know of your suspicions."

"You are right," I said; "I will. My absurd timidity has prevented my doing so sooner. I believe our lives can only be saved by laying the whole matter before him."

"Well, go and do it now," said Dick; "but for goodness' sake don't mix me up in the matter."

"I'll speak to him when he comes off the bridge," I answered; "and in the meantime I don't mean to lose sight of them."

"Let me know of the result," said my companion; and with a nod he strolled away in search, I fancy, of his partner at the dinner-table.

Left to myself, I bethought me of my retreat of the morning, and climbing on the bulwark I mounted into the quarter-boat, and lay down there. In it I could reconsider my course of action, and by raising my head I was able at any time to get a view of my disagreeable neighbours.

An hour passed, and the Captain was still on the bridge. He was talking to one of the passengers, a retired naval officer, and the two were deep in debate concerning some abstruse point in navigation. I could see the red tips of their cigars from where I lay. It was dark now, so dark that I could hardly make out the figures of Flannigan and his accomplice. They were still standing in the position which they had taken up after dinner. A few of the passengers were scattered about the deck, but many had gone below. A strange stillness seemed to pervade the air. The voices of the watch and the rattle of the wheel were the only sounds which broke the silence.

Another half-hour passed. The Captain was still upon the bridge. It seemed as if he would never come down. My nerves were in a state of unnatural tension, so much so that the sound of two steps upon the deck made me start up in a quiver of excitement. I peered over the edge of the boat, and saw that our suspicious passengers had crossed from the other side, and were standing almost directly beneath me. The light of a binnacle fell full upon the ghastly face of the ruffian Flannigan. Even in that short glance I saw that Muller had the ulster, whose use I knew so well, slung loosely over his arm. I sank back with a groan. It seemed that my fatal procrastination had sacrificed two hundred innocent lives.

I had read of the fiendish vengeance which awaited a spy. I knew that men with their lives in their hands would stick at nothing. All I could do was to cower at the bottom of the boat and listen silently to their whispered talk below.

"This place will do," said a voice.

"Yes, the leeward side is best."

"I wonder if the trigger will act?"

"I am sure it will."

"We were to let it off at ten, were we not?"

"Yes, at ten sharp. We have eight minutes yet." There was a pause. Then the voice began again -

"They'll hear the drop of the trigger, won't they?"

"It doesn't matter. It will be too late for anyone to prevent its going off."

"That's true. There will be some excitement among those we have left behind, won't there?"

"Rather. How long do you reckon it will be before they hear of us?"

"The first news will get in at about midnight at earliest."

"That will be my doing."

"No, mine."

"Ha, ha! we'll settle that."

There was a pause here. Then I heard Muller's voice in a ghastly whisper, "There's only five minutes more."

How slowly the moments seemed to pass! I could count them by the throbbing of my heart.

"It'll make a sensation on land," said a voice.

"Yes, it will make a noise in the newspapers."

I raised my head and peered over the side of the boat. There seemed no hope, no help. Death stared me in the face, whether I did or did not give the alarm. The Captain had at last left the bridge. The deck was deserted, save for those two dark figures crouching in the shadow of the boat.

Flannigan had a watch lying open in his hand.

"Three minutes more," he said. "Put it down upon the deck."

"No, put it here on the bulwarks."

It was the little square box. I knew by the sound that they had placed it near the davit, and almost exactly under my head.

I looked over again. Flannigan was pouring something out of a paper into his hand. It was white and granular - the same that I had seen him use in the morning. It was meant as a fuse, no doubt, for he shovelled it into the little box, and I heard the strange noise which had previously arrested my attention.

"A minute and a half more," he said. "Shall you or I pull the string?"

"I will pull it," said Muller.

He was kneeling down and holding the end in his hand. Flannigan stood behind with his arms folded, and an air of grim resolution upon his face.

I could stand it no longer. My nervous system seemed to give way in a moment.

"Stop!" I screamed, springing to my feet. "Stop misguided and unprincipled men!"

They both staggered backwards. I fancy they thought I was a spirit, with the moonlight streaming down upon my pale face.

I was brave enough now. I had gone too far to retreat.

"Cain was damned," I cried, "and he slew but one; would you have the blood of two hundred upon your souls?"

"He's mad!" said Flannigan. "Time's up. Let it off, Muller." I sprang down upon the deck.

"You shan't do it!" I said.

"By what right do you prevent us?"

"By every right, human and divine."

"It's no business of yours. Clear out of this."

"Never!" said I.

"Confound the fellow! There's too much at stake to stand on ceremony. I'll hold him, Muller, while you pull the trigger."

Next moment I was struggling in the herculean grasp of the Irishman. Resistance was useless; I was a child in his hands.

He pinned me up against the side of the vessel, and held me there.

"Now," he said, "look sharp. He can't prevent us."

I felt that I was standing on the verge of eternity. Half-strangled in the arms of the taller ruffian, I saw the other approach the fatal box. He stooped over it and seized the string. I breathed one prayer when I saw his grasp tighten upon it. Then came a sharp snap, a strange rasping noise. The trigger had fallen, the side of the box flew out, and let off - TWO GREY CARRIER PIGEONS!

Little more need be said. It is not a subject on which I care to dwell. The whole thing is too utterly disgusting and absurd. Perhaps the best thing I can do is to retire gracefully from the scene, and let the sporting correspondent of the New York Herald fill my unworthy place. Here is an extract clipped from its columns shortly after our departure from America: -

"Pigeon-flying Extraordinary. - A novel match has been brought off last week between the birds of John H. Flannigan, of Boston, and Jeremiah Muller, a well-known citizen of Lowell. Both men have devoted much time and attention to an improved breed of bird, and the challenge is an old-standing one. The pigeons were backed to a large amount, and there was considerable local interest in the result. The start was from the deck of the Transatlantic steamship Spartan, at ten o'clock on the evening of the day of starting, the vessel being then reckoned to be about a hundred miles from the land. The bird which reached home first was to be declared the winner. Considerable caution had, we believe, to be observed, as some captains have a prejudice against the bringing off of sporting events aboard their vessels. In spite of some little difficulty at the last moment, the trap was sprung almost exactly at ten o'clock.

"Muller's bird arrived in Lowell in an extreme state of exhaustion on the following morning, while Flannigan's has not been heard of. The backers of the latter have the satisfaction of knowing, however, that the whole affair has been characterised by extreme fairness. The pigeons were confined in a specially invented trap, which could only be opened by the spring. It was thus possible to feed them through an aperture in the top, but any tampering with their wings was quite out of the question. A few such matches would go far towards popularising pigeon-flying in America, and form an agreeable variety to the morbid exhibitions of human endurance which have assumed such proportions during the last few years."

SELECTING A GHOST, THE GHOSTS OF GORESTHORPE GRANGE

I am sure that Nature never intended me to be a self-made man. There are times when I can hardly bring myself to realise that twenty years of my life were spent behind the counter of a grocer's shop in the East End of London, and that it was through such an avenue that I reached a wealthy independence and the possession of Goresthorpe Grange. My habits are conservative, and my tastes refined and aristocratic. I have a soul which spurns the vulgar herd. Our family, the D'Odds, date back to a prehistoric era, as is to be inferred from the fact that their advent into British history is not commented on by any trustworthy historian. Some instinct tells me that the blood of a Crusader runs in my veins. Even now, after the lapse of so many years, such exclamations as "By'r Lady!" rise naturally to my lips, and I feel that, should circumstances require it, I am capable of rising in my stirrups and dealing an infidel a blow - say with a mace - which would considerably astonish him.

Goresthorpe Grange is a feudal mansion - or so it was termed in the advertisement which originally brought it under my notice. Its right to this adjective had a most remarkable effect upon its price, and the advantages gained may possibly be more sentimental than real. Still, it is soothing to me to know that I have slits in my staircase through which I can discharge arrows; and there is a sense of power in the fact of possessing a complicated apparatus by means of which I am enabled to pour molten lead upon the head of the casual visitor. These things chime in with my peculiar humour, and I do not grudge to pay for them. I am proud of my battlements and of the circular uncovered sewer which girds me round. I am proud of my portcullis and donjon and keep. There is but one thing wanting to round off the mediaevalism of my abode, and to render it symmetrically and completely antique. Goresthorpe Grange is not provided with a ghost.

Any man with old-fashioned tastes and ideas as to how such establishments should be conducted, would have been disappointed at the omission. In my case it was particularly unfortunate. From my childhood I had been an earnest student of the supernatural, and a firm believer in it. I have revelled in ghostly literature until there is hardly a tale bearing upon the subject which I have not perused. I learned the German language for the sole purpose of mastering a book upon demonology. When an infant I had secreted myself in dark rooms in the hope of seeing some of those bogies with which my nurse used to threaten me; and the same feeling is as strong in me now as then. It was a proud moment when I felt that a ghost was one of the luxuries which money might command.

It is true that there was no mention of an apparition in the advertisement. On reviewing the mildewed walls, however, and the shadowy corridors, I had taken it for granted that there was such a thing on the premises. As the presence of a kennel presupposes that of a dog, so I imagined that it was impossible that such desirable quarters should be untenanted by one or more restless shades. Good heavens, what can the noble family from whom I purchased it have been doing during these hundreds of years! Was there no member of it spirited enough to make away with his sweetheart, or take some other steps calculated to establish a hereditary spectre? Even now I can hardly write with patience upon the subject.

For a long time I hoped against hope. Never did rat squeak behind the wainscot, or rain drip upon the attic floor, without a wild thrill shooting through me as I thought that at last I had come upon traces of some unquiet soul. I felt no touch of fear upon these occasions. If it occurred in the night-time, I would send Mrs. D'Odd - who is a strong-minded woman - to investigate the matter, while I covered up my head with the bed clothes and indulged in an ecstacy of expectation. Alas, the result was always the same! The suspicious sound would be traced to some cause so absurdly natural and common place that the most fervid imagination could not clothe it with any of the glamour of romance.

I might have reconciled myself to this state of things, had it not been for Jorrocks of Havistock Farm. Jorrocks is a coarse, burly, matter-of-fact fellow, whom I only happened to know through the accidental circumstance of his fields adjoining my demesne. Yet this man, though utterly devoid of all appreciation of archaeological unities, is in possession of a well-authenticated and undeniable spectre. Its existence only dates back, I believe, to the reign of the Second George, when a young lady cut her throat upon hearing of the death of her lover at the battle of Dettingen. Still, even that gives the house an air of respectability, especially when coupled with blood stains upon the floor. Jorrocks is densely unconscious of his good fortune; and his language when he reverts to the apparition is painful to listen to. He little dreams how I covet every one of those moans and nocturnal wails which he describes with unnecessary objurgation. Things are indeed coming to a pretty pass when democratic spectres are allowed to desert the landed proprietors and annul every social distinction by taking refuge in the houses of the great unrecognised.

I have a large amount of perseverance. Nothing else could have raised me into my rightful sphere, considering the uncongenial atmosphere in which I spent the earlier part of my life. I felt now that a ghost must be secured, but how to set about securing one was more than either Mrs. D'Odd or myself was able to determine. My reading taught me that such phenomena are usually the outcome of crime. What crime was to be done, then, and who was to do it? A wild idea entered my mind that Watkins, the house-steward, might be prevailed upon - for a consideration - to immolate himself or someone else in the interests of the establishment. I put the matter to him in a half-jesting manner; but it did not seem to strike him in a favourable light. The other servants sympathised with him in his opinion - at least, I cannot account in any other way for their having left the house in a body the same afternoon.

"My dear," Mrs. D'Odd remarked to me one day after dinner, as I sat moodily sipping a cup of sack - I love the good old names - "my dear, that odious ghost of Jorrocks' has been gibbering again."

"Let it gibber!" I answered, recklessly.

Mrs. D'Odd struck a few chords on her virginal and looked thoughtfully into the fire.

"I'll tell you what it is, Argentine," she said at last, using the pet name which we usually substituted for Silas, "we must have a ghost sent down from London."

"How can you be so idiotic, Matilda?" I remarked, severely. "Who could get us such a thing?"

"My cousin, Jack Brocket, could," she answered, confidently.

Now, this cousin of Matilda's was rather a sore subject between us. He was a rakish, clever young fellow, who had tried his hand at many things, but wanted perseverance to succeed at any. He was, at that time, in chambers in London, professing to be a general agent, and really living, to a great extent, upon his wits. Matilda managed so that most of our business should pass through his hands, which certainly saved me a great deal of trouble; but I found that Jack's commission was generally considerably larger than all the other items of the bill put together. It was this fact which made me feel inclined to rebel against any further negotiations with the young gentleman.

"O yes, he could," insisted Mrs. D., seeing the look of disapprobation upon my face. "You remember how well he managed that business about the crest?"

"It was only a resuscitation of the old family coat-of-arms, my dear," I protested.

Matilda smiled in an irritating manner. "There was a resuscitation of the family portraits, too, dear," she remarked. "You must allow that Jack selected them very judiciously."

I thought of the long line of faces which adorned the walls of my banqueting-hall, from the burly Norman robber, through every gradation of casque, plume, and ruff, to the sombre Chesterfieldian individual who appears to have staggered against a pillar in his agony at the return of a maiden MS. which he grips convulsively in his right hand. I was fain to confess that in that instance he had done his work well, and that it was only fair to give him an order - with the usual commission - for a family spectre should such a thing be attainable.

It is one of my maxims to act promptly when once my mind is made up. Noon of the next day found me ascending the spiral stone staircase which leads to Mr. Brocket's chambers, and admiring the succession of arrows and fingers upon the whitewashed wall, all indicating the direction of that gentleman's sanctum. As it happened, artificial aids of the sort were entirely unnecessary, as an animated flap-dance overhead could proceed from no other quarter, though it was replaced by a deathly silence as I groped my way up the stair. The door was opened by a youth evidently astounded at the appearance of a client, and I was ushered into the presence of my young friend, who was writing furiously in a large ledger - upside down, as I afterwards discovered.

After the first greetings, I plunged into business at once. "Look here, Jack," I said, "I want you to get me a spirit, if you can."

"Spirits you mean!" shouted my wife's cousin, plunging his hand into the waste-paper basket and producing a bottle with the celerity of a conjuring trick. "Let's have a drink!"

I held up my hand as a mute appeal against such a proceeding so early in the day; but on lowering it again I found that I had almost involuntarily closed my fingers round the tumbler which my adviser had pressed upon me. I drank the contents hastily off, lest anyone should come in upon us and set me down as a toper. After all there was something very amusing about the young fellow's eccentricities.

"Not spirits," I explained, smilingly; "an apparition - a ghost. If such a thing is to be had, I should be very willing to negotiate."

"A ghost for Goresthorpe Grange?" inquired Mr. Brocket, with as much coolness as if I had asked for a drawing-room suite.

"Quite so," I answered.

"Easiest thing in the world," said my companion, filling up my glass again in spite of my remonstrance. "Let us see!" Here he took down a large red note-book, with all the letters of the alphabet in a fringe down the edge. "A ghost you said, didn't you? That's G. G - gems - gimlets - gas-pipes - gauntlets - guns - galleys. Ah, here we are. Ghosts. Volume nine, section six, page forty-one. Excuse me!" And Jack ran up a ladder and began rummaging among the pile of ledgers on a high shelf. I felt half inclined to empty my glass into the spittoon when his back was turned; but on second thoughts I disposed of it in a legitimate way.

"Here it is!" cried my London agent, jumping off the ladder with a crash, and depositing an enormous volume of manuscript upon the table. "I have all these things tabulated, so that I may lay my hands upon them in a moment. It's all right - it's quite weak" (here he filled our glasses again). "What were we looking up, again?"

"Ghosts," I suggested.

"Of course; page 41. Here we are. T.H. Fowler & Son, Dunkel Street, 'suppliers of mediums to the nobility and gentry; charms sold - love philtres - mummies - horoscopes cast.' Nothing in your line there, I suppose."

I shook my head despondently.

"'Frederick Tabb,'" continued my wife's cousin, "'sole channel of communication between the living and the dead. Proprietor of the spirits of Byron, Kirke White, Grimaldi, Tom Cribb, and Inigo Jones.' That's about the figure!"

"Nothing romantic enough there," I objected. "Good heavens! Fancy a ghost with a black eye and a handkerchief tied round its waist, or turning summersaults, and saying, 'How are you tomorrow?'" The very idea made me so warm that I emptied my glass and filled it again.

"Here is another," said my companion, "'Christopher McCarthy; bi-weekly seances - attended by all the eminent spirits of ancient and modern times. Nativities - charms - abracadabras, messages from the dead.' He might be able to help us. However, I shall have a hunt round myself to-morrow, and see some of these fellows. I know their haunts, and it's odd if I can't pick up something cheap. So there's an end of business," he concluded, hurling the ledger into the corner, "and now we'll have something to drink."

We had several things to drink - so many that my inventive faculties were dulled next morning, and I had some little difficulty in explaining to Mrs. D'Odd why it was that I hung my boots and spectacles upon a peg along with my other garments before retiring to rest. The new hopes excited by the confident manner in which my agent had undertaken the commission, caused me to rise superior to alcoholic reaction, and I paced about the rambling corridors and old-fashioned rooms, picturing to myself the appearance of my expected acquisition, and deciding what part of the building would harmonise best with its presence. After much consideration, I pitched upon the banqueting-hall as being, on the whole, most suitable for its reception. It was a long low room, hung round with valuable tapestry and interesting relics of the old family to whom it had belonged. Coats of mail and implements of war glimmered fitfully as the light of the fire played over them, and the wind crept under the door, moving the hangings to and fro with a ghastly rustling. At one end there was the raised dais, on which in ancient times the host and his guests used to spread their table, while a descent of a couple of steps led to the lower part of the hall, where the vassals and retainers held wassail. The floor was uncovered by any sort of carpet, but a layer of rushes had been scattered over it by my direction. In the whole room there was nothing to remind one of the nineteenth century; except, indeed, my own solid silver plate, stamped with the resuscitated family arms, which was laid out upon an oak table in the centre. This, I determined, should be the haunted room, supposing my wife's cousin to succeed in his negotiation with the spirit-mongers. There was nothing for it now but to wait patiently until I heard some news of the result of his inquiries.

A letter came in the course of a few days, which, if it was short, was at least encouraging. It was scribbled in pencil on the back of a playbill, and sealed apparently with a tobacco-stopper. "Am on the track," it said. "Nothing of the sort to be had from any professional spiritualist, but picked up a fellow in a pub yesterday who says he can manage it for you. Will send him down unless you wire to the contrary. Abrahams is his name, and he has done one or two of these jobs before." The letter wound up with some incoherent allusions to a cheque, and was signed by my affectionate cousin, John Brocket.

I need hardly say that I did not wire, but awaited the arrival of Mr. Abrahams with all impatience. In spite of my belief in the supernatural, I could scarcely credit the fact that any mortal could have such a command over the spirit-world as to deal in them and barter them against mere earthly gold. Still, I had Jack's word for it that such a trade existed; and here was a gentleman with a Judaical name ready to demonstrate it by proof positive. How vulgar and commonplace Jorrocks' eighteenth-century ghost would appear should I succeed in securing a real mediaeval apparition! I almost thought that one had been sent down in advance, for, as I walked round the moat that night before retiring to rest, I came upon a dark figure engaged in surveying the machinery of my portcullis and drawbridge. His start of surprise, however, and the manner in which he hurried off into the darkness, speedily convinced me of his earthly origin, and I put him down as some admirer of one of my female retainers mourning over the muddy Hellespont which divided him from his love. Whoever he may have been, he disappeared and did not return, though I loitered about for some time in the hope of catching a glimpse of him and exercising my feudal rights upon his person.

Jack Brocket was as good as his word. The shades of another evening were beginning to darken round Goresthorpe Grange, when a peal at the outer bell, and the sound of a fly pulling up, announced the arrival of Mr. Abrahams. I hurried down to meet him, half expecting to see a choice assortment of ghosts crowding in at his rear. Instead, however, of being the sallow-faced, melancholy-eyed man that I had pictured to myself, the ghost-dealer was a sturdy little podgy fellow, with a pair of wonderfully keen sparkling eyes and a mouth which was constantly stretched in a good-humoured, if somewhat artificial, grin. His sole stock-intrade seemed to consist of a small leather bag jealously locked and strapped, which emitted a metallic chink upon being placed on the stone flags in the hall.

"And 'ow are you, sir?" he asked, wringing my hand with the utmost effusion. "And the missus, 'ow is she? And all the others - 'ow's all their 'ealth?"

I intimated that we were all as well as could reasonably be expected, but Mr. Abrahams happened to catch a glimpse of Mrs. D'Odd in the distance, and at once plunged at her with another string of inquiries as to her health, delivered so volubly and with such an intense earnestness, that I half expected to see him terminate his cross-examination by feeling her pulse and demanding a sight of her tongue. All this time his little eyes rolled round and round, shifting perpetually from the floor to the ceiling, and from the ceiling to the walls, taking in apparently every article of furniture in a single comprehensive glance.

Having satisfied himself that neither of us was in a pathological condition, Mr. Abrahams suffered me to lead him upstairs, where a repast had been laid out for him to which he did ample justice. The mysterious little bag he carried along with him, and deposited it under his chair during the meal. It was not until the table had been cleared and we were left together that he broached the matter on which he had come down.

"I hunderstand," he remarked, puffing at a trichinopoly, "that you want my 'elp in fitting up this 'ere 'ouse with a happarition."

I acknowledged the correctness of his surmise, while mentally wondering at those restless eyes of his, which still danced about the room as if he were making an inventory of the contents.

"And you won't find a better man for the job, though I says it as shouldn't," continued my companion. "Wot did I say to the young gent wot spoke to me in the bar of the Lame Dog? 'Can you do it?' says he. 'Try me,' says I, 'me and my bag. Just try me.' I couldn't say fairer than that."

My respect for Jack Brocket's business capacities began to go up very considerably. He certainly seemed to have managed the matter wonderfully well. "You don't mean to say that you carry ghosts about in bags?" I remarked, with diffidence.

Mr. Abrahams smiled a smile of superior knowledge. "You wait," he said; "give me the right place and the right hour, with a little of the essence of Lucoptolycus" - here he produced a small bottle from his waistcoat pocket - "and you won't find no ghost that I ain't up to. You'll see them yourself, and pick your own, and I can't say fairer than that."

As all Mr. Abrahams' protestations of fairness were accompanied by a cunning leer and a wink from one or other of his wicked little eyes, the impression of candour was somewhat weakened.

"When are you going to do it?" I asked, reverentially.

"Ten minutes to one in the morning," said Mr. Abrahams, with decision. "Some says midnight, but I says ten to one, when there ain't such a crowd, and you can pick your own ghost. And now," he continued, rising to his feet, "suppose you trot me round the premises, and let me see where you wants it; for there's some places as attracts 'em, and some as they won't hear of - not if there was no other place in the world."

Mr. Abrahams inspected our corridors and chambers with a most critical and observant eye, fingering the old tapestry with the air of a connoisseur, and remarking in an undertone that it would "match uncommon nice." It was not until he reached the banqueting-hall, however, which I had myself picked out, that his admiration reached the pitch of enthusiasm. "Ere's the place!" he shouted, dancing, bag in hand, round the table on which my plate was lying, and looking not unlike some quaint little goblin himself. "Ere's the place; we won't get nothin' to beat this! A fine room - noble, solid, none of your electro-plate trash! That's the way as things ought to be done, sir. Plenty of room for 'em to glide here. Send up some brandy and the box of weeds; I'll sit here by the fire and do the preliminaries, which is more trouble than you'd think; for them ghosts carries on hawful at times, before they finds out who they've got to deal with. If you was in the room they'd tear you to pieces as like as not. You leave me alone to tackle them, and at half-past twelve come in, and I lay they'll be quiet enough by then."

Mr. Abrahams' request struck me as a reasonable one, so I left him with his feet upon the mantelpiece, and his chair in front of the fire, fortifying himself with stimulants against his refractory visitors. From the room beneath, in which I sat with Mrs. D'Odd, I could hear that, after sitting for some time, he rose up and paced about the hall with quick impatient steps. We then heard him try the lock of the door, and afterward drag some heavy article of furniture in the direction of the window, on which, apparently, he mounted, for I heard the creaking of the rusty hinges as the diamond-paned casement folded backward, and I knew it to be situated several feet above the little man's reach. Mrs. D'Odd says that she could distinguish his voice speaking in low and rapid whispers after this, but that may have been her imagination. I confess that I began to feel more impressed than I had deemed it possible to be. There was something awesome in the thought of the solitary mortal standing by the open window and summoning in from the gloom outside the spirits of the nether world. It was with a trepidation which I could hardly disguise from Matilda that I observed that the clock was pointing to half-past twelve, and that the time had come for me to share the vigil of my visitor.

He was sitting in his old position when I entered, and there were no signs of the mysterious movements which I had overheard, though his chubby face was flushed as with recent exertion.

"Are you succeeding all right?" I asked as I came in, putting on as careless an air as possible, but glancing involuntarily round the room to see if we were alone.

"Only your help is needed to complete the matter," said Mr. Abrahams, in a solemn voice. "You shall sit by me and partake of the essence of Lucoptolycus, which removes the scales from our earthly eyes. Whatever you may chance to see, speak not and make no movement, lest you break the spell." His manner was subdued, and his usual cockney vulgarity had entirely disappeared. I took the chair which he indicated, and awaited the result.

My companion cleared the rushes from the floor in our neighbourhood, and going down upon his hands and knees, described a half-circle with chalk, which enclosed the fireplace and ourselves. Round the edge of this half-circle he drew several hieroglyphics, not unlike the signs of the zodiac. He then stood up and uttered a long invocation, delivered so rapidly that it sounded like a single gigantic word in some uncouth guttural language. Having finished this prayer, if prayer it was, he pulled out the small bottle which he had produced before, and poured a couple of teaspoonfuls of clear transparent fluid into a phial, which he handed to me with an intimation that I should drink it.

The liquid had a faintly sweet odour, not unlike the aroma of certain sorts of apples. I hesitated a moment before applying it to my lips, but an impatient gesture from my companion overcame my scruples, and I tossed it off. The taste was not unpleasant; and, as it gave rise to no immediate effects, I leaned back in my chair and composed myself for what was to come. Mr. Abrahams seated himself beside me, and I felt that he was watching my face from time to time, while repeating some more of the invocations in which he had indulged before.

A sense of delicious warmth and languor began gradually to steal over me, partly, perhaps, from the heat of the fire, and partly from some unexplained cause. An uncontrollable impulse to sleep weighed down my eyelids, while at the same time my brain worked actively, and a hundred beautiful and pleasing ideas flitted through it. So utterly lethargic did I feel that, though I was aware that my companion put his hand over the region of my heart, as if to feel how it were beating, I did not attempt to prevent him, nor did I even ask him for the reason of his action. Everything in the room appeared to be reeling slowly round in a drowsy dance, of which I was the centre. The great elk's head at the far end wagged solemnly backward and forward, while the massive salvers on the tables performed cotillons with the claret-cooler and the epergne. My head fell upon my breast from sheer heaviness, and I should have become unconscious had I not been recalled to myself by the opening of the door at the other end of the hall.

This door led on to the raised dais, which, as I have mentioned, the heads of the house used to reserve for their own use. As it swung slowly back upon its hinges, I sat up in my chair, clutching at the arms, and staring with a horrified glare at the dark passage outside. Something was coming down it - something unformed and intangible, but still a something. Dim and shadowy, I saw it flit across the threshold, while a blast of ice-cold air swept down the room, which seemed to blow through me, chilling my very heart. I was aware of the mysterious presence, and then I heard it speak in a voice like the sighing of an east wind among pine-trees on the banks of a desolate sea.

It said: "I am the invisible nonentity. I have affinities and am subtle. I am electric, magnetic, and spiritualistic. I am the great ethereal sigh-heaver. I kill dogs. Mortal, wilt thou choose me?"

I was about to speak, but the words seemed to be choked in my throat; and, before I could get them out, the shadow flitted across the hall and vanished in the darkness at the other side, while a long-drawn melancholy sigh quivered through the apartment.

I turned my eyes toward the door once more, and beheld, to my astonishment, a very small old woman, who hobbled along the corridor and into the hall. She passed backward and forward several times, and then, crouching down at the very edge of the circle upon the floor, she disclosed a face the horrible malignity of which shall never be banished from my recollection. Every foul passion appeared to have left its mark upon that hideous countenance.

"Ha! ha!" she screamed, holding out her wizened hands like the talons of an unclean bird. "You see what I am. I am the fiendish old woman. I wear snuff-coloured silks. My curse descends on people. Sir Walter was partial to me. Shall I be thine, mortal?"

I endeavoured to shake my head in horror; on which she aimed a blow at me with her crutch, and vanished with an eldritch scream.

By this time my eyes turned naturally toward the open door, and I was hardly surprised to see a man walk in of tall and noble stature. His face was deadly pale, but was surmounted by a fringe of dark hair which fell in ringlets down his back. A short pointed beard covered his chin. He was dressed in loose-fitting clothes, made apparently of yellow satin, and a large white ruff surrounded his neck. He paced across the room with slow and majestic strides. Then turning, he addressed me in a sweet, exquisitely modulated voice.

"I am the cavalier," he remarked. "I pierce and am pierced. Here is my rapier. I clink steel. This is a blood stain over my heart. I can emit hollow groans. I am patronised by many old Conservative families. I am the original manor-house apparition. I work alone, or in company with shrieking damsels."

He bent his head courteously, as though awaiting my reply, but the same choking sensation prevented me from speaking; and, with a deep bow, he disappeared.

He had hardly gone before a feeling of intense horror stole over me, and I was aware of the presence of a ghastly creature in the room, of dim outlines and uncertain proportions. One moment it seemed to pervade the entire apartment, while at another it would become invisible, but always leaving behind it a distinct consciousness of its presence. Its voice, when it spoke, was quavering and gusty. It said: "I am the leaver of footsteps and the spiller of gouts of blood. I tramp upon corridors. Charles Dickens has alluded to me. I make strange and disagreeable noises. I snatch letters and place invisible hands on people's wrists. I am cheerful. I burst into peals of hideous laughter. Shall I do one now?" I raised my hand in a deprecating way, but too late to prevent one discordant outbreak which echoed through the room. Before I could lower it the apparition was gone.

I turned my head toward the door in time to see a man come hastily and stealthily into the chamber. He was a sunburnt powerfully built fellow, with ear-rings in his ears and a Barcelona handkerchief tied loosely round his neck. His head was bent upon his chest, and his whole aspect was that of one afflicted by intolerable remorse. He paced rapidly backward and forward like a caged tiger, and I observed that a drawn knife glittered in one of his hands, while he grasped what appeared to be a piece of parchment in the other. His voice, when he spoke, was deep and sonorous. He said, "I am a murderer. I am a ruffian. I crouch when I walk. I step noiselessly. I know something of the Spanish Main. I can do the lost treasure business. I have charts. Am able-bodied and a good walker. Capable of haunting a large park." He looked toward me beseechingly, but before I could make a sign I was paralysed by the horrible sight which appeared at the door.

It was a very tall man, if indeed, it might be called a man, for the gaunt bones were protruding through the corroding flesh, and the features were of a leaden hue. A winding-sheet was wrapped round the figure, and formed a hood over the head, from under the shadow of which two fiendish eyes, deep set in their grisly sockets, blazed and sparkled like red-hot coals. The lower jaw had fallen upon the breast, disclosing a withered, shrivelled tongue and two lines of black and jagged fangs. I shuddered and drew back as this fearful apparition advanced to the edge of the circle.

"I am the American blood-curdler," it said, in a voice which seemed to come in a hollow murmur from the earth beneath it. "None other is genuine. I am the embodiment of Edgar Allan Poe. I am circumstantial and horrible. I am a low-caste spirit-subduing spectre. Observe my blood and my bones. I am grisly and nauseous. No depending on artificial aid. Work with grave-clothes, a coffin-lid, and a galvanic battery. Turn hair white in a night." The creature stretched out its fleshless arms to me as if in entreaty, but I shook my head; and it vanished, leaving a low, sickening, repulsive odour behind it. I sank back in my chair, so overcome by terror and disgust that I would have very willingly resigned myself to dispensing with a ghost altogether, could I have been sure that this was the last of the hideous procession.

A faint sound of trailing garments warned me that it was not so. I looked up, and beheld a white figure emerging from the corridor into the light. As it stepped across the threshold I saw that it was that of a young and beautiful woman dressed in the fashion of a bygone day. Her hands were clasped in front of her, and her pale proud face bore traces of passion and of suffering. She crossed the hall with a gentle sound, like the rustling of autumn leaves, and then, turning her lovely and unutterably sad eyes upon me, she said. "I am the plaintive and sentimental, the beautiful and ill-used. I have been forsaken and betrayed. I shriek in the night-time and glide down passages. My antecedents are highly respectable and generally aristocratic. My tastes are aesthetic. Old oak furniture like this would do, with a few more coats of mail and plenty of tapestry. Will you not take me?"

Her voice died away in a beautiful cadence as she concluded, and she held out her hands as if in supplication. I am always sensitive to female influences. Besides, what would Jorrocks's ghost be to this? Could anything be in better taste? Would I not be exposing myself to the chance of injuring my nervous system by interviews with such creatures as my last visitor, unless I decided at once? She gave me a seraphic smile, as if she knew what was passing in my mind. That smile settled the matter. "She will do!" I cried; "I choose this one;" and as, in my enthusiasm, I took a step toward her I passed over the magic circle which had girdled me round.

"Argentine, we have been robbed!"

I had an indistinct consciousness of these words being spoken, or rather screamed, in my ear a great number of times without my being able to grasp their meaning. A violent throbbing in my head seemed to adapt itself to their rhythm, and I closed my eyes to the lullaby of "Robbed, robbed, robbed." A vigorous shake caused me to open them again, however, and the sight of Mrs. D'Odd in the scantiest of costumes and most furious of tempers was sufficiently impressive to recall all my scattered thoughts, and make me realise that I was lying on my back on the floor, with my head among the ashes which had fallen from last night's fire, and a small glass phial in my hand.

I staggered to my feet, but felt so weak and giddy that I was compelled to fall back into a chair. As my brain became clearer, stimulated by the exclamations of Matilda, I began gradually to recollect the events of the night. There was the door through which my supernatural visitors had filed. There was the circle of chalk with the hieroglyphics round the edge. There was the cigar-box and brandy-bottle which had been honoured by the attentions of Mr. Abrahams. But the seer himself - where was he? and what was this open window with a rope running out of it? And where, O where, was the pride of Goresthorpe Grange, the glorious plate which was to have been the delectation of generations of D'Odds? And why was Mrs. D. standing in the grey light of dawn, wringing her hands and repeating her monotonous refrain? It was only very gradually that my misty brain took these things in, and grasped the connection between them.

Reader, I have never seen Mr. Abrahams since; I have never seen the plate stamped with the resuscitated family crest; hardest of all, I have never caught a glimpse of the melancholy spectre with the trailing garments, nor do I expect that I ever shall. In fact my night's experiences have cured me of my mania for the supernatural, and quite reconciled me to inhabiting the humdrum nineteenth-century edifice on the outskirts of London which Mrs. D. has long had in her mind's eye.

As to the explanation of all that occurred - that is a matter which is open to several surmises. That Mr. Abrahams, the ghost-hunter, was identical with Jemmy Wilson, alias the Nottingham crackster, is considered more than probable at Scotland Yard, and certainly the description of that remarkable burglar tallied very well with the appearance of my visitor. The small bag which I have described was picked up in a neighbouring field next day, and found to contain a choice assortment of jemmies and centre-bits. Footmarks deeply imprinted in the mud on either side of the moat showed that an accomplice from below had received the sack of precious metals which had been let down through the open window. No doubt the pair of scoundrels, while looking round for a job, had overheard Jack Brocket's indiscreet inquiries, and promptly availed themselves of the tempting opening.

And now as to my less substantial visitors, and the curious grotesque vision which I had enjoyed - am I to lay it down to any real power over occult matters possessed by my Nottingham friend? For a long time I was doubtful upon the point, and eventually endeavoured to solve it by consulting a well-known analyst and medical man, sending him the few drops of the so-called essence of Lucoptolycus which remained in my phial. I append the letter which I received from him, only too happy to have the opportunity of winding up my little narrative by the weighty words of a man of learning:

"ARUNDEL STREET

"Dear Sir: Your very singular case has interested me extremely. The bottle which you sent contained a strong solution of chloral, and the quantity which you describe yourself as having swallowed must have amounted to at least eighty grains of the pure hydrate. This would of course have reduced you to a partial state of insensibility, gradually going on to complete coma. In this semi-unconscious state of chloralism it is not unusual for circumstantial and bizarre visions to present themselves - more especially to individuals unaccustomed to the use of the drug. You tell me in your note that your mind was saturated with ghostly literature, and that you had long taken a morbid interest in classifying and recalling the various forms in which apparitions have been said to appear. You must also remember that you were expecting to see something of that very nature, and that your nervous system was worked up to an unnatural state of tension. Under the circumstances, I think that, far from the sequel being an astonishing one, it would have been very surprising indeed to any one versed in narcotics had you not experienced some such effects. - I remain, dear sir, sincerely yours,

"T. E. STUBE, M.D.

"Argentine D'Odd, Esq. The Elms, Brixton

A FALSE START

"Is Dr. Horace Wilkinson at home?"

"I am he. Pray step in."

The visitor looked somewhat astonished at having the door opened to him by the master of the house.

"I wanted to have a few words."

The doctor, a pale, nervous young man, dressed in an ultra-professional, long black frock-coat, with a high, white collar cutting off his dapper side-whiskers in the centre, rubbed his hands together and smiled. In the thick, burly man in front of him he scented a patient, and it would be his first. His scanty resources had begun to run somewhat low, and, although he had his first quarter's rent safely locked away in the right-hand drawer of his desk, it was becoming a question with him how he should meet the current expenses of his very simple housekeeping. He bowed, therefore, waved his visitor in, closed the hall door in a careless fashion, as though his own presence thereat had been a purely accidental circumstance, and finally led the burly stranger into his scantily furnished front room, where he motioned him to a seat. Dr. Wilkinson planted himself behind his desk, and, placing his finger-tips together, he gazed with some apprehension at his companion. What was the matter with the man? He seemed very red in the face. Some of his old professors would have diagnosed his case by now, and would have electrified the patient by describing his own symptoms before he had said a word about them. Dr. Horace Wilkinson racked his brains for some clue, but Nature had fashioned him as a plodder - a very reliable plodder and nothing more. He could think of nothing save that the visitor's watch-chain had a very brassy appearance, with a corollary to the effect that he would be lucky if he got half-a-crown out of him. Still, even half-a-crown was something in those early days of struggle.

Whilst the doctor had been running his eyes over the stranger, the latter had been plunging his hands into pocket after pocket of his heavy coat. The heat of the weather, his dress, and this exercise of pocket-rummaging had all combined to still further redden his face, which had changed from brick to beet, with a gloss of moisture on his brow. This extreme ruddiness brought a clue at last to the observant doctor. Surely it was not to be attained without alcohol. In alcohol lay the secret of this man's trouble. Some little delicacy was needed, however, in showing him that he had read his case aright - that at a glance he had penetrated to the inmost sources of his ailments.

"It's very hot," observed the stranger, mopping his forehead.

"Yes, it is weather which tempts one to drink rather more beer than is good for one," answered Dr. Horace Wilkinson, looking very knowingly at his companion from over his finger-tips.

"Dear, dear, you shouldn't do that."

"I! I never touch beer."

"Neither do I. I've been an abstainer for twenty years."

This was depressing. Dr. Wilkinson blushed until he was nearly as red as the other. "May I ask what I can do for you?" he asked, picking up his stethoscope and tapping it gently against his thumb-nail.

"Yes, I was just going to tell you. I heard of your coming, but I couldn't get round before - " He broke into a nervous little cough.

"Yes?" said the doctor encouragingly.

"I should have been here three weeks ago, but you know how these things get put off." He coughed again behind his large red hand.

"I do not think that you need say anything more," said the doctor, taking over the case with an easy air of command. "Your cough is quite sufficient. It is entirely bronchial by the sound. No doubt the mischief is circumscribed at present, but there is always the danger that it may spread, so you have done wisely to come to me. A little judicious treatment will soon set you right. Your waistcoat, please, but not your shirt. Puff out your chest and say ninety-nine in a deep voice."

The red-faced man began to laugh. "It's all right, doctor," said he. "That cough comes from chewing tobacco, and I know it's a very bad habit. Nine-and-nine pence is what I have to say to you, for I'm the officer of the gas company, and they have a claim against you for that on the metre."

Dr. Horace Wilkinson collapsed into his chair. "Then you're not a patient?" he gasped.

"Never needed a doctor in my life, sir."

"Oh, that's all right." The doctor concealed his disappointment under an affectation of facetiousness. "You don't look as if you troubled them much. I don't know what we should do if everyone were as robust. I shall call at the company's offices and pay this small amount."

"If you could make it convenient, sir, now that I am here, it would save trouble - "

"Oh, certainly!" These eternal little sordid money troubles were more trying to the doctor than plain living or scanty food. He took out his purse and slid the contents on to the table. There were two half-crowns and some pennies. In his drawer he had ten golden sovereigns. But those were his rent. If he once broke in upon them he was lost. He would starve first.

"Dear me!" said he, with a smile, as at some strange, unheard-of incident. "I have run short of small change. I am afraid I shall have to call upon the company, after all."

"Very well, sir." The inspector rose, and with a practised glance around, which valued every article in the room, from the two-guinea carpet to the eight-shilling muslin curtains, he took his departure.

When he had gone Dr. Wilkinson rearranged his room, as was his habit a dozen times in the day. He laid out his large Quain's Dictionary of Medicine in the forefront of the table so as to impress the casual patient that he had ever the best authorities at his elbow. Then he cleared all the little instruments out of his pocket-case - the scissors, the forceps, the bistouries, the lancets - and he laid them all out beside the stethoscope, to make as good a show as possible. His ledger, day-book, and visiting-book were spread in front of him. There was no entry in any of them yet, but it would not look well to have the covers too glossy and new, so he rubbed them together and daubed ink over them. Neither would it be well that any patient should observe that his name was the first in the book, so he filled up the first page of each with notes of imaginary visits paid to nameless patients during the last three weeks. Having done all this, he rested his head upon his hands and relapsed into the terrible occupation of waiting.

Terrible enough at any time to the young professional man, but most of all to one who knows that the weeks, and even the days during which he can hold out are numbered. Economise as he would, the money would still slip away in the countless little claims which a man never understands until he lives under a rooftree of his own. Dr. Wilkinson could not deny, as he sat at his desk and looked at the little heap of silver and coppers, that his chances of being a successful practitioner in Sutton were rapidly vanishing away.

And yet it was a bustling, prosperous town, with so much money in it that it seemed strange that a man with a trained brain and dexterous fingers should be starved out of it for want of employment. At his desk, Dr. Horace Wilkinson could see the never-ending double current of people which ebbed and flowed in front of his window. It was a busy street, and the air was forever filled with the dull roar of life, the grinding of the wheels, and the patter of countless feet. Men, women, and children, thousands and thousands of them passed in the day, and yet each was hurrying on upon his own business, scarce glancing at the small brass plate, or wasting a thought upon the man who waited in the front room. And yet how many of them would obviously, glaringly have been the better for his professional assistance. Dyspeptic men, anemic women, blotched faces, bilious complexions - they flowed past him, they needing him, he needing them, and yet the remorseless bar of professional etiquette kept them forever apart. What could he do? Could he stand at his own front door, pluck the casual stranger by the sleeve, and whisper in his ear, "Sir, you will forgive me for remarking that you are suffering from a severe attack of acne rosacea, which makes you a peculiarly unpleasant object. Allow me to suggest that a small prescription containing arsenic, which will not cost you more than you often spend upon a single meal, will be very much to your advantage." Such an address would be a degradation to the high and lofty profession of Medicine, and there are no such sticklers for the ethics of that profession as some to whom she has been but a bitter and a grudging mother.

Dr. Horace Wilkinson was still looking moodily out of the window, when there came a sharp clang at the bell. Often it had rung, and with every ring his hopes had sprung up, only to dwindle away again, and change to leaden disappointment, as he faced some beggar or touting tradesman. But the doctor's spirit was young and elastic, and again, in spite of all experience, it responded to that exhilarating summons. He sprang to his feet, cast his eyes over the table, thrust out his medical books a little more prominently, and hurried to the door. A groan escaped him as he entered the hall. He could see through the half-glazed upper panels that a gypsy van, hung round with wicker tables and chairs, had halted before his door, and that a couple of the vagrants, with a baby, were waiting outside. He had learned by experience that it was better not even to parley with such people.

"I have nothing for you," said he, loosing the latch by an inch. "Go away!"

He closed the door, but the bell clanged once more. "Get away! Get away!" he cried impatiently, and walked back into his consulting-room. He had hardly seated himself when the bell went for the third time. In a towering passion he rushed back, flung open the door.

"What the - ?"

"If you please, sir, we need a doctor."

In an instant he was rubbing his hands again with his blandest professional smile. These were patients, then, whom he had tried to hunt from his doorstep - the very first patients, whom he had waited for so impatiently. They did not look very promising. The man, a tall, lank-haired gypsy, had gone back to the horse's head. There remained a small, hard-faced woman with a great bruise all round her eye. She wore a yellow silk handkerchief round her head, and a baby, tucked in a red shawl, was pressed to her bosom.

"Pray step in, madam," said Dr. Horace Wilkinson, with his very best sympathetic manner. In this case, at least, there could be no mistake as to diagnosis. "If you will sit on this sofa, I shall very soon make you feel much more comfortable."

He poured a little water from his carafe into a saucer, made a compress of lint, fastened it over the injured eye, and secured the whole with a spica bandage, secundum artem.

"Thank ye kindly, sir," said the woman, when his work was finished; "that's nice and warm, and may God bless your honour. But it wasn't about my eye at all that I came to see a doctor."

"Not your eye?" Dr. Horace Wilkinson was beginning to be a little doubtful as to the advantages of quick diagnosis. It is an excellent thing to be able to surprise a patient, but hitherto it was always the patient who had surprised him.

"The baby's got the measles."

The mother parted the red shawl, and exhibited a little dark, black-eyed gypsy baby, whose swarthy face was all flushed and mottled with a dark-red rash. The child breathed with a rattling sound, and it looked up at the doctor with eyes which were heavy with want of sleep and crusted together at the lids.

"Hum! Yes. Measles, sure enough - and a smart attack."

"I just wanted you to see her, sir, so that you could signify."

"Could what?"

"Signify, if anything happened."

"Oh, I see - certify."

"And now that you've seen it, sir, I'll go on, for Reuben - that's my man - is in a hurry."

"But don't you want any medicine?"

"Oh, now you've seen it, it's all right. I'll let you know if anything happens."

"But you must have some medicine. The child is very ill." He descended into the little room which he had fitted as a surgery, and he made up a two-ounce bottle of cooling medicine. In such cities as Sutton there are few patients who can afford to pay a fee to both doctor and chemist, so that unless the physician is prepared to play the part of both he will have little chance of making a living at either.

"There is your medicine, madam. You will find the directions upon the bottle. Keep the child warm and give it a light diet."

"Thank you kindly, sir." She shouldered her baby and marched for the door.

"Excuse me, madam," said the doctor nervously. "Don't you think it too small a matter to make a bill of? Perhaps it would be better if we had a settlement at once."

The gypsy woman looked at him reproachfully out of her one uncovered eye.

"Are you going to charge me for that?" she asked. "How much, then?"

"Well, say half-a-crown." He mentioned the sum in a half-jesting way, as though it were too small to take serious notice of, but the gypsy woman raised quite a scream at the mention of it.

"'Arf-a-crown! for that?"

"Well, my good woman, why not go to the poor doctor if you cannot afford a fee?"

She fumbled in her pocket, craning awkwardly to keep her grip upon the baby.

"Here's sevenpence," she said at last, holding out a little pile of copper coins. "I'll give you that and a wicker footstool."

"But my fee is half-a-crown." The doctor's views of the glory of his profession cried out against this wretched haggling, and yet what was he to do? "Where am I to get 'arf-a-crown? It is well for gentlefolk like you who sit in your grand houses, and can eat and drink what you like, an' charge 'arf-a-crown for just saying as much as, Ow d'ye do?' We can't pick up' arf-crowns like that. What we gets we earns 'ard. This sevenpence is just all I've got. You told me to feed the child light. She must feed light, for what she's to have is more than I know."

Whilst the woman had been speaking, Dr. Horace Wilkinson's eyes had wandered to the tiny heap of money upon the table, which represented all that separated him from absolute starvation, and he chuckled to himself at the grim joke that he should appear to this poor woman to be a being living in the lap of luxury. Then he picked up the odd coppers, leaving only the two half-crowns upon the table.

"Here you are," he said brusquely. "Never mind the fee, and take these coppers. They may be of some use to you. Good-bye!" He bowed her out, and closed the door behind her. After all she was the thin edge of the wedge. These wandering people have great powers of recommendation. All large practices have been built up from such foundations. The hangers-on to the kitchen recommend to the kitchen, they to the drawing-room, and so it spreads. At least he could say now that he had had a patient.

He went into the back room and lit the spirit-kettle to boil the water for his tea, laughing the while at the recollection of his recent interview. If all patients were like this one it could easily be reckoned how many it would take to ruin him completely. Putting aside the dirt upon his carpet and the loss of time, there were two pence gone upon the bandage, four pence or more upon the medicine, to say nothing of phial, cork, label, and paper. Then he had given her five pence, so that his first patient had absorbed altogether not less than one sixth of his available capital. If five more were to come he would be a broken man. He sat down upon the portmanteau and shook with laughter at the thought, while he measured out his one spoonful and a half of tea at one shilling eight pence into the brown earthenware teapot. Suddenly, however, the laugh faded from his face, and he cocked his ear towards the door, standing listening with a slanting head and a sidelong eye. There had been a rasping of wheels against the curb, the sound of steps outside, and then a loud peal at the bell. With his teaspoon in his hand he peeped round the corner and saw with amazement that a carriage and pair were waiting outside, and that a powdered footman was standing at the door. The spoon tinkled down upon the floor, and he stood gazing in bewilderment. Then, pulling himself together, he threw open the door.

"Young man," said the flunky, "tell your master, Dr. Wilkinson, that he is wanted just as quick as ever he can come to Lady Millbank, at the Towers. He is to come this very instant. We'd take him with us, but we have to go back to see if Dr. Mason is home yet. Just you stir your stumps and give him the message."

The footman nodded and was off in an instant, while the coachman lashed his horses and the carriage flew down the street.

Here was a new development. Dr. Horace Wilkinson stood at his door and tried to think it all out. Lady Millbank, of the Towers! People of wealth and position, no doubt. And a serious case, or why this haste and summoning of two doctors? But, then, why in the name of all that is wonderful should he be sent for?

He was obscure, unknown, without influence. There must be some mistake. Yes, that must be the true explanation; or was it possible that someone was attempting a cruel hoax upon him? At any rate, it was too positive a message to be disregarded. He must set off at once and settle the matter one way or the other.

But he had one source of information. At the corner of the street was a small shop where one of the oldest inhabitants dispensed newspapers and gossip. He could get information there if anywhere. He put on his well-brushed top hat, secreted instruments and bandages in all his pockets, and without waiting for his tea closed up his establishment and started off upon his adventure.

The stationer at the corner was a human directory to everyone and everything in Sutton, so that he soon had all the information which he wanted. Sir John Millbank was very well known in the town, it seemed. He was a merchant prince, an exporter of pens, three times mayor, and reported to be fully worth two millions sterling.

The Towers was his palatial seat, just outside the city. His wife had been an invalid for some years, and was growing worse. So far the whole thing seemed to be genuine enough. By some amazing chance these people really had sent for him.

And then another doubt assailed him, and he turned back into the shop.

"I am your neighbour, Dr. Horace Wilkinson," said he. "Is there any other medical man of that name in the town?"

No, the stationer was quite positive that there was not.

That was final, then. A great good fortune had come in his way, and he must take prompt advantage of it. He called a cab and drove furiously to the Towers, with his brain in a whirl, giddy with hope and delight at one moment, and sickened with fears and doubts at the next lest the case should in some way be beyond his powers, or lest he should find at some critical moment that he was without the instrument or appliance that was needed. Every strange and outré case of which he had ever heard or read came back into his mind, and long before he reached the Towers he had worked himself into a positive conviction that he would be instantly required to do a trephining at the least.

The Towers was a very large house, standing back amid trees, at the head of a winding drive. As he drove up the doctor sprang out, paid away half his worldly assets as a fare, and followed a stately footman who, having taken his name, led him through the oak-panelled, stained-glass hall, gorgeous with deers' heads and ancient armour, and ushered him into a large sitting-room beyond. A very irritable-looking, acid-faced man was seated in an armchair by the fireplace, while two young ladies in white were standing together in the bow window at the further end.

"Hullo! hullo! hullo! What's this - heh?" cried the irritable man. "Are you Dr. Wilkinson? Eh?"

"Yes, sir, I am Dr. Wilkinson."

"Really, now. You seem very young - much younger than I expected. Well, well, well, Mason's old, and yet he don't seem to know much about it. I suppose we must try the other end now. You're the Wilkinson who wrote something about the lungs? Heh?"

Here was a light! The only two letters which the doctor had ever written to The Lancet - modest little letters thrust away in a back column among the wrangles about medical ethics and the inquiries as to how much it took to keep a horse in the country - had been upon pulmonary disease. They had not been wasted, then. Some eye had picked them out and marked the name of the writer. Who could say that work was ever wasted, or that merit did not promptly meet with its reward?

"Yes, I have written on the subject."

"Ha! Well, then, where's Mason?"

"I have not the pleasure of his acquaintance."

"No? - that's queer too. He knows you and thinks a lot of your opinion. You're a stranger in the town, are you not?"

"Yes, I have only been here a very short time."

"That was what Mason said. He didn't give me the address. Said he would call on you and bring you, but when the wife got worse of course I inquired for you and sent for you direct. I sent for Mason, too, but he was out. However, we can't wait for him, so just run away upstairs and do what you can."

"Well, I am placed in a rather delicate position," said Dr. Horace Wilkinson, with some hesitation. "I am here, as I understand, to meet my colleague, Dr. Mason, in consultation. It would, perhaps, hardly be correct for me to see the patient in his absence. I think that I would rather wait."

"Would you, by Jove! Do you think I'll let my wife get worse while the doctor is coolly kicking his heels in the room below? No, sir, I am a plain man, and I tell you that you will either go up or go out."

The style of speech jarred upon the doctor's sense of the fitness of things, but still when a man's wife is ill much may be overlooked. He contented himself by bowing somewhat stiffly. "I shall go up, if you insist upon it," said he.

"I do insist upon it. And another thing, I won't have her thumped about all over the chest, or any hocus-pocus of the sort. She has bronchitis and asthma, and that's all. If you can cure it well and good. But it only weakens her to have you tapping and listening, and it does no good either."

Personal disrespect was a thing that the doctor could stand; but the profession was to him a holy thing, and a flippant word about it cut him to the quick.

"Thank you," said he, picking up his hat. "I have the honour to wish you a very good day. I do not care to undertake the responsibility of this case."

"Hullo! what's the matter now?"

"It is not my habit to give opinions without examining my patient. I wonder that you should suggest such a course to a medical man. I wish you good day."

But Sir John Millbank was a commercial man, and believed in the commercial principle that the more difficult a thing is to attain the more valuable it is. A doctor's opinion had been to him a mere matter of guineas. But here was a young man who seemed to care nothing either for his wealth or title. His respect for his judgment increased amazingly.

"Tut! tut!" said he; "Mason is not so thin-skinned. There! there! Have your way! Do what you like and I won't say another word. I'll just run upstairs and tell Lady Millbank that you are coming."

The door had hardly closed behind him when the two demure young ladies darted out of their corner, and fluttered with joy in front of the astonished doctor.

"Oh, well done! well done!" cried the taller, clapping her hands.

"Don't let him bully you, doctor," said the other. "Oh, it was so nice to hear you stand up to him. That's the way he does with poor Dr. Mason. Dr. Mason has never examined mamma yet. He always takes papa's word for everything. Hush, Maude; here he comes again." They subsided in an instant into their corner as silent and demure as ever.

Dr. Horace Wilkinson followed Sir John up the broad, thick-carpeted staircase, and into the darkened sick room. In a quarter of an hour he had sounded and sifted the case to the uttermost, and descended with the husband once more to the drawing-room. In front of the fireplace were standing two gentlemen, the one a very typical, clean-shaven, general practitioner, the other a striking-looking man of middle age, with pale blue eyes and a long red beard.

"Hullo, Mason, you've come at last!"

"Yes, Sir John, and I have brought, as I promised, Dr. Wilkinson with me."

"Dr. Wilkinson! Why, this is he."

Dr. Mason stared in astonishment. "I have never seen the gentleman before!" he cried.

"Nevertheless I am Dr. Wilkinson - Dr. Horace Wilkinson, of 114 Canal View."

"Good gracious, Sir John!" cried Dr. Mason.

"Did you think that in a case of such importance I should call in a junior local practitioner! This is Dr. Adam Wilkinson, lecturer on pulmonary diseases at Regent's College, London, physician upon the staff of the St. Swithin's Hospital, and author of a dozen works upon the subject. He happened to be in Sutton upon a visit, and I thought I would utilise his presence to have a first-rate opinion upon Lady Millbank."

"Thank you," said Sir John, dryly. "But I fear my wife is rather tired now, for she has just been very thoroughly examined by this young gentleman. I think we will let it stop at that for the present; though, of course, as you have had the trouble of coming here, I should be glad to have a note of your fees."

When Dr. Mason had departed, looking very disgusted, and his friend, the specialist, very amused, Sir John listened to all the young physician had to say about the case.

"Now, I'll tell you what," said he, when he had finished. "I'm a man of my word, d'ye see? When I like a man I freeze to him. I'm a good friend and a bad enemy. I believe in you, and I don't believe in Mason. From now on you are my doctor, and that of my family. Come and see my wife every day. How does that suit your book?"

"I am extremely grateful to you for your kind intentions toward me, but I am afraid there is no possible way in which I can avail myself of them."

"Heh! what d'ye mean?"

"I could not possibly take Dr. Mason's place in the middle of a case like this. It would be a most unprofessional act."

"Oh, well, go your own way!" cried Sir John, in despair. "Never was such a man for making difficulties. You've had a fair offer and you've refused it, and now you can just go your own way."

The millionaire stumped out of the room in a huff, and Dr. Horace Wilkinson made his way homeward to his spirit-lamp and his one-and-eight penny tea, with his first guinea in his pocket, and with a feeling that he had upheld the best traditions of his profession.

And yet this false start of his was a true start also, for it soon came to Dr. Mason's ears that his junior had had it in his power to carry off his best patient and had forborne to do so. To the honour of the profession be it said that such forbearance is the rule rather than the exception, and yet in this case, with so very junior a practitioner and so very wealthy a patient, the temptation was greater than is usual. There was a grateful note, a visit, a friendship, and now the well-known firm of Mason and Wilkinson is doing the largest family practice in Sutton.

THE THIRD GENERATION

Scudamore Lane, sloping down riverwards from just behind the Monument, lies at night in the shadow of two black and monstrous walls which loom high above the glimmer of the scattered gas lamps. The footpaths are narrow, and the causeway is paved with rounded cobblestones, so that the endless drays roar along it like breaking waves. A few old-fashioned houses lie scattered among the business premises, and in one of these, half-way down on the left-hand side, Dr. Horace Selby conducts his large practice. It is a singular street for so big a man; but a specialist who has an European reputation can afford to live where he likes. In his particular branch, too, patients do not always regard seclusion as a disadvantage.

It was only ten o'clock. The dull roar of the traffic which converged all day upon London Bridge had died away now to a mere confused murmur. It was raining heavily, and the gas shone dimly through the streaked and dripping glass, throwing little circles upon the glistening cobblestones. The air was full of the sounds of the rain, the thin swish of its fall, the heavier drip from the eaves, and the swirl and gurgle down the two steep gutters and through the sewer grating. There was only one figure in the whole length of Scudamore Lane. It was that of a man, and it stood outside the door of Dr. Horace Selby.

He had just rung and was waiting for an answer. The fanlight beat full upon the gleaming shoulders of his waterproof and upon his upturned features. It was a wan, sensitive, clear-cut face, with some subtle, nameless peculiarity in its expression, something of the startled horse in the white-rimmed eye, something too of the helpless child in the drawn cheek and the weakening of the lower lip. The man-servant knew the stranger as a patient at a bare glance at those frightened eyes. Such a look had been seen at that door many times before.

"Is the doctor in?"

The man hesitated.

"He has had a few friends to dinner, sir. He does not like to be disturbed outside his usual hours, sir."

"Tell him that I MUST see him. Tell him that it is of the very first importance. Here is my card." He fumbled with his trembling fingers in trying to draw one from his case. "Sir Francis Norton is the name. Tell him that Sir Francis Norton, of Deane Park, must see him without delay."

"Yes, sir." The butler closed his fingers upon the card and the half-sovereign which accompanied it. "Better hang your coat up here in the hall. It is very wet. Now if you will wait here in the consulting-room, I have no doubt that I shall be able to send the doctor in to you."

It was a large and lofty room in which the young baronet found himself. The carpet was so soft and thick that his feet made no sound as he walked across it. The two gas jets were turned only half-way up, and the dim light with the faint aromatic smell which filled the air had a vaguely religious suggestion. He sat down in a shining leather armchair by the smouldering fire and looked gloomily about him. Two sides of the room were taken up with books, fat and sombre, with broad gold lettering upon their backs. Beside him was the high, old-fashioned mantelpiece of white marble - the top of it strewed with cotton wadding and bandages, graduated measures, and little bottles. There was one with a broad neck just above him containing bluestone, and another narrower one with what looked like the ruins of a broken pipestem and "Caustic" outside upon a red label. Thermometers, hypodermic syringes bistouries and spatulas were scattered about both on the mantelpiece and on the central table on either side of the sloping desk. On the same table, to the right, stood copies of the five books which Dr. Horace Selby had written upon the subject with which his name is peculiarly associated, while on the left, on the top of a red medical directory, lay a huge glass model of a human eye the size of a turnip, which opened down the centre to expose the lens and double chamber within.

Sir Francis Norton had never been remarkable for his powers of observation, and yet he found himself watching these trifles with the keenest attention. Even the corrosion of the cork of an acid bottle caught his eye, and he wondered that the doctor did not use glass stoppers. Tiny scratches where the light glinted off from the table, little stains upon the leather of the desk, chemical formulae scribbled upon the labels of the phials - nothing was too slight to arrest his attention. And his sense of hearing was equally alert. The heavy ticking of the solemn black clock above the mantelpiece struck quite painfully upon his ears. Yet in spite of it, and in spite also of the thick, old-fashioned wooden partition, he could hear voices of men talking in the next room, and could even catch scraps of their conversation. "Second hand was bound to take it." "Why, you drew the last of them yourself."

"How could I play the queen when I knew that the ace was against me?" The phrases came in little spurts falling back into the dull murmur of conversation. And then suddenly he heard the creaking of a door and a step in the hall, and knew with a tingling mixture of impatience and horror that the crisis of his life was at hand.

Dr. Horace Selby was a large, portly man with an imposing presence. His nose and chin were bold and pronounced, yet his features were puffy, a combination which would blend more freely with the wig and cravat of the early Georges than with the close-cropped hair and black frock-coat of the end of the nineteenth century. He was clean shaven, for his mouth was too good to cover - large, flexible, and sensitive, with a kindly human softening at either corner which with his brown sympathetic eyes had drawn out many a shame- struck sinner's secret. Two masterful little bushy side-whiskers bristled out from under his ears spindling away upwards to merge in the thick curves of his brindled hair. To his patients there was something reassuring in the mere bulk and dignity of the man. A high and easy bearing in medicine as in war bears with it a hint of victories in the past, and a promise of others to come. Dr. Horace Selby's face was a consolation, and so too were the large, white, soothing hands, one of which he held out to his visitor.

"I am sorry to have kept you waiting. It is a conflict of duties, you perceive - a host's to his guests and an adviser's to his patient. But now I am entirely at your disposal, Sir Francis. But dear me, you are very cold."

"Yes, I am cold."

"And you are trembling all over. Tut, tut, this will never do! This miserable night has chilled you. Perhaps some little stimulant - "

"No, thank you. I would really rather not. And it is not the night which has chilled me. I am frightened, doctor."

The doctor half-turned in his chair, and he patted the arch of the young man's knee, as he might the neck of a restless horse.

"What then?" he asked, looking over his shoulder at the pale face with the startled eyes.

Twice the young man parted his lips. Then he stooped with a sudden gesture, and turning up the right leg of his trousers he pulled down his sock and thrust forward his shin. The doctor made a clicking noise with his tongue as he glanced at it.

"Both legs?"

"No, only one."

"Suddenly?"

"This morning."

"Hum."

The doctor pouted his lips, and drew his finger and thumb down the line of his chin. "Can you account for it?" he asked briskly.

"No."

A trace of sternness came into the large brown eyes.

"I need not point out to you that unless the most absolute frankness -"

The patient sprang from his chair. "So help me God!" he cried, "I have nothing in my life with which to reproach myself. Do you think that I would be such a fool as to come here and tell you lies. Once for all, I have nothing to regret." He was a pitiful, half-tragic and half-grotesque figure, as he stood with one trouser leg rolled to the knee, and that ever present horror still lurking in his eyes. A burst of merriment came from the card-players in the next room, and the two looked at each other in silence.

"Sit down," said the doctor abruptly, "your assurance is quite sufficient." He stooped and ran his finger down the line of the young man's shin, raising it at one point. "Hum, serpiginous," he murmured, shaking his head. "Any other symptoms?"

"My eyes have been a little weak."

"Let me see your teeth." He glanced at them, and again made the gentle, clicking sound of sympathy and disapprobation.

"Now your eye." He lit a lamp at the patient's elbow, and holding a small crystal lens to concentrate the light, he threw it obliquely upon the patient's eye. As he did so a glow of pleasure came over his large expressive face, a flush of such enthusiasm as the botanist feels when he packs the rare plant into his tin knapsack, or the astronomer when the long-sought comet first swims into the field of his telescope.

"This is very typical - very typical indeed," he murmured, turning to his desk and jotting down a few memoranda upon a sheet of paper. "Curiously enough, I am writing a monograph upon the subject. It is singular that you should have been able to furnish so well-marked a case." He had so forgotten the patient in his symptom, that he had assumed an almost congratulatory air towards its possessor. He reverted to human sympathy again, as his patient asked for particulars.

"My dear sir, there is no occasion for us to go into strictly professional details together," said he soothingly. "If, for example, I were to say that you have interstitial keratitis, how would you be the wiser? There are indications of a strumous diathesis. In broad terms, I may say that you have a constitutional and hereditary taint."

The young baronet sank back in his chair, and his chin fell forwards upon his chest. The doctor sprang to a side-table and poured out half a glass of liqueur brandy which he held to his patient's lips. A little fleck of colour came into his cheeks as he drank it down.

"Perhaps I spoke a little abruptly," said the doctor, "but you must have known the nature of your complaint. Why, otherwise, should you have come to me?"

"God help me, I suspected it; but only today when my leg grew bad. My father had a leg like this."

"It was from him, then - ?"

"No, from my grandfather. You have heard of Sir Rupert Norton, the great Corinthian?"

The doctor was a man of wide reading with a retentive memory. The name brought back instantly to him the remembrance of the sinister reputation of its owner - a notorious buck of the thirties - who had gambled and duelled and steeped himself in drink and debauchery, until even the vile set with whom he consorted had shrunk away from him in horror, and left him to a sinister old age with the barmaid wife whom he had married in some drunken frolic. As he looked at the young man still leaning back in the leather chair, there seemed for the instant to flicker up behind him some vague presentiment of that foul old dandy with his dangling seals, many-wreathed scarf, and dark satyric face. What was he now? An armful of bones in a mouldy box. But his deeds - they were living and rotting the blood in the veins of an innocent man.

"I see that you have heard of him," said the young baronet. "He died horribly, I have been told; but not more horribly than he had lived. My father was his only son. He was a studious man, fond of books and canaries and the country; but his innocent life did not save him."

"His symptoms were cutaneous, I understand."

"He wore gloves in the house. That was the first thing I can remember. And then it was his throat. And then his legs. He used to ask me so often about my own health, and I thought him so fussy, for how could I tell what the meaning of it was. He was always watching me - always with a sidelong eye fixed upon me. Now, at last, I know what he was watching for."

"Had you brothers or sisters?"

"None, thank God."

"Well, well, it is a sad case, and very typical of many which come in my way. You are no lonely sufferer, Sir Francis. There are many thousands who bear the same cross as you do."

"But where is the justice of it, doctor?" cried the young man, springing from his chair and pacing up and down the consulting-room. "If I were heir to my grandfather's sins as well as to their results, I could understand it, but I am of my father's type. I love all that is gentle and beautiful - music and poetry and art. The coarse and animal is abhorrent to me. Ask any of my friends and they would tell you that. And now that this vile, loathsome thing - ach, I am polluted to the marrow, soaked in abomination! And why? Haven't I a right to ask why? Did I do it? Was it my fault? Could I help being born? And look at me now, blighted and blasted, just as life was at its sweetest. Talk about the sins of the father - how about the sins of the Creator?" He shook his two clinched hands in the air - the poor impotent atom with his pin-point of brain caught in the whirl of the infinite.

The doctor rose and placing his hands upon his shoulders he pressed him back into his chair once more. "There, there, my dear lad," said he; "you must not excite yourself. You are trembling all over. Your nerves cannot stand it. We must take these great questions upon trust. What are we, after all? Half- evolved creatures in a transition stage, nearer perhaps to the Medusa on the one side than to perfected humanity on the other. With half a complete brain we can't expect to understand the whole of a complete fact, can we, now? It is all very dim and dark, no doubt; but I think that Pope's famous couplet sums up the whole matter, and from my heart, after fifty years of varied experience, I can say - "

But the young baronet gave a cry of impatience and disgust. "Words, words, words! You can sit comfortably there in your chair and say them - and think them too, no doubt. You've had your life, but I've never had mine. You've healthy blood in your veins; mine is putrid. And yet I am as innocent as you. What would words do for you if you were in this chair and I in that? Ah, it's such a mockery and a make-believe! Don't think me rude, though, doctor. I don't mean to be that. I only say that it is impossible for you or any other man to realise it. But I've a question to ask you, doctor. It's one on which my whole life must depend." He writhed his fingers together in an agony of apprehension.

"Speak out, my dear sir. I have every sympathy with you."

"Do you think - do you think the poison has spent itself on me? Do you think that if I had children they would suffer?"

"I can only give one answer to that. 'The third and fourth generation,' says the trite old text. You may in time eliminate it from your system, but many years must pass before you can think of marriage."

"I am to be married on Tuesday," whispered the patient.

It was the doctor's turn to be thrilled with horror. There were not many situations which would yield such a sensation to his seasoned nerves. He sat in silence while the babble of the card-table broke in upon them again. "We had a double ruff if you had returned a heart." "I was bound to clear the trumps." They were hot and angry about it.

"How could you?" cried the doctor severely. "It was criminal."

"You forget that I have only learned how I stand to-day." He put his two hands to his temples and pressed them convulsively. "You are a man of the world, Dr. Selby. You have seen or heard of such things before. Give me some advice. I'm in your hands. It is all very sudden and horrible, and I don't think I am strong enough to bear it."

The doctor's heavy brows thickened into two straight lines, and he bit his nails in perplexity.

"The marriage must not take place."

"Then what am I to do?"

"At all costs it must not take place."

"And I must give her up?"

"There can be no question about that."

The young man took out a pocketbook and drew from it a small photograph, holding it out towards the doctor. The firm face softened as he looked at it.

"It is very hard on you, no doubt. I can appreciate it more now that I have seen that. But there is no alternative at all. You must give up all thought of it."

"But this is madness, doctor - madness, I tell you. No, I won't raise my voice. I forgot myself. But realise it, man. I am to be married on Tuesday. This coming Tuesday, you understand. And all the world knows it. How can I put such a public affront upon her. It would be monstrous."

"None the less it must be done. My dear lad, there is no way out of it."

"You would have me simply write brutally and break the engagement at the last moment without a reason. I tell you I couldn't do it."

"I had a patient once who found himself in a somewhat similar situation some years ago," said the doctor thoughtfully. "His device was a singular one. He deliberately committed a penal offence, and so compelled the young lady's people to withdraw their consent to the marriage."

The young baronet shook his head. "My personal honour is as yet unstained," said he. "I have little else left, but that, at least, I will preserve."

"Well, well, it is a nice dilemma, and the choice lies with you."

"Have you no other suggestion?"

"You don't happen to have property in Australia?"

"None."

"But you have capital?"

"Yes."

"Then you could buy some. To-morrow morning would do. A thousand mining shares would be enough. Then you might write to say that urgent business affairs have compelled you to start at an hour's notice to inspect your property. That would give you six months, at any rate."

"Well, that would be possible. Yes, certainly, it would be possible. But think of her position. The house full of wedding presents - guests coming from a distance. It is awful. And you say that there is no alternative."

The doctor shrugged his shoulders.

"Well, then, I might write it now, and start to-morrow - eh? Perhaps you would let me use your desk. Thank you. I am so sorry to keep you from your guests so long. But I won't be a moment now."

He wrote an abrupt note of a few lines. Then with a sudden impulse he tore it to shreds and flung it into the fireplace.

"No, I can't sit down and tell her a lie, doctor," he said rising. "We must find some other way out of this. I will think it over and let you know my decision. You must allow me to double your fee as I have taken such an unconscionable time. Now good-bye, and thank you a thousand times for your sympathy and advice."

"Why, dear me, you haven't even got your prescription yet. This is the mixture, and I should recommend one of these powders every morning, and the chemist will put all directions upon the ointment box. You are placed in a cruel situation, but I trust that these may be but passing clouds. When may I hope to hear from you again?"

"To-morrow morning."

"Very good. How the rain is splashing in the street! You have your waterproof there. You will need it. Good-bye, then, until to-morrow."

He opened the door. A gust of cold, damp air swept into the hall. And yet the doctor stood for a minute or more watching the lonely figure which passed slowly through the yellow splotches of the gas lamps, and into the broad bars of darkness between. It was but his own shadow which trailed up the wall as he passed the lights, and yet it looked to the doctor's eye as though some huge and sombre figure walked by a manikin's side and led him silently up the lonely street.

Dr. Horace Selby heard again of his patient next morning, and rather earlier than he had expected. A paragraph in the Daily News caused him to push away his breakfast untasted, and turned him sick and faint while he read it. "A Deplorable Accident," it was headed, and it ran in this way:

"A fatal accident of a peculiarly painful character is reported from King William Street. About eleven o'clock last night a young man was observed while endeavouring to get out of the way of a hansom to slip and fall under the wheels of a heavy, two-horse dray. On being picked up his injuries were found to be of the most shocking character, and he expired while being conveyed to the hospital. An examination of his pocketbook and cardcase shows beyond any question that the deceased is none other than Sir Francis Norton, of Deane Park, who has only within the last year come into the baronetcy. The accident is made the more deplorable as the deceased, who was only just of age, was on the eve of being married to a young lady belonging to one of the oldest families in the South. With his wealth and his talents the ball of fortune was at his feet, and his many friends will be deeply grieved to know that his promising career has been cut short in so sudden and tragic a fashion."

AN EXCITING CHRISTMAS EVE

It has often seemed to me to be a very strange and curious thing that danger and trouble should follow those who are most anxious to lead a quiet and uneventful life. I myself have been such a one, and I find on looking back that it was in those very periods of my existence which might have been most confidently reckoned on as peaceful that some unexpected adventure has befallen me, like the thunder-bolt from an unclouded sky which shook the nerves of old Horace. Possibly my experience differs from that of other men, and I may have been especially unfortunate. If so, there is the more reason why I should mourn over my exceptional lot, and record it for the benefit of those more happily circumstanced.

Just compare my life with that of Leopold Walderich, and you will see what I complain of. We both come from Mulhausen, in Baden, and that is why I single him out as an example, though many others would do as well. He was a man who professed to be fond of adventure. Now listen to what occurred. We went to Heidelberg University together. I was quiet, studious, and unassuming; he was impetuous, reckless, and idle. For three years he reveled in every sort of riot, while I frequented the laboratories, and rarely deserted my books save for a hurried walk into the country when a pain in my head and ringing in my ears warned me that I was trifling with my constitution.

Yet during that period his life was comparatively uneventful, while my whole existence was a series of hairbreadth perils and escapes. I damaged my eyesight and nearly choked myself by the evolution of a poisonous gas. I swallowed a trichina in my ham, and was prostrated for weeks. I was hurled out of a second floor window by an English lunatic because I ventured to quote the solemn and serious passage in Schoppheim's Weltgeschichte which proves Waterloo to have been a purely Prussian victory, and throws grave doubts on the presence of any

British force nearer than Brussels! Twice I was nearly drowned, and once I should have been precipitated from the parapet of the schloss but for the assistance of this same Englishman. These are a few of the incidents which occurred to me while endeavouring to read in seclusion for my degree.

Even in smaller matters this luck of mine held good. I can well remember, for example, that on one occasion the wilder spirits of the Badischer Corps ventured upon an unusually hare-brained escapade. There was a farmer about a couple of miles from the town whose name was Nicholas Bodeck. This man had made himself obnoxious to the students, and they determined to play a prank upon him in return. An enormous number of little caps were accordingly made with the colours of the corps upon them, and the conspirators invaded his premises in the middle of the night and gummed them upon the heads of all the fowls.

They certainly had a very comical effect, as I had an opportunity of judging, for I happened to pass that way in the morning. I supposed that Walderich and his friends carried out their little joke for excitement, knowing the farmer to be a resolute man. They got no excitement from it, however; it was I who got that. Activity was never my strong point, but certainly I ran those two miles that morning with incredible speed - and so did the five men with pitch-forks who ran behind me!

These things may seem trivial, but, as you say in England, a straw shows which way the wind blows, and these were only indications of what was to come.

I took my degree in medicine, and found myself Herr Doctor Otto von Spee. I then graduated in science, receiving much applause for my thesis, "On the Explosive Compounds of the Tri-methyl Series". I was quoted as an authority in works of science, and my professors prophesied that a great career lay before me. My studies, however, were suddenly put an end to by the outbreak of the great war with France.

Waldenich volunteered into one of the crack regiments, fought in nearly every engagement, covered himself with glory, and came back unhurt to be decorated with the cross for valour. I was stationed in an ambulance which never even crossed the frontier, yet I succeeded in breaking my arm by tumbling over a stretcher, and in contracting erysipelas from one of the few wounds which came under my care. I got no medal or cross, and went back quietly to Berlin after it was all over, and there I settled as privat docent of chemistry and physics.

You will naturally ask what all this has to do with my Christmas story. You shall see in time that it is necessary I should tell you this, in order that you may appreciate that crowning event in my long list of misfortunes. You must remember also that I am a German and therefore somewhat long-winded perhaps, as my nation has the reputation of being. I have often admired the dashing, rattling manner of English story-tellers, but I fear if I were to attempt to imitate this it would be as if one of our own ponderous old Mulhausen storks were to adopt the pretty graceful airs of your Christmas robins. You shall hear in time all that I have to say about my Christmas Eve.

After I had settled in Berlin I endeavoured to combine the private practice of medicine with my labours as a privat docent, which corresponds to what you call a "coach" in England. For some years I pursued this plan, but I found that my practice, being largely among the lower classes, favoured my unfortunate propensity for getting into trouble, and I determined to abandon it.

I took a secluded house, therefore, in a quiet quarter of the city, and there I gave myself up to scientific research, pursuing principally the same train of investigation which had originally attracted me - namely, the chemistry of explosive compounds.

My expenses were small, and all the money which I could spare was laid out on scientific instruments and mechanical contrivances of different sorts. Soon I had a snug little laboratory which, if not as pretentious as that at Heidelberg, was quite as well fitted to supply my wants. It is true that the neighbours grumbled, and that Gretchen, my housekeeper, had to be quieted with a five-mark piece, after having been blown up three separate times, and blown down once while engaged in fixing an electric wire upon the summit of an outhouse. These little matters, however, were easily settled, and I found my life rapidly assuming a peaceful complexion, of which I had long despaired.

I was happy - and what is more I was becoming famous. My "Remarks on Cacodyl" in the "Monthly Archives of Science" created no small sensation, and Herr Raubenthal of Bonn characterised them as, "meisterlich," though dissenting from many of my deductions. I was enabled, however, in a later contribution to the same journal to recount certain experiments which were sufficient to convince that eminent savant that my view of the matter was the correct one.

After this victory I was universally recognised as an authority in my own special branch, and as one of the foremost living workers at explosives. The Government appointed me to the torpedo commission at Kiel, and many other honours were bestowed upon me. One of the consequences of this sudden accession of celebrity was that I found myself in great request as a lecturer, both at scientific gatherings and at those meetings for the education of the people which have become so common in the metropolis. By these means my name got into the daily papers as one learned in such matters, and to this it is that I ascribe the events which I am about to narrate.

It was a raw windy Christmas Eve. The sleet pattered against the window panes, and the blast howled among the skeleton branches of the gaunt poplar-trees in my garden. There were few people in the street, and those few had their coats buttoned up, and their chins upon their breasts, and hurried rapidly homewards, staggering along against the force of the storm. Even the big policeman outside had ceased to clank up and down, and was crouching in a doorway for protection.

Many a lonely man might have felt uncomfortable upon such a night, but I was too interested in my work to have time for any sympathy with the state of the weather. A submarine mine was engaging my attention, and in a leaden tank in front of me I had stuck a small pellet of my new explosive. The problem was how far its destructive capacities would be modified by the action of the water. The matter was too important to allow me to feel despondent. Besides, one of Gretchen's lovers was in the kitchen, and his gruff expressions of satisfaction, whether with her charms or my beer, or both, were sufficiently audible to banish any suspicion of loneliness.

I was raising my battery on to the table, and was connecting the wires carefully so as to explode the charge, when I heard a short, quick step outside the window, and immediately afterwards a loud knock at the outer door.

Now I very seldom had a call from any of my limited number of acquaintances, and certainly never upon such a night as this. I was astonished for a moment; then concluding that it was a visitor of Gretchen's, I continued to work at my apparatus.

To my very great surprise, after Gretchen had opened the door there was some muttering in the hall, and then a quiet tap at the entrance of my sanctum, followed by the appearance of a tall lady whom I could vow that I had never seen in my life before.

Her face was covered by a thick dark veil, and her dress was of the same sombre colour, so that I concluded her to be a widow. She walked in with a decisive energetic step, and after glancing round, seated herself quietly upon the sofa between the voltaic pile and my stand of reagents - all this without saying a word, or apparently taking the slightest notice of my presence.

"Good evening, madam," I remarked, when I had somehow recovered my composure.

"Would you do me a favour, doctor?" she replied, brusquely, in a harsh voice, which harmonised with her gaunt angular figure.

"Surely, madam," I answered, in my most elegant manner. I remember a girl at Heidelberg used to say that I had a very fascinating way sometimes. Of course it was only a joke, but still something must have put it into her head or she would never have said it. "What can I do for you?" I asked.

"You can send away that servant of yours, who is listening at the door."

At this moment, before I could move hand or foot, there were a succession of tremendous bumps, followed by a terrible crash and a prolonged scream. It was evident that my unhappy domestic had fallen downstairs in her attempt to avoid detection. I was about to rise, but the stranger arrested me.

"Never mind now," she said. "We can proceed to business."

I bowed my head to show that I was all attention.

"The fact is, doctor," she continued, "that I wish you to come back with me and give me your opinion upon a case."

"My dear madam," I answered, "I have long retired from the practice of my profession. If you go down the street, however, you will see the surgery of Doctor Benger, who is a most competent man, and who will be happy to accompany you."

"No, no," cried my companion, in great distress. "You or no one! You or no one! My poor dear husband cried out as I left him that Otto von Spee was the only man who could bring him back from the tomb. They will all be broken-hearted if I return without you. Besides, the professors at the hospital said that you were the only one in Europe who would be capable of dealing with it."

Now, devoted as I was to scientific research, I had always had a conviction in my mind that I had the makings in me of a first-class practical physician. It was inexpressibly consoling to hear that the heads of the profession had endorsed this opinion by referring a curious case to my judgment. The more I thought of it, however, the more extraordinary did it seem. "Are you sure?" I asked.

"Oh yes, quite sure."

"But I am a specialist - a student of explosives. I have had very little experience in practice. What is the matter with your husband?"

"He has a tumour."

"A tumour? I know nothing of tumours."

"Oh come, dear Doctor von Spee; come and look at it!" implored the female, producing a handkerchief from her pocket and beginning to sob convulsively.

It was too much. I had lived a secluded life, and had never before seen a female in distress.

"Madam," I said, "I shall be happy to accompany you."

I regretted that promise the moment it was uttered. There was a wild howl of wind in the chimney which reminded me of the inclemency of the night. However, my word was pledged, and there was no possibility of escape. I left the room with as cheerful an aspect as possible, while Gretchen wrapped a shawl round my neck and muffled me up to the best of her ability.

What could there be about this tumour, I wondered, which had induced the learned surgeons to refer it to my judgment - I who was rather an artillerist than a physician? Could it be that the growth was of such stony hardness that no knife could remove it, and that explosives were necessary for extraction? The idea was so comical that I could scarce refrain from laughing.

"Now, madam," I said re-entering the study, "I am at your disposal." As I spoke I knocked against the electric machine, causing a slight transmission of the current along the wires, so that the submarine mine exploded with a crash, blowing a little column of water into the air. Accustomed as I was to such accidents, I confess that I was considerably startled by the suddenness of the occurrence. My companion, however, sat perfectly impassive upon the sofa, and then rose without the slightest sign of surprise or emotion, and walked out of the room.

"She has the nerves of a grenadier," I mentally ejaculated, as I followed her into the street.

"Is it far?" I asked, as we started off through the storm.

"Not very far," she answered; "and I took the liberty of bringing a cab for you, for fear Herr Doctor might catch cold. Ah, here it comes."

As she spoke, a closed carriage dashed along the road, and pulled up beside us.

"Have you got Otto von Spee?" asked a sallow-faced man, letting down the window and protruding his head.

"Yes, here he is."

"Then shove him in."

For the moment I was inclined to regard the expression as a playful figure of speech, but my companion soon dispelled the delusion by seizing me by the collar and hurling me, with what seemed superhuman strength, into the vehicle. I fell upon the floor, and was dragged on to a seat by the man, while the other sprang in, slammed the door, and the horses dashed off at a furious gallop.

I lay back in a state of bewilderment, hardly able to realise what had occurred. It was pitch dark inside the carriage, but I could hear my two companions conversing in low whispers. Once I attempted to expostulate and demand an explanation of their conduct, but a threatening growl, and a rough hand placed over my mouth, warned me to be silent. I was neither a wealthy man nor particularly well connected, nor was I a politician. What then, could be the object of these people in kidnapping me in such an elaborate fashion? The more I pondered over it, the more mysterious did it seem.

Once we halted for a moment, and a third man got into the carriage, who also inquired anxiously whether Otto von Spee had been secured, and expressed his satisfaction on being answered in the affirmative. After this stoppage we rattled along even more quickly than before, the vehicle rocking from side to side with the velocity, and the clatter of the horses hoofs sounding above the howling of the gale. It seemed to me that we must have passed through every street in Berlin before, with a sudden jar, the coachman pulled up, and my captors intimated that I was to descend.

I had hardly time to look about me and realise the fact that I was in a narrow street in some low quarter of the city. A door opened in front of us, and the two men led me through it, while the herculean female followed us, effectually cutting off any hopes of escape.

We were in a long passage or corridor, feebly illuminated by a couple of flickering lamps, whose yellow glare seemed to intensify the darkness around them. After walking about twenty metres or more we came to a massive door, blocking our passage. One of my guardians struck it a blow with a stick which he carried in his hand, when it reverberated with a metallic clang, and swung open, closing with a snap behind us.

At this point I ventured to stop and expostulate with my companions once again. My only answer, however, was a shove from the individual behind me, which shot me through a half-opened door into a comfortable little chamber beyond. My captors followed in a more leisurely manner, and after turning the lock, they proceeded to seat themselves, motioning to me that I should do the same.

The room in which I found myself was small, but elegantly furnished. A fire was sparkling in the grate, and the bright colours of the handsome suite of furniture and variegated carpet helped to give it a cheering aspect. The pictures on the walls, however, went far towards neutralising this effect. They were very numerous, but every one of them treated of some unpleasant or murderous passage of history. Many of them were so distant that I was unable to decipher the inscriptions. To a scholar like myself, however, the majority were able to tell their own story. There was the lunatic Schtaps in the garden, making his attempt upon the life of the First Napoleon. Above it was a sketch of Orsini with his cowardly bomb, waiting silently among the loungers at the opera. A statuette of Ravaillac was placed upon a pedestal in the corner, while a large oil-painting of the strangling of the unhappy Emperor Paul in his bedchamber occupied the whole of one wall of the apartment.

These things did not tend to raise my spirits, and the appearance of my three companions was still less calculated to do so. I had several times doubted the sex of the individual who had seduced me from my comfortable home, but the veil had now been removed and revealed a dark moustache and sunburnt countenance, with a pair of searching, sinister eyes, which seemed to look into my very soul. Of the others, one was gaunt and cadaverous, the other insignificant-looking, with a straggling beard and unhealthy complexion.

"We are very sorry, Doctor von Spee, to be reduced to this necessity," said the last-mentioned individual, "but unhappily we had no other method of securing the pleasure of your society."

I bowed - a little sulkily, I am afraid.

"I must apologise for any little liberties I have taken, above all for having deprived you of the satisfaction of beholding my husband's remarkable tumour," said my original acquaintance.

I thought of the manner in which he had bundled me about like an empty portmanteau, and my bow was even more sulky than before.

"I trust, gentlemen," I remarked, "that since your practical joke has been so admirably carried out, you will now permit me to return to the studies which you have interrupted."

"Not so fast, Herr Doctor - not so fast," said the tall man, rising to his feet. "We have a little duty which you shall perform before you leave us. It is nothing more nor less than to give a few inquirers into the truth a lesson upon your own special subject. Might I beg you to step in this direction?"

He walked over to a side door, painted of the same colour as the paper on the wall, and held it persuasively open. Resistance was useless, as the other confederates had also risen, and were standing on either side of me. I yielded to circumstances, and walked out as directed.

We passed down a second passage, rather shorter than the first, and much more brilliantly illuminated. At the end of it a heavy velvet curtain was hung, which covered a green baize folding-door. This was swung open, and I found myself, to my astonishment, in a large room in which a considerable number of people were assembled. They were arranged in long rows, and sat so as to face a raised platform at one end of the apartment, on which was a single chair, with a small round table, littered with a number of objects.

My companions ushered me in, and our entrance was greeted with considerable applause. It was clear that we had been awaited, for there was a general movement of expectation throughout the assembly. Glancing round, I could see that the majority of the company were dressed as artisans or labourers. There were some, however, who were respectably and even fashionably attired, and a few whose blue coats and gilt shoulder-bands proclaimed them to be officers in the army. Their nationalities seemed almost as varied as their occupations. I could distinguish the dolichocephalic head of the Teuton, the round, curl-covered cranium of the Celt, and the prognathous jaw and savage features of the Slav. I could almost have imagined myself looking into one of the cabinets of casts in my friend Landerstein's anthropological museum.

However, I had not much time for wonder or reflection. One of my guardians led me across the room, and I found myself standing at the table, which I have already mentioned as being situated upon a raised dais. My appearance in this situation was the signal for a fresh outburst of applause, which, with clapping of hands and drumming of sticks upon the floor, lasted for some considerable time.

When it had subsided, the gaunt man who had come with me in the carriage walked up to the dais and addressed a few words to the audience. "Gentlemen," he said, "you will perceive that the committee have succeeded in keeping their promise and of bringing the celebrated - ("beruhmte" was the word he used) - Doctor Otto von Spee to address you." Here there was renewed applause.

"Doctor," he continued, turning to me, "I think a few words of public explanation will not be amiss in this matter. You are well known as an authority upon explosives. Now all these gentlemen and myself have an interest in this subject, and would gladly listen to your views upon it. We are particularly anxious that you should give us clear and precise directions as to the method of preparing dynamite, guncotton, and other such substances, as we sometimes have a little difficulty in obtaining such things for our experiments. You shall also tell us about the effect of temperature, water, and other agents upon these substances, the best method of storing them, and the way of using them to the greatest advantage. For our part, we shall listen attentively and treat you well, always provided that you make no attempt to summon aid or to escape. Should you be so ill-advised as to do either" - here he slapped his pocket - "you shall become as intimately acquainted with projectiles as you now are with explosives." I cannot say that this struck me as a good joke, but it seemed to meet considerable favour among the audience.

"I wish to add a few words to the remarks of our learned president," said a small man, rising up from among the first line of the company. "I have placed upon the table such materials as I could lay my hands upon in order that the learned doctor may be able to illustrate his discourse by any experiments which he may think appropriate. I may warn him, in conclusion, to speak somewhat slowly and distinctly, as some of his hearers are but imperfectly acquainted with the German language."

Here was my old luck again with a vengeance! At a time when Walderich and every gay dog in Berlin were snoring peacefully in their beds, I - I, Doctor Otto von Spee, the modest man of science - was lecturing to a murderous secret organisation - for my audience could be nothing else - and teaching them to forge the weapons with which they were to attack society and everything which should be treasured and revered. And on such a night as this too! Should I, then, put it in their power to convert a house into an arsenal, to destroy the stability of the Fatherland, and even perhaps attempt the life of my beloved kaiser? Never! I swore it - never!

Most small men who wear spectacles are obstinate. I am a small man with spectacles, and I was no exception to the rule. I clenched my teeth, and felt that ruat caelum, never a word should pass my lips that might be of any help to them. I should not refuse to lecture, but I was determined to avoid those very points upon which they desired to be instructed.

I was not allowed much time for meditation. An ominous murmur among the audience, and a shuffling of feet upon the floor, betokened their impatience. I must say, however, that many of them seemed actuated with rather kindly feelings towards me, more particularly one stoutish individual of a well-marked Celtic type, who, not content with smiling all over his florid countenance, waved his arms occasionally in motions intended to indicate sympathy and inspire confidence.

I stepped up to the table, which was covered all over with such objects as were thought to have a bearing upon my subject. Some of them were rather curious - a lump of salt, an iron teapot, part of the broken axle of a wheel, and a large pair of kitchen bellows. Others were more appropriate. There was a piece of guncotton which could not have weighed less than a couple of pounds, coarse cotton, starch, various acids, a Bunsen burner, tubes of fulminate of mercury, some dynamite powder, and a large pitcher of water. There was also a carafe and tumbler for my own use, should I feel so disposed.

"Meine herren," I began, with perhaps a slight quaver in my voice, "we have met here tonight for the purpose of studying dynamite and other explosives." It flowed naturally from my lips, as it was the stereotyped formula with which my discourses at the Educationische Institut were usually commenced. My audience seemed, however, to be much amused, and the florid Celt was convulsed with admiration and merriment. Even the forbidding-looking man who had been referred to as the president condescended to smile his approval and remark that I adapted myself readily to my circumstances.

"These substances," I continued, "are powerful agents either for good or for evil. For good when used for the quarrying of rocks, the removal of impediments to navigation, or the destruction of houses during a conflagration. For evil - "

"I think you had better pass on to something more practical," said the president, grimly.

"On dipping starch into certain liquids," I resumed, "it is found to assume an explosive property. The attention of a learned countryman of ours, the chemist Schonbein, was directed to the fact, and he found that by treating cotton in a similar manner the effect was enormously increased. Schonbein was a man respected among his contemporaries, devoted to his country, and loyal - "

"Pass on!" said the president.

"After being treated in this fashion," I continued, "the cotton is found to gain eighty per cent in weight. This substance is more susceptible to an increase of temperature than gunpowder, igniting at 300° Fahrenheit, while the latter requires a heat of 560° for its explosion. Guncotton can also be exploded by a blow, which is not the case with a mixture of carbon, sulphur, and saltpetre."

Here there were some angry murmurs among the company, and the president interrupted me for the third time.

"These gentlemen complain," he said, "that you have left no definite impression upon their minds as to how the substance is manufactured. Perhaps you will kindly dwell more fully upon the point."

"I have no further remarks to make," I said.

There was another threatening murmur, and the president took something out of the pocket of his coat, and toyed with it negligently. "I think you had better reconsider your decision," he remarked.

Most little men with spectacles are timid. Again I was no exception to the rule. I am ashamed to say that the peril of my Fatherland and even of my kaiser suddenly vanished from my recollection. I only realised that I, Otto von Spee, was standing upon the brink of eternity. After all, I argued, they could find out for themselves in any book upon chemistry. Why should my valuable life be sacrificed for such a trifle? I resumed my lecture with somewhat undignified haste.

"Guncotton is manufactured by steeping cotton waste in nitric acid. The explosion is caused by the oxygen of the acid combining with the carbon of the wool. It should be well cleaned with water after manufacture, otherwise the superfluous nitric acid acts directly upon the wool, charring it and gradually reducing it to a gummy mass. During this process heat is often evolved sufficient to explode the cotton, so that it is a dangerous matter to neglect the cleaning. After this a little sulphuric acid may be used to get rid of the moisture, when the substance is ready for use."

There was considerable applause at this point of my discourse, several of the audience taking notes of my remarks.

While I had been speaking I had been making a careful survey of the room in the hope of seeing some possibility of escape. The dais upon which I stood extended as far as the side wall, in which there was a window. The window was half open, and, could I reach it, there appeared to be a deserted looking garden outside, which might communicate with the street. No one could intercept me before I reached the window, but then there was the deadly weapon with which my cadaverous acquaintance was still trifling. He was sitting on the other side, and the table would partially protect me should I venture upon a dash. Could I screw up my courage to make an attempt? Not yet, at any rate.

"General von Link," I continued, "the Austrian artillerist, is one of our leading authorities upon guncotton. He experimented upon it in field-pieces, but - "

"Never mind that," said the president.

"After being manufactured, guncotton may be compressed under water. When compressed it is perfectly safe, and cannot be discharged. This sample which we have upon the table is not compressed. No amount of heat will have any effect upon the wet cotton. In an experiment tried in England a storehouse containing guncotton was burned down without there being any explosion. If, however, a charge of fulminated mercury, or a small piece of dry cotton, be fired in connection with a damp disc, it will be sufficient to discharge it. I shall now proceed to demonstrate this to you by an experiment."

An idea had come into my mind. Upon the table there was lying a mixture of sugar and chlorate of potash, used with sulphuric acid as a fuse for mining purposes. A bottle of the acid was also ready to my hand. I knew the white dense cloud of smoke which is raised by the imperfect combustion of these bodies. Could I make it serve as a screen between the weapon of the president and myself?

For a moment the plan seemed wild and unfeasible; still, it offered some chance of escape, and the more I thought it over the more reconciled I became to it. Of course, even after getting through the window there was the possibility that the garden might prove to be a cul-de-sac, and that my pursuers might overtake me. But then, on the other hand, I had no guarantee that I might not be murdered at the conclusion of my lecture. From what I knew of the habits of such men I considered it to be extremely probable. It was better to risk - but no, I would not think of what I was risking.

"I am now going to show you the effect of fulminate of mercury upon a small piece of damp cotton," I said, shaking out the sugar and chlorate of potash upon the edge of the table and pushing the large piece of cotton to the other end to be out of danger from the effects of the explosion.

"You will observe that the fact of the substance having been soaked with water does not in any way hinder its action." Here I poured the sulphuric acid over the mixture, dropped the bottle, and fled for the window amid a perfect cloud of smoke.

Most little men with spectacles are not remarkable for activity. Ha! there at last I proved myself to be an exception. I seemed hardly to put my foot to the ground between leaving the table and shooting out through the window as the equestrians fly through hoops in the circus. I was well outside before the sharp crack which I was expecting sounded in the chamber behind me, and then -

Ah! what then? How can I ever hope to describe it? There was a low, deep rumble, which seemed to shake the ground, swelling and swelling in sound until it culminated in a roar which split the very heavens. Flames danced before my eyes, burning wood and stones and débris came clattering down around me, and as I stared about me in bewilderment I received a crushing blow upon the head, and fell.

How long I may have remained unconscious it is difficult to say. Some time, at any rate, for when I came to myself I was stretched upon the bed in my own little chamber at home, while the devoted Gretchen bathed my temples with vinegar and water. In the doorway were standing a couple of stalwart polizei diener, who bobbed their helmeted heads and grinned their satisfaction on seeing that I was returning to consciousness.

It was some while before I could recall anything of what had passed. Then gradually came the recollection of my mysterious visitor, of the wild drive through the storm, of the impromptu lecture on dynamite, and lastly of some strange and unaccountable accident. Strange it still remains, but I think that when we reflect that the table was between the bullet and me, and that on that table were two pounds of guncotton liable to ignition at a blow, we have not very far to go for an explanation. I have fired a pistol at a distance into a small piece of the same substance since that occasion with very much the same result.

And where was the house? you will ask, and what was the fate of its inmates? Ah! there my lips are sealed. The police of the Fatherland are active and cunning, and they have commanded me to say nothing - not even to my dearest friend - upon either point. No doubt they have their reasons for it, and I must obey. Perhaps they wish other conspirators to imagine that more has been found out than is actually the case. I may say, however, that it is not conducive to long life or perfect health to be present on such an occasion. That, at least, no one can object to.

I am nearly well again now, thanks to Gretchen and Dr Benger, who lives down the road. I can hobble about, and my neighbours are already beginning to complain of the noxious vapours which I evolve. I fear I have not quite the same enthusiasm, however, upon the subject of explosives as I entertained before my midnight lecture on dynamite. The subject seems to have lost many of its charms. It may be that in the course of time I may return to my first love once again; at present, however, I remain a quiet privat docent of the more elementary branches of chemistry. It is that very quietness which weighs upon my mind. I fear that I am on the verge of some other unexpected adventure. There is one thing, however, upon which I am unalterably determined. Should every relative that I have in the world, with the Imperial family and half the population of Berlin, be clamouring at my door for medical advice, I shall never again protrude my head after nightfall. I am content to work away in my own little groove, and have laid aside for ever the pretensions to be looked upon as a practical physician which I entertained before that eventful Christmas Eve.

THE CABMAN'S STORY

We had to take a "growler," for the day looked rather threatening and we agreed that it would be a very bad way of beginning our holiday by getting wet, especially when Fanny was only just coming round from the whooping cough. Holidays were rather scarce with us, and when we took one we generally arranged some little treat, and went in for enjoying ourselves. On this occasion we were starting off from Hammersmith to the Alexandra Palace in all the dignity of a four-wheeler. What with the wife and her sister, and Tommy and Fanny and Jack, the inside was pretty well filled up, so I had to look out for myself. I didn't adopt the plan of John Gilpin under similar circumstances, but I took my waterproof and climbed up beside the driver.

This driver was a knowing-looking old veteran, with a weather-beaten face and white side whiskers. It has always seemed to me that a London cabman is about the shrewdest of the human race, but this specimen struck me as looking like the shrewdest of the cabmen. I tried to draw him out a bit as we jogged along, for I am always fond of a chat; but he was a bit rusty until I oiled his tongue with glass of gin when we got as far as the "Green Anchor." Then he rattled away quickly enough, and some of what he said is worth trying to put down in black and white.

"Wouldn't a hansom pay me better?" he said, in answer to a question of mine. "Why, of course it would. But look at the position! A four-wheeler's a respectable conveyance, and the driver of it's a respectable man, but you can't say that of a rattling, splashing 'ansom. Any boy would do for that job. Now, to my mind money hain't to be compared to position, whatever a man's trade may be."

"Certainly not!" I answered.

"Besides, I've saved my little penny, and I'm got too old to change my ways. I've begun on a growler, and I'll end on one. If you'll believe me, sir, I've been on the streets for seven-and-forty year."

"That's a long time," I said.

"Well, it's long for our trade," he replied. "You see, there ain't no other in the world that takes the steam out of a man so quickly - what with wet and cold and late hours, and maybe no hours at all. There's few that lasts at it as long as I have."

"You must have seen a deal of the world during that time," I remarked. "There are few men who can have greater opportunities of seeing life."

"The world!" he grunted, flicking up the horse with his whip. "I've seen enough of it to be well-nigh sick of it. As to life, if you'd said death, you'd ha' been nearer the mark."

"Death!" I ejaculated.

"Yes, death," he said. "Why, bless your soul, sir, if I was to write down all I've seen since I've been in the trade, there's not a man in London would believe me, unless maybe some o' the other cabbies. I tell ye I took a dead man for a fare once, and drove about with him nigh half the night. Oh, you needn't look shocked, sir, for this wasn't the cab - no, nor the last one I had neither."

"How did it happen?" I asked, feeling glad, in spite of his assurance, that Matilda had not heard of the episode.

"Well, it's an old story now," said the driver, putting a small piece of very black tobacco into the corner of his mouth. "I daresay it's twenty odd years since it happened, but it's not the kind o' thing as slips out of a man's memory. It was very late one night, and I was working my hardest to pick up something good, for I'd made a poor day's work of it. The theatres had all come out, and though I kept up and down the Strand till nigh one o'clock, I got nothing but one eighteen penny job. I was thinking of giving it up and going home, when it struck me that I might as well make a bit of a circuit, and see if I couldn't drop across something. Pretty soon I gave a gentleman a lift as far as the Oxford Road, and then I drove through St. John's Wood on my way home. By that time it would be about half-past one, and the streets were quite quiet and deserted, for the night was cloudy and it was beginning to rain. I was putting on the pace as well as my tired beast would go, for we both wanted to get back to our suppers, when I heard a woman's voice hail me out of a side street. I turned back, and there in about the darkest part of the road was standing two ladies -

real ladies, mind you, for it would take a deal of darkness before I would mistake one for the other. One was elderly and stoutish; the other was young, and had a veil over her face. Between them there was a man in evening dress, whom they were supporting on each side, while his back was propped up against a lamp-post. He seemed beyond taking care of himself altogether, for his head was sunk down on his chest, and he'd have fallen if they hadn't held him.

"'Cabman,' said the stout lady, with a very shaky voice, 'I wish you would help us in this painful business.' Those were her very identical words.

"'Cert'nly, mum,' I says for I saw my way to a good thing. 'What can I do for the young lady and yourself?' I mentioned the other in order to console her like, for she was sobbing behind her veil something pitiful.

"'The fact is, cabman,' she answers, 'this gentleman is my daughter's husband. They have only just been married, and we are visiting at a friend's house near here. My son-in-law has just returned in a state of complete intoxication, and my daughter and I have brought him out in the hope of seeing a cab in which we could send him home, for we have most particular reasons for not wishing our friends to see him in this state, and as yet they are ignorant of it. If you would drive him to his house and leave him there, you would do us both a very great kindness, and we can easily account to our hosts for his absence. '

"I thought this rather a rum start, but I agreed, and no sooner had I said the word than the old one she pulls open the door, and she and the other, without waiting for me to bear a hand, bundled him in between them.

"'Where to?' I asked.

"'Forty-seven, Orange Grove, Clapham,' she said. 'Hoffman is the name. You'll easily waken the servants. '

"'And how about the fare?' I suggested, for I thought maybe there might be a difficulty in collecting it at the end of the journey.

"'Here it is,' said the young one, slipping what I felt to be a sovereign into my hand, and at the same time giving it a sort of a grateful squeeze, which made me feel as if I'd drive anywhere to get her out of trouble.

"Well, off I went, leaving them standing by the side of the road. The horse was well-nigh beat, but at last I found my way to 47, Orange Grove. It was a biggish house, and all quiet, as you may suppose, at that hour. I rang the bell, and at last down came a servant a man, he was.

"'I've got the master here,' I said.

"'Got who?' he asked.

"'Why Mr. Hoffman - your master. He's in the cab, not quite himself. This is number forty-seven, ain't it?'

"'Yes, it's forty-seven, right enough; but my master's Captain Ritchie, and he's away in India, so you've got the wrong house. '

"'That was the number they gave me,' I said, 'But maybe he's come to himself by this time, and can give us some information. He was dead drunk an hour ago. '

"Down we went to the cab, the two of us, and opened the door. He had slipped off the seat and was lying all in a heap on the floor.

"'Now, then, sir,' I shouted. 'Wake up and give us your address. '

"He didn't answer.

"I gave another shake. 'Pull yourself together,' I roared. 'Give us your name, and tell us where you live. '

"He didn't answer again. I couldn't even hear the sound of breathing. Then a kind of queer feeling came over me, and I put down my hand and felt his face. It was as cold as lead. The cove's dead, mate,' I said.

"The servant struck a match, and we had a look at my passenger. He was a young, good-looking fellow, but his face wore an expression of pain, and his jaw hung down. He was evidently not only dead, but had been dead some time.

"'What shall we do?' said the flunkey. He was as white as death himself, and his hair bristled with fear.

"'I'll drive to the nearest police station,' I answered; and so I did, leaving him shivering on the pavement. There I gave up my fare, and that was the last I ever saw of him."

"Did you never hear any more of it?" I asked.

"Hear! I thought I should never hear the end of it, what with examinations and inquests and one thing and another. The doctors proved that he must have been dead at the time he was shoved into the cab. Just before the inquest four little blue spots came out on one side of his neck, and one on the other, and they said only a woman's hand could have fitted over them, so they brought in a verdict of willful murder; but, bless you, they had managed it so neatly that there was not a clue to the women, nor to the man either, for everything by which he might have been identified had been removed from his pockets. The police were fairly puzzled by that case. I've always thought what a bit o' luck it was that I got my fare, for I wouldn't have had much chance of it if it hadn't been paid in advance."

My friend the driver began to get very husky about the throat at this stage of the proceedings, and slackened his speed very noticeably as we approached a large public-house, so that I felt constrained to offer him another gin, which he graciously accepted. The ladies had some wine, too, and I followed the example of my companion on the box, so that we all started refreshed.

"The police and me's been mixed up a good deal," continued the veteran resuming his reminiscences: "They took the best customer I ever had away from me. I'd have made my fortune if they'd let him carry on his little game a while longer."

Here, with the coquetry of one who knows that his words are of interest, the driver began to look around him with an air of abstraction and to comment upon the weather.

"Well, what about your customer and the police?" I asked.

"It's not much to tell," he said, coming back to his subject. "One morning I was driving across Vauxhall Bridge when I was hailed by a crooked old man with a pair of spectacles on, who was standing at the Middlesex end, with a big leather bag in his hand. 'Drive anywhere you like,' he said; 'only don't drive fast for I'm getting old, and it shakes me to pieces. 'He jumped in, and shut himself up, closing the windows, and I trotted about with him for three hours, before he let me know that he had had enough. When I stopped, out he hopped with his big bag in his hand.

"'I say cabbie! ' he said, after he had paid his fare.

"'Yes, sir,' said I, touching my hat.

"'You seem to be a decent sort of fellow, and you don't go in the break- neck way of some of your kind. I don't mind giving you the same job every day. The doctors recommend gentle exercise of the sort, and you may as well drive me as another. Just pick me up at the same place tomorrow. '

"Well, to make a long story short, I used to find the little man in his place every morning, always with his black bag, and for nigh on to four months never a day passed without his having his three hours' drive and paying his fare like a man at the end of it. I shifted into new quarters on the strength of it, and was able to buy a new set of harness. I don't say as I altogether swallowed the story of the doctors having recommended him on a hot day to go about in a growler with both windows up. However, it's a bad thing in this world to be too knowing, so though I own I felt a bit curious at times, I never put myself out o' the way to find out what the little game was. One day, I was driving tap to my usual place of dropping him - for by this time we had got into the way of going a regular beat every morning - when I saw a policeman waiting, with a perky sort of look about him, as if he had some job on hand. When the cab stopped out jumped the little man with his bag right into the arms of the 'bobby. '

"'I arrest you, John Malone,' says the policeman.

"'On what charge?' he answers as cool as a turnip.

"'On the charge of forging Bank of England notes,' says the 'bobby'.

"'Oh, then the game is up! ' he cries, and with that he pulls off his spectacles, and his wig and whiskers, and there he was, as smart a young fellow as you'd wish to see.

"'Good-bye, cabby,' he cried, as they led him off, and that was the last I saw of him, marching along between two of them, and another behind with the bag."

"And why did he take a cab?" I asked, much interested.

"Well, you see, he had all his plant for making the notes in that bag. If he were to lock himself up in his lodging several hours a day it would soon set people wondering, to say nothing of the chance of eyes at the window or key-hole. Again, you see, if he took a house all on his own hook, without servant nor anyone, it would look queer. So he made up his mind as the best way of working it was to carry it on in a closed cab, and I don't know that he wasn't right. He was known to the police however, and that was how they spotted him. Drat that van! It was as near as a touch to my off-wheel.

"Bless you, if I was to tell you all the thieves and burglars, and even murderers, as have been in my growler one time or another, you'd think I'd given the whole Newgate Calendar a lift, though to be sure this young chap as I spoke of was the only one as ever reg'lar set up in business there. There was one though as I reckon to be worse than all the others put together, if he was what I think him to be. It's often laid heavy on my mind that I didn't have that chap collared before it was too late, for I might have saved some mischief. It was about ten years ago - I never was a good hand for dates - that I picked up a stout-built sailor-sort of fellow, with a reddish moustache, who wanted to be taken down to the docks. After this chap as I told you of had taken such liberties with the premises I'd had a little bit of a glass slit let in front here - the same that your little boy's flattening his nose against at this moment - so as I could prevent any such games in the future, and have an idea, whenever I wished, of what was going on inside. Well, something or another about this sailor fellow made me suspicious of him, and I took a look at what he was after. He was sitting on the seat, sir, with a big lump o' coal in his lap, and was a looking at it most attentive. Now this seemed to me rather a rum start, so I kept on watching of him, for as you'll see, my window's not a very large one, and it's easier to see through it than to be seen. Well, he pulls a spring or something, and out jumps one of the sides of this bit of coal, and then I saw it was really a hollow box, painted, you see, and made rough so as to look like the other. I couldn't make head or tail of it anyhow, and indeed I'd pretty near forgot all about it when there came news of the explosion at Bemerhaven, and people began to talk about coal torpedoes. Then I knew as in all probability I'd carried the man who managed the business, and I gave word to the police, but they never could make anything of it. You know what a coal torpedo is, don't you? Well, you see, a cove insures his ship for more than its value, and then off he goes and makes a box like a bit o'coal, and fills it chock full with dynamite, or some other cowardly stuff of the sort. He drops this box among the other coals on the quay when the vessel is filling her bunkers, and then in course of time box is shoveled on to the furnaces, when of course the whole ship is blown sky high. They say there's many a good ship gone to the bottom like that."

"You've certainly had some queer experiences," I said.

"Why bless you!" remarked the driver, "I've hardly got fairly started yet, and here we are at the 'Alexandry. 'I could tell you many another story as strange as these - and true, mind ye, true as Gospel. If ever your missus looks in need of a breath of fresh air you send round for me - Copper Street, number ninety-four - and I'll give her a turn into the country, and if you'll come up beside me on the box, I'll tell you a good deal that may surprise you. But there's your little lad a hollering to you like mad, and the wife wants to get out, and the other one's a tapping at the window with a parasol. Take care how you get down, sir! That's right! Don't forget number ninety-four! Good-day missus! Good-day, sir!" And the growler rumbled heavily away until I lost sight both of it and of its communicative driver among the crowd of holiday-makers who thronged the road which led to the Palace.

THE BLOOD-STONE TRAGEDY: A DRUIDICAL STORY

'HUSH!' said my fellow-traveller, holding up his hand with a warning gesture, and glancing at his wife, who was snugly ensconced amongst her rugs in the corner. 'Hush!'

'My dear sir,' I remonstrated, 'my reference to Doctor Price-'

'Hush!' interrupted my companion, in a more authoritative voice. 'Not a word!'

Now, this was very mysterious conduct. The gentleman who curtailed my remarks so brusquely had entered the carriage at Rugby with his wife, and we had been whiling away an hour or so of our journey by retailing our views upon current subjects to each other. Having chatted over one topic or another, some unlucky impulse had led me to refer to Dr Price and his recent attempt at the revival of Druidism by the cremation of an infant. To my surprise my allusion had a marked effect upon my companion, who became much agitated, and checked me in the decisive manner which I have quoted.

'Ah! it's all right,' he resumed, bending over and looking down at his wife. 'She is asleep. Come over here into the far corner, so that she cannot hear us if she wakes.'

I obeyed this mysterious injunction, with many surmises in my mind as to the cause of so much precaution.

'It's a painful subject to her,' he said, nodding his head in the direction of the sleeping woman. 'I have known her have an attack of acute mania on hearing an allusion made to it.'

'Made to what?'

'To Druidism.'

'What an extraordinary thing!' I ejaculated.

'I have been keeping the papers from her during the last week,' continued my acquaintance, 'so that she should not hear of this escapade of the doctor. I am convinced it would have a very bad effect upon her mind.'

'Indeed!' I remarked not without a growing conviction that my companion was a little wrong in the upper storey.

'Ah! of course, you don't understand,' he said, smiling at my evident bewilderment. 'The fact is, that just before our marriage some ten years ago - my wife had a very terrible experience in connection with Druidism. It did not get into the papers at the time, but there are a good many people alive who can testify to the facts. It shattered her nervous system, and anything which recalls it knocks her over very much.'

With this short preface, my new friend, leaning well forward and speaking in a low voice, with many precautionary glances at his sleeping wife, told me the story of her extraordinary adventure. I have endeavoured to set it down in his own words as far as I can, but I cannot imitate the earnestness of his manner, nor the weird effect produced by the flickering carriage-lamp, and the presence of the unconscious heroine of this strange story.

'I don't know whether you know Wales well,' he began; 'but even if you do, it is not at all likely that you have ever journeyed as far as Llanduran.' It is an out-of-the-way little mountain village up in the north, not far from the sea, a place which is hardly marked in the maps, and where no tourist ever goes unless he stumbles upon it by accident. This was our fate in the autumn of '72, and we were so taken by the pretty surroundings and the primitive peasantry, that we made it our resting-place for some time. We were a fairly large party - my brother Stephen and his wife, my present wife, with her two brothers, and three friends of mine from London. Altogether we had a very jolly time of it, and astonished the quiet-living Cymric population not a little, until our holiday was brought to an abrupt and tragic termination.

I must tell you that my wife - or Miss Madison, as she was in those days was of a most adventurous disposition. She appeared to be absolutely insensible to fear. I was continually remonstrating with her as to the risks which she ran, and her brothers did all they could to restrain her, but without avail. The more we spoke, the more daring would she become. We were compelled, at last, to leave her behind when we intended to do any serious mountaineering, for fear she should meet with some accident.

One morning, when we came down to breakfast, we learned to our surprise that Miss Madison had been seen to leave the inn alone at early dawn, in her walking-dress, and to take the direction of the mountains. Her intention, evidently, was to steal a march upon us by visiting alone some of those places which we had gone to without her. We were all rather alarmed by this escapade of the wild girl; but our alarm deepened into positive terror when the whole day passed without our hearing a word of her. The district was a notoriously dangerous one. The mountains, without being remarkably high, were jagged and steep, and intersected by numerous chasms. Several fatal accidents had occurred of late in the vicinity. No wonder then, that I felt a sinking at my heart when I left the inn that night at the head of a party with torches in search of the woman whom I had already begun to love.

I will tell you the story now from her point of view, and give you that facts which we heard afterwards from her own lips.

Leaving the inn, then, and laughing to herself at the way in which she was giving us the slip, she made the best of her way into the mountains. The morning was a beautiful one, and the crisp, bracing air increased her natural activity and endurance, so that she had walked a very long way before the thought of fatigue entered her mind. She had gone on at random, following the little goat-paths from one rugged valley to another, until she had lost sight of all the familiar landmarks, and found herself in a desolate labyrinth, surrounded on every side by precipitous crags, and without the smallest sign of human life. Many women would have been terrified in her position, but, as I have said, she was constitutionally brave; so finding it hopeless to retrace her steps, she pushed on, in the hope of reaching some eminence from which she could catch a glimpse of the outside world.

As she advanced, the scenery became bleaker and more dismal. The mountains in those regions are always desolate, being hardly picturesque enough to attract tourists, and too barren to allow anyone to settle among them. She stumbled along among great boulders, and along the bed of a dried-up stream, with lofty granite walls on each side of her without break or opening. Following the track of the old torrent, she traced it at last to a place where there had evidently been a cascade, as the bed of the stream descended precipitously for thirty or forty feet. Hoping by ascending to obtain some idea of her whereabouts, my wife clambered up this steep incline, and succeeded with some difficulty in reaching the top.

The sight before her was an extraordinary one. The gap through which the stream had forced its way was the only entrance to a little ravine, surrounded on all sides by high, dark cliffs. This secluded nook formed a cul-de-sac about two hundred yards long and fifty broad, ringed in by fir trees, which sprouted from the base of the rocky walls. In the centre of the clear space in the middle was a large flat slab, round which were placed a number of stones, standing upon their ends, and forming a double circle. This arrangement was evidently artificial, and my wife looked round, in the hope of seeing some signs of human life. To her great delight she perceived among the trees a rough sort of hut, to which she hurried, with the intention of getting some refreshment if possible, and then of inquiring her way homewards.

The rude door of this wooden dwelling was ajar, and Miss Madison, after knocking several times without receiving an answer, pushed her way in.

The room in which she found herself was a small one, and furnished in the roughest manner possible. A heap of goat-skins in the corner appeared to have been utilised as a bed, and a large block of wood in the centre was evidently intended as a table, as the remains of a meal, in the shape of a couple of bones, were lying upon it. What struck the young lady most, however, in this extraordinary apartment were the walls, which were thickly covered with curious inscriptions, painted on it in dark letters. These were in some unknown language, which she conjectured to be Welsh; but there were others, especially over the door and in the centre of each wall, which were evidently designed as symbols or charms, consisting of the same letter, repeated a number of times in different shapes and forms.

My wife was standing in the door-way, regarding all these strange things with natural curiosity, when she became aware of a shadow which intervened between her and the sun. Turning round, she saw behind her the most extraordinary mortal that she had ever beheld. He was an elderly man, with long, floating hair and a grizzled beard, which descended over his breast. He could not have been less than six feet four inches high, and the breadth of his shoulders and length of his arms denoted extraordinary strength, while the great club upon which he leaned might have served him either as a support or as a weapon. His dress was a sort of ragged gown, which had been originally white, but was now weather-stained and dirty. What struck my wife, however, more than either his other features or his strange attire, were his eyes, which were of a light, almost colourless blue, but which projected considerably, and shifted from one object to another without remaining still for an instant.

"Hail, lady!" he exclaimed, advancing towards Miss Madison, and speaking in a well-modulated voice. "For five moons I have waited for you. Why hast thou tarried so long?"

Considerably astonished, but more amused than frightened, the young lady took a step or two back from this strange apparition, who walked slowly forwards, waving his hands rhythmically from side to side.

"The blood-stone is dry!" he cried, "the blood-stone is dry! Shall it be said that in the days of the fifteenth avatar there was no man who would honour the old gods, and no woman who would dare lie down upon the blood-stone? Britain's noblest and fairest have stretched themselves upon that cold couch. You are worthy of the honour, maiden. Thy cheek is unblanched, and thy hand is steady. So should she be whom the high gods select."

My wife had begun by this time to realise that the man in front of her was a maniac, though she had not yet fathomed the meaning of his strange words. She endeavoured to conceal her fright as much as possible, however and to conciliate her fierce-looking companion.

"You must lead a lonely life, sir," she said. "Who are you, and why do you dwell up here alone?"

"Who am I?" he cried, tossing his long, thin arms in the air. "I am Ap-Griffiths, of the pure blood of Arisdenna, seventieth in descent from the high priest Mona, who was second brother to the great Queen Boadicea.

Woman, I am the last of the Druids. All round," he continued, mournfully, "men have left the old creed. None bow to the high gods now. Only we are staunch and true, maiden; you and I the slayer and the slain."

Thoroughly alarmed by this time, my wife endeavoured to edge away to the mouth of the little glen, but the maniac, who was wildly excited, caught her by the wrist and dragged her over to the spot where the stones were.

"Have I not done it well!" he cried. "There have been many larger, but none more complete. What is there wanting? Here is the blood-stone," pointing to the flat slab in the centre; "it has been dry for many years, but when you lie on it, maiden, with the flames roaring around you, and when your life-blood hisses upon the hot stone, then the gods will know that there are believers yet. Nay, do not shudder and shrink. Your vile body may be charred and tortured, but your spirit will soar above the stars, ever exulting in a happiness which no words can depict. Mark my stones. Thirty-four without, and twenty-three within, according to the direction of the learned and holy Mona. I have a trench, too, around the blood-stone, and my instrument is as it should be." Here he drew a long, keen knife from his bosom. "All has been ready for months, save only the victim, and now the great gods have sent me that also."

My wife was, as I have already told you, a woman of great courage and resource. It was evident to her in a moment that to attempt to escape was impossible, in the presence of so agile and powerful an adversary. Her only hope of safety lay in humouring and outwitting him. She wined towards him, therefore, and assumed as much calmness as she could, while she asked the terrible question -

"When am I to be sacrificed?"

"At the middle hour of the night," said the maniac, with decision.

She felt instinctively that it was useless to plead her sex, her age, or her helplessness to this sanguinary fanatic. The sun was already low down on the horizon, and there would be only a few hours to pass before she should find herself stretched upon the fatal blood-stone. Her last chance lay in the use she might make of that short period.

"I am ignorant," she said, "of many of the things of which you speak; I have much to learn before I can die."

"You are right, maiden," he said; "there is much which none can teach in these latter days save those who still have the priestly blood in their veins. Come with me into my dwelling, and I will discourse with you concerning many things, that when thy soul is loosened from its bonds it may know whither it speedeth."

'With these words the Druid, as I will call him, led Miss Madison into the hut, and commanded her to be seated on a rough wooden bench which stood opposite the door. He himself lay down upon a couple of goat-skins at her feet, and began to talk to her with great volubility and earnestness. Much of his conversation was unintelligible to her, and occasionally he would break into rude doggerel verses, but she could understand enough to gather that he was laying down the precepts of the old British faith. Poor girl! Her mind was too full of horror to allow her to pay much attention to his disquisition. Certain death seemed to stare her in the face and death in its most horrible form. Look which way she would, there seemed to be no possibility of escape. Through the half-open door she could see that the night was drawing in. The Druid observed it too, for suddenly ceasing his harangue, he sprang to his feet and seized a great chopper which leaned against the wall.

"I must leave you for a time, maiden," he said. "There is much to be done before the darkness comes. The wood is to be cut for the funeral pyre, for I swear to you that none who ever lay upon that hard bridal couch shall have had a more seemly ending than thine shall be."

With these words he hurried out of the hut, and Miss Madison could tell by the crashing sound that he was cutting among the fir trees which surrounded the valley.

For a moment a ray of hope came into her mind. Might she not slip past him while he was engaged in his work, and gain the mouth of the ravine without his detecting her? She rose with the determination to risk everything upon the chance, when to her unutterable horror, she found that the cunning miscreant had, in some unaccountable way, managed to slip the noose of a rope round her ankles while he lay at her feet, and that she was firmly pinioned to the bench. It was only then that the relentless cruelty and unbending resolution of the monster who had captured her came fully home to her. She screamed piteously for aid, though she knew that her cries were as useless as her struggles would be. She was entirely at the mercy of the maniac.

He came back upon hearing her cries, and stood in the doorway, looking down at her with a look of melancholy upon his face. It was so dark now that it was difficult for her to distinguish his features.

"Lady," he said. "this is not what I had hoped. How shall thy courage bear thee up at the supreme moment if thou shrinkest now? You have been honoured above all women by the selection of the gods. Canst thou not prove thyself worthy of the choice? Learn, too, that thy cries are of no avail, for there is no human ear for many a mile. Thou art not the only one on whom death will come to-night. When the red light of thy pyre tinges the crags of Conmorris, and thy holocaust is completed, then Ap-Griffiths, the last of the priestly line, shall pass away with his mission gloriously fulfilled. My life, as well as yours, maiden, terminates at the coming of the fifteenth avatar, which my knowledge teaches me will be at the twelfth hour of this night."

Driven to desperation, my poor wife prayed and begged for mercy from the madman, using every possible entreaty and expostulation to prevent him from carrying out his murderous design. Her prayers, however, had the exactly opposite effect, for, flying into a paroxysm of rage, the Druid sprang upon her, forcing her down on the bench, to which she was already pinioned.

"Wicked and ungrateful Woman!" he roared, winding a cord round her body, and securing her more firmly than before, "would you persuade the only faithful one to turn false? Not a word more, or I must silence your tongue. You have already committed a grievous sin."

With these words, he seized his chopper once more, and went back to his work, cutting great faggots, and piling them around the fatal blood-stone.

Gradually the darkness of night settled down upon the little valley. The poor girl stretched, more dead than alive, upon the rough bench; she could distinguish the gaunt outlines of the madman as he wielded his chopper with demoniacal fury. Then the sound ceased, and she lost sight of him in the gloom. When the moon came out, however, she perceived him once more, kneeling among the perpendicular stones. He was bowing his head, waving his arms and giving other symptoms of being engaged in religious devotion. Then he stood up, and burst into a rude, wild chant, which reverberated through the little ravine, and was echoed back from the rocky walls.

During this time, the very possibility of escape had ceased to occur to Miss Madison. Suddenly, however, her senses, strained to an unnatural tension, detected a sound in the distance. She listened once more in a quiver of excitement, and again it seemed to her that the breeze bore a faint note to her ear, not unlike the sound of a horn. Could it be that her friends had hit upon the right track? She lay perfectly still, able to hear the beatings of her own heart. For five minutes all was silence, save the monotonous chant of the maniac. Then again the same long wail struck upon her ear, apparently rather louder and more near than before. The Druid seemed to hear it, too, for he ceased his incantation, and paced uneasily backwards and forwards.

By her calculation it could not be more than eleven o'clock. She had, therefore, an hour before her if the maniac adhered to his former plan. The suspense was agonising. She lay, with her eyes shut, counting the seconds, and waiting for a repetition of the sound; but all was as silent as the grave.

Minute passed after minute. Half the hour was gone without any sign of her rescuers. Another quarter passed, and the madman began to take a last look at the pyre, and to make his final preparations. Then he struck a light, and ignited the base of the mound of sticks. The dry, resinous pine-wood crackled and spluttered, while long tongues of flame licked round the borders of the fatal blood-stone. He approached the door of the hut. "The time has come, maiden!" he said.

It must have been a weird sight - the column of fire shooting up into the air, throwing fantastic shadows among the gaunt fir trees and the Druidical stones, within the circle of light the white-clad maniac, and in front of him the shrinking girl! He was in the very act of undoing the cords which bound her, when, from the mouth of the glen came a loud peal from a horn, and a chorus of human voices, all shouting together. The light of the fire had attracted the rescue party.

The Druid started like a hunted beast. "Too late!" he roared; "too late! Thy doom is sealed! Thou must die!" He caught up the bench and the prostrate woman, and, running with incredible speed, he laid her beside the roaring flames, while he drew his long knife from his bosom. My poor wife's last recollection is of the fierce face looking down at her, the savage, colourless eyes, and the uplifted knife.

When she came to herself, friendly faces were around her. Her head was pillowed upon my breast, and the first word that passed her dear lips was my name. The Druid was lying on his back, some little way off, with his head cut open. I shall never get such a stick again as the old friend which I broke that night over his crazy skull. It was touch and go, though, for if I had got up one moment later, the fellow's knife would have been in Mary's heart.

'We got her down to the inn at Llanduran, but she developed brain fever next day, and for weeks her life was despaired of. Such an impression has the adventure made upon her that the least incident which may recall it has a very bad effect upon her. That is why I have concealed the episode of Dr Price from her knowledge.'

'And the Druid?' I asked.

'Oh, he turned out to be a very well-known man of science and archaeologist. He had been erratic in his conduct, and was therefore confined in the Merthyr Lunatic Asylum, but he escaped some six months before, and all clue to his whereabouts was lost. He must have spent the whole time in this nook among the mountains, practising his pagan rites, and living on the goats and anything he could pick up.'

'What became of him, then?'

'Oh, that is about the queerest thing in the whole queer story. Whether the crack with my stick depressed some bump, or how it acted, I don't know; but the fact remains that when he had recovered his senses he was as sane as you and I, and hass as far as I know, remained so ever since. They kept him in the asylum for some time for fear of a relapse, but they let him out eventually. Hush! she's waking up. Yes, they will have a lively time at the beginning of the next session, to all appearance. Don't you think so, my dear?'

Essays/Articles

MY FAVOURITE NOVELIST AND HIS BEST BOOK

If some fairy godmother were to lead me into the reading room of the British Museum, and to say to me, "Upon these walls you will find the works of all the great story tellers of the world. Look at them well, weigh one against the other, and when you have quite made up your mind which is the greatest, you will you self be endowed with that writer's virtues and failings," I should then, I think, approach the question with a keener sense of criticism and a more resolute effort to be clear in my own literary aims. But I know that the task would be a hard one, for I am catholic in my tastes, and every form of fiction - be it good of its kind - appeals to my admiration as freely as every flower in a garden. I have no sympathy for the petty critics who cannot enjoy Flaubert without belittling Scott, or relish a romance without sneering at the modern problem novel. They are all good - if they be but good of their kind - and there is room and to spare for all of them, if they serve to interest some section of the public.

The idea that the writing of a novel is a sort of exact science, only to be approached in certain ways and along certain lines, by realism or by romance, is the utmost pedantry and cant. Here is the writer and there is the audience. Let him seek his subject where he will. Let him treat it how he will. But let him hold that audience - and if he continue to hold it long enough to show that his power does not spring from any passing fashion, he has then a real vocation, whether he deal with the court of a medieval king or that of an East End slum.

But to recur to the stupendous offer of my fairy godmother, I can imagine myself seated in the midst of that enormous room, and gazing round at the books which line it, while I carefully consider which are those which I shall henceforth claim as my own. I review in my mind all those great writers whom I have admired and revered. I try to see their faults as well as their beauties. I turn to Tolstoy, and I am attracted by his earnestness and by his power of detail, but I am repelled by his looseness of construction and by his unreasonable and impracticable mysticism. I covet the literary but not the moral conscience of Zola. I long for the human humor of Dickens and the polished worldliness of Thackeray, but in each case deplore their want of form, their lack of that sense of construction which has been the weakest point of our English novelists. There are many great names left, but of them all there are three over which I should linger, if such a choice were mine - Scott, Dumas, Maupassant.

Maupassant, with all his faults of taste, was such a natural, instinctive story teller, so concise, so admirably balanced, with such a range of sympathies. Of the great masters of fiction none, perhaps, combined high imagination with actual knowledge of life so fully as he. Some of his tales are, I grant, indefensible, but a French writer is to be judged by the standard of his own country, and it may at least be said of him that he is never coarse for the sake of coarseness, and that the humor or the drama of the situation is its excuse, if not its justification.

And yet, as my good godmother waits impatiently for my choice, I pass my favorite of all short story writers regretfully by, and I turn to the full blooded, fiery Creole, the man of a hundred books and plays innumerable, the father of the Musketeers, and the grandfather of much of the fiction of today. Who can judge him impartially, for who is there who does not owe him a debt of gratitude ? His colossal imagination, his great sweep, the masterful way in which he molds history to his own uses, these give him a place apart. Boy or man, simpleton or philosopher, all can find what they want in his pages.

But if I am to choose between him and Scott, I must become advocatus diaboli, and seek for the flaws as well as the beauties of my Dumas. And it must be confessed that they abound. Amidst all this rattle of incident I catch but dim and uncertain glimpses of the world in which these people lived. I learn little - and that little I mistrust. These St. Vitus' dance conversations, too, which jerk and jump in little spasmodic sentences with unnecessary questions and gratuitous answers, do they not bear some relation to the daily column of some journal which had to be filled with its feuilleton ? And then again, when a character becomes superhuman - like Porthos, who dies pulling down a mountain and slaying a regiment - he becomes not impressive, but grotesque. No, I will pass the Norman Frenchman, and I will pass the shock headed Creole, and I will fix my aspirations upon the canny Scotch lawyer, the man with the lame leg and the peaked head, who, with the heartiest contempt for his own profession, hardly deigning to acknowledge his work after he had done it, found time between his dogs, his plantations, and his sheriff's court to write the series of novels which has made the name of Scott immortal.

For apart from the fact of his being the first - which, ceteris paribus, must give him an overwhelming share of the credit - how many points there are in which Scott was the master of Dumas, and how few in which he was his inferior. Let us grant that the Frenchman treated his women characters with more freedom, if with less reverence. Granted, also, that there is a certain touch and go quality about his story telling which is racial. But beyond this everything is in Scott's favor - his sanity, his restraint, his accuracy to history, his dignity, his power of realizing and reproducing a historical character as he reproduced Louis XI, from the "Croniques" of Philippe de Comines, his exact knowledge, his humor. In the latter quality there can be no comparison between the two. Take the four comic servants of the musketeers, and compare them with Friar Tuck, with Dandie Dinmont, or, best of all, with Dugald Dalgetty, and you see the difference between a marionette and a human creature.

But the most odious of all comparisons are those between two people whom you admire, and I should never have ventured upon so ungracious a task had I not been forced to justify myself for choosing the one, rather than the other, as my ideal. Let me speak rather of Scott's own virtues, without reference to any rival.

First, as to his beautiful reverence for woman : is there in the whole list of his books one single scene which verges upon coarseness, or is there one precept to be gathered from them which is not gallant and manly ? I acknowledge that it is not the primary duty of a novel to teach ethics; but granting that it fulfils all other conditions of a good novel, then it would be absurd to say that this is not an added merit.

And then there is the fullness and accuracy of his knowledge. He knows the peculiarities of every class and of every trade. His fowlers speak like fowlers, his soldiers like soldiers, his physicians like the leeches of the period. He had a unique power of concentrating all his wide reading so as to build up a single definite picture. Take the work of his old age, Count Robert of Paris. Who has ever realized the old Greek empire, grotesque, bloodstained, and yet venerable, as he has done in this book, which is usually quoted as the least successful of his writings? A student who had spent his whole life in studying the subject confessed that he had never realized it until this tired old giant came along and made the whole thing clear by a single flash of his imagination.

It is worthy of note that Scott never wrote a line of fiction until after he was forty - in which he resembled many of the greatest novelists, for this art is the latest of all to mature. To describe life one must know it. Having once begun, he wrote with great rapidity, in spite of many distractions. The wise critics who are so ready to accuse modern writers of over production should remember that Scott turned out as many as three novels a year, each of them exceeding in length the average book of today. If the modern cannot justify his books by their merit, he can at least quote the aphorism of Dr. Johnson, who said that if a tree only produced crab apples, the tree which produced many of them was better than the one which produced few. On the whole, then, whether I take his quantity or his quality, his literary merit or his clean and noble moral influence, I should from all ages and all races place the author of Ivanhoe and of Quentin Durward at the highest pinnacle of his profession. But before choosing my favorite novelist I should have, as I have shown, to hesitate and to weigh one against the other. This would not be so in the case of my favorite novel. There my mind is entirely made up. It is a book by none of the great men whom I have mentioned, but it is one which, if the author could always have kept to that high level, would have placed him higher than them all. It is Charles Reade's Cloister and the Hearth. Some books are great on account of the intellect which is shown in them, and some on account of the heart, but I do not know where I can find a book in which the highest qualities of head and of heart go together as they do in this one. From that noble and sonorous opening paragraph :

There is a musty Chronicle written in tolerable Latin, and in it a chapter where every sentence holds a fact. Here is told with harsh brevity the strange history of a pair who lived untrumpeted and died unsung four hundred years ago, and lie now as unpitied on that stern page as fossils in a rock. Thus, living or dead, Fate is still unjust to them. For if I can but show you what lies below that dry Chronicler's words, me thinks you will correct the indifference of centuries, and give those two sore tried souls a place in your heart for a day -

down to the last ringing sentence:

The words of a genius so high as his are not born to die; their immediate work upon mankind fulfilled, they may seem to lie torpid ; but at each fresh shower of intelligence Time pours upon their students they prove their immortal race; they revive, they spring from the dust of great libraries, they bud, they flower, they fruit, they seed, from generation to generation and from age to age -

I have never found so much accurate knowledge and ripe wisdom and passionate human emotion within the covers of any single book.

The story is to be told in a few sentences, and sounds bald enough, as all stories do when reduced to pure statement. A young Dutchman, Gerard, the son of Ali, somewhere about the year 1450 marries a girl, Margaret - sweetest of all heroines of fiction - and has a child, known in after years as the great Erasmus. Persecuted at home, he journeys across Europe to Rome, to earn some money by his ornamental manuscripts, which are rapidly being ousted by the printing press. While at Rome a false report of the death of Margaret reaches his ears, and, in his agony, he joins the priest hood and becomes a preaching friar. As such he visits Holland and finds the poor, faithful Margaret still waiting for him. His vows stand between her and him, so they live as friends and die as the novelist tells us. There lies the whole of the story, and it is from the struggle between the church and human love, the life of the home and that of the cloister, that the book takes its title. Such an indictment against celibacy of the clergy has never yet been penned.

But the wonder of the book is the extraordinary clearness and power with which the middle-ages, in many countries and from many points of view, are laid before us. As Mr. Hornung has picturesquely remarked, it is a searchlight thrown across medieval Europe. And it is a human medievalism, neither stiff nor conventional nor unnatural, but palpitating with rude life and with primitive emotions. We are convinced, as we read, that even such the people must have been, and so they must have thought and lived. The atmosphere is so perfect and so consistent that we drift back into that dreadful life, and wake at the end of a chapter with a start and a sigh of relief to feel that we are living in a cleaner, fresher world, where force has been tempered by law and bigotry by reason.

We see the castle of the brutal and ignorant noble which dominates the road. We see also the monastery, where a little spark of learning and humanity still glimmers amid that widespread darkness. We realize the inns, their discomforts and their dangers, the great woods swarming with robbers, the incessant wars, the grossness and superstition of the people, and yet the picture is lightened, as life is lightened, by the traits of kindliness and mobility which in all ages, and under every condition, will break out in human nature; the self sacrifice which springs from love, the loyalty of friends, the kindliness of women, and the devotion of the poorer clergy.

Wonderfully reproduced, also, is that atmosphere of wonder and of adventure which pervaded the world in a time when there always hung a mirage over the horizon. A man knew the city in which he was born - perhaps also a little of the country around it; but over the river, or beyond the mountains, it was all a land of mystery, a place where anything might befall him. If he traveled, it was along villainous, deeply rutted roads, with danger like a hedge upon either side of them, and the chances of an ambuscade at every defile. Printing was coming, the Reformation was coming, the revival of learning was just at hand, but the greater part of Europe still lay in that blackest night which precedes the dawn.

I do not know that Charles Reade has anywhere left it upon record how many books went to the making of this one, but it is evident that only very wide reading could give him the store of knowledge from which he draws so freely. And it is necessary not only to collect such knowledge, but to digest and to assimilate it, before it can be used in a natural fashion, without any savor of pedantry. Sir Walter Besant, who is himself an authority upon this epoch, mentions Erasmus, Froissart,

Deschamps, Esquillart, Gringoire, Villon, and Luther among the roots from which this great book has sprung.

Consider the many sides of life which are treated here - all of them with the greatest minuteness of detail. We begin with the well ordered routine of provincial Holland, the thrifty, spotless, tile lined house of the burgher, with a passing glance into the palace of the Duke of Burgundy. We learn many things, incidentally and allusively, as such things should be learned in a novel, of the house keeping of these people, of their dress, of their lives, of the Dutch school of painters, of the mystery plays, of their hunting, their archery, their views of existence. Then you start upon that wonderfully vivid journey from Holland to Rome. You pass into medieval Germany, you visit the slovenly inns, the dirty, drunken, good hearted people, the sluggish but honest traders. You are introduced to the old world soldier, and to that more deadly man, the old world physician. At Düsseldorf you strike the Rhine, the broad green highway which binds southern and northern Europe. You visit good abbeys and bad ones, consort with saints and sinners, take your chances with amorous hostesses and murderous hosts, learn incidentally the methods of scientific warfare in the middle ages, and the more complex methods of scientific begging, and so pass on through Burgundy and down to the sea.

And then there is the Roman section, with its sketch of the renaissance, its dilettante cardinals who stand for the new dispensation, and its fanatical preaching friars who represent the old ; its artists, its collectors, its debauched society, its hired assassins, and its very human and tolerant pope. Finally there is the somber and elaborate finale, which draws the life of the cloister and the life of the cell, and the moving study of that poor saint whose troubles arose from never having heard that pithy Western maxim, "One world at a time." When you look back on all this wide field of information you feel that it is not a mere book, but the distillation of a whole library, which you have been reading.

So much for the head, but it is the qualities of heart which seem to me to be the greater of the two. With what tenderness the piteous story is told ! How warm and true is Reade's sympathy with all that is human and good ! The great heart of the man sets the whole book throbbing. From the first meeting of Gerard and Margaret, when he plucks the straws to suck the soup, until he is laid in his coffin and stern old Brother Jerome lays the auburn tress upon his body, no such love story, so natural, so beautiful, and so tender, has been told in our time. You feel that the author has fulfilled that first essential for deeply moving others - he has been deeply moved himself. Sad as it is, it is not maudlin or forced, but the solemn and tender sadness of life which has something sweet forever mixed with its bitterness. I know no scene in fiction which affects me so powerfully as the death of Margaret. The man who can read that chapter with dry eyes is a man whom I do not wish to know.

There is no work of man which is not open to adverse criticism. Perfection never has and never will be attained. In Reade's case the imperfections, the irritating and superficial tricks of manner, are so obtrusive that they catch the eye to the exclusion, sometimes, of the rare qualities which lie beneath them. That a man of his judgment and discernment should try to emphasize a point by using large type, like a sensational daily paper, is a psychological curiosity. His style can be sonorous and beautiful, as in the opening and closing passages which I have quoted, but it can also be abrupt, jerky, and incoherent to an exasperating extent. But at least it was his own - "his skin and not his shirt," as Carlyle expressed it - and that is something in these days, when "style" is usually a short word for affectation.

Bad also are Charles Reade's familiarities with his reader and with his characters, his trick of nicknaming them, his occasionally clumsy playfulness, his eternal asides, his habit of destroying the illusion by alluding to modern matters in what purports to be an ancient chronicle. But when all this has been most freely discounted, there still remains enough virtue in this novel to make it, in my eyes, the wisest and the most beautiful I have ever read.

Play

THE CROWN DIAMOND: AN EVENING WITH SHERLOCK HOLMES

—⚬⚬⚬—

Dramatis Personae

MR. SHERLOCK HOLMES (The famous Detective).

DR. WATSON (His Friend).

BILLY (Page to MR. HOLMES).

COL. SEBASTIAN MORAN (An intellectual Criminal.)

SAM MERTON (A Boxer.)

SCENE

MR. HOLMES'S room in Baker Street. It presents the usual features, but there is a deep bow window to it, and across there is drawn a curtain running upon a brass rod fastened across eight feet above the ground and enclosing the recess of the window.

Enter Watson and Billy

Watson:	Well, Billy, when will he be back?
Billy:	I'm sure I couldn't say sir.
Watson:	When did you see him last?
Billy:	I really couldn't tell you.
Watson:	What, you couldn't tell me?
Billy:	No sir. There was a clergyman looked in yesterday and there was an old bookmaker and there was a workman.
Watson:	Well?
Billy:	But I'm not sure they weren't all Mr. Holmes. You see he's very hot on a chase just now.
Watson:	Oh!
Billy:	He neither eats nor sleeps. Well you've lived with him

	same as me. You know what he's like when he's after some one.
Watson:	I know.
Billy:	He's a responsibility sir, that he is. It's a real worry to me sometimes. When I asked him if he would order dinner, he said. "Yes, I'll have chops and mashed potatoes at 7:30 the day after to morrow." "Won't you eat before then sir?" I asked. "I haven't time, Billy. I'm busy," said he. He gets thinner and paler and his eyes get brighter. It's awful to see him.
Watson:	Tut, tut, this will never do. I must certainly stop and see him.
Billy:	Yes sir, it will ease my mind.
Watson:	But what is he after?
Billy:	It's this case of the Crown Diamond.
Watson:	What the hundred thousand pound burglary?
Billy:	Yes, sir. They must get it back sir. Why we had the Prime Minister and the Home Secretary both sitting on that very sofa. Mr. Holmes promised he'd do his very best for them. Quite nice he was to them. Put them at their ease in a moment.
Watson:	Dear me! I've read about it in the paper. But I say, Billy, what have you been doing to the room? What's this curtain?
Billy:	I don't know, sir. Mr. Holmes had it put there three days ago. But we've got something funny behind it.
Watson:	Something funny?
Billy (laughing):	Yes, sir. He had it made.
	(*Billy goes to the curtain and draws it across, disclosing a wax image of Holmes seated in a chair, back to the audience.*)
Watson:	Good heavens, Billy!
Billy:	Yes, sir. It's like him, sir. (Picks the head off and exhibits it.)

Watson:	It's wonderful! But what's it for, Billy?
Billy:	You see, sir, he's anxious that those who watch him should think he's at home sometimes when he isn't. There's the bell, sir. (Replaces head, draws curtain.) I must go.

(Billy goes out.)

(Watson sits down, lights a cigarette, and opens a paper. Enter a tall, bent OLD WOMAN in black with veil and side-curls.)

Watson (rising):	Good day, Ma'm.
Woman:	You're not Mr. Holmes?
Watson:	No, Ma'm. I'm his friend, Dr. Watson.
Woman:	I knew you couldn't be Mr. Holmes. I'd always heard he was a handsome man.
Watson (aside):	Upon my word!
Woman:	But I must see him at once.
Watson:	I assure you he is not in.
Woman:	I don't believe you.
Watson:	What!
Woman:	You have a sly, deceitful face - oh, yes, a wicked, scheming face. Come, young man, where is he?
Watson:	Really, Madam...!
Woman:	Very well, I'll find him for myself. He's in there, I believe. (Walks toward bedroom door.)
Watson (rising and crossing):	That is his bedroom. Really, Madam, this is outrageous!
Woman:	I wonder what he keeps in this safe. *(She approaces it, and as she does so the lights go out, and the room is in darkness save for "DON'T TOUCH" in red fire over the safe. Four red lights spring up, and between them the inscription "DON'T TOUCH!" After a few seconds the lights go on again, and HOLMES is standing beside Watson.)*

Watson:	Good heavens, Holmes!
Holmes:	Neat little alarm, is it not, Watson? My own invention. You tread on a loose plank and so connect the circuit, or I can turn it on myself. It prevents inquisitive people becoming too inquisitive. When I come back I know if anyone has been fooling with my things. It switches off again automatically, as you saw.
Watson:	But my dear fellow, why this disguise?
Holmes:	A little comic relief, Watson. When I saw you sitting there looking so solemn, I really couldn't help it. But I assure you there is nothing comic in the business I am engaged upon. Good heavens! (Rushes across room, and draws curtain, which has been left partly open.)
Watson:	Why, what is it?
Holmes:	Danger, Watson. Airguns, Watson. I'm expecting something this evening.
Watson:	Expecting what, Holmes?
Holmes (lighting pipe):	Expecting to be murdered, Watson.
Watson:	No, no, you are joking, Holmes!
Holmes:	Even my limited sense of humour could evolve a better joke than that, Watson. No, it is a fact. And in case it should come off - it's about a two to one chance - it would perhaps be as well that you should burden your memory with the name and address of the murderer.
Watson:	Holmes!
Holmes:	You can give it to Scotland Yard with my love and a parting blessing. Moran is the name. Colonel Sebastian Moran. Write it down, Watson, write it down! 136, Moorside Gardens, N.W. Got it?
Watson:	But surely something can be done, Holmes. Couldn't you have this fellow arrested?
Holmes:	Yes, Watson, I could. That's what's worrying him so.
Watson:	But why don't you?
Holmes:	Because I don't know where the diamond is.

Watson:	What diamond?
Holmes:	Yes, yes, the great yellow Crown Diamond, seventy seven carats, lad, and without flaw. I have two fish in the net. But I haven't got the stone there. And what's the use of taking them? It's the stone I'm after.
Watson:	Is this Colonel Moran one of the fish in the net?
Holmes:	Yes, and he's a shark. He bites. The other is Sam Merton the boxer. Not a bad fellow, Sam, but the Colonel has used him. Sam's not a shark. He's a big silly gudgeon. But he's flopping about in my net, all the same.
Watson:	Where is this Colonel Moran?
Holmes:	I've been at his elbow all morning. Once he picked up my parasol. "By your leave, Ma'm," said he. Life is full of whimsical happenings. I followed him to old Straubenzee's workshop in the Minories. Straubenzee made the airgun - fine bit of work, I understand.
Watson:	An airgun?
Holmes:	The idea was to shoot me through the window. I had to put up that curtain. By the way, have you seen the dummy? (Draws curtain.)

(Watson nods.)

Ah! Billy has been showing you the sights. It may get a bullet through its beautiful wax head at any moment.

(Enter Billy.)

Well, Billy?

Billy:	Colonel Sebastian Moran, sir.
Holmes:	Ah! the man himself. I rather expected it. Grasp the nettle, Watson. A man of nerve! He felt my toe on his heels. (Looks out of window.) And there is Sam Merton in the street - the faithful but fatuous Sam. Where is the Colonel, Billy?
Billy:	Waiting-room, sir.
Holmes:	Show him up when I ring.

Billy:	Yes, sir.
Holmes:	Oh, by the way, Billy, if I am not in the room show him in just the same.
Billy:	Very good, sir.

(Billy goes out.)

Watson:	I'll stay with you, Holmes.
Holmes:	No, my dear fellow, you would be horribly in the way (Goes to the table and scribbles a note.)
Watson:	He may murder you.
Holmes:	I shouldn't be surprised.
Watson:	I can't possibly leave you.
Holmes:	Yes, you can, my dear Watson, for you've always played the game, and I am very sure that you will play it to end. Take this note to Scotland Yard. Come back with the police. The fellow's arrest will follow.
Watson:	I'll do that with joy.
Holmes:	And before you return I have just time to find where the diamond is. (Rings bell.) This way, Watson. We'll go together. I rather want to see my shark without his seeing me.

(Watson and Holmes go into the bedroom.)
(Enter Billy and Colonel Sebastian Moran, who is a fierce big man, flashily dressed, with a heavy cudgel.)

Billy:	Colonel Sebastian Moran.

(Billy goes out.)

(Colonel Moran looks round, advances slowly into the room and starts as he sees the dummy figure sitting in the window. He stares at it, then crouches, grips his stick, and advances on tip-toe. When close to the figure he raises his stick. Holmes comes quickly out of the bedroom door.)

Holmes:	Don't break it, Colonel, don't break it.

Colonel (staggering back): Good Lord!

Holmes:	It's such a pretty little thing. Tavernier, the French modeller, made it. He is as good at waxwork as Straubenzee is at airguns. (Shuts curtains.)
Colonel:	Airguns, sir. Airguns! What do you mean?
Holmes:	Put your hat and stick on the side table. Thank you. Pray take a seat. Would you care to put your revolver out also? Oh, very good, if you prefer to sit upon it.

(The Colonel sits down.)

| Colonel: | I wanted to have five minutes' chat with you. |

(Holmes sits down near him and crosses his leg.)

	I won't deny that I intended to assault you just now.
Holmes:	It struck me that some idea of that sort had crossed your mind.
Colonel:	And with reason, sir, with reason.
Holmes:	But why this attention?
Colonel:	Because you have gone out of your way to annoy me. Because you have put your creatures on my track.
Holmes:	My creatures?
Colonel:	I have had them followed. I know that they come to report to you here.
Holmes:	No, I assure you.
Colonel:	Tut, sir! Other people can observe as well as you. Yesterday there was an old sporting man; to-day it was an elderly lady. They held me in view all day.
Holmes:	Really, sir, you compliment me! Old Baron Dowson, before he was hanged at Newgate, was good enough to say that in my case what the law had gained the stage had lost. And now you come along with your kindly words. In the name of the elderly lady and of the sporting gentleman I thank you. There was also an out-of-work plumber who was an artistic dream - you seem to have overlooked him.

Colonel: It was you... you!

Holmes: Your humble servant! If you doubt it, you can see the parasol upon the settee which you so politely handed to me this morning down in the Minories.

Colonel: If I had known you might never -

Holmes: Never have seen this humble home again. I was well aware of it. But it happens you didn't know, and here we are, quite chatty and comfortable.

Colonel: What you say only makes matters worse. It was not your agents, but you yourself, who have dogged me. Why have you done this?

Holmes: You used to shoot tigers?

Colonel: Yes, sir.

Holmes: But why?

Colonel: Pshaw! Why does any man shoot a tiger? excitement. The danger.

Holmes: And no doubt the satisfaction of freeing the country from a pest, which devastates it and lives on the population.

Colonel: Exactly.

Holmes: My reasons in a nutshell.

COLONEL (springing to his feet): Insolent!

Holmes: Sit down, sir, sit down! There was another more practical reason.

Colonel: Well?

Holmes: I want that yellow Crown Diamond.

Colonel: Upon my word! Well, go on.

Holmes: You knew that I was after you for that. The reason why you are here to-night is to find out how much I know about the matter. Well, you can take it that I know all about it, save one thing, which you are about to tell me.

Colonel (sneering): And, pray, what is that?

Holmes: Where the diamond is.

Colonel: Oh, you want to know that, do you? How the devil
                 should I know where it is?

Holmes: You not only know, but you are about to tell me.

Colonel: Oh, indeed!

Holmes: You can't bluff me, Colonel. You're absolute plate glass. I
                 see to the very back of your mind.

Colonel: Then of course you see where the diamond is.

Holmes: Ah! then you do know. You have admitted it.

Colonel: I admit nothing.

Holmes: Now, Colonel, if you will be reasonable we can do
                 business together. If not you may get hurt.

Colonel: And you talk about bluff!

Holmes (raising a book from the table): Do you know what I keep
                 inside this book?

Colonel: No, sir, I do not.

Holmes: You.

Colonel: Me!

Holmes: Yes, sir, you. You're all here, every action of your vile
                 and dangerous life.

Colonel: Damn you, Holmes! Don't go too far.

Holmes: Some interesting details, Colonel. The real facts as to the
                 death of Miss Minnie Warrender of Laburnum Grove.
                 All here, Colonel.

Colonel: You - you devil!

Holmes: And the story of young Arbothnot, who was found
                 drowned in the Regents Canal just before his intended
                 exposure of you for cheating at cards.

Colonel: I - I never hurt the boy.

Holmes: But he died at a very seasonable time. Do you want
                 some more, Colonel? Plenty of it here. How about the
                 robbery in the train deluxe to the Riviera, February
                 13th, 1892? How about the forged cheque on the Credit
                 Lyonnais the same year?

Colonel:	No, you're wrong there.
Holmes:	Then I'm right on the others. Now, Colonel, you are a card-player. When the other fellow holds all the trumps it saves time to throw down your hand.
Colonel:	If there was a word of truth in all this, would I have been a free man all these years?
Holmes:	I was not consulted. There were missing links in the police case. But I have a way of finding missing links. You may take it from me that I could do so.
Colonel:	Bluff! Mr. Holmes, bluff!
Holmes:	Oh, you wish me to prove my words! Well, if I touch this bell it means the police, and from that instant the matter is out of my hands. Shall I?
Colonel:	What has all this to do with the jewel you speak of?
Holmes:	Gently, Colonel! Restrain that eager mind. Let me get to the point in my own hum-drum way. I have all this against you, and I also have a clear case against both you and your fighting bully in this case of the Crown Diamond.
Colonel:	Indeed!
Holmes:	I have the cabman who took you to Whitehall, and the cabman who brought you away. I have the commissionaire who saw you beside the case. I have Ikey Cohen who refused to cut it up for you. Ikey has peached, and the game is up.
Colonel:	Hell!
Holmes:	That's the hand I play from. But there's one card missing. I don't know where this king of diamonds is.
Colonel:	You never shall know.
Holmes:	Tut! tut! don't turn nasty. Now, consider. You're going to be locked up for twenty years. So is Sam Merton. What good are you going to get out of your diamond? None in world. But if you let me know where it is... well, I'll compound a felony. We don't want you or Sam. We

want the stone. Give up, and so far as I am concerned you can go free so long as you behave yourself in the future. If you make another slip, then God help you. But this time my commission is to get the stone, not you. (Rings bell.)

Colonel: But if I refuse?

Holmes: Then, alas, it must be you, not the stone.

(Enter Billy.)

Billy: Yes, sir.

Holmes(to the Colonel): I think we had better have your friend Sam at this conference. Billy, you will see a large and very ugly gentleman outside the front door. Ask him to come up, will you?

Billy: Yes, sir. Suppose he won't come, sir?

Holmes: No force, Billy! Don't be rough with him. If you tell him Colonel Moran wants him, he will come.

Billy: Yes, sir.

(Billy goes out.)

Colonel: What's the meaning of this, then?

Holmes: My friend Watson was with me just now. I told him that I had a shark and a gudgeon in my net. Now, I'm drawing the net and up they come together.

COLONEL (leaning forward): You won't die in your bed Holmes!

Holmes: D'you know, I have often had the same idea. For that matter, your own finish is more likely to be perpendicular than horizontal. But these anticipations are morbid. Let us give ourselves up to the unrestrained enjoyment of the present. No good fingering your revolver, my friend, for you know perfectly well that you dare not use it. Nasty, noisy things, revolvers. Better stick to airguns, Colonel Moran. Ah! ... I think I hear the footsteps of your estimable partner.

(Enter Billy.)

Billy: Mr. Sam Merton.

(Enter Sam Merton, in check suit and loud necktie, yellow overcoat.)

Holmes: Good day, Mr. Merton. Rather damp in the street, is it
                not?

(Billy goes out.)

Merton (to the Colonel): What's the game? What's up?

Holmes: If I may put it in a nutshell, Mr. Merton, I should say it
                is all up.

Merton (to the Colonel): Is this cove tryin' to be funny - or what?
                I'm not in the funny mood myself.

Holmes: You'll feel even less humourous as the evening advances,
                I think I can promise you that. Now, look here, Colonel.
                I'm a busy man and I can't waste time. I'm going into the
                bedroom. Pray make yourselves entirely at home in my
                absence. You can explain to your friend how the matter
                lies. I shall try over the Barcarolle upon my violin.
                (Looks at watch.) In five minutes I shall return for your
                final answer. You quite grasp the alternative, don't you?
                Shall we take you, or shall we have the stone?

(Holmes goes into his bedroom, taking his violin with him.)

Merton: What's that? He knows about the stone!

Colonel: Yes, he knows a dashed sight too much about it. I'm not
                sure that he doesn't know all about it.

Merton: Good Lord!

Colonel: Ikey Cohen has split.

Merton: He has, has he? I'll do him down a thick 'un for that.

Colonel: But that won't help us. We've got to make up our minds
                what to do.

Merton: Half a mo'. He's not listening, is he? (Approaches
                bedroom door.) No, it's shut. Look to me as if it was
                locked.

(Music begins.)

| | Ah! there he is, safe enough. (Goes to curtain.) Here, I say! (Draws it back, disclosing the figure.) Here's that cove again, blast him! |

Ah! there he is, safe enough. (Goes to curtain.) Here, I say! (Draws it back, disclosing the figure.) Here's that cove again, blast him!

Colonel: Tut! it's a dummy. Never mind it.

Merton: A fake, is it? (Examines it, and turns the head) By Gosh, I wish I could twist his own as easy. Well, strike me! Madame Tussaud ain't in it!

(As Merton returns towards the Colonel, the lights suddenly go out, and the red "DON'T TOUCH" signal goes up. After a few seconds the lights readjust them selves. Figures must transpose at that moment.)

Well, dash my buttons! Look 'ere, Guv'nor, this is gettin' on my nerves. Is it unsweetened gin, or what?

Colonel: Tut! it is some childish hanky-panky of this fellow Holmes, a spring or an alarm or something. Look here, there's no time to lose. He can lag us for the diamond.

Merton: The hell he can!

Colonel: But he'll let us slip if we only tell him where the stone is.

Merton: What, give up the swag! Give up a hundred thousand!

Colonel: It's one or the other.

Merton: No way out? You've got the brains, Guv'nor. Surely you can think a way out of it.

Colonel: Wait a bit! I've fooled better men than he. Here's the stone in my secret pocket. It can be out of England tonight, cut into four pieces in Amsterdam before Saturday. He knows nothing of Van Seddor.

Merton: I thought Van Seddor was to wait till next week.

Colonel: Yes, he was. But now he must get the next boat. One or other of us must slip round with the stone to the "Excelsior" and tell him.

Merton: But the false bottom ain't in the hat-box yet!

Colonel: Well, he must take it as it is and chance it. There's not a moment to lose. As to Holmes, we can fool him enough. You see, he won't arrest us if he thinks he can get the

	stone. We'll put him on the wrong track about it, and before he finds it is the wrong track, the stone will be in Amsterdam, and we out of the country.
Merton:	That's prime.
Colonel:	You go off now, and tell Van Seddor to get a move on him. I'll see this sucker and fill him up with a bogus confession. The stone's in Liverpool - that's what I'll tell him. By the time he finds it isn't, there won't be much of it left, and we'll be on blue water. (He looks carefully round him, then draws a small leather box from his pocket, and holds it out.) Here is the Crown Diamond.

Holmes (taking it, as he rises from his chair): I thank you.

Colonel (staggering back): Curse you, Holmes! (Puts hand in pocket.)

Merton:	To hell with him!
Holmes:	No violence, gentlemen; no violence, I beg of you. It must be very clear to you that your position is an impossible one. The police are waiting below.
Colonel:	You - you devil! How did you get there?
Holmes:	The device is obvious but effective; lights off for a moment and the rest is common sense. It gave me a chance of listening to your racy conversation which would have been painfully constrained by a knowledge of my presence. No, Colonel, no. I am covering you with a .450 Derringer through the pocket of my dressing-gown. (Rings bell.)

(Enter Billy.)

Send them up, Billy.

(Billy goes out.)

Colonel:	Well, you've got us, damn you!
Merton:	A fair cop... But I say, what about that bloomin' fiddle?
Holmes:	Ah, yes, these modern gramophones! Wonderful invention. Wonderful!

CURTAIN

www.ingramcontent.com/pod-product-compliance
Lightning Source LLC
Chambersburg PA
CBHW030351030726
47497CB00002B/293